This book is for Jason Smith.

All is order there, and elegance,
pleasure, peace, and opulence.

— 'Invitation to the Voyage'

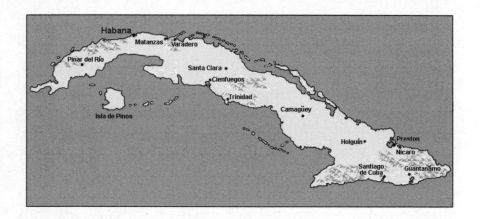

RACHEL KUSHNER

◆

TELEX
FROM CUBA

Complete and Unabridged

CHARNWOOD
Leicester

First published in Great Britain in 2014 by
Vintage
London

First Charnwood Edition
published 2015
by arrangement with
Vintage
The Random House Group Limited
London

The moral right of the author has been asserted

The epigraph from 'Invitation to the Voyage' is by
Baudelaire, translated by Richard Howard

This book is a work of fiction. Names, characters,
places, and incidents either are products of the
author's imagination or are used fictitiously. Any
resemblance to actual events or locales or persons,
living or dead, is entirely coincidental.

A catalogue record for this book is available
from the British Library.

ISBN 978–1–4448–2492–6

Published by
F. A. Thorpe (Publishing)
Anstey, Leicestershire

Set by Words & Graphics Ltd.
Anstey, Leicestershire
Printed and bound in Great Britain by
T. J. International Ltd., Padstow, Cornwall

This book is printed on acid-free paper

Prologue

Everly Lederer, January 1952

There it was on the globe, a dashed line of darker blue on the lighter blue Atlantic. Words in faint italic script: *Tropic of Cancer*. The adults told her to stop asking what it was, as if the dull reply they gave would satisfy: 'A latitude, in this case twenty-three and a half degrees.' She pictured daisy chains of seaweed stretching across the water toward a distant horizon. On the globe were different shades of blue wrapping around the continents in layers. But how could there be geographical zones in the sea, which belongs to no country? Divisions on a surface that is indifferent to rain, to borders, that can hold no object in place? She'd seen an old globe that had one ocean wrapping the Earth, called Ocean. In place of the North Pole was a region marked 'Heaven.' In place of the South Pole, 'Hell.'

She selected the color black from a list of topics and wrote her book report, despite feeling that reducing *Treasure Island* to various things colored black was unfaithful to the story, which was not about black, but perhaps how boys need fathers, and how sometimes children are more clever than adults and not prone to the same vices. The Jolly Roger was black, and there was Black Dog, who showed up mysteriously at the

1

Admiral Benbow, demanding rum. There were black nights on the deserted island, creeping around in shadows amid yet more blackness: the black of danger. Also, the 'black spots' that pirates handed out — a sort of threat. A death sentence, really. 'Who tipped me the black spot?' asked Silver. This death sentence, a stain of wood ash on a leaf of paper. The leaf, torn from a Bible, which now had a hole cut into Revelation. And holes are black as well.

She'd read about Sargasso, a nomadic seaweed city, and hoped they would encounter some. Other things floated on the ocean as well: jetsam, which is what sailors toss overboard to lighten their load, and flotsam, things caught and pushed out to sea, such as coconuts, which rolled up on the shores of Europe in a time before anyone knew what lay to the west. Maybe coconuts still washed up, but they weren't eerie and enchanting now that you could buy one at the store. In that earlier time, people displayed them as exotic charms. Or cut them open. A strange white fluid poured out, greasy and foul-smelling. Not poisonous, just spoiled from such a long and difficult journey, a fruit thousands of miles from its home under the green fronds of a palm tree.

To get from green to red is easy: they are twins. Thin membranes, like retinae, attached at their backing. Her father saw red as green, and green as red. A permanent condition, he assured her. And there was a red grass native to the Antilles from which you could make green dye.

Now picture red velvet drapes.

Part them.

Beyond is a room with perfect acoustics. In it, a gleaming black piano. She can see her face in its surface, like she's leaning over a shallow pan of water. She sits down to play — Chopin, a prelude for saying good-byes, for dreaming in a minor key.

Spin the globe slowly, once, and return to where the dashed blue line skims above the island of Cuba.

She will cross the Tropic of Cancer and begin her new life.

PART ONE

1

It was the first thing I saw when I opened my
eyes that morning. An orange rectangle, the color
of hot lava, hovering on the wall of my bedroom.
It was from the light, which was streaming through
the window in a dusty ray, playing on the wall
like a slow and quiet movie. Just this strange,
orange light. I was sure that at any moment it
would vanish, like when a rainbow appears and
immediately starts to fade, and you look where
you saw it moments before and it's gone, just the
faintest color, and even that faint color you might
be imagining from the memory of what you just
saw.

I went to the window and looked out. The sky
was a hazy violet, like the color of the delicate
skin under Mother's eyes, half circles that went
dark when she was tired. The sun was a blurred,
dark red orb. You could look directly at it through
the haze, like a jewel under layers of tissue. I
figured we were in for some kind of curious
weather. In eastern Cuba, there were mornings
I'd wake up and sense immediately that the weather
had radically turned. I could see the bay from my
window, and if a tropical storm was approaching,
the sunrise would spread ribbons of light into the
dense clouds piling up on the water's horizon,
turning them rose-colored like they were glowing

7

from inside. I loved the feeling of waking up to some drastic change, knowing that when I went downstairs the servants would be rushing around, taking the patio furniture inside and nailing boards over the windows, the air outside warm and gusting, the first giant wave surging in a glassy, green wall and drenching the embankment just beyond our garden. If a storm had already approached, I'd wake up to rain pouring down over the house, my room so dark I had to turn on the bedside lamp just to read the clock. Change was exciting to me, and when I woke up that morning and saw a rectangle of orange light, bright as embers, on my bedroom wall, it seemed like something special was about to happen.

It was early, and Mother and Daddy were still asleep. My brother, Del, had been gone for three weeks at that point, ever since we'd returned from our Christmas vacation in Havana. Daddy didn't talk about it openly, but I knew Del was up in the mountains with Raúl's column. I'd never been much for the pool hall in Mayarí, but I started hanging around down there after he disappeared. In Preston it was difficult to get information about the rebels. The Cubans all knew what was going on, but they kept quiet around Americans. The company was putting a lot of pressure on workers to stay away from anyone involved with the rebels. Who's going to talk to the boss's thirteen-year-old son? Down in Mayarí, people got drunk and opened their mouths. The week before, an old campesino grabbed me by the shoulder. He put his face up to mine, so close I could smell his rummy breath. He said something about Del. He said he was still young, but that he would be one of the great ones. A liberator of the people. Like Bolívar.

I could hear Annie making breakfast, opening and shutting drawers. I put on my slippers and went downstairs. It was so dark in the kitchen I could barely see. Annie had latched all the windows and closed the jalousies. I asked why she didn't open the shutters or put on a light.

Servants have their funny ways — superstitions — and you never know what they're up to. Annie didn't like to go out at dusk. If Mother insisted she run some errand, Annie put a scarf over her mouth. She said evil spirits tried to fly into women's mouths at dusk. Annie and our laundress, Darcina, both listened to this cockeyed faith healer Clavelito on radio CMQ. Darcina sometimes cried at night. She said she missed sleeping in a bed with her children. Mother bought her a portable to keep her company and ended up buying one for Annie as well, just to be fair. Mother was big on fairness. Clavelito told folks to set a glass of water on top of the radio, something about his voice blessing the water, and Annie and Darcina both did.

Annie said she'd closed the shutters on account of the air. There was an awful haze, and it was tickling her nose and making her hoarse. She said it must have been those guajiros burning their trash again. Annie didn't like the campesinos. She was a house servant, and that's a different class.

I sat down in the kitchen with the new issue of

Unifruitco, our company magazine. It came out bimonthly, meaning the news was always a bit stale. This was January 1958, and on the front page was a photo of my brother and Phillip Mackey posing with a swordfish they'd caught in Nipe Bay, back in October. They'd won first prize in the fall fishing tournament. It was strange to see that photograph, now that both of them were gone and my brother no longer cared about things such as fishing tournaments. On the next page was Daddy with Batista and Ambassador Smith on our yacht the *Mollie and Me*. I flipped through the pages while Annie made pastry dough. She cut the dough into circles, put cheese and guava paste into the little circles, folded them over into half moons, and spread them on a baking sheet. Annie's pastelitos de guayaba, warm from the oven, were the most delicious things in the world. Some of the Americans in Preston didn't allow their servants to cook native. Mother was considerably more open-minded about these things, and she absolutely loved some of the Cuban dishes. Mother didn't cook. She made lists for Annie. Annie would take a huge red snapper and stuff it with potatoes, olives, and celery, then marinate it in butter and lime juice and bake it in the oven. That was my favorite. Six months earlier, in the summer of '57, when I turned thirteen, Annie said that because I was a young man and would be grown up before she knew it, she wanted to make me a rum cake for my wedding. Thirteen-year-old boys are not exactly thinking about marriage. Sure I'd fooled around with

10

girls, but there wasn't any formal courtship going on. A rum cake will keep for ten or fifteen years, and Annie figured that was enough time for me to grow up and find a wife. She had the guys at the company machine shop make a five-tier tin just for that cake. The tin was painted white, with Kimball C. Stites handpainted on top, and handles on the sides for pulling out the cake layers. I don't know what happened to the cake or the tin with my name on it. Lost in the rush of leaving, like so many of our things.

Annie was putting her pastelitos in the oven when I heard Daddy's footsteps pounding down the stairs, and Mother calling after him, 'Malcolm! Malcolm, please in God's name be *careful!*'

I ran into the foyer and met Daddy at the bottom of the stairs. He didn't look at me, just charged past like I was invisible, opened the front door, and took the veranda steps two at a time. I followed him, running down the garden path in my pajamas. He went around to the servants' quarters behind the house and pounded on Hilton Hardy's door. Hilton was Daddy's chauffeur.

'Hilton! Wake up!' He pounded on the door again. That was when I noticed Daddy still had on his rumpled pajama shirt underneath his suit jacket.

'Mr. Stites, Mr. Hardy visiting his people in Cayo Mambí,' Annie called from the window of the butler's pantry, her voice muffled through the shut jalousies. 'He got permission from Mrs. Stites.'

Daddy swore out loud and rushed to the garage where Hilton kept the company limousine, a shiny black Buick. We had two of them

11

— Dynaflows, with the chromed, oval-shaped ventiports along the front fenders. Daddy opened the garage doors and got in the car, but he didn't start it. He got back out and shouted up to the house, 'Annie! Where does Hilton keep the keys to this goddamn thing?'

'On a hook in there, Mr. Stites. Mr. Hardy have all the keys on hooks,' she called back.

Daddy found the keys, revved the Buick, and backed it out of the garage. I watched from the path and didn't dare ask what was happening. He roared down the driveway, wheels spitting up gravel, and took a right on La Avenida.

That was the first time in my life I ever saw Daddy behind the wheel of his own car. He always had a driver. Daddy wore a white duck suit every day, perfectly creased, the bejesus starched out of it. A white shirt, white tie, and his panama hat. Every afternoon Hilton Hardy took him on his rounds in the Buick limousine. At each stop a secretary served Daddy a two-cent demitasse of Cuban coffee. They knew exactly what time he was coming and just how he liked his demitasse: a thimble-sized shot, no sugar. A 'demi demi,' he used to say. According to him, he never got sick because his stomach was coated with the stuff. Daddy was old-fashioned. He had his habits and he took his time. He was not a man who rushed.

★   ★   ★

I remember how the cane cutters lived: in one-room shacks called bohios. Dirt floors, a pot in the middle of the room, no windows, no plumbing, no electricity. The only light was what came through the open doorway and filtered into the cracks between the thatched palm walls. They slept in hammacas. They were squatters, but the company tolerated it because they had to live somewhere during the harvest. The rest of the year — the dead time, they called it — they were desolajos. I don't know what they did. Wandered the countryside looking for work and food, I guess. In the shantytown where the cane cutters lived — it's called a batey — there were naked children running everywhere. None of those people had shoes, and their feet had hard shells of calloused skin around them. They cooked their meals outdoors, on mangrove charcoal. Got their water from a spigot at the edge of the cane fields. They had to carry their water in hand buckets, but the company let them take as much as they wanted. It was certainly a better deal than the mine workers got over in Nicaro. Those people were employees of the U.S. government, and they had to get their water from the river — the Levisa River — where they dumped the tailings from the nickel mine. The Nicaro workers drank from the river, bathed in the river, washed their clothes in the river. If you wash your bike in the Levisa River after it rains, it gets shiny clean. That's a Cuban thing. I don't know why, but it really works. After it rained, everybody was down there, boys and grown men wading into the river in their underwear, washing cars and bicycles.

The American kids on La Avenida weren't supposed to go beyond the gates of Preston, down to the cane cutters' batey. I think it was a company policy. Inside the gates was okay. Beyond the gates, you were looking for trouble. But Hatch Allain's son Curtis Junior and I went down there all the time. We were boys, and curious. We sneaked into native dances. Curtis liked Cuban girls. That was a thing — some of the American kids only dated Cubans. Phillip Mackey and Everly Lederer's sister Stevie from over in Nicaro were both like that, and they both got shipped off to boarding school in the States. Though in Phillip's case it wasn't just girls but the trouble he and my brother got into together, helping the rebels. The Cuban girls never gave poor Curtis the chance to get in any trouble. He was dirty and his ears stuck out, and the girls just didn't like him. I tried to tell him that you have to be a little aloof, a little bit take-it-or-leave-it, even if it isn't how you really feel, but Curtis just didn't get it.

It was Daddy's idea to give the cane cutters plots of land so they could feed themselves, grow yucca and sweet potatoes. He believed in self-sufficiency. He brought over Rev. Crim, who ran United Fruit's agricultural school. The cane cutters' kids were mostly illiterate. They studied practical things: farming, housekeeping, Methodist values. Daddy was conscientious about offering education, but he wouldn't have taken urchins up off the street like my mother wanted to do. My mother was a real liberal. She fed people at the back door. She would have had them inside the house if my father didn't put limits on her. If there was a child out in the batey

14

who was ill or crippled or retarded, or had some sort of disease, Mother sent someone to pick him or her up and take the child to the company hospital. Christmastime, she went out into the countryside on her horse with gifts and toys. She wanted to go alone, but my father wouldn't allow it. A United Fruit security guard rode along behind her. I guess they were more like police officers than guards; they carried guns and guamparas — that's like a machete, with a big, flat blade for slapping people. My mother rode her horse all over the countryside. She once brought the *National Geographic* folks on a tour, and they took a lot of pictures. That is still the finest magazine to me. When my mother rode up, the Cubans streamed out of their houses and gathered around her. They loved her. They wanted to touch her. She had that effect.

When Daddy first laid eyes on her, he was visiting his brother up near Crawfordsville, Indiana. Mother had run out of gas. Daddy saw her walking along the side of the road and he said here came this angel. Mother had been a May Queen, and she was president of Kappa Kappa Gamma at DePauw. I had to return her sorority pin when she died. Harlan Sanders — that's Colonel Sanders — he was from Indiana, and always in love with Mother. We were his guests at the Sanders Motor Court once, on our way to Cumberland Falls. You could tell he had that fatal thing for Mother. His hands shook and his face turned red when he greeted us. I think Daddy was amused. He didn't mind showing her off. Mother was a beautiful woman, and she took fine care of herself. Never washed her face with soap, only cold cream, and she was health-conscious. She had the servants making yogurt back when it was still a very unusual thing to eat. Every night she sat at her desk and brushed her hair a hundred times before she went to bed. You notice those things as a boy. Twice or three times a year Daddy would take us to Miami to shop for Mother's clothes. He'd arrange for a private room at Burdine's. He, Del, and I would sit with Mother as the models came out in various things. If we liked what the model wore, Mother tried it on and came out and took a spin. If we agreed that it looked nice, Daddy bought it. Mother said she would never wear anything that her men didn't approve of. At first I didn't want to spend the afternoon in a fitting room. But then I got to liking the ritual of it, and how nice Mother dressed herself. When Del started palling around with Phillip Mackey, Del grew less interested in family things and stopped coming with us to Miami. It wasn't as fun going without him, but it made Mother happy that I was there, and I took pride in helping her choose outfits, in being the son she could depend on. Later, when I was at military school, we dressed up for dances and functions and I knew how to put myself together because of Mother. I cared about these things. Mother said elegance was taking a plain outfit and accenting it with one flashy detail — a tie, maybe. I still think of her when I get dressed up.

Dirt shacks, no running water — the way those people lived, it's just how life was to me. I was a child. Mother didn't like it, but Daddy reminded her that the company paid them higher wages than any Cuban-owned sugar operation. Mother thought it was just terrible the way the Cuban plantations did business. It broke her heart, the idea of a race of people exploiting their own kind. The cane cutters were all Jamaicans, of course — not a single one of them was Cuban — but I knew what she meant: native people taking advantage of other native people, brown against black, that kind of thing. She was proud of Daddy, proud of the fact that the United Fruit Company upheld a certain standard, paid better wages than they had to, just to be decent. She said she hoped it would influence the Cubans to treat their own kind a bit better.

★   ★   ★

I knew something terrible had happened, watching Daddy take off like that, still wearing his pajama shirt. I ran back in to get dressed and heard Mother on the phone with Mr. LaDue, apologizing for calling so early. 'Mr. Stites wanted me to call and inform you that there's a fire in the cane fields,' she said. Of course it was a fire. Nothing else could have made that strange, orange light. 'He wanted me to tell you he's gone out there.' Even in a crisis, Mother was formal, always proper and composed. She was like that up to the very end. And it wasn't easy for her, believe me. To lose everything. And not just the house, our whole world, but to have her oldest son up there with those people.

Mother was in the kitchen talking to Annie, and I figured it was best to keep quiet and slip out without her noticing. Our house was next to the seawall, at the very end of La Avenida, across the street from my school, the Preston Academy for American Children. I opened the gate and headed right, toward the town square. La Avenida was the managers' row, with a locked gate and guards at the entrance. There was a pecking order in Preston, and we were at the end of the row, in the biggest house, with our own private guards, one in the daytime and one at night. The night guards were called serenos, and one sat on our steps until dawn. It was still early — barely 6:00 A.M. — and the street was peaceful and quiet. The only sound I heard was Mrs. LaDue's peacocks. Each house on La Avenida had an arbor at the front gate with bougainvillea, and beyond each gate, exquisite gardens. The company gardeners kept those places immaculate. A breeze was ruffling the bougainvillea, and bright pink leaves were blowing along the sidewalk. The new *Unifruitco*, rolled up with a rubber band, was sitting on every porch. I passed the swimming pool, where the week before we'd had a big poolside cookout for the Cabot Lodges, who were down visiting. Henry Cabot Lodge was an older fellow, but he'd been on the swim team at Harvard, and he was going off the high dive with us kids, doing flips and jackknives. The Cabot Lodges had returned to Boston a few days earlier. Now the pool was deserted and quiet. I noticed something

18

settling on the surface of the water, a grayish film. It was ash floating down from the air.

The guard station was at the end of the avenue. I waved to the guard and kept going. From the town square, where company headquarters and Daddy's office were, I could see the mill off to the right. During the harvest, the mill ran on a twenty-four-hour schedule, lit up like a Christmas tree. Crushers going, cane syrup boiling, centrifugals humming. I expected to see steam drifting from the mill's two giant chimneys, but they were both cold. Cars loaded with cut cane were sitting on the train tracks just outside the mill, waiting to be rolled in and emptied into the crushers. You can't cut cane and leave it sitting — it turns acidic and dries out. The entire extraction process was designed for that not to happen.

The smell of boiling cane syrup — the meladura, it's called — used to fill the air in Preston. A warm, malty smell. I loved that smell. I can smell it right now. There was a different smell in the air that morning, not exactly familiar. I headed toward the rail crossing. I figured the flagman might know what was happening and where to find Daddy. Beyond the tennis courts were the golf course, the polo fields, then nothing but cane for miles and miles. A yellowish mutt, one of those scrawny little Cuban dogs, trotted along beside me. As I got closer to the fields, that peculiar smell was getting stronger. The dog was zigzagging and putting his nose up to sniff. The air smelled like burned sugar, a tangy, black carbon smell, like

19

when one of Annie's pies bubbled over and dripped onto the bottom of the oven.

There was no flagman at the crossing, which seemed odd. Three tracks converged, and cars were always coming in. A railroad car half-filled with freshly hacked cane sat there, abandoned like someone had suddenly decided to stop working. I stepped over the ties and took the access road past a row of workers' shanties. The workers usually had cook fires going out there in the morning, for boiling sweet potatoes that they ate while they worked in the fields. But there was no one around. Maybe it's idiotic, but I remember thinking, *If there are no cook fires, how did the cane catch fire?*

From the access road I saw a plume of black smoke going up. My next thought was that we'd been bombed. The week before, Batista had dropped white phosphorus over the Sierra Cristal, the mountains above us where the rebels were hiding. The smoke drifted over Preston, and the next day we had rain, and the rainwater covered the town with greasy soot. Rain fell in the mountains, too, but the fires up there kept burning. Water won't put out white phosphorus; it loves moisture. The fires burned for days, killing animals and a few of the guajiros who lived up there. Guajiros, that's one thing. Americans is another. Batista wouldn't have bombed us. We were practically the only support he had left in eastern Cuba.

I saw Daddy pull up in the black Buick, about a quarter mile down the road. He had Hatch and Rudy Allain riding with him. Hatch was the plantation boss. His brother, Rudy, was the guy who fixed all the mill machinery and irrigation equipment. The fire was in the southern part of our fields. As I got closer, heat baked my face and the front of my clothes. I heard the dry, licking sound of flames. Through waves of heat I could see Daddy talking to Rudy, and old Mr. LaDue running toward them from the other direction. A couple of lower management guys came hauling up the road in a company truck. Rudy yelled something to Daddy. I was close now, but I couldn't hear what he said. There was a burst that sounded like an explosion. Cane is volatile, especially when it's ready for cutting. Black smoke was filtering up so fast it looked like water running backward. Daddy picked up a cane cutter's machete and headed toward the narrow break between two burning fields. He ran right in and disappeared in the smoke and flames.

★　★　★

In Daddy's office at company headquarters there was a big map of Oriente. Oriente was where we lived, and it was Cuba's largest, poorest, blackest province. It has the best climate and most fertile land for growing sugarcane. Castro has it all divided up now, I don't know why; another cockeyed thing like changing the name of our town, Preston, to 'Guatemala' — which makes no sense at all. Back then the entire eastern half of the island was all one province, Oriente. On the map in Daddy's office, United Fruit's

21

property was marked in green. Practically the whole map was green — 330,000 acres of arable land — with one small area of gray that wasn't ours marked 'owned by others.' People have no idea, the scale of things. Fourteen thousand cane cutters. Eight hundred fifty railcars. Our own machine shops, to repair every part in the mill. Our own airstrip. Two company DC-3s, a Lockheed Lodestar and Daddy's Cessna Bobcat, which he used for hedgehopping — surveying land or popping over to Banes, the other company mill town thirty miles away. We had our own fleet of sugar boats that went back and forth to Boston. You could sit in the Pan-American Club, which had a bank of panoramic windows perched out over the water like the prow of an ocean liner, and watch the boats coming in and being loaded with bags of raw sugar. During cutting season, our mill processed fifteen million pounds of sugar a day.

The cane cutters were always paid their wages at the end of the season. Before the terrible thing that happened to him, Mr. Flamm, the paymaster, calculated their earnings in a giant ledger book. The workers lined up along the road, and Mr. Flamm unzipped a green leather moneybag and doled out pesos. The moneybag had a big lock on it at the end of the zipper, and the company logo embossed on the front. As each worker received his pay, Mr. Flamm crossed him off the list. He had the workers sign next to their names that they'd received their earnings in full. These guys were mostly from Jamaica. They spoke the king's English, but practically none of

them could sign their name. They were supposed to just put a check next to it instead. Some of them didn't have last names, just nicknames. Hatch Allain stood by to make sure there was no monkey business. It was all handled in cash. They were paid straight cash, minus whatever they'd charged at the company store, the almacén. If they'd drawn off their pay, it was recorded in the ledger book. The company let them draw off their wages so they could eat before payday. None of them owned cars or mules, and they had to do their shopping in Preston. For a while, the company paid them at the end of each workday, but Daddy said it was better to hold off and pay them at the end of the season. The reason was that some of those guys who came over from Jamaica to cut the cane found out they didn't like it so much. They deserted, never paid the company for their boat passage from Kingston. Cutting cane is brutal, brutal work, some of the hardest work in the world. Bending over all day long under broiling sun, hitting the cane with a flat-blade machete. Leaves so sharp they'll slice you to ribbons. People get sun-stroke; there were heart attacks in our fields. They have to work fast because the sugar starts to turn. The acid content rises and it ferments if the cane sits for more than a few hours. The workers cut the cane and stripped it of leaves. Tied it into bundles and loaded the bundles onto oxcarts, and from oxcarts onto cane cars, which were shunted straight into the mill for processing. It was an eighteen-hour workday, with maybe four hours of sleep. Those

23

guys were up before dawn, and after dark they worked by the light of oil pots. If you pay people at the very end of cutting season, they stick around and finish the job.

The cane cutters in Preston hadn't always been Jamaican. Up through the forties, the company hired mostly Haitians. Every year Daddy went by ship to Cap-Haïtien to bring a bunch of them to Cuba for cutting season. He had a gentleman over there, an absolutely elegant Frenchman named Mr. Bloussé, who contracted for so many workers to come over and cut our cane. I was just a little teeny kid, but I remember one of those ships, a double-stacked tramp steamer, docked in the Preston bay and packed with them, black arms hanging out the open sides. They unloaded those guys from the ship and transported them in open railcars. They might have been cane cars, come to think of it. The cane cars are just cages, with oval-shaped iron bars that bow out like a whale's rib cage, to hold cane stalks. They trundled the Haitians out to a compound, kind of a pen, and dosed them with salts. The doctor from the company hospital would go and have a look at them, Dr. Romero, who gave health certificates for servants — every servant had to have a certificate or they couldn't work in your home. The men were examined and left in the pen for several days to make sure they didn't have any communicable diseases, ophthalmia, or what have you. There was some nasty stuff on those ships. That one can make you blind.

When I was boy we had iceboxes, and the ice came in a burlap sugar sack surrounded by

sawdust to keep it from melting. Every day a little horse came down La Avenida pulling a cart, and the iceman delivered our hundred-pound block of ice. After payday, and just before they shipped the cane cutters back to Haiti on those double-deckers, the Haitians would go down to Mayarí and buy trunks and fill them with things to take home, gaudy silk shirts in red or yellow, trinkets, bottles of Cuban rum, that sort of thing. One fellow bought a trunk, then went and got himself a hundred-pound block of ice. Without telling anybody, this guy put the ice in his trunk and carried it with him onto the ship. When they docked in Le Cap he wanted to kill the captain because he said the captain stole his ice.

★ ★ ★

We'd had cane fires before. When I was six, lightning hit, and several hundred acres burned. The company roused the workers, and they had almost a thousand guys out there hacking into the breaks with machetes to widen them and prevent the fire from jumping the road. They backburned so that when the fire got to the break there was nothing left to fuel it. Cane fires are notoriously difficult to put out. That morning, I could see flames spreading out across the southern part of our fields. I couldn't imagine how they would get the fire under control, even with every last worker out there helping.

Rudy was talking to Mr. LaDue and some other guys when I came running up. I'd never cut a break, but I grabbed a machete that was leaning against the little shed where poor Mr. Flamm — may he rest in peace — used to pay the workers. Mr. Flamm was a delicate little guy in wire-framed glasses, and they'd built him the shed so he wouldn't have to stand in the sun as he doled out wages to the cane cutters. The machete was heavy. I couldn't have swung it worth a damn, but I was willing to try. I started heading toward the break where Daddy had gone in. Rudy grabbed me by the shoulders and blocked my way. 'Hold on, son,' he said. 'We don't need you burning yourself up in that field.' Just then, two guys pulled up in a truck and yelled to Rudy that they couldn't get the main valve open. Rudy said to come with him. We ran over and hopped into one of the trucks. He drove us down the access road a ways and parked. There was a spigot there, the opening to the main irrigation line. Rudy bent down and started loosening the bolt on the spigot with a wrench. He took the bolt off and turned the valve wheel counterclockwise. Nothing happened. No water came out. He spun the wheel. It was all the way open.

'God*damnit.*' He threw his wrench on the ground. The air was thick with smoke, and one of Rudy's eyes was red and irritated. His other eye was glass. I started coughing and inched my shirt up over my mouth.

He spun the open wheel again. 'We're shit out of luck, K.C.'

More guys were arriving, fellows from company headquarters. Daddy's secretary, Mr. Suarez, was with them — he might have been the

26

only Cuban in the bunch. They had machetes, and scarves tied around their mouths. They went in at the break near the busted main valve. There were no cane cutters out there. No mill workers, either. Just management — agriculture guys and pencil pushers from the offices.

'The batey is a ghost town,' Hatch Allain, the plantation boss, yelled, walking toward us. 'I've got the guards knocking on doors, getting people up around town. We should have at least a hundred guys out here soon.'

The heat from the flames pressed against my face like I was getting a sunburn. I kept coughing, although I had the shirt up over my mouth. How Daddy could stand it in the thick of the fire is beyond me.

Mr. LaDue came down the road, and Rudy called to him that the valve was busted and there wasn't any water. Mr. LaDue looked even older than usual. His face was half-shaved. He had shaving cream on his neck.

'If we don't get the fire stopped at the access road, the whole town is going up,' he told Rudy.

As more men appeared, Rudy and Hatch were yelling instructions, where to go into the cane fields and how deep to cut. I wanted to help out. I said, 'Rudy, Hatch, put me to work.' But Rudy said I should go home and have my mother call Mr. Smith, the American ambassador. What Ambassador Smith could do about a cane fire was beyond me, but I did what he said.

The cloud of smoke from the fire was shifting out over the bay. It looked like a massive black ocean liner moving across the sky. Ash was flaking down over the town as I ran back to the house to give Mother Rudy's message. It was like falling snow, lacy gray flakes that sifted through the air and wafted back up on the hot drafts from the blaze. Maybe it was more like fake snow in a snow dome than real snow. It just whirled around, a circular blizzard of cane ash.

★ ★ ★

Mr. Bloussé, who contracted the workers from Haiti, came to visit us once in Preston. He was dashing like a movie star, blond hair pomaded and shiny, a silk ascot tied around his neck. He wore French-tailored shirts with black onyx cuff links and military jodhpurs. A servant stood behind him, a young Haitian boy who was quiet as a mouse, a curious boy. Mr. Bloussé would snap his fingers and say something to the boy in French, and the boy would scamper off to run some errand. I figured he spoke only French or some version of it, a native patois, but on one occasion Mr. Bloussé's little Haitian boy spoke to me in English. Mr. Bloussé was in the parlor with Daddy, and the boy stopped me in the hall and asked if we had any books he could look at. This boy carried luggage and shined Mr. Bloussé's shoes. He stood patiently in the hall like he didn't have a thought in his head. And yet apparently he was able to read, and in *English*. I gave him some magazines to look at, and asked him how he learned. He said Mr. Bloussé taught him. That it was part of his training. I don't know what sort of training. Later, that same boy ended up working for the Lederer family in Nicaro. One of the Lederers' daughters, Everly, the redhead, used to follow him around. It was the same boy, but he was a grown-up by then — just one more Haitian servant in Nicaro, except he had this curious history, which I knew about.

Mr. Bloussé brought Luxenil lace for Mother, and for Daddy a bottle of expensive cognac. He and Daddy drank and smoked cigars late every night. Daddy collected liquors from all over the world. On a mahogany cart he had miniature glass bears from Russia filled with kümmel, and bottles of yellow and green Chartreuse — the yellow glowed; it looked like it had a lightbulb shining up through the glass from underneath. He had orgeat and syrupy white crème de menthe in cut-crystal decanters. Spanish cider, and pear brandy that had a whole pear floating in the bottle. That one was from Portugal. The bottle was clear and the fruit loomed up like a fish under the surface of a pond. The younger guys in management came over to sit in the parlor, drink cognac, and visit with Mr. Bloussé. He'd been in the French Foreign Legion, he'd traveled all over the world. Zanzibar, you name it. Everybody admired him. He was wealthy, with a magnificent estate in Cap-Haïtien. I remember him talking about his three daughters. They were just old enough to get married, maybe seventeen or eighteen. Some of the guys in management wanted to set up meetings with Mr. Bloussé, to court the daughters. I imagined them as tropical French princesses, pretty girls in elaborate costumes, hand servants fanning them with palm fronds in a courtyard.

★ ★ ★

'Yes, I'm aware that His Excellency is in Havana, but my husband feels he ought to know,' Mother said to someone at the embassy.

'Call the fire department? Yes, ma'am.'

'Well, I'm not sure *why* he wanted me to call, but there must have been some reason. If you could forward the message, that this is Evelyn Stites, calling on behalf of Malcolm Stites, and we've got quite a blaze on our hands.'

'Yes, ma'am, we've called the fire department.'

Mother was too polite to tell the embassy receptionist that this was United Fruit territory, and we *were* the fire department.

After she made the call, Mother started crying and held on to me and wouldn't let go. Crying was something Daddy didn't tolerate. I knew this was her chance to get it out. I didn't tell her what Mr. LaDue had said about the town going up in flames. I didn't need to. Through the window we could both see Ho, our gardener, aiming his hose up to wet the roof and the sides of the house.

By noon, the smoke coming from the cane fields was so thick it blotted out the sun. It was the middle of the day and we had the dregs of twilight, like it was nine o'clock on a summer night. Mother and Annie and the other servants were rushing around putting damp towels up against the window sashes and under the doors.

Ambassador Smith's secretary, or maybe his secretary's secretary, called to say she was still trying but had not yet located His Excellency. Ambassador Smith was never in his office when Daddy needed him. If the workers went on strike, or there was some misunderstanding with Batista's people about export dues, Daddy called and the ambassador took his sweet time dealing with it, busy playing golf at the yacht club or hosting a charity ball. He was a real high society New England type, Yale University, all of that. The Havana Yacht Club was so exclusive that they blackballed the president of Cuba. Batista was a mulatto from Banes, the other United Fruit town. His father had worked for us as a cane cutter. Batista had worked for us, too, for the company railroad. He started out as an assistant to a chauffeur on a company line car — that's an automobile with flanged wheels, it runs on the track — and was eventually promoted to flagman.

I was in the parlor listening to the radio, to see if I could find out what was happening in the mountains. It hadn't occurred to me that the fire was deliberately set, but my instinct had been to try to tune in the rebels' wireless broadcast, Radio Rebelde. It was on the twenty-meter band, at 5:00 and 9:00 P.M.. every night, and came in perfectly clear. Daddy didn't allow it, but I listened when he wasn't around, thinking maybe I could find out something about my brother. They talked about Raúl's column, and this and that victory, and the horrific phosphorus bombings in the mountains, and once I heard something about 'brave foreigners' helping the

31

cause. But no one ever mentioned Del by name. It seems surprising in retrospect that they missed such a whopping opportunity for propaganda. The oldest son of enemy number one, the head of La United, had joined the cause, and they aren't using it.

When the fellows from Preston and Nicaro were kidnapped a few months later — in the summer of that year, 1958 — the rebels invited a photojournalist from *Life* to go up to the Sierra Maestra and visit their camp. From the magazine pictures it looked like those guys were having one hell of a party up there, kidnappers and hostages drinking rum and smoking cigars, goofing off and lying around barefoot in hammocks. Mr. Lederer from Nicaro posed with a rebel's hip holster, a drawn gun, and the caption said the Cubans had nicknamed him 'Desperado.' What sort of kidnapping is that? The rebels managed to look like real heroes — romantic-type revolutionaries — right there in the pages of *Life* magazine. It would have been quite a scandal that they had an American boy on their side. And not just any boy, but a poster child for American 'imperialismo' — Delmore Stites, son of Malcolm Stites, manager of the United Fruit Company's Cuba Division.

I fiddled with the radio set and finally got Rebelde. It sounded like they'd closed down the highway east of Camagüey. They had a reputation for overstating their advances, and I didn't really believe it. I heard the parlor door open and quickly switched off the broadcast. A man covered with soot was standing in the doorway. He looked like a chimney sweep, charred from head to toe. The hair on his head was burned off in patches. It was Daddy. His eyebrows were gone. So was his mustache. He had a banged-up gas can in his hand, a green and yellow company can like the ones in Rudy's machine shop. He stood there and didn't say a word, just tossed the gas can on the parlor floor. It bounced on the wood, empty. Daddy never wore anything but the white ducks. He was the picture of a United Fruit man, tall and intimidating in his perfectly pressed suit. And here he was, his white pants filthy, jacket gone. Wearing his pajama shirt, the sleeves rolled up, burned patches on his hands and arms that were the color of raw steak.

The dented gas can lay on the parlor floor, its cap missing. Daddy stood over it in his burned, soot-smeared clothes. He looked too dirty to sit down on his own furniture.

'Found this out there in the fields,' he said.

I couldn't tell if I was supposed to respond or keep quiet. I knew what it meant. Someone set the fire. If the cane operation was anybody's, it was Daddy's. The idea that people would want to destroy it, it was like they wanted to destroy him. And us.

'It's disgusting what these people are willing to do.' He started coughing. 'Those son of a bitches.' His voice was almost gone from the smoke. 'Those goddamn son of a bitches. This is what they call *negotiating?*'

Daddy sat down in the chair across from me and put his head in his hands.

'They say they want to do business, work out a

33

deal. And the next thing you know, they're trying to burn us to the ground.'

I didn't know it at the time, but Daddy had been sending messages up into the mountains, trying to negotiate with Raúl. By that point, the American managers in Oriente saw the writing on the wall and everybody was scrambling to keep the door open with the rebels, hoping to keep their operations running, their sweetheart deals and tax-free status, in case the rebels were suddenly the new government. Daddy was still dealing with Batista, of course — he was the president — but Batista had lost control of Oriente. That was a fact, but people in Havana, Ambassador Smith, and Batista's army generals — these guys were in denial. So Daddy had taken it upon himself to get a line of communication going. I'm sure he was trying to get Del back as well. The problem was that Del didn't want to come home.

'We had a deal,' Daddy said, 'and the deal was, I work with them and they leave us alone. I sent a letter up there to Raúl Castro. They've got it in writing. And they turn around and attack us.'

My father had never confided in me about these sorts of things. Work was work, and he hung it up at the door; that was his rule.

'I personally *promised* this faggot Raúl that I'd get Dulles on the horn and stop the arms shipments. And I did — I held up my end of the bargain — and this is what I get: a bunch of natives running out of the hills and starting fires.'

* * *

The gray area marked 'owned by others' on the map in Daddy's office was a decent-sized plantation near Birán, fifteen miles southwest of us. It belonged to Don Ángel Castro, Fidel and Raúl's father. He had acquired a lot of property down there for some unusual reason. I don't know how he did it — moving fence lines, probably. He sold his cane to us, but he wouldn't sell the land. Everybody knew the family. The kids, especially Raúl and Fidel, would lurk down in Mayarí, at the pool halls and the cockfights, when they were visiting from Havana, where they all went off to school. Later, Fidel said that when they were growing up they weren't allowed into Preston, or invited to any of our social functions or permitted to use our beaches. But they were not employees of the United Fruit Company, and it was all private property, every last bit of it. And even if they had been employees, Cubans weren't allowed certain places, like the Pan-American Club. But they wouldn't have *wanted* to go to our club. Everybody kept to themselves. American with American. Cuban with Cuban. Jamaican with Jamaican. I remember thinking Raúl was a fruity type. People said he was like that. You know what I mean. A maricón. And they said he had a Chinese mother — he was Oriental-looking, and people were suspicious about that. I don't know if there was more to it than just gossip. Fidel's mother was the old man's maid — Lina — she had a withered arm from polio. Del and I used to go hunting up in Birán, guinea hens and blue pigeons, and we'd see Don Ángel sitting on the porch in his

35

guayabera, a big cigar in his mouth. We always stopped and said hello. The first time he invited us up for a glass of water, I couldn't help staring at Lina's withered arm, fascinated the way boys are. That place was in true guajiro style, the house up on stilts, with chickens and goats running around underneath it.

Months before the fire started, Daddy had begun to suspect that some of the cane cutters were rebel sympathizers. He had Rev. Crim reporting on the workers. And you might call it racist, especially nowadays, but it was reasonable to assume that anybody black — whether they were Cuban, Haitian, Jamaican — was trouble. Two months before the fire was set, one of the cane cutters had gone into Mr. Flamm's office to see him. He wanted chits so he could draw off his pay and get credit at the almacén. But he'd already overdrawn what he would make for the whole cutting season. Some of these guys were foolish about that. They'd get chits to buy appliances at the company store and turn around and sell them in Mayarí for a quarter of what they were worth, just to have the money. Spend it on rotgut or lottery tickets. By the time payday rolled around they had nothing coming. They were working like dogs for no pay, just to get out of debt with the company. This cane cutter and Mr. Flamm had an argument. Mr. Flamm wouldn't give him any store credit and tried to show him the books and explain why, but the guy wasn't having any of it. What a shame. There is no reason to bring a machete into company headquarters. Mr. Flamm was a little teeny man in his wire-framed glasses. If only somebody had stopped the guy before he went in carrying that machete. After that, Hatch said no blacks in the offices. Mr. Flamm bled to death right there in the accounting office. That's not politics, it's mental illness. There were lots of cane cutters, thousands of them, and as I said, they barely had names. They came over on boats from Kingston and lived in these hovels. The one who killed Mr. Flamm ran off. I don't know if they ever caught him.

★ ★ ★

The company guys who wanted to court Mr. Bloussé's daughters came to our house to meet with Mr. Bloussé. There were three of them, and they showed up with their hair combed flat, in dinner jackets, smelling of Vitalis. They were bachelors, bored and lonely. They had good pay, no expenses, free housing; everything was provided by the company. But there was no place to go, nothing to spend the money on, and they couldn't date the Cuban girls. At least not the upper-class, light-skinned girls. The Cubans didn't allow it: Americans were mongrels as far as they were concerned. We didn't have the right blood. Rich Cubans, the planters and politicians, they sent their children to be educated in Europe — Paris or Madrid — not the United States. They wanted their daughters to marry Spanish aristocrats, not some rube from Kansas. If these fellows did manage to get a date with a Cuban girl, they were expected to sit on the porch with her mother, her sister, her grandmother — a stern dueña in a black lace shawl, policing the situation. In Oriente, you never went out with a young Cuban girl alone. But these guys weren't used to any of that, so they cut corners. Daddy said he lost a lot of good people, really fine employees, because of the trouble they got themselves into with Cuban women. Daddy was sensitive about those things. We may have owned the land, but Daddy had to deal with Cubans to keep things running smoothly with Batista, the Rural Guard, these sorts of Latin factotums, and it was better to fire an employee than to offend anyone. Daddy made it a policy to send fat old Jamaican women to work in bachelors' homes. The younger the employee, the fatter and older and uglier the maid. No young, pretty servants for those guys. Daddy himself always had a male secretary. He worked late hours, and said he didn't want his secretary leaving to go fix dinner for her family.

Mr. Bloussé came back to Preston and he brought his wife and the three daughters. They stayed at the company hotel down by the docks — like everything else in town, I'm sure it's fallen into an awful state at this point. I've seen pictures and it's terrible how they haven't taken care of those places. They cram ten families in each house and let the buildings rot, no paint, no maintenance. It was a very elegant hotel, with dark red walls and mahogany furniture. Mr. Bloussé and his wife and daughters checked in and then came to our house for dinner. When they arrived, Mother's mouth nearly dropped to the floor. Mr. Bloussé's wife was Haitian — she was black, and I mean *black*, and so were the daughters. Annie didn't want to serve them. I think she felt it was an insult to have to wait on other blacks, and such dark ones, too. There are codes to these things. The bachelors who'd come over to impress Mr. Bloussé with their greased hair and Vitalis, they got wind of it and none of them showed up to meet the daughters. The courtships were called off. The guys all joked about it afterward, said Mr. Bloussé was a nigger-lover and a mud shark. But I never heard Daddy mention it. I knew he disapproved of race mixing. The Cubans did it sometimes, they dated black, and they called their girlfriends mi negrita. And the Chinamen married Cubans because they had to. There weren't any Chinese women. Maybe that's why people accused the Chinamen of being homosexuals. And why people accused Raúl Castro of it — because he looked part Chinese. We had two Chinamen at the house, one for the vegetable garden and one for the flowers. Daddy had a whole village of them, to work the centrifugals at the sugar mill. It was hot as Hades in that room. As the centrifugals stirred the boiling cane syrup, the last impurities bubbled up and the sugar crystals got spun out. The Chinamen wore little underwear like Speedo bathing suits as they worked. The Cubans refused to do that job because of the heat. Each Chinaman had a cup of salt and a bucket of water, and they wore the little Speedos because it was like 140 degrees in there. They would just sweat, sweat, sweat.

'As you can see,' Mr. Bloussé said to Daddy that night when we sat down to dinner, 'I'm doing my part to *blanchir* the population.' He gestured to the wife and daughters. During dinner, Mr. Bloussé told a story about a ship where ophthalmia spread. Everyone on the ship, including the captain and his helmsman, caught it and went blind, and they plowed right into another steamer. Daddy laughed and seemed relaxed, as if he admired Mr. Bloussé as much as he had before we knew he had a colored family. I was a young boy and this was confusing to me, why something Daddy disapproved of was suddenly okay. I figured it had to do with Mr. Bloussé being French and exotic and debonair. Like maybe the very rich didn't have to abide by the same rules as everybody else. Mother and Daddy didn't even want me hugging Annie so tightly. Mother was a liberal, but not too liberal. Mother said Annie's smell rubbed off on me — she'd sniff me to check. Annie did have a smell, sort of musky. I loved it. I can smell it right now. When I was little I let her hug me when they weren't around. She squeezed me tight. It was a wonderful, safe feeling, my face buried in her apron so I could barely breathe. She called me muñnequito, her little doll. I don't remember if she had any children of her own. Maybe she did, but I think they lived in Mayarí. Annie lived with us. Once, in a taxicab here in Tampa, the driver was some type of black Caribbean and his cab smelled like Annie.

* * *

40

With no water to put out the fires, Daddy said we would have to wait for them to burn themselves out. The men kept on cutting breaks, putting down flame retardant along the access road, backburning, and we had to just hope for the best. At about five o'clock that evening, Rudy Allain came to our house. He was blackened from head to toe with cane ash. I couldn't remember Rudy ever coming to our house before. Certainly not inside, as a guest. As I said, there was a pecking order in Preston, always someone to answer to. Daddy wasn't Rudy's boss. Rudy was a few notches down the chain. Rudy and his brother, Hatch, were different from us socially, you could say. Coarse people from Louisiana who knew how to handle workers. They didn't live on La Avenida. Daddy had them in two brick houses down by the mill.

Daddy and Rudy sat in the kitchen, talking. Rudy told Daddy the rebels had drained our gasoline supply, and there was nothing in the pumps. They'd done it the previous night, just before they torched our fields. Rudy said whoever had done it must have had keys to the shop. Keys to the fuel pumps. Known where the valves for the irrigation lines were in order to cut off the water. Rudy said maybe an insider was helping them. Maybe an American, he said, and then pointed out again that it had to be someone with keys. Hilton kept all of Daddy's company keys on hooks in the garage, a label on each set. I remembered hearing Hilton tell Daddy that he needed masters to make new copies, that some of the keys were missing. That was right after Del disappeared.

41

Daddy stood up from the table. 'Goddamnit, Rudy. My son is gone, probably kidnapped by these lunatics. For all I know he's lashed to a tree, eating bark, and you're telling me he came down here and torched the town where he was born? Where both of my children were born?'

'I'm not saying he started the fire, Mr. Stites — '

'Then what the hell *are* you saying?'

'Nothing, sir. I'm sorry if I implied — I hope the boy is okay is all.'

Del was okay, and Daddy knew it. For starters, he hadn't been kidnapped. He went gladly. He wasn't on our side.

★ ★ ★

The fire burned late into the night. From our upstairs windows we could see a reddish glow, and smoke backlit by the glow. The rebels had blocked our train lines and the road into Preston. Daddy was putting in calls to Ambassador Smith, hoping he'd get us help from Guantánamo. Maybe they could send a firefighting vessel up the coast, one of those things that pumped ocean water. But then the town transformers had to be shut down because of fire danger, and we had no phone line. Mother, Daddy, and I sat around with hurricane lamps going. Mother tried to keep the mood light. She knew how to handle a crisis, and she and I played canasta. What else was there to do? There's something relaxing about that game. Bastista played it obsessively. Some people say that's why his government collapsed. The rebels were taking over, and meanwhile he was at the presidential palace playing canasta, his aides standing behind the other players, signaling discreetly what cards they held. Annie made us cold sandwiches and we ate those while we played. Daddy paced and cursed Smith — he'd been warning the ambassador that all hell was about to break loose, but Smith kept insisting that Fidel was just a ruffian in the hills. The ambassador was out of touch with what was happening in Oriente. He'd come recently to Santiago, and his reception was about as warm and friendly as what those Venezuelans gave Nixon a few months after the fire, in May of '58. Rocks whistling through the air. When Smith arrived in Santiago, the Rural Guard had been cracking down as a warning to the rebels. They'd killed a few students, and people were livid. That was his last visit. I think he preferred the yacht club in Havana.

Rudy came back to our house later that night, to tell Daddy that all we had left in Preston for drinking water was the rain that had collected in the molasses tanks.

★ ★ ★

The company never had operations in Haiti. Daddy said it wasn't the right political climate for business. In Cuba, we Americans had our traditions, our own world. The company had a set of arrangements with Batista, annual payments, and in return there were no taxes, no tariffs, and we didn't have to bother with the labor unions or any labor laws. We exported raw sugar, and nobody raised a stink. We sent our sugar up to Boston for

43

processing, to the Revere Sugar Refinery. Batista came to our house. He and Daddy got along fine. I don't know that they were friends exactly, but they had an understanding.

I'm sure you know the slaves had a revolution in Haiti. A hundred years before slavery was abolished in Cuba, slaves were running the show over there. But instead of voting in a real government, those guys ran buck wild. Put jeweled crowns on their heads and acted like crazed despots, strutting around with white babies on pikes. But what can you expect of a revolution that began with the pounding of African drums, slaves communicating by voodoo? Bloody mayhem is what. Freed slaves running amok in generals' coats with all the medals and the gold epaulets, and nude from the waist down. They gave themselves ridiculous titles: Chevalier, Viceroy, Generalissimo. The whole thing seems like a bad fever dream. French landowners wallowing in the squalor of their own destroyed estates, lying under the open taps in their own wine cellars, drinking themselves sick. I think they were happy to finally own nothing. Rule no one. Burned mansions, burned crops — the slaves in Haiti torched everything. Of course, slavery is terrible, and as I said, cutting cane is brutal, brutal work. But the slaves were forced, and that's the difference. On some of the plantations the masters made them wear tin face masks so they wouldn't eat the cane. Can you imagine? We let them eat the cane, I mean not as a policy, but nobody had to wear any mask. I'm sure it cost more to make those masks than to lose a few stalks of cane.

Preston was eerily quiet that night. There weren't any trains. Normally, I could hear them from our house, rolling through all night. I would lie in the dark and listen to that long, low whistle, and imagine the train's round yellow headlight cutting a beam through the nighttime mist, which came in off the bay and hung over our fields, a floating lake of ghostly white. From the tone of the train's whistle I'd tell myself, there's the Number Thirty-two. The Number Forty-one. El Veintiuno, El Veintiocho. These were all steam engines, and I knew them by their sound. When I was much younger, Annie came to lie in bed with me some nights. If Mother and Daddy were at a cocktail party or if I was scared and felt like visiting with somebody, Annie came and listened to the trains with me. She knew them, too. All the servants did. The engine whistles were like voices, each one different.

★ ★ ★

Maybe we should have seen it coming. It takes a while to put things together. You can't always do it while it's happening to you. A week before the fire started, the rebels closed down the main highway east of Las Tunas. That meant they had control of Oriente, so much of which was owned by Americans. Us, and the American government, who ran the Nicaro nickel mine. Batista was persona non grata with the Cubans, and we were caught in the middle. Fidel and Raúl, these

45

were local boys, and I think Daddy was hoping he could reason with them. But after the embargo on U.S. sales of military planes to Cuba, that was in March of '57, Batista put pressure on Daddy to convince John Foster Dulles — Mr. Dulles was a friend of Daddy's and a stock-holder and his brother Allen was on the company's board — to find a loophole and get a sale of bombers through. Daddy did that, he spoke to Mr. Dulles, and they set up a pretty crazy scheme. Later, Mr. Dulles told Congress that the Cubans had received the wrong shipment — *before* the embargo — and the new shipment was simply making good on an old arms deal. Batista got his B-26 bombers. This was in the late fall of 1957. Del disappeared at Christmas that year. It was almost a month later, January 1958, when they torched our cane fields. Batista had been strafing the rebels with his American planes, and the rebels were furious. This is why they attacked us, because of the American bombers. Daddy's deal with Batista wrecked Daddy's deal with the rebels. These guys who started the fires, most of them had been United Fruit employees. We were the biggest employer in the whole region. The worst part was that Daddy's oldest son was up in the mountains, getting bombed by American planes that Daddy had helped Batista to buy.

★   ★   ★

But we'd been through this kind of thing before. There was a revolution in 1933, before I was born, when they overthrew Machado. Mother and Daddy lived in Guaro at the time, a few miles inland from Preston. Daddy was super-intendent in charge of agriculture, and the company gave him a house out in the country, right on the Guaro River. Mother and Daddy hid behind a table as bullets shattered the window glass. It was a good table, Mother said, four-inch-thick mahogany. She said they'd be dead if they hadn't had such a fine table. There were troublemakers right outside the house. The U.S. government sent gunboats out onto Nipe Bay to protect the Americans. Mother and Daddy hid and waited for a skyrocket, the signal to get to the gunboats by any means possible. But no skyrockets went off. Sumner Welles, who was the American ambassador at the time, told President Machado he better leave the island, and the rebels called off the shooting. Mother said it was amazing. Just like that, the American ambassador snaps his fingers and it's quiet outside.

★　★　★

Months before that fire started, Daddy had already been shipping our mahogany furniture back to the States, piece by piece, but I hadn't thought to ask why. I was born at the company hospital in Preston. Up to that point I'd spent my entire life in Oriente Province, on the property of the United Fruit Company. I was a boy, and it was my world. I wasn't ready to give it up.

2

'But I didn't know girls like you even *had* relatives,' the United Fruit executive said, shouting over the engine drone of the airplane.

Rachel K had told him that her grandfather, Ferdinand K, had spent time near where they were flying, in northeastern Oriente.

'What the hell kind of last name is 'K' anyhow?' the executive asked.

She said she didn't know. Maybe it stood for something, but she never found out what. Her grandfather came over from Europe at the turn of the century, worked on a plantation for someone called Dumois.

'That means your grandfather worked for us. We bought out Dumois ages ago. They owned Cayo Saetía. There's an old plantation house. We own it now.'

'Just think,' he said, 'your grandfather probably lived in the servants' quarters of the Saetía place.' He shook his head. 'What is the point of living your way of life, doing those . . . whatever you call them . . . Pam-Pam Room 'shimmy shows,' if you've got an actual lineage? A family and everything.'

He gave instructions to the pilot. 'We'll fly right over it.'

Her grandfather had come to Cuba to

48

document the Spanish-American War, but ended up filming the hardwood fires around Dumois' plantation instead. Forests of campeachy, purple-heart, and mahogany that were burned to make way for sugarcane, fires so magnificent and hot they cracked his camera lens. He decided it was safer to stay in Havana and construct dioramic magic tricks. And so he blew up the USS *Maine* in a hotel sink with Chinese firecrackers and sold the reels as war footage.

A French adventurer, her mother had said, which didn't explain why Ferdinand had spoken mostly German. He'd started his own film company in Havana, named it after Rachel K's grandmother Irene, 'Irene Fantoscope.' They had a scheme to advertise commercial messages on clouds floating over the city. It was either moronic or brilliant. Either way, it hadn't worked. Ferdinand got syphilis and died. He left Irene with a small child — Rachel K's mother — who must have had similar taste in men, because she, too, ended up alone and penniless with her own child, Rachel K.

★　★　★

Far down below, the sugarcane swished, turning green or silver according to the direction it was blown, like brushed velvet nap.

She'd been reluctant at first to go with the executive to Oriente. He'd always struck her as a person who was dangerous because he didn't know which parts of him were rotten, or even that he harbored rot.

49

'All this belongs to us,' he said, as they flew low over the green cane fields. 'Three hundred thousand acres.'

Maybe he wasn't dangerous after all. He simply wanted a showgirl to marvel over his sugar empire.

He'd brought along a half-full bottle of whiskey and plenty of ice. They drank it, the executive shouting up to the pilot every so often with instructions, then pointing out this and that to Rachel K. The company sugar mill, the company town. The company 'choo-choo trains,' he called them.

'You be a good girl and finish this up.' He poured more whiskey into her glass. The bottle was empty and they must have been drunk, but it was difficult to gauge drunkenness when she was sitting still, crammed into a tiny plane.

'We toss the empties,' he said, 'to test the soil. The higher the bottle bounces, the richer the loam. That's how we know what to buy. Don't even have to bother landing.'

He insisted that she drop the empty whiskey bottle from the window of the plane. It was Dewar's, she later remembered. Dewar's White Label. She'd watched the clear glass bottle plunging down into the green. The executive claimed that it bounced, but she didn't see anything. Just green.

They landed at company headquarters some-where along the northern coast, a place called Preston. Damp heat closed in around her, and sweat rolled down the sides of her face. 'Not used to it, are you?' he said, grinning. 'Humid,

humid, humid — it's perfect for the cane.'

He pointed toward rows of large and ornate haciendas along the edge of a blue-green bay. 'We live over there. She and the boys are gone for a couple days, shopping in Santiago.' He gripped Rachel K by the waist with both hands. 'And I'm gone on hooky.' Without letting go, he told her, 'I have to confess: I sometimes find myself wanting to stuff you in a footlocker.' And then he added, in a bewildered tone, 'Why do I feel this way?' As if she might know the answer.

She pulled away and skipped down an alley of bananas, a pale-green canopy of long, floppy leaves, taller than she was and loaded with dank and heavy clusters of bananas.

She put her hand around the trunk of a banana plant and felt its cool pulse.

'They're full of water,' the executive called after her, 'pure water.'

* * *

At the airport in Havana where he landed his company plane, Stites — that was his name, she could never remember it and called him 'you' — got her a taxi into town.

He put his hand on her head. 'Look, I'm sad, too, that our little trip is over, but try not to pout.'

'Okay.' She assumed a pouty look and got in the taxi.

She went home and lay in the bath, relieved to be alone after two days of performing the executive's idea of her, that they were having an

51

'affair,' as he put it, that she cared about his sugarcane. After her bath, she painted on her fishnets. Using a sable cosmetic brush and a pot of liquid mascara, she drew lines that crossed at angles to make diamonds, her foot lodged on the windowsill of her kitchenette. This ritual took several hours to complete. Like prayer, it was a quiet, obliterative meditation that opened up an empty space in her thoughts.

★ ★ ★

President Prio showed up at the Cabaret Tokio that night.

'You've been gone,' he said. 'Handsome missed you.'

Handsome was what she called him, a nickname, though Prio was not, in truth, so handsome. He was president and vain. They sat together in his private booth, decorated like a Roman grotto with panorama-print classical scenery, plaster figurines, and purple-leafed wandering Jew tumbling down the walls like ivy. Prio gave her an opal pendant and a silk dress with a secret pocket. She kissed his mustache and let him practice his speeches on her.

He rehearsed his grand civic plans, announcing he would build a new Havana aqueduct, schools for the children in the slums, and a botanical garden open to the public, with a special aviary for African birds. This was just talk. Mostly, Prio liked to have a good time. The press ridiculed him for his expensive tastes: caviar, Russian vodka, fourteen-carat toilet flush handles. Photos had been in the newspaper of him and his prime minister, Tony, jumping over the sofas in the Green Room of the president's palace, in pursuit of young girls clad in short shorts. They were taken during one of Prio's notorious 'white' parties, plenty of cocaine for everyone. After the photos were leaked, Tony moved to Venezuela and started a construction firm. Prio went out only in dark sunglasses. His wife had black illusion veils sewn to the inside of all her pillbox hats. The two of them and the children got in and out of limousines as quickly as they could, turning away from photographers' flashes.

'How about a walk. An ice cream cone?' he said to Rachel K.

She hadn't expected a walk, an ice cream. She'd expected *go to the palace Green Room and cooperate fully*. But his tenderness — opals, dresses, ice cream cones — was part of why she liked him best, of the presidents she'd known. Not because he spoiled her, but because he could be embarrassing and sentimental, a fragile man who needed comforting. When the press rejected him, he sulked to Rachel K; his wife rejected him as well.

They left the club and went to nearby La Rampa, a grand avenue of deluxe sundae parlors where the rich strolled and licked. Exclusive confection boutiques that would later be replaced by an enormous state-run ice cream emporium, a concrete spaceship that gave away twenty-five thousand bowls of government-issue vanilla and strawberry every day, a drab and massive enterprise that would be the future government's elaborate fuck you to the rich, to the presidents and their escorts, who'd strolled and licked along La Rampa in Havana's diamond days.

Prio chose chocolate and she guava, a fruit that tasted deliciously unnatural, more like feminine poisons, perfume, or shampoo, than something you were supposed to eat. They were strolling and licking and window-shopping along La Rampa, Rachel K laughing at Prio, who looked unpresidential, she said, with ice cream in his mustache. A member of his dark-suited security team, who normally walked a few paces behind, approached and tapped Prio's shoulder. The man leaned in and whispered something. Prio blanched. He turned to Rachel K.

'I must leave you now. Lelo here will take you back to the club.'

★　★　★

That night on La Rampa, March 10, 1952, was Prio's last night as president. With the military's cooperation, Fulgencio Batista staged a coup. Batista had telephoned from Miami, promising to buy all the officers new uniforms. In return they gave undying loyalty and surrounded the palace with tanks.

'Easy as ordering a birthday cake from Schrafft's,' Rachel K later heard an American at the Cabaret Tokio remark loudly. One moment Prio was laughing and window-shopping, his wife and children fast asleep in the private wing of the palace. An hour later he and his family were huddled in the piss elegance of the

54

Dominican embassy, booking airline tickets out. They settled in Miami. Prio wrote to Rachel K that he planned to enroll in theater classes and pursue his lifelong dream of becoming an actor. People talked about the coup as the end of democracy. Until later in the week, when the American ambassador endorsed the new government. Batista had been president before, a celebrated army general the Americans knew and liked.

Stites came back to Havana a few days after the coup. He came to the Tokio whistling and happy, said he'd met with Batista. 'A damn good fellow,' he said. 'Used to work for us.'

Rachel K missed Prio, but suspected he might have been relieved to have the presidency stolen from him. He'd put up no fight, chocolate ice cream still frosting the tines of his mustache, a curiously eager tone to his voice, despite his look of alarm. 'Lelo here will take you back to the club.' *Because this should go unwitnessed. Where do I sign?*

★ ★ ★

A couple of weeks after the coup, she watched from a crack between the closed stage curtains as two of Batista's security guards entered the Pam-Pam Room and waited by the bar. One was talking to La Paloma, probably trying to get a freebie, testing out his new role as a state security thug. The other glowered, fingering the contours of a gun in his waistband.

Opening notes floated from the piano.

She stood behind the curtains, waiting for her cue.

'Introducing, from Paris!'

If she says she's from Paris, she's from Paris, was her sentiment. Being from Paris meant filing her nails to a point and lacquering them in Hemorrhage Red, drinking beer with grenadine, and dressing like a zazou, in painted-on fishnets, short skirts, and stacked wooden heels. Eating mouthfuls of cocaine and douching with champagne. She once heard an actual French girl tell the stage manager that she and Rachel K had worked together 'for years' at the Moulin Rouge. It was mysterious and wonderful. Worked together for years at the Moulin Rouge! Maybe we have, Rachel K thought, maybe we have. She believed that people are born every minute of their lives, and what they are in each of those minutes is what they are completely. Zazou, and from Paris, are things she does. Things she is by virtue of doing them. It was a lie whose logic and condition the other dancers understood. Prio, too, understood. Batista didn't, but he liked her anyway, stupidly suggesting that eventually she'd accept her *cubanidad*. 'Like I know my skin color,' he told her, 'and no longer bother with the powder.'

The accompanist began to play an old-fashioned danzón.

'Zazou dancer, Rachel K!'

She stepped out. The blue lights were angled toward her, and in them she could see mostly a screen of curling smoke, and through the smoky screen the men in the front two or three rows.

Those in the back didn't matter — the men near the stage laid down bills, and it was for them that she danced. But tonight there was one in the back who intrigued her. She couldn't see him but knew he was there, at a table by himself. He'd been coming around ever since Batista took over, maybe a foreign dignitary. The girls were calling him 'the German.' The bartender said he was French. He seemed confident, amused, self-contained. Each evening he'd been there, his presence distracted her, like he knew that she knew that he was watching her, while pretending not to, and his gaze colored her every movement. She wanted to talk to him but sensed it wasn't yet the moment, as if there were a tacit agreement between them that they would continue for some time with this ritual of him watching her and pretending not to. She danced for him, invisible to her in the back of the Pam-Pam Room.

'The president is waiting for you,' the stage manager said as she finished her show. On her way to Batista's booth she passed near the Frenchman's table, thinking they would silently communicate once again. But his table was empty. He'd left.

3

'Who tipped me the black spot?' Everly Lederer asked in her fake pirate's brogue. It was Silver's question, from *Treasure Island*.

Her father kept loading suitcases into the trunk.

'If I'm moving to an island, I need a knife,' she announced, leaning up to the front seat. Her mother said to sit back.

In *Treasure Island*, when a pirate died, the first thing you did was rifle his sea clothes and locate his knife. An island was full of danger: malaria-infested bogs, disease that would turn your eyes the color of lemon peel, poisonous snakes, and double-crossing pirates like Barbecue. She'd need a knife to cut down branches and make a sleeping lean-to in the woods, to cut open biscuits to eat with fried junk, like Jim Hawkins.

On their way to Miami, they stayed at a motor court in Georgia called the Admiral Benbow. The same name as the inn run by Jim Hawkins and his mother, where Billy Bones died. In Billy Bones's trunk Jim found the treasure map, and the adventure began. But the Admiral Benbow where they stayed was nothing like the one in *Treasure Island*. It was crowded with tough-looking southern families, kids cannon-balling into the pool and adults yelling at them or swatting them with newspapers. Everly watched a man and woman who talked in hushed voices, dangling their arms over the second-floor balcony of the motel, smoke drifting from the man's cigarette in a lazy trail. The man and a woman descended the rickety metal staircase, the woman's high heels — 'pumps,' her mother called them — clicking down the stairs. The man and the woman didn't say good-bye or even look at each other. They separated and walked off in opposite directions. For a moment Everly thought they would count paces and both turn around and draw like in the movies — the Westerns, that is. But neither the man nor the woman turned around. They weren't counting paces. They were just walking, the woman in her click-click pumps. Each got into a different car and drove out of the parking lot.

As they were checking out of their room the next the morning, her father said something about the Admiral 'Bimbo.' Her older sister, Stevie, laughed loudly. 'Admiral Bimbo! Ha-ha!' Stevie liked to be in on the adults' jokes, even if she had to fake that she'd understood. Their father grabbed her by the elbow and shushed her.

★   ★   ★

They left their car at the Miami port building, to be loaded on a lower deck, and stood behind a rope waiting for a maharaja to board before the regular people were allowed on the ship. She'd seen a picture of a maharaja in the encyclopedia and was expecting a man in a jeweled turban, shoes with curled-up toes, a chain of decorated elephants following behind him. Though she figured there might not be any elephants.

The maharaja finally appeared, making his way up the gangplank, porters behind him wheeling carts stacked with enormous brass-latched leather trunks. He was a frail, balding man in a dark suit and soft-collared shirt. No curled-up shoes and no elephants. Not even a turban.

What made him a maharaja, she asked her father, if he looked just like a normal businessman, too puny to carry his own luggage? Her father said his bank account. He said the man was in trouble with the government of India, that he'd taken money that wasn't his. He boarded first with a lot of fuss and ceremony, her father said, but he'd been run out of his country. Her father said the maharaja was on French leave. What did it mean? That he'd sneaked away.

Her mother and father seemed to hate people for being rich, and yet they wanted to be rich themselves. Money was always a problem. That's why they were going to Cuba, where her father would have a higher salary and be a boss. Her mother said if they had to live in a jungle for George Lederer to get the salary and respect he deserved, well then, they'd live in a jungle.

Everly was keen on the idea of living in a jungle. Why not? But her mother talked about it like it was something they were forcing themselves to do. Her mother said she was tired of living on 'slender means,' which made Everly picture well-fitting men's pants with narrow legs, even after she was told what it meant. If her parents ever did get rich, their old selves would hate their new selves. Though maybe it wouldn't matter, because they would have forgotten their old selves, erased by their new selves, since self was self and there couldn't be more than one in a single body.

The maharaja's troubles had been in the newspaper, and from the way her father spoke, she guessed the other adults in line must have read the article, too. It seemed more lonely and shameful than a privilege to walk up the gangplank with so many eyes staring. She felt sorry for the little maharaja, a man who had too many bags to carry by himself, and what was the difference, really, between a grown-up's shame and a child's shame? She was always feeling sorry for people and sometimes this led to feeling sorry for herself. Sympathy was messy business, and where did you stop the flow of it? She would think of something, a memory of something unpleasant, like being spanked in the department store or shoved into the shower with her clothes on. When she had her tantrums she couldn't stop them once they'd started, so her father would stop them for her by putting her in the shower. Everly had once put Tinker in the shower for misbehaving. At first he was scared, but then he liked it. He was a dog and didn't understand that it was a punishment. Later, Tinker ran away.

The line to board the ship began to move. Her mother nervously clutched the travel papers and passport, one slim green booklet for her and the three girls. There was a folded-up letter in the passport from the State Department. The letter reminded them that they were emissaries of the United States and should act accordingly. Everly held her younger sister Duffy's hand as they walked up the gangplank. The sun was low, and the sky had turned the color of ripe watermelon. Florida was all soft and artificial colors. Pink houses, turquoise water, perfumy flowers, and huge gnarled trees with moss caught in the branches like torn lace. The air had an underwater cast to it, a greenish-blue that laved over them as they moved through the thick humidity, up the gangplank and onto the ship. She looked out to where the sea's horizon met the watermelon sky. Already she felt closer to this mysterious place, the tropics. She pictured an island in a sea of tepid green glass, a foamy ruffle of waves lapping its shore. Beyond the shore, an endless mesh of jungle plants. The smell of ripe fruit. A forgotten lagoon surrounded by palm trees reflected in the silver mirror of the water. At the entrance to the lagoon, green vines as thick as theater drapes, waiting to be parted.

They were finishing dinner in the ship's dining room when rain began slapping against the thick glass of the portholes in violent bursts, like someone was tossing buckets of water. Stevie was reading from a list of diversions in the guidebook. '*Ping-Pong, deck tennis, and shuffle-board. Skeeball and bingo on the Lido. And with parental permission, children are invited to take a guided tour of the bridge.*' She finished reading and put the guidebook in her purse to keep as a souvenir. Stevie was documenting her life as it happened. Everly was not. Documenting life as it happened seemed like a way of not experiencing it. As if posing for photographs, or focusing on what to save and call a souvenir, made the present instantly the past. You had to choose one or the other was Everly's feeling. Try to shape a moment into a memory you could save and look at later, or have the moment as it was happening, but you couldn't have both. Everly had not saved the homemade newspaper, the *Lederer Times*, which she'd spent an entire weekend working on before they left Oak Ridge. Just threw it away along with a huge box of schoolwork and drawings. My things, she'd thought, to destroy if I want to. Her father had printed copies of her newspaper on his Teletype machine at work. She had intended to make a daily, then scaled it down to a monthly, but only ended up making one edition — 'March 1952.' It had three articles: 'Largest Hailstone Ever Recorded' — six inches in diameter, with a drawing to illustrate the story. 'Timothy Hodgkiss Says You Can Die from Eating a Cigar,' a rumor that was confirmed by the school nurse. And 'Lederers Are Moving to Cuba!' with more illustrations and a story that included a few fibs, like that Everly would be getting a pet monkey from China, so young that he wore a diaper and would have to be fed green coconut milk from a bottle. And her own pet parrot, like the one that sat on Barbecue's shoulder in *Treasure Island*, except hers wouldn't be called Cap'n Flint. He'd be called Jim Hawkins, and he'd recite lines from the book. 'I'll tip you the black spot!' the parrot would say, but only to people who were mean. It seemed incredible that parrots could talk. And that they could live for a hundred years, which meant Duffy would have to take care of the parrot after Everly was dead, a detail she included in her article. Her mother said it was 'morbid.' What did it mean? That you weren't supposed to think about death.

Out the dining room window, rain pocked the surface of the sea, making dimpled patterns that changed as the wind shifted the angle of the rain. The wind crescendoed and decrescendoed, sounding like the braided voices of distressed people. The week before, at Everly's final piano lesson with Mrs. Vanderveer, Mrs. Vanderveer had played a Chopin prelude to demonstrate a proper crescendo and decrescendo. Everly's favorites were the Chopin preludes. They were all in a minor key, and she only liked music in a minor key. And music that called for damper pedal. In private, she used the damper pedal more than the sheet music indicated, which made her feel thoughtful and dramatic. For the decrescendo, Mrs. Vanderveer had leaned low and delicate over the keys, pressing them softer and softer, notes melting away in the final stanza like a glassy sliver of candy on the tongue, nothing remaining after the note but a vibration, a silent thing that hung in the room. A feeling that was there even though you couldn't see it and it made no sound.

But she was lazy and didn't practice enough, only played her favorite things and ignored those that were too difficult, or in a happy key, went to

64

her lesson with her hands dirty, her fingernails uncut. At her last lesson she'd been overcome with regret. She wouldn't have any more chances to please Mrs. Vanderveer by practicing diligently and coming prepared, trimming her nails and scrubbing out the dirt. Life was going to be like this. You only understood how to behave and appreciate things when they were being taken away from you.

The ship began to rock, left and then right, and the horizon moved up and down through the window. Duffy started to cry. A man's voice came through a speaker, echoing loudly through the dining room. 'The captain requests that all passengers please return to their cabins.' Her mother wrapped several uneaten dinner rolls in napkins and put them in her pocketbook. As they all got up to file out of the dining room, the ship leaned again, and the floor of the room tilted up like a Whirl-a-Wheel. A cartful of dirty dishes crashed sideways, and a giant coffee urn spilled over and began glugging a lake of coffee onto the floor.

No one was allowed up on deck.

'Darn. No bingo on the Lido,' Stevie said.

Duffy bounced up and down on the bed. 'Bingo on the Lido! Bingo on the Lido!' When she was worn out from jumping up and down, the room was quiet except for her panting and the sound of the rain.

They would cross the Tropic of Cancer sometime during the night. Maybe they were crossing it now, Everly thought, picturing the prow of their ship slicing tracelessly through that invisible border and into the tropics, a zone between Cancer and Capricorn that went around Earth like a person's belt around her waist.

When Everly told the school librarian, Miss Jiggs, that her family was moving to Cuba, Miss Jiggs pulled out a book called *Empire in Green and Gold*. Perfect yellow bananas dressed like flamenco dancers in red lipstick and pearls danced across the bottom border of the book's pages. The book said Cuba was the world's sugar bowl. Everly pictured a pink crystal bowl, beveled on the edges and filled with glinting white sugar. A pink crystal lid, cut like a gemstone. The sort of thing Mrs. Vanderveer would have brought out for tea service.

Everyone else was asleep. She lay in bed next to Stevie and listened to the wind and waited for lightning to illuminate the cabin like a photographer's flash. Was lightning white, or was it purple? It looked white but left a residue of purple, like the shapes that floated across the backs of her eyelids when she pressed on them. She counted Mississippi seconds until thunder and got to seven. The lightning was far away, but she couldn't remember the formula for how far. Their room moved up and down, and their only window was a small, round porthole. She felt like she was in a tin can turned on its side.

When she woke, the ship was calm and there was no sound of rain. The quiet seemed especially so for having followed the stormy night. She could see a thin line of colored light feathering the horizon, a peek of the sun's red petticoat. The ocean had a dullish shine like something that had been glazed in butter and then chilled in the refrigerator. She pitched herself up against the window to see the water better, looking for some indication that they had passed through that dashed line and into the tropics, but it was hard to know what to look for. After all her daydreaming in front of the globe, peering like a giant over the tiny letters of 'Tropic of Cancer,' she was in the place that the globe depicted. And yet the globe seemed more real. A map illustrated relationships among islands and seas and continents. The water she could see from the ship porthole illustrated nothing — just water, with no daisy chains or markers of any kind. She'd read about a woman from Guernsey who threw a bottle into the ocean with a message inside. It floated all the way to Africa and was tossed up on the beach at Dakar. The man who found it wrote to the woman from Guernsey. Upon receiving his letter, she invited him to dinner. The newspaper article didn't say whether he was planning to attend. It seemed like an awfully long way to go.

The clock read 5:00 A.M. What now?

It was early, but there was nothing to do but get dressed — quietly, or someone would tell her to go back to bed. She put on the new outfit she'd gotten at the Miami Sears, a brown, dotted Swiss dress with a white pinafore. She hated dresses. She wanted to wear denim pants with rolled cuffs and checked Western shirts like Hopalong Cassidy. Her father sometimes called her Tex instead of Everly. He meant to tease her, but she enjoyed the nickname and sometimes thought of herself as Tex, Tex Lederer. It had a ring. She'd once seen real cowboys. They came to an Oak Ridge square dance, government-hired construction people who lived beyond the security fence in Clinton. 'Hillbillies,' her mother had called them. They showed up in pointy boots and cowboy hats and Western shirts, the fancy kind with white piping. They got drunk and acted rowdy and started a fight. The hillbillies weren't invited back, and at the next dance an armed security guard sat by the door. Her mother said they'd only been included to make the dance, with its hay bales and Western band, seem more authentic. 'Authenticity,' she'd said, 'is not always a good idea.'

At the Sears in Miami, everyone got to pick out something special for Cuba. Her father, a stack of short-sleeved Dacron shirts. Stevie, a white leatherette tambourine bag. And Duffy, a doll called Scribbles that had a blank face and a pack of special colored markers for drawing one onto it. Everly knew immediately what she wanted: a knife from a display case in the camping department. It was the knife she needed for going to an island, like Jim Hawkins would have worn looped onto his belt. But her mother insisted she get a dress. There was a showdown in the children's department. She wanted a knife, just like Stevie wanted a purse. She didn't want a stupid dress. Her mother was too tired to fight and struck a deal. They left Sears with the knife, in a brown leather case, and the dotted Swiss dress.

'Everybody up and washed and ready for

customs. Everly? Stevie?' her mother called from the adjoining room.

'I'm dressed, Mother,' Everly said.

'Then wake your sisters and remind them to comb their hair. Let me see you.'

Everly stood in the doorway.

'Oh, Everly, can't you go without the glasses, just for today? They make you look cross-eyed.'

'I *am* cross-eyed, Mother.'

'But it's so much more noticeable with those Coke bottles over your eyes. You can see without them, and it won't kill you. Just until we get through customs.'

Their mother had talked about customs like they'd get tipped the black spot if they weren't careful. Everly imagined stern men in uniforms with holstered guns, looking them over. If she and her sisters were unkempt, poorly dressed, if their hair wasn't parted straight, if she felt like Tex instead of Everly and insisted on wearing filthy dungarees and a ratty boy's shirt, they'd be turned away and have to go back to Oak Ridge. A city of mud and barbed wire, where her father was a low man on the totem pole.

★   ★   ★

Everly and her sisters pressed up against the passenger rail as the ship readied to dock. A deep, resonant horn sounded, and the ship moved toward the shore, kicking up a thick wake as it slowed. A stone castle towered on one end of the curve of land. On the other end, a massive factory jutted out into the bay, a miniature city

69

of blinking white lights and enormous silver tanks with ladders on their sides. Chimneys emitted orange flames against a plume of black.

'That must be Shell's new refinery,' her father said.

It looked just like Oak Ridge, big industrial buildings with smokestacks that shot puffs of steam and plumes of smoke. Steam and smoke were different, and she enjoyed observing the difference between them. Steam came off a cup of hot coffee, and Tennessee roads after summer rain. Smoke poured out of Gamble Valley, the Negro neighborhood in Oak Ridge, always on fire, and hovered in the air near K-25, the secret facility where her father worked. Air that was sour if you breathed through your mouth, and poisonous-smelling. K-25 hummed and crackled with electricity. There was a giant magnet somewhere inside the complex of buildings, and people said if you got too close to the fence, the force of the magnet would pull the hobnails out of your shoes and knock you flat on the ground. Everly's Brownie leader had made the girls all take their shoes off when their troop walked past. They picked through the mud in their socks, single file.

They were getting close to the Havana waterfront, and she could see church spires and three- and four-decker buildings in pale pinks and yellows and blues. The harbor was a cloudy brown, with bits of garbage floating in it, empty bottles and soap bubbles and wood scraps. Cuban boys, thin and shirtless, with smooth chests and skin that was a chocolaty purple, gathered along

70

the dock. One of them, taller than the rest, cupped his hands around his mouth and shouted in English, 'Throw down a quarter!'

The ship was getting close enough that she could see the boys' faces. They waved, smiling as if she and the other American passengers were their personal friends.

'Throw down a quarter!' the tall boy yelled again, louder this time.

Someone threw a coin. It sailed over the deck railing and plunked into the water. The boys cheered, and three of them dived in. They emerged from the dark, oily, and iridescent-skinned water, treading with their arms and legs, bobbing up and down in the water, which rose up in waves and slapped against the dock. Drops of water glinted like stardust in the boys' kinky hair. They shouted up at the deck, gesturing for more coins. Someone pitched another over the railing. The boys shot toward it. There was a scramble, bodies splashing wildly, right near the ship's giant propellers, which churned up soft and water-bloated garbage. One of the boys popped through the murk, his face the same dark color as the mush-strewn water, almost indistinguishable if it weren't for the tinsel of drops glinting in his strange halo of hair. He smiled, and a coin flashed from between his teeth.

'Look at them!' her mother said. 'Performing like seals!'

They did look like seals, with their smooth, purple-skinned bodies, diving into the water, then skimming under the surface in fluid motions.

The gangplank went down, and people streamed off the ship. Workers in gloves and grease-streaked clothes unloaded the ship's cargo. Crates swung on huge cranes, then were lowered slowly to the dock. The men stood in a line, yelling to one another in Spanish and tossing boxes from hand to hand, then stacking them on dollies. More men took the dollies and wheeled them into the customs building. They all wore a crude sort of rope shoe and moved cargo with lit cigarettes dangling from their mouths. They were all Negroes, with darker skin than the boys on the dock, a blackish-purple like the powdery black center of a tulip's cup. Everly thought of Mavis, their maid in Oak Ridge, the only colored person she knew. Mavis looked at the floor and said *Yes, ma'am* and *No, ma'am* when Everly's mother gave orders. Told her to turn off that God-awful gospel radio. Mavis's husband waited in the backyard when he came to fetch her. He kept his eyes on the ground and stood far from the house. These men on the waterfront laughed and shouted, and when a pretty woman in a clinging dress passed along the gangplank, they all stared at her bottom, which jiggled as she walked. One of them whistled.

Everly's mother yanked her arm. 'Don't stare, young lady!' The men were allowed to stare at the lady's bottom. Everly was not.

They sat in customs for hours, in a dimly lighted room with mint green walls and fans that hung down from a high ceiling, the rotors spinning so slowly they created no breeze. Duffy drew various faces on Scribbles, and Stevie read from what their father, teasing, had called a dime-store romance. When he first said it, Everly thought it meant the book was about people who fell in love in a dime store. Everly sneaked stares at a pair of twins, teenage daughters of another family who were also moving to Nicaro. They were big-boned, horsey-looking girls with over-sized teeth like white Chiclets, wearing identical blue dresses and matching ribbons in their hair. They were blond, the sort that people seemed to find pretty for the reason that they were blond, even if their faces weren't particularly nice. Everly got away with staring at the horsey twins because her mother was busy filling out forms and couldn't tell her not to. She didn't understand how it was that some people resisted the urge to stare. Where did they put their eyes? Hers locked onto other people's faces. She had to look, and only when someone returned her gaze did she look away.

The twins walked over and introduced themselves. Their names were Pamela and Val. Pamela said their father was in charge of construction at the Nicaro plant.

'My father's in charge of nickel,' Everly said.

'Your father can't be 'in charge' of nickel,' Pamela said. 'Maybe he's running some *aspect* of it.' She turned to Val and said something in French. Val said something back, also in French.

A customs official in a beige military uniform and amber sunglasses approached and asked the twins something in Spanish. Pamela answered, speaking in the same rapid-fire manner as the man in the amber glasses, her shift from English to Spanish completely natural. Everly asked where they were from.

'Hmm. Let's see. Tela, Limón, Buenos Aires,' Val said, counting on her fingers, 'Bogotá, Panama City — '

'Our father built the port in Limón,' Pamela said. 'Last year we were in Bolivia. But then troublemakers started rioting.'

'Daddy tried to help the government,' Val added.

'But the troublemakers ended up taking over, and all the good people had to get out of there fast.'

'And now we get here and there's practically a revolution.'

'Or whatever they're calling it.'

'Father says it's a coup d'état,' Pamela said, 'because they gave President Prio the boot.'

'What's a cootay-tah?' Everly asked.

'Oh, God, there's Mom,' Val said. Both girls quickly stood up.

A woman was rushing toward them through the crowded room. She had a broad, ruddy face and the same lank blond hair as her daughters, her scalp blushing pink from underneath.

'I've been looking all over for you girls.' Her voice was loud but hoarse, like she'd been yelling too much. She looked like someone who might yell a lot.

'Your father is ready to sell you both to the circus,' she wheezed.

There weren't any twins in the circus. They would have been too ordinary. Triplets, maybe.

She was thinking about the circus, about the paper cones that were dipped in a drum and came out wrapped in turbans of pink cotton batting, and the machine where you could record your own voice, when Pamela and Val dutifully followed their mother away.

Pamela turned back and said, 'See you in Nicaro, kid.'

* * *

She stood with her family under the sun's stabbing heat in front of the port building, waiting for the car to be rolled out. Beyond the building, a boardwalk stretched as far as she could see. Large waves crashed against the boardwalk and shot into the air like saltwater confetti, then slopped onto the pedestrian walkway. A man standing on the corner yelled 'Lotería! Lotcría!' and waved a long pole with strips of paper attached, printed with rows of numbers. The air was hot and moist, like fevered human breath wafting around her. Stevie fanned herself with the menu from dinner the night before, another souvenir for her scrap-book. The street and all the buildings seemed coated in a combination of auto soot and ocean brine. A stench of urine rose from the sidewalk, an anonymous insult. Her mother took a bleached cotton handkerchief out of her pocketbook and held it over her nose. All that fuss, Everly and her sisters with scrubbed faces and combed hair, in their froufrou dresses. She felt like a tea doily, damp and frilly and out of place.

A man missing an arm was rooting through the garbage can near them. He pulled a paper food container out of the trash, leaned his head back, and tipped the container to his mouth. Rice spilled out over his face. None of it made it into his mouth, but the man chewed frantically, then dumped the container and began walking in circles. Clever-looking women milled around, shooting one another mysterious looks. The women were purple-skinned like the boys who dove for coins, but their hair wasn't like the boys' hair. It was pressed flat and pulled back like a white person's hair. One of the women blotted her underarms with what looked like pages from a book. They were pages from a book. The woman retrieved a paperback from her purse, ripped out two more pages, and blotted her forehead. Boys carrying wooden boxes filled with tins of shoe polish, brushes, and spit rags roamed around like stray dogs looking for scraps. A man stumbled among them, his hand clamped to a bottle in a creased and grease-splotched paper sack. The soles of his shoes were coming unglued, flapping as he walked.

Everly looked up and saw an enormous rat jumping from a palm tree. It landed on the oily sidewalk and charged toward a woman who was sleeping in a doorway. Someone whistled a watch-out whistle, and the woman stirred awake and pulled up her legs just before the rat darted past. She wore no shoes, only a ripped dress that was the grayish dinge of the rags Mavis used to polish their good silverware.

'Wow, look at that,' Stevie said, pointing at a

poster mounted on a kiosk, a large color photo-graph of women in elaborate sequined costumes, wearing chandeliers on their heads, draped in strings of pearls. *THE CABARET TOKIO — THE PLACE TO BE IN HAVANA!* the poster announced. And underneath, *VISIT OUR FAMOUS PAMPAM ROOM, FEATURING, FROM PARIS, ZAZOU DANCER RACHEL K!*

'Daddy, can we go there?' Stevie asked.

The answer would, of course, be no. Their parents were too cheap for that, but Everly admired her sister's optimism.

Their father stepped closer and stared at the photograph. 'It's for adults,' he said.

'How come?' Stevie asked.

'Because it's a burlesque.'

A burlesque. Everly thought she might have seen one, when she and Stevie sneaked into the wrong movie one Saturday afternoon. On the screen, a woman was dancing in a saloon, singing in a high, breathy voice. *You can touch my cherries, but you cannot touch my plums.* The audience was all adults, and mostly men. She whispered to Stevie that they were in the wrong theater, but Stevie shushed her. They watched the woman perform her song, her white breasts practically falling out of the top of her dress, which seemed more of an undergarment, like their mother's merry widow. But this woman had a different kind of body than their mother. When the song was finished, she and Stevie ran out of the theater. They pushed the double doors and were pitched into the flooding light and noise of the lobby, where kids stood in line to buy buckets of popcorn and paper cups of cola with crushed ice. Everly felt queer, like she had done something naughty that she couldn't reverse. Stevie kept singing the song as they walked home. *You can touch my cherries, but you cannot touch my plums*.

A dockworker pulled up in their Studebaker. Their familiar car had crossed the Tropic of Cancer, too, and here it was in this dirty and exotic, underwater-feeling place. It looked the same, with its forest green paint and shiny, bullet-nosed grille, except that a purple-colored man was driving it, his arm hanging casually out the window. He slammed on the brakes, and the car screeched to a stop. Her mother winced. The man got out. He stood leaning against the driver's side. Her father thanked him, but the man wouldn't step aside until her father produced a coin.

As they were driving away, someone called after them, 'Excuse me — sir! Americano!' Her father put on the brake.

'George, do *not* talk to these people!' her mother said. 'Keep the car moving!'

They bumped down the street. Two men ran behind the car yelling, 'Americanos! Americanos!' Her mother put her head out the window, looked back down the street. 'Drive faster!' she said. One of the men running after them yelled, 'Hey, lady, take me with you!' The others running beside him all laughed. 'I'm very good!' he shouted. 'I'm very nice!'

Everly watched out the back window. People running on foot can't keep up with an automobile for long. Not even a dog can keep up with a car. The men were getting smaller. They were a block behind them now, but still running and laughing. The car picked up speed, went through a yellow light, and the men faded out of view.

4

Blue lights flip on. Smoky haze drifts above the tables.

'Introducing, from Paris, zazou dancer Rachel K!'

Rachel K steps from behind a Chinois screen. She is draped in black chiffon and a cascade of rooster tail feathers that glint metallic green under the lights.

★ ★ ★

The Frenchman remembers zazou. It was a jazz thing during the war. Girls in chunky heels and fishnets, with dark lipstick and parasols. Or maybe it was berets — he can't recall. Boys in zoot suits, an unseemly glisten of salad oil in their hair. They were bohemians who struck poses near the outdoor tables at the Café de Flore, begging cigarettes and slurping the soup people left in the bottom of their bowls. The point of it was more than just poverty. It was a form of protest. But by the time the zazou were being rounded up by German patrols, he was far away from Paris. Marching waist-deep into a cold apocalypse with a panzerfaust over his shoulder.

The Tokio marquee had said *French Variety Dancer*, but watching her through his aubergine-tinted dictator's glasses, he senses immediately she isn't French. Whatever she is or isn't, she looks like a liar and he likes liars. He imagines there is someone for whom honesty is a potent seduction, but he is not that sentimental someone. Seduction, he knows, is a slew of projections, disguises, denials. What can you claim to accurately know about anyone, much less a stranger to whom you're attracted? And yet you can claim, accurately, that a person is evasive and that their evasions interest you.

This Frenchman, a certain Christian de La Mazière — ex-Charlemagne Division Waffen SS, minor aristocrat, memoirist, and traitor to the state of France — had taken an airplane from Paris to Havana the day after he heard about the coup. He caught a limousine from the airport, then ran a bubble bath in the sunken marble tub at his suite in the Hotel Nacional. Ordered a split of Perrier-Jouët, two boiled eggs, and a saltshaker. Ate his light lunch and headed for the Cabaret Tokio.

He sat in the back of the Pam-Pam Room and watched Rachel K's show, her golden sartouche whipping like a lasso as she swung around a pole, no less graceful than a ballerina, though ballet dancers were like porcelain figurines, elegantly molded and coldly unsexed, while Rachel K was warm-looking, soft-contoured flesh. A gaudy spill of platinum hair and those barely bobbing firm-jelly breasts that are not only rare, a happy coincidence of genetics and luck, but utterly time-sensitive, existing only in a slim window of youth. Youth was no miracle, he knew. Or it was a banal miracle. And yet he loved the blunt perfection of young flesh. Unreflective, knowing only its own moment-to-moment existence. She had a narrow face, dark eyes, the full lips and large teeth of a Manouche Gypsy or a German Jew. *Zazou* — of all things! The framing made her seem oddly knowing, despite her blunt and stupid and perfect flesh.

La Mazière watched her kneel before the blue lights and smile coyly for the men at the front tables. They were serious and stoic, and he understood that the cabaret was their church, her show an engrossing sermon they took in with naive and absolute faith. He was serious, too, but while the other men watched her with awe, an exotic creature as mysterious as conical rays of divine light coming through a stained-glass window, he'd immediately seen something he was sure they could not. She'd gauzed her person in persona, but he sensed the person slipping through, person and persona in an elaborate tangle.

He studied her with detached desire, in no hurry to get closer. He was patient, almost perversely so. The delay of pleasure, after all, was a more refined and intense category of pleasure.

★ ★ ★

He began going to the Tokio nightly, showing up just as it was her turn to dance. He sat in a shadowy back corner of the Pam-Pam Room where the tables were always empty. He had a clear view of the stage as well as the hallway that led to the private booths, where drunk and enthusiastic businessmen clumsily swatted the booth curtains out of their way and ducked in with girls who wore sly, proud looks on their faces, the men and the girls each thinking it was they who'd triumphed over the other. He watched the Tokio bartender, a man with down-turned eyes that made his face melancholy, like a song in a minor key. He observed as the sad bartender ritually played canasta with two bored and customerless dancers, girls whom La Mazière guessed had no choice but to bide their time waiting for specialty clientele. One was much too thin, with an unappealing, shovel-like pelvis. The other, maximally fleshy and six feet tall, a regular giantess. One evening, after watching the giantess lose at canasta and circulate the room twice, approaching him on both sweeps, La Mazière dug out a couple of pesos for a lap dance. He suspected Rachel K might notice he'd bought company, though it was part of the game for him to pay attention to everyone in the room but her. For two weeks now, he'd avoided her gaze, and she'd avoided his. Because what he waited for felt inevitable, he could sample a giantess, get her squirming and giggling and moving her brown Caribbean hips in just the right way, and do it with full concentration.

The girl on his lap slowed to a steady gyration, her eyes closed. He sensed she might have taken the liberty of falling asleep, but her sleepy movements were no less effective. Her skin was perfectly smooth, her sequins glinting splendidly under the colored cabaret lights. He imagined that she and probably all the girls in the club, despite their showgirl glamour, were from the filthy ring of desperation that surrounded the city. If its center was staked with neon-pulsing casinos, on Havana's outskirts were miles and miles of slums with no electricity, no running water, and smokily typhoid trash fires. It was a combination he relished, sometimes preferring his high- and his low-grade pleasures mixed instead of pure. Proust's Marcel bequeathed his aunt Léonie's couch to a bordello, and whenever he visited the place to tease 'Rachel, when of the Lord' (but never buy her services), he was unnerved to see tarts flopped on its pink velvet cushions. A favorite detail of a favorite literature, and yet La Mazière knew what Marcel didn't, that there is nothing more perfect and appropriate than pink velvet plush flattening under a whore's ass. La Mazière didn't care if he reclined on luxurious furniture in the lobby of the Ritz or in a squalid Saint-Denis cathouse. Ate his steak at Maxim's or at a colonial outpost in Djibouti, a backwater of salt factories and scorching temperatures on the bacterial mouth of the Red Sea. Properly seared steak is everywhere the same. He had even argued, adamantly, that a juicier cut could be eaten in Djibouti, not naming out loud the special ingredient that tenderized the meat: contradiction.

The Pam-Pam Room dancers had mostly left him to himself at his lone back table, having pegged him as quirky, disinterested, and cheap. Until he got the giantess gyrating on his lap. The next evening, girls fluttered around him. They thought he was German and kept saying, 'Das ist gut, ja? Das ist gut?' He nodded, smiled distantly, and said, 'Ja, gut' in his French accent. He ordered a rum drink with crushed mint and morphine crystals dissolving in a slush of ice. Sipped his drink and stole looks at Rachel K as he tickled the girl on his lap, who erupted in giggles. The girl straddled him. Took his tinted dictator's glasses and tried them on. Placed her hand on his crotch.

'Das ist gut?' she asked, smiling, pressing with her hand, his tinted glasses slipping down her nose.

'Ja,' he replied, 'gut.'

* * *

Three weeks after the coup, La Mazière watched on the television in his hotel suite as Batista made his official acceptance speech. Perhaps the president had waited thinking the memory would fade that there wasn't any election. He was a mulatto with soft features, a faint severity straining his smile, a mean streak that couldn't quite be suppressed. His general's uniform was littered with medals and badges, stripes and ribbons. Those guys could never resist. Soon the people would be calling him 'Bottle Caps,' which is what the Dominicans called President Trujillo. La Mazière thought of Darnand pinning his French decorations — 'bonbons' — to his new Sturmbannführer's uniform, when he became de facto head of the Vichy Milice. Medals Darnand had won fighting the Germans on the Maginot Line, pinned under his new silver-stitched SS insignia.

85

Batista smiled and made his face handsome. 'I am a dictator *with* the people,' he said.

Prio was now in exile. Batista home. Everyone switching places as the chips fell. Darnand and the entire Vichy government fled to Germany, but the stakes were so much higher. Darnand, Laval, Pétain. These weren't small-time factotums from a banana republic and there wasn't any Miami, a place to cool their heels and wait things out playing canasta under a lanai. Darnand was captured. Brought to Paris. Executed.

That was a dark time. La Mazière preferred the early, glory days in occupied Paris, when royalists and scum roamed with pockets full of cash, La Mazière among them, savoring the hushed feeling of the curfewed city at dusk, riding through the streets in a black Mercedes under the violet-blushing emptiness of the Parisian sky. What had he cared the city was 'annexed'? Or that Hitler surveyed the Champs-Élysées and visited Sacré-Coeur? The nightmare of the 1930s, of working-class people and their 'paid' vacations invading the Côte d'Azure, was finally over. France had been heading for socialist ruin. Maybe the Germans, he'd believed, were what they needed to finally stamp out the vile ideas of the so-called Popular Front. Parisians blamed the Germans for the tanks that burned on the outskirts of Paris, covering the city in grease and ash. They blamed the Germans for their own quick and miserable defeat, for the toxic soot that coated the cherries on their trees. But they'd brought this failure on themselves. The soot was from their own captured tanks, French tanks. They could contemplate why Germany was strong and France was weak as they ate shoe leather and burned furniture to keep warm. La Mazière never had to eat blighted cherries or boiled shoe leather. As part of the new elite of moneyed riffraff, he lived extremely well, dined at Le Boeuf sur le Toit and Maxim's, which did booming business, packed for all-night parties of crystal-clinking pandemonium. An impossible time, that time in Paris. Impossible as it was happening.

The television switched to footage of Batista stepping off a plane and kneeling to kiss the tarmac, apparently overcome with love for his country.

Perverse, he knew, to compare occupied Paris, people like Darnand, with this little republic and its General Bottle Caps. And yet something about the place activated familiar sensations, a mixture of dread and privilege, with Americans in shiny Cadillacs instead of Germans in Mercedes. But Havana was so much sultrier, starrier. The girls were purple-mouthed. The cinema palaces had retractable roofs. There was no notoriety and no shame, and instead, a power shuffle that was an open call to opportunists. A new president who reeked of insecurity. An old president in exile, eager to return home. Both would be looking for help. La Mazière could help them.

And there was this girl, a Gypsy or Jew, and either way she couldn't disguise it. She seemed formed from his own memories and longings, and yet unknowable. A cipher in pasties, painted like a doll. She had a stained, gloating air about her, like the girls who'd ridden topless on carousel horses at Fifine's on the rue Saint-Denis. The carousel revolving at a slow, erotic keel, the girls floating up and down like lithe, buttery-bodied centaurs. Later those same girls ate veal with German officers, while most of the population stood in ration lines, waiting for bread so moldy and stale they had to chop it with an ax.

'Das ist gut?' The Tokio girls asked him, no idea who he was.

'Ja,' he answered, and honestly, 'gut.'

★   ★   ★

He was at his table in the back when Batista showed up at the club with several bodyguards who hustled him to a private booth down a roped-off hallway. This was predictable, politicians in titty bars. And yet it surprised La Mazière to see Rachel K escorted beyond the rope by Batista's security detail, and led into the general's booth. It surprised and intrigued him. Soon it would be time to finally break the wax seal on their silent conversation of glances.

The next evening, when she passed near his table, he stared at her coolly. In her cycle of periodically eyeing him, she was forced to meet his gaze.

He nodded almost imperceptibly.

She came toward him.

'You're an ambassador or something?' she asked.

Her voice, to his great relief, was slightly low and calm. A high and squeaky voice could have ruined everything.

La Mazière said yes, exactly, an ambassador, but they both knew it was a lie, that ambassador was a code for something complex and possibly unspeakable.

He took a moment to examine her. The plump mouth. The chemical blond hair. She was wearing black fishnet stockings — La Mazière could see their pattern in the dim blue light. He liked the diaphanous allure of fishnets. They were an enticement in the guise of a barrier, like a beaded curtain hung over a doorway says 'come in,' not 'stay out,' its beads telegraphing that what's inside is enchanted and special. He touched her knee, and to his surprise, her skin felt slightly cool — bare and smooth. He ran his finger up her thigh carefully, as though drawing a line on dew-frosted glass. It left a skin-toned smear in the cross-hook pattern of her fishnets, which apparently were made not of thread but of ink.

'An illusion — a painting,' he said, and looked at her with a bemused smile. He had a vague memory of Parisian women wearing paint-on stockings during the war. But that was all over. This was 1952. The girl had made her own perverse style out of France's wartime scarcity. He was impressed. And what was supposed to be an enticement, a fine membrane of netting that begged not just 'remove me' but also 'rip me to shreds' could not be ripped to shreds. It could be removed, of course, with water and soap, but such a ritual, without the purpose of gaining sexual access, would have no meaning. Why bother, when he could have her as she was? Her stockings were as material as the sun shadow of chain-link fence on a prison wall. He thought of Inge, the German girl with whom he'd toured the Rhineland before enlisting in the Charlemagne Division. Little Inge, who insisted he tear through her intricate cat's cradle of garters and stays, girdle, corset, and underwear. He would burst through snaps and panels, and tug tight-fitting elasticized garments down around the German girl's knees, dismantling underwear fortifications to penetrate the frontier of her pretend virginity. Sometimes he became impatient, pried his hand into her underwear and jerked the crotch panel to the inside of her thigh, to clear the way. The tearing sound of unforgiving fabric would cause Inge to let out a little moan, as if the fabric itself were the delicate folds of her innocence. With paint-on stockings, there was nothing to burst through. No garters, stays, or snaps. Only flesh.

Rachel K nodded, yes, that she'd painted them on. 'They were perfect, too — until you marked me.' She extended her legs to survey her work. 'They took me all day to finish.'

'You spent an entire day painting your legs?' he asked, amused.

'Some girls spend hours plucking their eyebrows,' she said. 'Burning sugar cubes and dropping them in absinthe.'

He nodded. 'And you do this instead.'

'I do lots of things.'

'I'm sure you do,' he said. 'It does say 'variety' dancer, after all. *French* variety dancer, no less.' It was a style of flirting, exposing her fabrications to provoke her into new ones.

'Maybe my dance is French-*style*,' she said. 'But it's more than that. My grandfather, Ferdinand K, was French.'

'K could be a number of things, mademoiselle,' La Mazière said, touching her cheek with the back of his hand. 'But K is not French.'

'They said he was French.'

'"They"?'

'Actually, my mother.'

'And she was — '

'A nothing. A stranger who left me here when I was thirteen.'

La Mazière said thirteen seemed rather young for a debut in her line of work. Not in the Tropics, Rachel K replied, where girls reach puberty at ten. She told him how the Tokio dressing room attendants had draped her in spangles, pom-poms, and gold sartouche trim. They were kind, middle-aged women with smoky voices and thick masks of makeup. They'd crimped her locks and painted her mouth in lipstick imported from Paris, a reddish-black, like blood gone dark from asphyxiation. Covered her breasts with tasseled pasties and put her onstage in the Pam-Pam Room. Voilà. Here she was.

She and her mother had ducked into the Tokio from the blinding sun of midday Havana. You'll be better off, her mother said. Cuba was a heartless place owned by men in New York, and it made more sense to part ways than wander the streets together, pathetic urchins that no one wanted to help. It was so dark inside the club that Rachel K could barely see. They waited at the Pam-Pam Room bar until a manager appeared from a back office, trailing cigar smoke. He breathed audibly, and in his labored breath she understood that he'd taken her on. That was ten years ago. She'd been at the Tokio so long now it was a kind of mother to her. It gave her life a shape. Other girls passed through. They regarded cabaret dancing as momentary and sordid, always hoping for some politician or businessman to rescue them. Because the Tokio gave her life a shape and never sent her fretting over imagined alternatives, she was free in a way the other girls weren't. She had longings as well, but they weren't an illness to be cured. They were part of her.

Sometimes it seemed her entire adolescence had been lived in the dressing room mirrors of the Cabaret Tokio. She'd spent hours gazing into them, locked out and wanting to get inside, where the world was the same, but silvery and greenish, doubled and reversed. The same, but different. When she was alone in the dressing room she'd press her cheek to the silver and look sidelong into the mirror, hoping to catch a glimpse — of what? — whatever its invisible secret was. She had faith that there was some secret at the heart of invisibility, even if faith meant allowing for the possibility that there was no secret, that invisibility had no heart. If she knew the mirror's secret, she'd know how to pass through to the other side. To a greenish-silver province that was her world, but reversed.

Now it occurred to her that she never looked

at mirrors as mystery spaces anymore. Maybe she'd passed through without knowing it.

'You have friends in high places,' La Mazière said to her. 'The president makes his grand entrance, with full security detail — '

'Who says they're friends?'

'Ah. How right you are. Friendship is built on loyalty. Not services rendered by a coquette.'

'Friendliness is a service. In any case, I preferred the old president, Prio.'

'But of course. 'Democratically elected,' a man of the people — '

'I didn't *vote* for him. He was a friend. But he's gone, and I'm not hearing any violins.'

La Mazière smiled. 'You're too busy cavorting with his enemy.' He had his two hands clasped around her thigh, a garter belt of human fingers banding her leg. 'If this was Paris, after the' — he paused and made quotes with his fingers — ''Liberation,' they'd shave your head, mademoiselle.' He stroked her coarse blond hair with the attention of a hairdresser assessing locks he was about to shear.

The French women who'd cavorted with Germans couldn't hide their Nazi trysts any better than their ears, while La Mazière had woven incredible fabrications and spent his jail time in a luxury cell. His labor assignment, organizing the warden's formal dinner parties. Until a yellow telex arrived, pardoning him after only five years.

He was grabbing locks of Rachel K's hair and running them through his fingers, pulling firmly at her scalp.

93

'*Friendliness is a service*,' he said. 'Of course. You need privacy. Ease of mobility. People get in the way, don't they?'

They really did, she thought. Even Prio. Near the end, he came around too often, and she felt a wearying boredom in having to keep fixing herself into the same persona, something familiar and consistent he could recognize.

'Friendship,' La Mazière said, tugging her hair to angle her face toward his, 'is a barbaric concept.'

He was looking at her, and she had the funny feeling that if time and everyone suspended in its viscous grip were just then frozen, only the two of them would be left as they were, sentient and unfrozen.

'What do you like to do,' he asked, 'besides paint your legs?'

All men at the Tokio asked this. *What do you like?* It was part of the tête-à-tête of her profession, but what the men wanted was something from a limited variety of set responses: *I like pleasing you. I like squirming on your lap. I like being coquettish and slutty. Giggly and deferent. I like to fantasize about a man just like you watching me take my clothes off. I think about it when I'm alone, and I have to put my own little girl hands in my underwear, just to stop the longing to be on your lap.* Gullibility was beside the point: hearing these things was a performance the men were paying for. They didn't really want to know what she liked, and it never would have occurred to her to tell them. But she figured that the Frenchman,

94

with his bemused half smile, was too clever to want such an obvious put-on. He seemed to understand flirtation — real flirtation, and not a bluntly performed simulation of it. She suspected that if she said 'I like squirming on your lap' he'd laugh his head off, and at her expense.

'I like those few days of the year when it's cold here, at the end of hurricane season,' she said. 'It's cold enough you need a sweater. And at night, blankets. But I don't fall asleep with blankets over me. I leave them down at the end of the bed and make myself fall asleep uncovered. When I wake up later in the night, freezing cold, I reach down and pull up all the blankets.'

La Mazière pictured her making herself fall asleep cold and uncovered in order to feel warmth with more intensity. He couldn't help but imagine being the warm body that smothered this petite girl, cold and naked, on a mattress. Though he didn't want to be just the warmth, he realized, but the cold as well. What preceded, in this fantasy, was him stripping the bed and leaving her shivering in nothing. Maybe underwear. Him making her cold, and then warm.

He looked at her face, so obviously middle European. 'I think you should tell me your story,' he said. Not that he didn't believe the orphaned-at-a-burlesque-club tale, but he wanted something else. He wasn't sure whether he wanted a made-up story or a true story, or even what the difference was. People talked about character, a defining sort of substance. But deception was a substance as well, as relevant and admirable as what it concealed. If it concealed anything, that is.

95

'Okay here's a story,' she said. 'A man named Ferdinand K came over from France. He worked in cinema, met a girl named Irene, my grandmother. They had a baby — my mother — the nothing. Then they both dropped dead of venereal diseases. My mother, the orphan, was a street urchin. I don't know who my father is. I told you the rest of it already.'

'You've told me circumstances. Not story.'

'Okay, fine. Maybe you should tell me *your* story,' she said, catching his eye through the tinted lenses, '*Ambassador*.'

He smiled as if to say, No problem. Watch me give you nothing. 'I'm Christian de La Mazière. And okay, I'm not an ambassador.' He paused. 'I'm a journalist.'

'You're lying,' she said.

'There is that possibility.'

'And you know what else? I have a feeling you dismiss lowly 'circumstances' because you're not willing to cough up your own story.'

'Why should I divulge what is meaningless?' he said. 'A banal dossier of 'this was my grandfather, I was steered into this or that profession.' My existence is free of those tedious things.'

'I bet the opposite is true. I bet your 'tedious' past is a prison.'

'It isn't a prison,' he said. 'You'll see.'

If only it were tedious, he thought, but didn't say out loud. If only.

★   ★   ★

In fact it was sordid and remarkable to have been an incidental SS. Left with no war, no army, no country, only floating memories of medals and Maxim's and going to fight the Bolsheviks, thinking Fascism was better than Stalin and that he was fighting for heritage and class, and then knowing that he wasn't. That it had nothing to do with politics or ideals, only passion. Of course, there were some with ideals. Not him. Even if he had conviction — you might call it rare — the conviction to enlist at the Hotel Majestic on a stifling, hot August day in 1944, hours before the Allies rolled in. He'd explained his story as best he could in his memoir *The Helmeted Dreamer*, making his way, chapter by chapter, through the reasonings and events of his life like rows of a shark's teeth. When the memoir came out he garnered instant cachet, coeds and housewives practically lining up to sleep with a remorscful former Nazi. Overtures to which he responded with special gratitude, though these engagements were marked by a poignant and troubling intimacy.

Why he enlisted, he still wasn't sure. He had tried to explain his Huguenot and royalist heritage, a fight against cowardly defeat, against so-called Allies who murdered thirteen hundred French sailors at Mers el-Kábir, in one devastating blow. The impression that the German Army made on a demoralized country and its disheveled, ruined military. The thrill of German boys loitering in the lobby of the Ritz, their muscles pressing up against the perfectly creased fabric of their well-fitting uniforms,

97

anxious to polish his boots. But how to make people understand what had really been at stake? The magnificent glimmer of a traumschloss — a dream castle — and the dream of a glorious Europe. Two great nations, France and Germany, flowing into one historic river, heirs to the rule of Charlemagne. And there was pride, the issue of pride. Rather than manufacture a despicable fiction about having worked all along for the Resistance, he'd chosen honor. The women, especially, were sympathetic to this reasoning. Women always preferred bravery to cowardice, regardless of politics or ethics.

In the end, these reasons, even reason itself, were beside the point. It had been a pure sacrifice, empty of reasons. A bigger, more grand self-erasure. On his way to enlist on that hot August day, the war already lost, he saw people shuttling into the Velodrome. He won't deny that he saw them being led inside. He was a helmeted dreamer who waited in a German uniform while Marshal Pétain, their 'brave leader' of a crumbling Vichy regime, dozed in his chambers. Pétain in his kepi with the scrambled eggs braid, who refused to see them, the few who were ready to keep going, the only people — correction, the only *person* — with the conviction to fight to lose, to test nothing but extremes. They all caved, and Pétain slept in his kepi with the scrambled eggs braid.

He was a man who had to go it alone, fight with conviction and for nothing, a dream castle, with men who didn't speak his language. The only one who didn't cave.

★ ★ ★

And so here he was, at a burlesque club below the Tropic of Cancer, in a damp city where dreams were marbled with nothingness.

She'd disappeared. He was so lost in thought he hadn't noticed.

It was time for her show. The blue lights flipped on.

'Introducing, from Paris, zazou dancer Rachel K!'

5

Her mother said it was an insurance policy: Dubuque hams, specially ordered from their Oak Ridge grocer. A just-in-case because the native food might be inedible. Seven bulky teardrop cans that Everly and her sisters had to wedge their feet between in the backseat of the Studebaker for the past three days as they made their way across the length of the island. An eighth ham, which they'd opened, was in a cooler of ice that Duffy propped her legs on as she drew faces on Scribbles. Erased them with a special sponge and drew on new ones.

They stopped at an Esso station. Marjorie Lederer handed out sandwiches she'd made in their hotel room that morning in Santa Clara, having found a store that sold American things, white bread and mustard to go with the ham.

'Does ham come from Hamburg?' Everly asked.

No one replied.

'Will we be taking a tram?' She knew they weren't taking a tram. She liked the word. It looked, on paper, like it should have something on the end of it. A *b*, maybe. Tramb.

She sensed there was a new policy in the car, of the adults not answering her questions. If they were going to ignore her, she would ask whatever she felt like asking.

'Is it 'morbid' if I think about other people

dying, or only myself?'

'If a person had a face like Scribbles, would she be a brand-new person every time her face got erased and redrawn? Or would she only be tricking people into thinking she was new?'

Duffy was putting eyelashes on Scribbles, swoopy and outsized like the legs of a tarantula. Even after you were dead, Everly thought, you were trapped in your own face. That is, if anyone had taken photographs of you, which was likely. What if she could change her face and not be permanently trapped in the one she was born with? Or just erase her features? When Scribbles's face was blank, you really could not tell what she was thinking. Surely there were advantages to being able to make your face occasionally blank, erase it and go around like that.

As they were getting gasoline, a man approached the car carrying a basket covered with cloths.

'Americanos! Vende Puffs!' he called. 'Hot puffs! Carne o guayaba! Meat or jam!'

George Lederer said no gracias.

'Puffs! Hot puffs!'

A Cuban father waiting at the other gasoline pump bought some and handed them to his children in the backseat.

'I want a hot puff,' Everly said. 'A meat one.'

She was given a ham sandwich, which seemed plain and ordinary and did not belong. A familiar thing you didn't want to see at a gas station somewhere in Cuba, electric green all around. You wanted to eat a puff, whatever it was. A hot puff. Meat or jam, they both sounded good.

Her father drove and her mother navigated.

There were tall palm trees along the road, and in the folds between the green hills, clusters of funny little shacks. They looked like yellow jacket hives, molded clumps of mud and leaves. Everly asked if people lived in them. Her father said they did, that they were native huts. That's how the Cubans live, he said, in huts.

★   ★   ★

There were fewer huts, and mostly sugarcane fields, when they had to stop because a river was rushing over the road.

Her father turned off the car, and everyone sat quietly, waiting as he tried to figure out what they should do. They heard animal hooves, a Cuban family in a horse-drawn wagon. The horse stalled when he reached the water, but the driver whipped him to keep going. The horse stepped slowly into the water, deeper and deeper, dragging the wagon after it, until the wheels were three-quarters submerged.

Two men were working on the side of the road, hitting a fence post with a large rock. Each wore the straw hats that all the men, once they'd left Havana, seemed to wear. Her father walked over to them. They listened as he communicated with hand gestures and broken sentences.

He said 'Auto,' and pointed at the car.

He said 'Water,' making a wavelike hand motion. 'Is it possible to cross?'

One of them nodded. 'Sí, sí.'

Her father smiled cheerfully, as he and one of the Cubans walked toward the car. He announced that the nice man had offered to guide it across for them.

'George, this person cannot drive our car,' Marjorie Lederer said. 'I won't allow it.'

George Lederer was in charge of everything, but he had to be in charge exactly her mother's way.

'This man,' her mother said, 'cannot even speak English.'

The man took off his hat, wiped his forehead on his shirtsleeve, and smiled politely at Marjorie Lederer.

'He doesn't even understand me! And this is the person you're giving our car keys to?'

'Dear, these men are locals,' George Lederer said, 'and I think it might be worth — '

'It might be worth *what?*'

'Letting them help us, dear.'

'Fine.' Marjorie Lederer opened her door and announced to the girls that their father was figuring this one out on his own while she sat in the bar just up the road. Anyone who wanted to come could come. Everly and her sisters got out and followed her.

George Lederer was always talking to strangers, which irritated and embarrassed Everly's mother. Everly could tell when other people didn't feel like chatting. Her father kept on anyway, talking to strangers in line at the bank or the bakery, telling them his name, what type of work he did, what he was buying or sending or depositing. 'Sending this to Cuba,' he'd said to a woman behind him in line at the Oak Ridge post office, pointing to the address on the package he

103

was carrying. 'The whole family is moving there.' At the Oak Ridge bakery, he told stories to the people in line. 'Grandma Lederer was a baker — right, Everly? She lives in St. Louis. She's retired now, but she ran a bakery downtown. I worked there as a child. She and my father made cheesecakes in flat, rectangular pans that were too big to fit on the shelves. They put the cakes on the floor to cool. One night, when I was very small, probably six years old, I got out of bed to get a drink of water. It was dark and I didn't see the cake on the floor and I stepped in it.' He could go on and on this way. It was embarrassing, but when her mother scolded her father, it made Everly want to try not to be embarrassed by him.

The bar was open-air, covered by a palm-leaf roof. Everly's mother ordered drinks, and the bartender lined up four ice-filled glasses, poured lemonade into them, and trickled red syrup over. It sifted down among the cubes in the glasses like a red dye. As they sipped their red lemonade, rain began to patter on the bar's thatched roof, making a gentle, creaking sound like water hitting a wicker basket.

The man spoke some English, and he asked her mother where they were from and where they were going.

'You arrive in Cuba,' he said, 'just in time for el golpe.'

Her mother asked what he meant.

'The change in the government, señora. A week ago. It was, how you say, con mucha fuerza. President Prio, he is no more presidente. He's left to Miami, in un hotel lindo. Batista, el dictador, el general, he is presidente now. But with no vote. You did not hear?'

Her mother said no, no one had mentioned it in Havana. Had it been announced?

Yes, of course, he said, but everything was back to normal now. 'For one whole day the radio station plays only music. The next day, they make the announcement. But maybe it was not in the American papers.'

Everly's mother said it might have been, but she hadn't had time to read a newspaper since they'd arrived. They'd left Havana immediately and had been on the road for the past few days, navigating maps and trying to get three children and twenty-one suitcases and a Studebaker all the way to Nicaro.

'And hams,' Duffy said. 'We have seven hams!'
'Eight,' Everly said.
'We have eight hams!'

★ ★ ★

They had turned around and were taking another route on account of the washed-out road. To Preston, the United Fruit town across the channel, where a boat could take them to Nicaro.

'There was a golpe!' Duffy said.
'What's a golpe?' George Lederer asked.
'I was getting to that,' their mother said, explaining that it was something the bartender mentioned. Some sort of major Cuban political event had occurred, and the old president had

105

gone to Miami and was now apparently staying at a place called the Hotel Lindo, which was probably a heck of a lot nicer than the fleabag where the Lederers had stayed. The way the bartender had explained it, it hadn't made much sense. Something about them playing only music on the radio station, and now everything was back to normal. But what if there was trouble?

George Lederer said he was pretty sure there wasn't any trouble, that the American government would never have asked twenty-six men and their families to move to a place that wasn't stable.

She said she hoped he was right. But that she planned to look up this word 'golpe' as soon as they got to Nicaro.

'Golpe!' Duffy shouted.

'Golpe! Golpe! Golpe!'

'Okay, Duffy,' they said, 'that's enough.'

6

Del and I had just caught a hammerhead shark, and we were down on the dock cleaning it with cleavers when we first met the Allains. This was in the summer of 1951. That shark bled like a slaughterhouse cow. We'd caught him with a hand line, right off the pier in Preston. When he struck the line he almost snapped it. I figured we'd cut him loose, have the novelty of being able to say a shark bit our line. But Del starts struggling with the line, barking orders at me to hold on and slacken, pull and slacken. I couldn't believe he actually thought we could catch that thing, or that it was worth trying. 'Del, there's no way — he'll drag us in,' I said. But Del wasn't listening. He was leaning against the line so hard I was sure it would break, frantically coiling it to one of the anchors on the dock as if nothing else in the world mattered. I didn't think there was the slimmest chance we could catch the shark, but I did what he told me.

It took us most of the night to tire the shark out. Just before dawn, it seemed like it was giving up. I tugged on the line and it didn't tug back. I remember feeling suddenly lousy. Sometimes you want something purely for the sake of wanting it, and when you finally get it, you only feel regret. Del said it was safe to go down. 'Into the water?' I said. 'Are you crazy?' There was no way I was getting into the water with a shark.

Hammerheads have skin like ground glass. Just grazing against them, they can turn flesh to hamburger. Del said it was dying, and that he'd go down and get a rope around its tail so we could hoist it out. I imagined the shark summoning just enough energy to lash at the bastards responsible for ending its happy life. Del stripped his shirt off and dove in. I felt the shark tug, just a final soft wriggle, and then it was still.

By the time we pulled it out, the sun was coming up. Our hands were completely shredded from the line. Del whacked him with a mallet, and it was over. Later we got our picture in our company magazine, *Unifruitco*, with a little article about the Stites boys catching a shark off Preston dock. They wrote 'kidney-headed shark,' but it's the same thing as a hammerhead. Nipe Bay was crawling with sharks. A month before we caught ours, a Pan Am seaplane hit a log and busted apart as it came in for a landing. Those poor people. Some of them survived the impact, only to get ripped apart by hungry hammerheads. Afterward, a couple of Cuban fishermen caught one, and when they opened it up they found women's jewelry in its gut.

As Del and I were cleaning the shark, a company launch pulled up to the dock. We were both delirious, and suddenly we hear these people shouting and carrying on — Americans, with southern accents, but not like Daddy's people. These people talked like real hillbillies. I looked up and a rowdy family with maybe seven kids came scrambling onto the dock. I think every one of them was barefoot, wearing overalls

108

like Tom Sawyer or something. They were yelling and chasing one another around as their bags were being unloaded from the boat. They crowded around us to get a look at the hammerhead, which are pretty weird-looking if you've never seen one. Sandpaper skin, a head like a forked tail, with these dull, cretinous eyes jutting from each side. There was a pile of innards next to me, organs and weird gunk we'd scraped out of the body cavity. One of the boys pointed and asked what we did with that stuff. I said toss it. He picked up what looked like a piece of intestine and started swinging it around as if it was seaweed. Tee-Tee was there, I remember because I'd never seen anyone with eyes like hers — ice blue, like a wolf's eyes. She was barefoot like the rest of them, and she stepped right into the dark pool of blood around the shark. She looked down at us, her stringy hair falling into her face, and said we could attract more of them if we tossed a chunk of its flesh back into the water.

I was eight and Del must have been twelve, and we'd never met anyone like the Allains. United Fruit had hired Hatch Allain and his brother, Rudy, and the two of them brought everybody over, even Grandmother Pearly. Pearly, who weighed about eighty pounds soaking wet and kept a .32 Derringer in the pocket of her apron. Rudy was a fix-it guy, he ran the machine shop, and Hatch was the plantation boss. Hatch was a giant, with these huge hands, huge elbows. Daddy said the company hired him because he'd worked on Louisiana plantations and he knew how to handle black people. Daddy didn't say it so politely, but you get the idea. Hatch had that name for a reason — I think it was short for Hatchet. The workers were scared to death of him. He'd killed a man in Louisiana, and that's why the Allains came to Cuba. They couldn't go back to the States, or Hatch would be sent to prison. It was supposed to be a secret, but everyone knew. It was part of what made Hatch, Hatch and the Allains, the Allains.

By the time Hatch and his wife, Flordelis, left Cuba, they had nine kids. When I think of Flordelis Allain I think of her pregnant. It seemed like she was the entire time I knew her. In Rudy's clan there were six kids and his wife, Marthize — everyone called her Mars. Hatch's son Curtis Junior was my age and he and I were buddies from day one. That's how it is with kids sometimes. When you're a good match, you're best friends in a day. But then again, you can become enemies in a day, which is what happened later with me and Curtis.

Tee-Tee, Hatch's oldest, was Del's age. That girl must have been almost six feet tall, lanky, with these long, bruised, dirty legs. Pale skin, almost colorless, like a baby's flesh. She was attractive in a sort of peculiar way. Del had a crush on her from that moment on the dock. As I was thinking what a weird girl she was, Del was falling in love. The first year the Allains were in the Preston school with us, Del gave Tee-Tee a heart-shaped box of candy on Valentine's Day. He'd bought it with his own money at the almacén. We were all on the playground, and Del walked up to her and mumbled something like 'here.' Del was shy. He was one of those people who once you found a subject he cared about, he livened up and had plenty to say, but otherwise he gave you almost nothing. Tee-Tee snatched the heart-shaped box out of his hands, sat down on the seawall, and tore it open. Poor Del. She didn't even thank him. She ate all the candies, plucked them out of their pleated paper liners until the box was empty. Rooted around to make sure she hadn't missed any, and wiped her hands on her skirt. Stared at him with this blank expression, licking chocolate off her fingers, rough and indifferent as an alley cat. I bought Valentine candy at the almacén, too, but I gave mine to Mother.

The Allains didn't mix with the other Americans in Preston. They were different socially, you could say. They were Cajuns, from a small town in southern Louisiana, and they did things in their own style. They didn't go to the Pan-American Club or play golf or polo or tennis or croquet or any of it. The Christmas pageant, the moonlit barge dances on the bay, yacht outings — there was always some sort of organized company fun happening, but you didn't see the Allains at these things. I suppose they probably weren't invited. But they wouldn't have wanted to go to those events. They'd rather cook at the house or go fishing or hunting, camp out on the beach. Daddy had them in two squat brick houses down by the sugar mill and the hump yard where all the railroad cars sat. There were laundry lines strung between the two

111

places, connecting them into one ragged compound, with diapers and kids' T-shirts and Hatch and Rudy's work coveralls flapping in the breeze that came over the seawall. Shredded clothes that didn't look much different clean from dirty. I don't know where they all slept — there must have been four or five of them to a room, so close to the sugar mill they were practically underneath it. The mill whistle was deafening down there, and during crushing season it blew on the hour every hour, twenty-four hours a day. This was how a lot of the Cubans kept track of time — not everyone had money to buy a watch. I think Daddy housed Hatch and Rudy down there to make sure there was no trouble. If something happened, they were two steps from the mill.

That first week after the Allains arrived in Preston, Curtis Junior and I rode our bikes out to the airstrip together. On our way back into town he asked if I wanted to eat with them. That was something different. They cooked outside and they ate outside. Grilled everything on a fifty-gallon drum that Rudy cut in half and welded onto a stand. We all sat together, both families and all of the kids, at two picnic tables pushed end to end. Adults, kids — everybody shouted. The babies cried, wearing nothing but diapers; the other kids in barely anything more, barefoot, standing up on the picnic benches so they could reach what they wanted off the table. At our house, dinner was a formal affair. Daddy insisted on it. Daddy wore a white duck suit, white tie. Mother was dressed nicely, her hair done up, a little rouge on her cheeks, perfume, though not much: Mother said you should only be able to detect a woman's scent when you lean to embrace her. Children were to be seen and not heard, unless Daddy asked us a question directly. Del and I had to be downstairs at six o'clock on the button, washed up and dressed for dinner, and nobody ate until my father said grace. Our butler, Henry Das — he was half Jamaican and half Hindu — served the courses. Daddy was from an old Mississippi family, and Henry Das wore white starched jackets and black bow ties. He stood at the door to the kitchen, still as a statue while we ate. Dinner was three or four courses, the table set with polished silver, good china, finger bowls. A Cuban lawyer came to dinner at our house once, and after we'd finished eating, he took out his pocket comb, dipped it in his finger bowl, and ran the comb through his hair. Mother was horrified, but she didn't say anything, of course. Even when Mr. Bloussé arrived with the Haitian wife and the black daughters, Mother was polite. Treated them like she'd treat anyone. She had a little silver bell at her end of the table. When she rang it, Henry Das came to see what we needed, walking with his perfect posture. That man was pure grace. When dinner ended, if there was a game happening out on the avenue, stickball or kick the can, Del and I wouldn't be excused until after coffee was served. We could hear kids shouting and running around, but we had to stay at the table until Daddy gave the word. After dinner we went out and played until dark.

Mother read, or painted with watercolors, or wrote letters to people in the States. Daddy sat on the front veranda listening to the nightly stock quotes on the radio. After the stock quotes was Lowell Thomas, and when Lowell Thomas said 'So long until tomorrow,' Daddy called out that it was time to come in and get ready for bed.

I'm pretty sure the Allains were the only Americans in Preston who didn't have servants. This was highly unusual. In Cuba, the Anglos all had servants. We always had eight or nine people working at our house. Having a staff was part of how you did things in the tropics — they knew how to run a household, haggle with the vendors, maintain everything in that heat, with all that rain. And labor was cheap. But the Allains had no staff. They didn't live on La Avenida, as I said — they lived in two squat brick houses practically in the armpit of the mill. That's the pecking order for you. Rudy and Hatch weren't management, they were blue-collar overseers, and they seemed happy next to the mill and the hump yard. I don't think they would have wanted to live on La Avenida, with butlers, cooks, houseboys, gardeners, handymen, chauffeurs, and laundresses, all of that.

Flordelis and Mars set big bowls on the outdoor table. They cooked Cajun, which I had never eaten. Oysters, some kind of blackened fish, corn bread, cracklins, rice, black-eyed peas. Delicious, spicy, salt-of-the-earth food. I miss it still. They started serving themselves and so did I, too, just reached in like everyone else and piled

114

what I wanted on my plate. Manners isn't just being proper, it's doing things as they're done at the home of your hosts. I wasn't taught that; it's something you pick up as you go. Putting your arm across somebody's face? That was politeness to them. Hatch and Rudy's mother, Pearly, came out of the house after everyone had started eating. She was in curlers, bobby pins sticking out every which way. Her head looked like a queen's mace. 'You got a date later on?' Hatch asked her. 'Maybe I do,' Pearly said. 'That is when I get done whuppin' your ass.' That is the only person I ever saw give lip to Hatch Allain. After she sat down, Pearly took the little handgun out of her apron pocket and set it gently on the table. I think it was a joke, because everybody laughed. Rudy said, 'Watch out somebody don't get shot tonight.' Mother had the little silver bell next to her place setting, to ring Henry Das. Pearly had the .32 Derringer.

Curtis's baby brother, Chinaman, threw food all during dinner and nobody cared. In fact, they seemed to delight in it. His name was Clovis, but they called him Chinaman because he was a chubby little guy and he had slanty eyes. All those kids had funny names, except for Curtis Junior, who was always just Curtis. Hatch was Curtis Senior but I never heard anyone call him that. I don't know what Curtis Junior's doing now — probably in Louisiana with ten kids of his own. I haven't talked to him in forty years. Hatch and Rudy are dead, I'm sure. Pearly's probably buried with that gun in her apron pocket.

Chinaman was maybe two years old, but he knew what he was doing: holding court. It was stiff competition to get the spotlight at the Allain table. After dinner Rudy put his two hands around his right eye and squeezed. His eye popped completely out. I couldn't believe it. He dropped it on the table like a jumbo jawbreaker — clunk! It was glass. He reached down and turned it so it was staring right at me. 'Here's looking at you, kid,' he said. Then he picked it up and bounced it in his hand. 'Yep,' he said, 'the price you pay for pissing off Marthize Allain. But I'm working on forgiving her.' He looked at me. 'I'll share something with you, son: it ain't eye for an eye between a man and his wife. It's something else. What do you think, Mars?' He was cupping the glass eye, turning it in his fingers. 'What would you call it?'

Everyone was quiet. I looked around, and the kids were staring at their plates, except for Tee-Tee, who had this awkward smirk, like here we go again, and in front of the clueless dinner guest. I figured Rudy was joking, although it didn't seem like a very funny joke. Mars stared at him. Then she started clearing dinner and went into the house with a stack of dirty plates. After she left, everyone sat quietly. Finally, Hatch spoke. 'If you don't shut your trap, Rudy, she might just take out the other one.'

Mars really had gouged his eye out. Years back, when they were all living in Louisiana, she and Rudy had a terrible argument. She broke an empty liquor bottle against the kitchen counter and jabbed the jagged end at him, not meaning to actually hurt him. He lunged toward her to grab it, and the broken end went into his eye. Busted his yolk. You have to wonder what that does to a marriage. She'd done this unforgivable thing to Rudy. And Rudy had experienced a horrific loss because of it — his eye, for Christ's sake. And now they were stuck with each other.

At our house, Annie made flan, flambé, elaborate triple-layer cakes. Every afternoon, the smell rose up from the kitchen and filled the house. Henry Das would bring dessert out on a rolling tea cart and serve it on Mother's special cake plates with her silver server. After the table was cleared at the Allains that night, Mars put out a halved watermelon on an old board. We each hacked off our own piece, and everyone spit their seeds in the dust. The adults all smoked. Rudy said he was out of loose tobacco, and Mars offered him one of her pre-rolled cigarettes. He took it and bit the filter off and spit the filter on the ground. He said smoking a cigarette with a filter on it was like — he paused, trying to think of what it was like — 'like suckin' on a titty through a brassiere,' he said.

After dinner they brought out the instruments. Curtis Junior and his cousin Mitty played fiddle and accordion, and Genevieve, Eglantine, and Tee-Tee took turns dancing on a piece of linoleum. Eglantine — or Giddle, as they called her — had tap shoes. The rest of the girls did a sort of fake tap dance in bare feet. I remember the metal taps on Giddle's soles click-clacking on the playground blacktop — she wore them to school every day, like they were just normal shoes. Rudy's littlest, Panda, she sang. Panda was maybe seven years old and she had this strange, beautiful voice, not in a conventional sense, but she had something special and they all knew it. Panda had long, dirty blond hair, always a big snarl right at the back of her head, a plum-colored birthmark around one eye. She once came to school in her nightgown. I have no idea why. Miss Sparks sent her home and told her to come back dressed properly. I guess kids wear what they want to, pajamas, tap dancing shoes, when there are a lot of them and not much supervision. Curtis and Mitty dressed like guajiros, pants cut off at the knee, a rope through the belt loops, no socks, canvas tennis shoes with holes in them. Even Tee-Tee, good-looking in her peculiar way, was just as dirty as the rest of them.

Panda sang, and Curtis and Mitty played accompaniment. Hatch kept time, slapping an enormous hand on an enormous thigh, and sipping from a bottle of Methuselah rum. Now, that's what you call rotgut. Thirty cents a liter at the almacén. The United Fruit executives drank Dewar's White Label scotch whiskey. It was the company's official drink. A gentleman named Joseph P. Kennedy, JFK's father, ran the Dewar's franchise in the States, and he was a friend of Daddy's. It's no secret that United Fruit people were involved in the Bay of Pigs. And the son of the CEO of the company that distilled our official whiskey is who they all later blamed for deserting them, for the missed opportunity to get the sugar empire back.

Dewar's White Label is what the younger guys drank as well, the bachelors who hung around at the Pan-American Club, sat on the terrace watching the dockhands load three-hundred-pound sugar sacks. This was United Fruit management, and there were rituals, ways of doing pretty much everything. You wore a white duck suit with the bejesus starched out of it; you lived in a house full of servants; your children were raised by Jamaican nannies; you listened to the company stock quotes on the portable; you sent your kids to bed when Lowell Thomas said 'So long until tomorrow,' and you sipped your Dewar's White Label scotch whiskey. The Allain brothers wore oil-stained coveralls; their wives did all the cooking and cleaning and laundry; their children ran wild; and Hatch drank from that jug of rotgut like it was an elixir from heaven.

That first night I had dinner there — supper, they called it — Daddy made me strip down in the garage, and Hilton Hardy hosed me off before I was allowed to come into the main house. Daddy didn't object to my going down to the Allains. He just didn't want me 'traipsing it into the house.' 'It' meaning lower class — not a thing you could catch. I think Daddy figured if I was going to be friends with Curtis, he wanted me to remain aware of the differences between us. Eventually I stopped having to strip down and hose off in the garage, and could just return home from the Allains like I'd been on a normal outing. Daddy would still pretend to grab lice out of my hair, or he'd tell Annie to check me for fleas, but he was only kidding.

Before we had the fight, Curtis and I did everything together, built forts, made slingshots, swam in the river, rode our bikes out to the airstrip to shoot doves. Rudy took us down to Mayarí in a company truck, to buy fireworks and shotgun shells. Every Sunday the Allains had a huge cookout — venison, oysters, lobster, you name it — and I was always invited. They treated me like one of their own, especially after I found Panda for them. Panda disappeared on a Saturday afternoon and Mars was a wreck, wringing her hands and crying. Rudy and Hatch got a search party together. I remember them loading shotguns in the kitchen. They were convinced someone had kidnapped her, and they went down to the cane cutters' batey, did a sweep from shack to shack to see if someone had her down there. They combed the town and no one could find her, a seven-year-old girl, just plain disappeared. But Panda was a funny child, not at all like the rest of them. She was in her own world, and I had a feeling she might have just walked off, maybe for a little peace and quiet. The second day she was missing, I was walking through the hump yard, along the railroad tracks. Just ahead of me was Daddy's Pullman car, the sun glinting off its dark green paint, with yellow lettering along its side that said *United Fruit Company*. Daddy used it for trips to Havana. The company had the DC-3s, and Daddy could have taken one and been there in an hour, but he was old-fashioned. All the old United Fruit gentlemen were like that. Occasionally he flew, but often, when Daddy went to

120

Havana, they'd latch his Pullman car to the main line in Holguín, and from there it was an overnight ride. The car was elegant — red velvet drapery, velvet upholstery, a teakwood-paneled office, gold faucets in the washroom, a dining room with silver, Wedgwood china, white tablecloths. It was cleaned on a regular schedule, and sometimes the cleaning ladies forgot to lock it up.

As I walked along the side of the car, I heard this little voice through the closed windows. I opened the door, and there was Panda, hair all knotted and hanging in her face, that birthmark like a wine stain spreading out around her eye. She was singing and talking to herself, sitting on the floor playing with a doll, making it move around like it was talking to her. She'd brought a suitcase, and she had stuff strewn everywhere. She looked up at me. 'We're going to Havana!' she said. I told her everyone was worried, that maybe we ought to go see Mars and let her know Panda was okay. She told me she was sick of sharing a bed with Genevieve, that Genevieve kicked her in her sleep. I almost felt sad to have to take her home. Not every personality is suited to a family like the Allains.

Curtis and I did a lot of fishing, and we'd give what we caught to Mars and Flordelis for the Sunday cookouts. Sometimes it was me, Curtis, and Del. Saturday night we packed bedrolls, sandwiches, and fishing gear, a radio set maybe, and loaded them on a popshot, which is a little four-wheeled open car that runs on the railroad tracks, with a lever to control it. You put the popshot in gear by pushing the lever, and there were pulleys that slackened to slow it down, and you had a brake. We'd take it down to the end of the pier, put out crab cages, and spend the night down there. If we had the radio set we'd listen to Clavelito's show, for kicks. It came on at 8:00 P.M., and they syndicated it all over the island. Sometimes, at dusk, I'd ride my bike along the access road between the cane fields and the workers' shanties. You could hear this eerie echo, all the radios tuned to Clavelito's show, his strange high voice coming from the dark bohíos. They had batteries but no electricity. Clavelito cured people over the radio. I mean supposedly. He made predictions on winning lottery numbers — that's the other thing the Cubans were addicted to besides Clavelito, the lotería. Sometimes he played the guitar and sang. We joked about Clavelito curing people by telling them to put a glass of water on their radio as he spoke. Then they'd drink the water. But there must have been something to the guy, a charisma, because why else would we have listened? The truth is I listened all the time. Everybody did.

★   ★   ★

The serious fishing was over at Cayo Saetía, and Hatch decided to organize a trip and take us boys. This was about a year after the Allains arrived, when Curtis and I had the fight.

Saetía was a perfectly protected cove, with pink sand that sparkled like it had ground-up diamonds in it, and reefs that were teeming with sea life. You could stick a pole with a sharp hook on the end of it into the clear green water and pull out one octopus after another, lay dip nets, and when you dragged them out they were filled with enormous green lobsters. The island was covered with tropical fruit trees — mango, papaya, breadfruit, rose apple, soursop, mamey, flowers as big as your head drooping off the trees and vines. There was an opening in the reef to get into the bay, and boats could clear it only at high tide. It was scary going in, but it was the best fishing in eastern Cuba. Saetía was United Fruit Company property, and Cubans weren't allowed to go there. Poachers tried to come in all the time. The company had a guard patrolling the bay to keep them out. In 1947, Fidel Castro supposedly swam several miles to the shores of Saetía, after an aborted invasion of the Dominican Republic he and some other Cubans had planned, in hopes of overthrowing the dictator Trujillo. I hear Raúl Castro owns Saetía now, that it's his private vacation spot, which doesn't surprise me. Whatever was ours, those brothers made a point of making theirs. Fidel still talks about Saetía and Preston and the rest of it when he makes his multihour speeches.

We were all thrilled about the fishing trip, five days of living off the sea. Del stayed home, and at the time I couldn't figure out why — I thought he was crazy to miss out. I'm sure it was because of Tee-Tee. He was always trying to figure out where she'd be and what she'd be doing. She definitely wouldn't be over at Saetía, catching octopus with a bunch of boys, and maybe he hoped that with Hatch and the boys gone, he might have a chance at seeing her. I remember that Mother was happy that Del was staying, because Daddy had gone to Havana to meet with Batista. This was March of 1952. Batista had taken over in a coup, and there were all sorts of negotiations to figure out with the company. Daddy knew about the coup before it even happened. Deke Havelin, a businessman in Havana who was a family friend, sent a telex to let him know. The Americans all considered it a positive thing. Certainly Daddy did. United Fruit had a relationship with Batista — he'd grown up in a United Fruit town, had even worked for the company, and he was very probusiness. I think Daddy respected Batista, but it was difficult to tell how much Daddy respected anyone. He had a way of treating you like you were a very clever person, and then again a total idiot.

Mitty, Curtis, a nephew of Mr. LaDue's who was visiting from Missouri, and I all helped load the boat with supplies — rice, cooking oil, sugar, coffee. Hatch passed a case of his Methuselah rum to me and told me to be careful, and to handle it like it was a carton of hen's eggs. We had three Cubans with us, an old guy named Perequín and his two grown boys. The sons rowed, and the old man sat in the boat chewing on his cigar — he didn't really smoke, he just chewed on a cold cigar stub jammed in his mouth. Barely talked, but he knew everything about the sea. He and his sons guided us through the reef, took care of the boats, cooked for us.

The first two days were paradise. We caught yellowtail, black grouper — we called it cherna — red grouper, strawberry snapper, and octopus, which the old man and his sons pounded on rocks and hung up on a line to dry. They chopped it into little pieces, boiled it, fried it, and stirred it in with a pot of rice. They cooked what we caught and served everything with fried plantains, rice, beans, and thick wedges of avocado. Saetía had once been a company orchard. Mostly citrus, but there were avocado trees as well, so heavy with fruit they were all leaning over. We ate heaping plates of food, and then everybody collapsed right on the beach. We slept on company sugar sacks, clean ones, laid over ficus leaves that we stripped from the trees. The second night it rained, and the Cubans put up canvas and we slept under that.

There was an old United Fruit guesthouse on Saetía, near the main cove. When I was little we used to stay there. It looked like something from Savannah, Georgia, three floors of ornate, wraparound balconies. When we had important visitors from Havana or the States, the company threw elaborate parties at the Saetía guesthouse. We took the seventy-five-foot company yacht over, the *Mollie and Me*, and if that wasn't big enough, they'd strap a sand barge behind the yacht and tow the rest of the guests. The house had twenty bedrooms, beautiful mahogany and purple-heartwood furniture, a giant old-fashioned staircase with a curved balustrade. Crystal chandeliers, all the linens monogrammed with UF Co on them. A full staff lived in the house, just to

125

take care of it. They had stopped growing citrus on Saetía years earlier; it wasn't profitable the way sugar was. The fruit had to be shipped in air-conditioned containers, it was a small crop, and they didn't want to deal with it anymore. For a while, they had just one Jamaican lady living in the house. Little by little, the company let it go. By the time we went fishing with Hatch, no one lived there. We still had our big company picnics on the beach at Saetía, and people would sit on the steps of the house for shade, but the place was falling apart, windows all boarded over. It was still painted United Fruit's trademark mustard yellow, but the paint was faded and peeling, half the red clay tiles had slid off the roof, and porch floorboards were missing where the wood had rotted. Perequín said it was haunted.

The door of that house was maybe twelve feet tall, and nailed shut. Our third day at Saetía Curtis and I pried it open with a claw hammer. There were little bats hanging upside down on the top of the door frame, asleep — the middle of the day is the middle of their night. When we finally got the door open, they stayed attached to the frame, hanging upside down like decoration, like those tassels along the bottom of a curtain. Curtis carried a flashlight, and we each had a twenty-gauge shotgun. I don't know what we thought — shoot a ghost, maybe. The furniture was covered with white sheets, and cobwebs hung from every corner, wafting in the air that blew in through the front door. It was the same house where I had stayed as a little boy, but it wasn't the same house. It had been a showpiece

126

for the company, and now it was an abandoned wreck, the floor covered with dirt and mouse droppings. It smelled of dampness and mold and trapped air. There were beehives wedged against the hardwood beams of the dining room ceiling, and Curtis and I aimed our shotguns up at the hives and fired to knock them down and get the honey out. We put huge holes into the ceiling of the dining room, where my family had hosted formal dinners with the Cabots and the Lodges, the du Ponts and the Bacardi people.

On a mild night in the old days, the servants made up beds on the second- and third-floor balconies, and we slept out there. I was maybe three years old, but I remember lying in an outdoor bed, listening for the watchman to blow his conch to announce a ship was coming in, which told the pilots to go out and meet it. They'd raise a flag, one or two flags, which told you how many ships, and how many pilots they needed. The head watchman, Chatsworth — Chatty, we called him — gave me a conch shell and taught me how to blow it. Mother had it preserved for me in leaded silver. Chatty said that during World War II, he watched from Saetía as our United Fruit ships got shelled by German U-boats. We lost an entire company fleet.

I wanted to see the upstairs rooms where we used to stay. 'You first,' Curtis said. Beyond the curve of the balustrade we couldn't see anything, just darkness. The smell of mildew drifted down the stairs. 'I'll let you hold the flashlight,' I offered, 'if you go first.' Curtis didn't buy that. We went up side by side, stopping every few steps to shine the flashlight around and listen for creepy noises. At the top of the stairs was a hallway, all the doors along it shut. I toed one of the doors — it wasn't latched, and it swung open and banged against the inside wall. Light leaked in through the slats of the shuttered balcony. The room was empty, no furniture, nothing but a stack of newspapers tied with cord — ancient editions of the *Havana Post*, the pink pages faded to a yellowish-peach. Suddenly we heard a noise. We both practically jumped through the ceiling. It was just the watchman blowing his conch. We went into the room and opened the balcony shutters to get a look.

The day was perfectly clear, no mist on the water, and from the balcony we could see out over the reef, to the larger, sparkling blue of Nipe Bay. There was a boat heading for Levisa — that's Nicaro's bay, where the nickel processing plant was. Whenever it rained, which it just had, the roads turned to mud, and no one could get past Mayarí up to Nicaro. Instead they forked left into Preston and took boats from our dock through the channel, past Saetía and into Levisa Bay. The nickel mine in Nicaro, which was owned by the U.S. government, had just reopened. The government built it during World War II, and shut it down when the war ended. They were starting it up again because of the war in Korea. They needed nickel for armor plating, airplane cladding, all sorts of munitions. It was a serious operation, and a bunch of Americans were coming over to run it.

The boat passing by was filled with people,

American-looking in their fancy travel clothes, ladies in white cotton gloves, and kids who had that fussy Sears catalog look about them, all of them pale as ghosts. One woman had a nervous little dog in her lap that kept yapping at the oarsmen, the oarsmen laughing back at the little dog like it was the stupidest thing they'd ever seen. 'Yap yap yap!' Its little bark echoed across the bay. I said I'd heard they were all coming over to work in Nicaro.

'Another boatload of losers,' Curtis said. He started carrying on about people coming to Cuba once they've screwed things up at home. He said people used to move West in frontier times when they'd screwed up, got a bad reputation, or had trouble with the law. Go to a new town, the next county over, where no one knew them. 'Now they just come here,' he said.

'Maybe some people like it better over here, and that's why they come,' I said.

'You telling me all these Americans move here because they *want* to? To live with a bunch of niggers on the edge of a swamp?'

'I was born here, Curtis. My father's been here since he graduated from agriculture school. He moved my mother over. It's our home.'

'Uncle Rudy says it's a loser's paradise.'

'I don't know what losers he's talking about. My father's not a loser.'

'Not here he ain't,' Curtis said. 'He's *el jefe*. The big boss. Like Uncle Rudy says: *if you can't serve in heaven, might as well rule in hell.*'

'Just because your father killed someone' — I'd never said a word to Curtis about Hatch's

129

murder rap, it just came out — 'doesn't mean everyone around here is a fugitive. That's *your* family.'

'How do you know what your father did before he moved here? Maybe he knocked up some girl, a cousin or something, and he had to scram — '

That's when I punched him. It's possible I knocked him out with one punch. Curtis fell back and landed on the balustrade of the balcony, and the balustrade must have been rotten because it gave way. He pitched off the balcony, backward. I leaned over the edge, panicked, and almost fell off myself. He'd dropped two stories. Landed flat on his back on the sandy ground. I hadn't meant to hit him so hard. I knew how to box, and hitting hard came naturally. The Cubans had a boxing ring set up in the cockfighting round when it wasn't cockfighting season, and I went down there and sparred. They had a guy from the mill, Luís Galindez, who coached me and Del. Later, when I went to military academy, I was on the boxing team and everyone called me Cuba, Cuba Stites.

I ran down the hall, took the main stairs to the foyer two at a time, flew through the lobby and past all that sheet-draped furniture, raising dust and sending that damp, moldy smell up to my nose. The front door was open and light flooded in, so bright I couldn't see a thing, light flooding through like it was a door into heaven. The inside of the house felt like a completely different world than the one outside — different light, a different climate — much cooler, and the sound of the ocean muted through the boarded windows. I remember hoping that when I got outside, I wouldn't have punched Curtis, and he wouldn't have fallen two stories off the balcony, like it was just a nightmare dreamed up by the house. Maybe that's what Perequín meant when he said it was haunted, a place that lets your imagination run wild, or where you end up accidentally pitching another kid off a balcony.

Curtis's face was covered with blood, and he was out cold, either from the punch or from the fall, or maybe both. I shouted for help. Hatch and Perequín came running over. Hatch was calm. He asked me what happened, picked up Curtis, and carried him down to the shore. I wish I wouldn't have seen it, but Curtis peed in his pants in Hatch's arms. I guess that's what happens when the body's in shock and you're unconscious. Hatch laid him down in one of the boats, and we set off for Preston, to take him to the company hospital. Perequín was whispering Hail Marys and shaking his head while he rowed. He said it was the house, that he knew there was trouble inside. Hatch had a balled-up shirt pressed to Curtis's nose, to try to stop the bleeding. Hatch said, 'Son, wake up. Can you hear me? Son?' Curtis's eyes fluttered. Hatch shook him gently. Curtis finally came-to. He opened his eyes, sat up, and started swinging at me like a wild man. Hatch pinned him down. 'Hey, hey, easy, Curtis. You better just rest.' Curtis closed his eyes. He was out cold again.

We had him under Doctor Romero's care in maybe an hour. Curtis woke up, and Doctor

Romero said he seemed okay, that he had a concussion and they would monitor him for a few days to make sure there was nothing seriously wrong. Dr. Romero said that he weathered the fall because he was a kid and flexible and strong. His nose wasn't broken; faces just bleed a lot, this I know from boxing.

While Curtis was in the hospital, I couldn't stop thinking about what had happened and what he'd said about the Americans going to Nicaro. I started wondering if maybe people did come to Cuba because they had to, because they'd failed in some way at home and needed to escape this or that fate. Hatch Allain killed a man with his bare hands — that's what everybody said. But whether or not you actually committed a crime, moving to another country meant getting away from all the people who had decided what kind of person you were and how you were supposed to live your life. Like Panda moving into Daddy's Pullman car, except Panda hadn't done anything wrong. She just wanted a fresh start, away from her family. But let's say you had done something wrong, committed a crime. A fresh start in a place like Cuba meant you could be wanted by the law at home, and it wouldn't matter because you were under a different set of laws. Not Cuba's laws. You were under the company's laws.

Did the company care that Hatch had killed a man? They knew about his murder rap. At the end there was a lot of talk of where the Allains would go because they couldn't go back to the States. The company hired Hatch because he knew how to handle black people. 'Take care of niggers' is what Daddy said. But what if the company hired him *because* he was a murderer? There was a Rural Guard in Oriente, a special army that patrolled the countryside to protect landowners. One of the captains, Sosa Blanco, had been in prison for murder. Near the end, he torched the workers' shanties in Nicaro and was stringing the blacks up in trees around Mayarí. He was a monster who was useful to Batista and his military cronies, perfect for scaring the hell out of everybody and ruling with an iron hand. That's what people said about Hatch — that he ruled with an iron hand. Then again they said it about Daddy, and Daddy wasn't escaping any murder rap. Daddy was an upstanding citizen, a Mississippi gentleman in a white duck suit. His father owned a country store and most of the land in the county where Daddy was from. But the workers were scared of Daddy, and so was I. And maybe like with Hatch, what was scary about him was part of what made him a good jefe.

I don't like to think of Hatch Allain as any kind of monster. You could feel his power, but he was nothing but kind to me. I beat up his kid and knocked him off a second-story balcony, and Hatch wasn't angry about it. In the hospital waiting room, worried as hell about Curtis, Hatch was joking around and calling me 'slugger.' In a lot of ways he was gentler with me than my own father. When I was six years old, Daddy dragged me out into the yard, by the servants' quarters and the garage where we kept the two Buick limousines. There was a pig tied up back there, a gift from some of the sugar mill workers. At Christmas, the employees who got on well with Daddy would bring him a pig. Daddy hit the pig with a hammer. The poor animal squealed something horrible. I was just a little kid and I hadn't seen anything so rough before. I started crying and begging him to stop. He had a grim expression, and he hit the pig with the hammer again, and again. There was blood everywhere. The obvious lesson is that pigs are food and not pets, and it's a father's duty to make his child understand this. But I think Daddy also wanted me to understand that life is violent and arbitrary and unfair — that it's not easy, like a child might think, especially a child like me, living in a paradise, coddled by Mother and by Annie, no worries, always having a ball. He beat that pig to death with a hammer in our backyard, and he made me watch.

★　★　★

While Curtis was in the hospital that week, more Nicaro people arrived. The rains didn't let up, and the Levisa River flooded the road up to Nicaro, so everybody had to come into Preston instead. They stayed at the company hotel and waited to be taken over to Nicaro in launches. These people and their kids were on the town square, they were at the almacén, at the Pan-American Club. Mother entertained some of them. Daddy was still in Havana, ironing things out with Batista and his new ministers.

134

That's when the Mackeys first came to our house. The Mackeys' son, Phillip, was Del's age, and those two hit it off immediately. Phillip was a class clown, an instant ringleader. We all went to the movies in a big group, and Phillip stood up in front of the screen, cutting into the projector's beam and doing hand puppets. Someone threw a hot dog at him. He caught it with one hand and took a bite out of it. Everybody's personality was on display, the talent show that happens when there are a lot of kids, and it became immediately apparent who was going to be most popular. Like at summer camp, there was a mad grab, social cliques forming, but Curtis wasn't part of it. Eventually he and I made peace, but for a while the Nicaro kids were the new thing. A bunch of them, Phillip Mackey, the Lederer girls, and some others came to Preston every weekend. The boys would all go fishing, or we'd have cookouts at the swimming pool.

The week the Nicaro people were arriving in Preston, Mother invited the Lederers over for lunch. Annie made arroz con pollo, and the three Lederer girls wolfed it down and asked for seconds. Their mother said she was surprised they would eat anything besides a hamburger. After lunch, we all sat in the parlor, and Everly Lederer played piano. I remember that there was a tussle between her and her mother; maybe Everly didn't want to play. What she played sounded nice, different from what Mother played on the piano. Mother played old show tunes, Tin Pan Alley — not classical music. I was enjoying it, and amused at this little girl who was so serious and dramatic, bent over the keys. But then she hit a wrong note, and then another, and got frustrated and stopped playing. She banged the keyboard with the side of her hand and ran out of the room. Mrs. Lederer said she had a temper, and that she was awfully sorry for the behavior. Mother ran after her. She told Everly Lederer that it was our old stupid piano, that it was out of tune. It was so humid in Oriente that the piano tuner would come, and by the next day the piano was out of tune and he had to come back again. 'It's the piano,' Mother said, 'it's not you.'

Afterward I took Everly and Stevie on a tour; that was my job with all the new Nicaro kids that week. I was going to just take a loop around town, show them the movie theater, the swimming pool, the mill, our school. But when we passed near Daddy's Pullman car, I decided to take them inside. I showed the Lederer girls where Daddy slept, and the compartment where I slept when I went with him on trips, the little transom window that I could slide open above my single bed to get a breeze going if I wanted one, the worktable with flip-down seats where I did my homework, Daddy sitting across from me running company numbers. I told them how a porter would come in and bring me a cherry cola, serve Daddy his demi-demi. And how the porter never spilled anything no matter what, even when the train was rounding a bend and leaning over to one side. Daddy's Pullman car was special to me. It felt like I was showing them something private — my own bedroom, or some other bedroom, almost more private than my real one, which I only wished for and thought about. The older girl, Stevie, was unimpressed. But Everly seemed to understand that it was a kid's fort on wheels, a place where you could sit and enjoy the green landscape rolling past, and daydream.

Mother was gentle with all children, but she had a soft spot for Everly Lederer. I think I did, too, although I didn't quite realize it at the time. I was nine years old, and at that age you're not so aware, or reflective, when you're drawn to someone. I think Everly was about eight, cross-eyed, with these thick glasses, fire-red hair, couldn't be in the sun for thirty seconds before she burned pink as a boiled lobster, and feisty. At a kids' pool party the next weekend, she saw me and Del and Phillip Mackey going off the high dive and insisted on doing the same. She landed flat on her belly — you could hear it when she hit the water. That poor girl. It must have hurt like hell, but she pretended everything was fine. Got out of the pool and limped over to her towel and wouldn't let anyone come near her.

7

Everly had fibbed to some of the kids in Oak Ridge that she'd be getting a pet monkey in Cuba, but someone in Preston really did have a monkey.

Its name was Poncho and it belonged to Mr. and Mrs. LaDue. Everly's mother said the LaDues were 'empty nesters' and that Mrs. LaDue believed that the monkey was her child. But no one would keep a child in a big cage out in the yard, and especially not at midday, when the child would have nowhere to hide from the blazing sun. The LaDues had peacocks that were allowed to wander free, waddling and preening under the shade of the LaDues' tree ferns, while Poncho hung from the bars on the roof of his metal cage, looking at Everly. He blinked just like people blinked, and let her know with his bloodshot eyes that he was suffering from boredom, like a person might suffer from boredom. His look was passive — as though he accepted his fate, a life of hanging from the roof of a cage — but also questioning. He was trying to figure out if Everly might be sympathetic, though whether or not he wanted sympathy, she wasn't sure. He was bored and passive and questioning, but he seemed to know that he and Everly were different types of beings, and he wasn't planning on letting the matter go.

★ ★ ★

Her family had arrived in Preston late the night before. After three days of dark country roads, they were suddenly on an avenue lined with old-fashioned streetlamps, frosted white globes arranged in clusters like grapes, huge homes with yellow-lit windows. They spent the night at the United Fruit Company hotel, in a large suite with old-fashioned four-poster beds that creaked when you got into them, and heavy cotton sheets that had been ironed, her mother pointed out approvingly, adding that the place was remarkably fancy for a company hotel. 'It's the United FRUIT Company,' Duffy shouted, 'and there are pineapples on the bedposts!' 'Last call for alcohol,' George Lederer said, picking up Duffy, who screamed and kicked her legs. 'Last call' meant Duffy was in that crazed state just before passing out.

In the morning they went shopping at the United Fruit commissary. George Lederer said everybody could pick something, but it was like at Sears again, and what Everly chose wasn't 'acceptable..' Duffy got a toy six-shooter, though they took it away from her right outside the store because she wouldn't stop pointing it at her own head. Stevie chose a Little Lady box set with eau de cologne, soaps, and powder. Everly wanted a pair of lazy tongs that were hanging on a nail behind the counter. 'What on earth do you need those for?' her father asked. 'Don't you want a Little Lady box set like your sister?' She insisted on the lazy tongs, which turned out to be as much fun as she'd predicted, though later, when they had settled in Nicaro, they banned her from

139

bringing them in the car after she used the tongs to pinch her father's ear while he was driving. 'I'm just reminding you I'm *here*,' Everly said. 'Don't be sassy,' her mother replied, 'that was an accident.' They'd forgotten her at a gas station in Mayarí, on a trip into a town one Sunday for church services. She'd gone to use the bathroom as the attendant was filling their car. She didn't really need to use the bathroom. She had a *National Geographic* and wanted a few minutes alone, reading her magazine on the toilet. She lost track of time, and when she came out, they were gone. 'Are you scared?' the gas station attendant asked her in Spanish. 'No,' she said, knowing the car would reappear in the station and that they'd be arguing in the front seat about whose fault it was, everyone rankled like it was she who'd done something wrong. The attendant gave her a cup of cane juice and let her sit in the office, but she'd barely begun to relax and enjoy herself when she saw the Studebaker pulling up.

★   ★   ★

Preston was a whole day of visiting before they got on a boat for Nicaro in the early evening. Lunch at Mrs. Stites's, and then afternoon tea at the LaDues, because Mr. LaDue's cousin knew the pastor at the Lederers' church in Oak Ridge. It seemed like her mother's version of her father talking to strangers in line at the post office and the bakery. *I was barefoot and I stepped right in it. They cut around my footprints and sold it anyway. But perhaps I shouldn't be telling you this. You might be buying cheesecake!* The stranger's shut-down look. Polite, but hoping not to encourage him. Her mother 'networked.' Her father was 'inappropriately friendly,' which was why her mother managed him in social situations, hovered close, and intervened if she didn't like what he said.

Mrs. Stites had a gentle manner and a pretty smile, and she smelled faintly like flowers. The Stiteses had a baby grand piano, and when her mother mentioned that Everly had taken lessons in Oak Ridge, Mrs. Stites asked if she would play them something. Everly was embarrassed and didn't want to, but Mrs. Stites was so nice about it, it seemed like she actually wanted Everly to play. She agreed, and not because it was something her mother wanted her to do. She chose a Mozart piece she knew by heart, but she flubbed a difficult trill and then lost her place and couldn't finish. Mrs. Stites acted as though nothing was wrong and Everly's behavior was the most normal thing in the world. She told Everly she could come and play their piano anytime she wanted. Usually it was Stevie whom the adults took a shine to. But Mrs. Stites chose Everly, despite the tantrum she'd had right in the Stiteses' living room. Everly figured there must have been some mistake. But Mrs. Stites was insistent and said to come back the next weekend, that they'd have lunch and play duets together.

The boys, K.C. and Delmore, both had sun-bleached hair and tanned skin like they belonged on a Coppertone billboard. Delmore was about Stevie's age, but he didn't express much interest in talking to her. K.C. took them into his father's private train car, red velvet drapes, red velvet-upholstered seats, and red carpeting. It looked like the inside of a mouth. Lining the walls above the windows were mirrors tinted a goldish-pink — champagne, Everly later learned, was the name of the color. K.C. said the mirrors were there so you could see the landscape twice — out the windows, and also in reflection. Why look at a mirror, Stevie asked, when you could just look at the real thing? But Everly liked the idea. Maybe you'd see something in the reflection that you'd missed in the landscape itself. And besides, it would be goldish-pink now. Even I look okay, she thought, in a gold-pink mirror.

Two girls, an older and a younger one, poked their heads into the Pullman car. The younger one had a huge birthmark around her eye. She asked if they were going on a trip. 'I forgot to tell you,' K.C. said to Everly and Stevie, 'that this is actually Panda's Pullman car.' 'No, it isn't!' the girl squealed, delighted by the idea that maybe it was.

The two girls tagged along with them as they walked around town. Click click click click went the older girl's shoes. They were tap-dancing shoes. 'Why are you wearing those?' Stevie asked. 'Because I feel like it,' the girl said. Later, Everly suspected they were the only shoes Giddle Allain had. But maybe it was how she got to be such a good tap dancer. She was already wearing the shoes and could practice at any moment. K.C. took them by the Allains' and they met the whole family. They were each offered a piece of cut sugarcane, which Hatch Allain sent Mitty to retrieve from a cane car just beyond the house. Hatch showed them how to strip it and eat it.

'We do *not* say 'Chinaman,'' her mother scolded, when Everly and Stevie returned to the hotel.

'But it's his name! That's what they call him!'

Which only confirmed to Marjorie Lederer that the Allains were not just common but downright crude. 'Roughnecks,' her father called them. Giddle Allain had invited Everly and Stevie to come back sometime to spend the night.

'They can't stay at your house!' Duffy blurted, when Giddle and Panda came to the dock to say good-bye as the Lederers were getting on the launch for Nicaro. 'Mother won't allow it!'

'She just likes us to sleep at home,' Everly said as hurt rolled over Giddle's face. Rolled over but then was gone. Giddle didn't care what people thought. None of them did. Roughnecks or not, the Allains, as Everly got to know them, did not cry or complain. No one watched out for them and told them to clean up or wear a dress or do their homework. They dressed themselves and told themselves where to go and what to eat and who to hang around with. They didn't sleep on ironed sheets. They didn't *have* sheets. Everly saw the beds in the room the three girls shared — just mattresses, with the striped mattress ticking you weren't supposed to see unless the

143

maid was changing the bed. Panda was the only one who might have been the least bit delicate. Traipsing around in her nightgown, clutching a piece of foam rubber like it was a teddy bear. On the foam, which looked like a hunk of ceiling insulation, she'd written 'Panda's pillow' in magic marker, so no one else would use it.

★ ★ ★

Marjorie Lederer took notes on everything she observed at the Stiteses' and the LaDues'. She said these people had been living in Cuba for a long time and knew how to make a life in the jungle. She would pay attention. Everly had paid attention and took her own notes, like never to hold Poncho again if they were invited back to the LaDues' house.

'He doesn't bite,' Mrs. LaDue had said, encouraging Everly to hold him. 'Snuggle her baby' is how Mrs. LaDue had put it. And if he did bite, she added, it wouldn't hurt because Poncho's teeth had been removed. He didn't scratch because his fingernails had been removed. And he wasn't aggressive because he'd been 'neutered.' Everly held him and he really was like a baby, curled up against her, his long, thin fingers playing with the buttons on her shirt. Although he didn't have nails, his fingers were as careful, deliberate, and wrinkly as human fingers. His eyes, as moist and expressive as human eyes.

A human trapped inside a monkey trapped inside a cage. But when she tried to put him down, he screeched like a vicious animal.

PART TWO

8

IN HAVANA AS IN PARIS . . .
MADAME MASIGLI SHOPS AT JEAN
PATOU.

We're proud to offer Her Excellency
Masigli's favorite scent, COLONY, cele-
brating the tropics since 1938. Available in
perfume, cologne water, talcum, lotion, and
soap.

Visit our exclusive showroom, Prado 157
between Colón and Refugio, or purchase
by mail order through El Encanto.

Blythe Carrington closed the catalog and sat
powdering her complexion, perspiring through
the powder, then powdering again. It was useless.
Sweat and humidity were turning her makeup to
paste. She gave up and downed the last of her
lukewarm stinger.

The temperature hadn't dipped under eighty-
five degrees since she and Mr. Carrington and
their twin daughters, Val and Pamela, arrived in
Nicaro four weeks ago. Unlike their neighbors,
the Lederers on one side and the Billings on the
other, who showed up with wardrobes of
synthetic cloth that not only transformed body
odor to an inorganic stench but also melted after
one day in the climate of eastern Cuba, Blythe
Carrington wore cotton and hadn't been a bit

surprised to encounter damp tropical heat. She'd spent her adult life suspended in it. But tonight the air was heavy and windless as the air in a shut closet, though instead of mothballs she smelled oxide dust. The plant had begun production, the managers too impatient to wait for the new chimney scrubbers to arrive from the States. And so the town was coated in oxide dust — reddish, and blending grittily with the humidity. To make matters worse, Tip Carrington had used up the last of the cube ice, and so lukewarm stingers.

She was already slightly drunk, what she thought of as twilight drunk: a special moment when she was still sober enough to *notice* she was drunk, caring more about certain things and less about others, her vision blurring around the edges like a camera with a twinkle filter on its lens. And she was already irritated with her husband, who'd dressed, greased his hair, and patted on cologne with the attentive optimism of a horny bachelor.

As she went to fix another drink, Val and Pamela came into the living room.

'Mom,' Val said, 'I think it's only fair to let us go to the party. There aren't any kids our age in town, so we should be promoted to adult things.'

Blythe Carrington replied that no one else was bringing teenagers, that it was a meet-and-greet expressly for employees and their wives. Pamela, more hotheaded than her sister, protested that no one was bringing teenagers because there *weren't* any teenagers. She said they'd been carted off to live in this muddy two-bit nowhere and get followed around by a weird eight-year-old like Everly Lederer. Pamela marched down the hall and slammed a door, then opened it so she could slam it again. A nasty little habit she'd learned from her father. When Tip Carrington had successfully broken every door in their house in Bolivia, he'd resorted to slamming kitchen cabinets, and had broken all of those as well. Blythe Carrington knew about anger, but she didn't bother with doors. Fix yourself another room-temperature stinger. That was Blythe Carrington's answer to everything.

'I hate this place!' Pamela yelled. 'It's ugly and we have to live under a disgusting factory. My shoes are all ruined because these idiotic people haven't paved our road.'

Why Pamela had developed this irrational homesickness for Bolivia was beyond Blythe Carrington. Another corrupt hellhole where her husband had screwed the maid, the laundress, his secretary, and his assistant's secretary. Where they'd lived a life of tenuous appearances and outright lies. And where her husband's engineering job at the silver mine had lasted only so long as the hostile locals remained firmly under the company's shit hammer. Which wasn't long. When the revolution began, they ran for their lives. Her husband's employees — the same miners who'd brought gifts, little hand-woven native things, to the house after Tip Carrington successfully negotiated a better ration card system for them — were suddenly the angry mob lobbing medium- and large-sized rocks at their car as they fled to the port in Sulaco. Even the

149

wives had flung rocks.

Blythe Carrington placated Val and Pamela by telling them they could order whatever they wanted from the El Encanto catalog on her dressing table. Val retrieved it, happy to shop, and to shop expensively.

'Here, Pamela,' Val said. 'Colony perfume by Jean Patou. From *France*.'

'I *love* Colony perfume,' Pamela said, folding the page corner to mark it. 'And it's only forty-five dollars.'

★ ★ ★

When the jeep arrived to take the Carringtons to the party the moon had just appeared, rose-colored and hanging low and giant like a ripe mango. Probably the nickel dust, giving it that hue. Mist was settling in the air, and Blythe Carrington felt relieved to be outside, under that moon and free, for a moment, of her own petty irritations. They were going to a party, and the party might actually be fun. Over the past three weeks people had been arriving in dribbles, moving in along the manager's row. She'd met a few of the wives at the ice factory and the club, and gotten a vague sense of who might make tolerable company, who not. But tonight was the first official gathering, and everyone would be there.

The party host was this mysterious Gonzalez character whom people had been gossiping about since the Carringtons arrived. The 'Cuban millionaire' who'd finagled his way into the nickel mining operation. They were all going up to his hunting lodge on the Cabonico River. She wasn't sure what to expect, and that alone was reason for hope.

The jeep fetched Mr. and Mrs. Lederer, and they made their way up the steep, rutted, and narrow road to Lito Gonzalez's remote lodge. Branches xylophoned down the sides of the jeep as it forced its way through the foliage that strangled the road's throat. They ducked under a fig tree, and giant water-filled leaves upturned like ladles, raining into the jeep. Figs plopped on the hood like soft leather pouches.

The river rushed loudly as they pulled up in front of a three-story house that looked like it had been slapped together with driftwood and rusty nails.

'My God,' Blythe Carrington said, 'a polite person would call this 'rustic.' I call it a dump.'

The house was on stilts, pitched over the river, and the entire structure seemed to be listing to one side. Ivy and lianas coiled up and around the eaves of its sagging roof. More vines smothered the exterior and hung down from the power lines in tangled masses, like drain clogs of human hair.

Lito Gonzalez greeted the four of them as they entered the dimly lit foyer, pronouncing their names slowly, carefully. He was wearing pressed gabardine — the jacket with an excess of shoulder padding, the pants with an excess of pleats girdling his large middle.

★   ★   ★

New management people and their wives, some of whom Mrs. Lederer had met, others she'd only seen in town, were crowded around the bar, where white-jacketed Negroes were pouring drinks from a cart of gleaming liquor bottles. Mrs. Lederer tried not to seem too eager as she waited her turn to get a drink. She felt slightly frantic, like this was a department store white sale and the best linens would be gone before you knew it. The girls were at home in Nicaro, where they would be watched over by the new houseboy, and she was planning on getting good and drunk.

'Never get tight at a company affair,' *Fortune* magazine advised in the issue devoted to management social mores. Marjorie Lederer had read it cover to cover and taken notes. But after only three weeks in Cuba she'd come to understand that management people drank. And did they ever.

Tip Carrington commandeered the bar and mixed up a batch of martinis, making the task into an impromptu tutorial for the benefit of the three Jamaican bartenders. He explained to them that extra dry meant not a little bit, but the merest *suggestion* of vermouth, in a sense *none*. Which he demonstrated by tipping the vermouth bottle over the shaker, and righting it before any actual alcohol poured from the spout.

'It's a gesture of the wrist — like a dance,' he excitedly explained to the bartenders. 'You boys like those native dances, right? Rumba?'

Tip Carrington leaned the vermouth bottle again, leaned it back. He capped the stainless steel canister of gin and ice, shook it up and down — another kind of dance — and strained it into an empty canister.

The men talked business and the women compared notes on settling in, as Tip Carrington circulated the party with a fogged cocktail shaker, filling people's drinks.

'Is the freezer they gave you auto-defrost?' one of the wives asked. 'Because I don't think mine is, and I was promised an auto-defrost. I specifically asked — '

'But what do you plan on filling it with? I mean, I just can't get over the lack of produce,' one of the women said, 'no peas, no celery, no carrots. Only tropical things. We've got alligator pears coming out our ears, and my kids won't eat them. Yesterday I broke down and paid a dollar twenty-five for a head of lettuce at the commissary in Preston.'

'Aren't you on the produce vendor's route? He comes by the house, the cutest thing, ringing a bell. A little old Chinaman named Lumling. I send the houseboys out, and they haggle with him.'

'The Chinese vendor?' Mrs. Lederer asked. 'But I was told he grows with night soil.' Night soil being the only polite term she could think of to convey that the Chinese vendor was fertilizing his turnips with human waste.

'The produce can't possibly be as bad as the dairy products, which, as you know, come from Gonzalez's dairy. Mrs. Billings took a tour of the place and said it was *most* unsanitary. Just absolutely *dreadful*. Cows urinating and defecating practically into the milk. I've half a mind to order a home pasteurizer.'

'Well, don't order it from the Sears in Havana. They'll ship you a vacuum cleaner instead — *by accident*, of course.'

One of the women commented that the heat was making her listless, and Blythe Carrington said cheerfully that people everywhere were listless, and at least they had something to blame it on.

'Has anyone noticed that the air in Nicaro — I daresay, the *heat itself* — seems rust-colored?'

'The factory,' Mrs. Carrington said. 'Nickel oxide.'

Charmaine Mackey, whose husband, Hubert Mackey, was the new general manager, patted her face with a handkerchief and said she couldn't believe how infernal the weather had been, and what bad timing it was for setting up a household. Blythe Carrington said her advice was to stock up on cube ice. She said it went quickly in this heat, and that all you could do to stay cool was keep your drink fresh and the fans on high.

'Don't they say it's deleterious to one's health to drink in equatorial zones?' Mrs. Mackey asked. 'I read it in the brochure the company sent, *Tips for Anglos*.'

'*Deleterious?*' Mrs. Carrington said, suppressing her desire to smack Mrs. Mackey right there at the party, in front of the other women. 'Forgive me, Mrs. Mackey, but I'm not sure if I know the term.'

'Bad for the health,' Mrs. Mackey replied, nervously clutching her handkerchief to dampen

154

the shake of her hands. She'd seen a doctor for the problem. He'd prescribed something for nerves, but the medication, and the idea that she suffered from nerves, had made her hands shake more. It was a stupid thing to have said, and she knew better. Her neighbor Mrs. Billings had informed Mrs. Mackey that Mrs. Carrington had a drinking problem. 'It'll end badly,' Mrs. Billings had said. Mrs. Mackey had nodded, wondering silently *what* would end badly. A great deal of her time was spent not understanding what other people meant when they made these ominous, sweeping, and vague statements. *It'll end badly*. Statements that often were lost on Mr. Mackey as well, but Mr. Mackey seemed perfectly comfortable not understanding, didn't notice there was anything to miss, especially now that his hearing was partly compromised in one ear. When they'd arrived, a month earlier, Hubert had insisted that quinine, their company-allotted malarial vaccine, was harmless. In his fear of tropical diseases, he'd ingested more than five times the recommended dose and lost the hearing in his right ear. He insisted that his hearing was restored, 'good as new,' but several times she caught him switching to people's left as he conversed. The only normal one of them was Phillip. How did they manage to have such a normal son? Phillip could have been spokesman for the Boy Scouts of America. He could have been on television.

Blythe Carrington took a deep breath and said that Mrs. Mackey might recall that she and Mr. Carrington had just relocated from Bolivia. And

155

that due to her husband's engineering career, they had been living in Central and South America for most of their adult lives. That it might be the case that Mr. and Mrs. Mackey were from Peoria — or was it Moline? — but she and Mr. Carrington were more from Lima, from Caracas, from Panama City, than they were from anywhere else. And whatever 'they' were saying about whether and how much booze was good for you, she could assure Mrs. Mackey that a person could drink herself to oblivion in the tropics and wake up feeling like a million bucks.

'Carlsbad, New Mexico,' Mrs. Mackey said. But Blythe Carrington wasn't listening. 'We're from *Carlsbad, New Mexico,*' she repeated, but there was no point. Blythe Carrington was a bully, and she didn't care where the Mackeys were from. Earlier in the day, Mrs. Mackey had run into her in the beauty parlor. Mrs. Carrington had been friendly, but even her friendliness was confrontational. 'Some of the gals are going down to the club for happy hour,' Mrs. Carrington had said from under her domed dryer. 'Meet there at five.' Mrs. Mackey had leaned forward from her own domed dryer, thanked Mrs. Carrington for the invitation but said she thought she'd go home and rest before the party. Mrs. Carrington shrugged. 'Whatever suits you.'

'How was your rest?' Mrs. Carrington had asked her when the Mackeys arrived at Mr. Gonzalez's.

Upon returning from the beauty parlor, Mrs. Mackey had gone out to the laundry shed to make sure the new laundress was following directions, ironing Mr. Mackey's suit on low, as she'd instructed and then repeated with emphasis. These people, it was hard to tell if they listened. The company sent them over and they'd knock at the kitchen door and announce that they were your houseboy, your gardener, your cook, with a curious mix of shyness and dogged insistence. You almost had no choice but to let them in, was Charmaine Mackey's feeling, even if they made her nervous with their yellow and bloodshot eyes, their impossible Jamaican accents, and their pink hands, which forced you to feel sorry for them somehow. She hated their pink hands. Before she'd gotten to the laundry-shed door, what she saw through the window stopped her in her tracks. Lenore, the new laundress, had taken a long drink of water from a pitcher and was holding the liquid in her mouth with her cheeks puffed out. She blew out a magnificent spray, all over Mr. Mackey's suit laid out on the ironing table. Mrs. Mackey opened the door. The air inside the laundry shed was inhumanly hot, heavy with the smell of starch and heated cloth. 'Lenore, what on God's Earth are you doing?'

'I press your husband's suit, just like you ask,' Lenore said, sweat rolling down her neck. She stared at Mrs. Mackey with her googly and bloodshot eyes. 'You got to wet the linen, or it don't press.'

Mrs. Mackey turned around and walked back to the house, trying to shut out the staccato bark of Mrs. Billings's young poodle on the other side of the fence, the sound like a knife to the temple over and over again, driving Mrs. Mackey to fantasize ugly thoughts about stabbing a puppy, thoughts she wouldn't have shared even with a doctor, but she shared little with doctors. She sat in their offices trying to divine what it was a normal person might say and then said it, took the pills they gave her, and now she had shaky hands.

Yap! Yap! Yap! Yap! Yap! Was it normal that she wanted to knife a puppy? Or that the laundress was spraying saliva-flecked water all over her husband's clothes? It was difficult to know what was normal. When she'd been pregnant with Phillip, Hubert had caught her eating chalk. He called the doctor, sure that his nut-job wife would finally have to be committed. But the doctor said it was *normal*, the behavioral symptom of a relatively common nutrient deficiency, and that all she needed was a multivitamin.

* * *

'Just think, our very own Edward G. Robinson,' Mrs. Billings whispered to her husband, glancing over at Lito Gonzalez. Mr. Billings was in charge of nickel mine security, and though his job didn't entail keeping tabs on the other mine managers, he didn't need to, because his wife had this so zealously covered. Throughout the evening, Mrs. Billings tried out her code name of 'Edward G. Robinson' on the other Americans, referring to Mr. Gonzalez, assuming he would have no idea who the famous Hollywood actor was, or that he happened to not only look just like him, that carplike face, but also exuded the same unseemly qualities. 'Five foot five — with lifts in his shoes,' she said to one person. And to someone else, 'Five foot *three*, with lifts in his shoes.' Earlier that week Mrs. Billings had seen Gonzalez pull up to the plant's executive offices in a brand-new Cadillac. She'd watched him leave the offices, as she narrated to the other women, get into that car, shiny and white like a gigantic bar of soap, and drive half a block to the company mailboxes. 'And *then*,' she said, 'he got *back* into that enormous showy car — I mean, go ahead and buy the tackiest thing Detroit has to offer — and he *drove* the half a block back to his office at the plant.'

A waiter came around with a tray of drinks, shallow bowls of some sort of rum drink with thin slices of lime floating on the surface like discs of green stained glass, undissolved sugar and crushed ice crusted around the rim of each little bowl. 'I'll take one of those delicious-looking things,' Blythe Carrington said, scooping one up into her hand. She took a sip from the edge of the bowl. 'Positively *deleterious*,' she said, sugar crystals gleaming on her upper lip.

'Did you read the bit about him in *The New York Times* piece on Nicaro?' Mrs. Lederer asked. 'I found the whole thing confusing. Gonzalez is new to the company, but they said he operated 'concessions' when the mine first opened, during World War II. What kind of 'concessions' was he running?' The term made Mrs. Lederer think of hot dog and popcorn stands at baseball games.

'A shack with a red light over the door,' Mrs. Carrington replied.

'I'm not sure I understand.'

'A *whorehouse*, Mrs. Lederer,' Mrs. Carrington said, enunciating like she was talking to a child. 'Apparently he did quite a business before the Americans went and shut him down. Hypocrites,' Mrs. Carrington snorted. 'Now you can expect them to go over to Levisa — '

' "Them"?' Mrs. Lederer asked.

'The men, Mrs. Lederer. They don't want one in Nicaro, so they'll go to Levisa, is what I'm saying.'

'Does Gonzalez have a family?' someone asked.

'I hear he's a widower,' another said.

'What I hear is what I could've told you by common sense alone,' Mrs. Billings said, and then lowered her voice, '*only homosexuals drive Cadillacs.*'

★ ★ ★

Mrs. Lederer was making her way back from the bathroom when she saw Charmaine Mackey standing in the hallway by herself, looking glamorous despite her ill-fitting and plain black dress, accented with only a wan strand of what Mrs. Lederer assumed were cultured pearls. Mrs. Mackey was one of those naturally good-looking and trim-figured women who didn't have to compensate with distracting patterns and bright makeup, or adjust garments to disguise bulges and deficiencies. She had no style and nevertheless managed to look perfect. And moreover, to make style and effort seem gaudy and in poor taste. Mrs. Lederer suddenly felt ungainly in her size-fourteen persimmon-orange dress. Her size-eleven persimmon-orange pumps.

'Good evening, Mrs. Mackey. How positively smart you look.'

Mrs. Mackey smiled shyly.

'I've been meaning to ask you,' Mrs. Lederer said, 'are you on the wives' committee, by chance?'

Mrs. Mackey shook her head. 'I don't think so.'

'We're meeting to discuss getting a better commissary in Nicaro, so we don't have to take the boat over to Preston just to pick up a loaf of bread. You should come to the meeting, if you're interested. We're also going to discuss the construction of the pool. Mr. Carrington has agreed to present the plans.'

'A swimming pool. Right.'

Mrs. Mackey sensed that any other boss's wife might know about construction projects. Perhaps Phillip had mentioned the pool. She couldn't recall. Hubert had not mentioned it. There were lots of things Hubert didn't mention, but this was her own fault. She sometimes pretended to care about these kinds of things, but she could never remember the details, which proved to everyone, even Phillip, that she didn't care, and that there was no point in anyone telling her anything. At the dinner table these days, Hubert spoke expressly to Phillip and not to her. Still, she nodded and pretended to listen as he went on about nickel processing and the pilot plant,

Cuban politics and labor laws, and this and that about the problems between Gonzalez and the Government Services Administration, which oversaw the Nicaro Nickel Company.

'Did you read the piece in this morning's paper about Mr. Neutra?' Mrs. Lederer asked her. 'It's very exciting that he's been commissioned for a project in Havana — it's going to be a stunning example of tropical modern.'

'Is he with the mining concern?' Mrs. Mackey distractedly removed a compact from her handbag and opened it to check her lipstick.

'Richard Neutra? Oh, heavens, no, dear. He's a famous Austrian architect — the most famous.'

'Good evening, Mrs. Lederer.' It was the woman from French Guiana, whose name Mrs. Lederer could not quite recall and didn't dare mispronounce.

Mrs. Mackey excused herself somewhat abruptly, but Mrs. Lederer didn't mind and was even slightly relieved. The woman from French Guiana would know who Neutra was. She had a sober, European air, and from the moment Mrs. Lederer had seen her at the bakery a few days earlier, she'd imagined they might become friends, talk about modern art and articles they'd both read in *The New Yorker*.

The woman held up her drink and gestured around the room. 'This place is fantastic, isn't it?'

'It's certainly unique,' Mrs. Lederer ventured, locking eyes with her and assuming they could collectively agree that it was not fantastic, that it was a complete horror.

'Oh, I don't know if it *is* unique, Mrs. Lederer. It strikes me as very traditional. This is a real Cuban hunting lodge. Did you see the cast-iron boot scraper by the door? It must be a hundred and fifty years old. I have to remember to ask Lito about that remarkable piece.'

Lito? Mrs. Lederer wouldn't have called him by his first name, never in a million years, though twice already this evening he had entreated her to do so. But perhaps there was some elegant subtlety to the gesture, as if it were true class to pretend their unctuous host was on equal footing.

'Perhaps we could go over to Preston together next week,' Mrs. Lederer ventured. 'A ladies' trip to the *friseur*.'

'You mean the hairdresser? I hate to give myself away, Mrs. Lederer, but I brush mine fifty times and tie it in a knot.'

★ ★ ★

Alone, Charmaine Mackey felt invisible, the laughter and conversation merging into one loud sound that was more like silence, as though the revelry were taking place behind glass, a transparent barrier dividing her from everyone else in the room. She squeezed past people drunkenly unaware that they were blocking her passage, went through a set of doors and out onto the terrace. There were servants outside, setting the tables for dinner. The terrace jutted out over the river, and the enveloping sound of rushing water was grabbing her thoughts and carrying them away on its swift current. How anyone could live with that noise and not lose his mind was beyond her.

Mrs. Lederer seemed like the type who expected a great deal from the world. She'd been saying something about Austria or an Austrian, and all Charmaine Mackey could think of was the phrase 'mother-of-pearl.' She'd taken out her abalone-shell compact to check her lipstick, to avoid looking Mrs. Lederer in the eye. When had it gotten to the point that she couldn't look people in the eye? It had suddenly occurred to her, as she blocked Mrs. Lederer's gaze with the compact in her hand, what mother-of-pearl meant. The oyster is the *mother* of the *pearl*, the bed in which the pearl, a grain of sand coated in a milky something, is born. A beautiful thing formed from irritation, its mother pried open with human hands, the pearl removed to live its life with a hole drilled through it, strung together with other hole-drilled babies. The mother made the pearl, but she was worth far less. She was practically junk. They inlaid mother-of-pearl in tables and crushed cigarettes into ashtrays made out of it.

On the boat that had taken them from Preston to Nicaro for the first time, Charmaine had seen a huge patch of something purple, some sort of flotsam — bluish-purple, oddly shaped balloons, like bladders, that were riding on the surface of the water. One of the Lederer daughters, the redhead, had pointed and said that they were Portuguese man-o'-wars. It was a kind of jellyfish, the child explained, though the child

164

had said 'species' instead of 'kind.' There must have been hundreds of them. They surrounded the boat and moved toward the shore like the Spanish Armada. Charmaine had never seen them, wouldn't have known what they were called. It was unsettling when children knew things she didn't. 'Do you know the best way to kill an octopus?' Phillip asked her one afternoon. Was she supposed to know? 'I'm sorry, Phillip, no. I don't know.' 'You pop it in a bag of seawater and put it in the freezer,' he said. 'It dies in its sleep!' Oh, she thought, relieved. I'm not supposed to know. He wanted to tell me how. These tiny confusions were endless. The biggest problem with children wasn't that they knew about sea life, animal trivia, it was the manner in which they drew pleasure from these things, their capacity for delight, a special kind of accusation. *See my wonderful mantle of innocence? Isn't it precious? How come you don't have one? You're nothing like what I'll be when I'm a grown-up. What's wrong with you?*

'Mrs. Mackey, you are lost in thought.'

It was Mr. Gonzalez.

'Oh, I . . . yes, I was lost in thought.'

'You seem like a person who thinks about things carefully.'

I do? she wondered. How do you measure?

Mr. Gonzalez offered to show her around the hunting lodge. Charity, she assumed, because she'd been standing in the foyer by herself. The Americans were all suspicious of Mr. Gonzalez — her husband acted as though the man were an unconvicted killer — but she'd found him

165

reasonably polite the few times they'd met. She accepted his offer, and enjoyed a fleeting twinge of her own version of power: doing what she sensed she was not supposed to. Like asking Blythe Carrington if drinking below the Tropic of Cancer was bad for you, knowing somewhere in the back of her mind that Blythe Carrington was definitely an alcoholic. It was in these timid forays that Mrs. Mackey felt the vague shape of her own self, as if her essence hid in the margins and could be felt only when these margins were crossed.

'You are without a refreshment, Mrs. Mackey. May I get you something? A lemonade?'

Mrs. Mackey said impulsively that she wanted a Tom Collins. She didn't even know what was in a Tom Collins. It was a drink she'd heard of.

'That's with gin?' Mr. Gonzalez asked.

He was asking, she later realized, because he wasn't sure, but she assumed he was implying, like her husband might imply, that a nervous woman shouldn't drink.

'I'm not a teetotaler, Mr. Gonzalez, although I might seem like one.'

Though until that moment, the truth was she had been a teetotaler. Her doctor had said drinking could interfere with her medication. But her medication was already interfering, and so perhaps it needed its own interference.

Mr. Gonzalez fetched her the Tom Collins, which tasted quite good. Then he led her down a hallway to what he announced was his trophy room. The lighting was dim and low, dissolving into folds of darkness near the ceiling. Mrs.

Mackey looked up at the faces of animals that had been cleaved at the shoulders and nailed or glued to lacquered plaques that hung from the walls. It was morbid ornamentation, she thought, but also funny. As if the animals were standing behind those painted plywood sets at the fair, putting their heads through the circular holes, placing themselves in the scenery depicted on the plywood. Or maybe they were bursting into the room, their bodies lodged partway through the walls. Were they staring at her? And were they grimacing, or did they have more of a mug shot expression, the face you made when you wanted to make no face at all?

She said she remembered hearing that General Batista had some sort of hunting reserve not far from here, where they shipped in exotic game from Africa.

Mr. Gonzalez said yes, that was right. Near Gibara, he said.

'You're a friend of President Batista's?' she asked, an unfamiliar sense of ease coming over her. Tingly but diffuse, like there was a less abrupt transition between her and the outside world. She was a person, a body, at a party, and her presence there felt natural, like a body in a body-temperature swimming pool. It must have been the drink. All this time, she'd avoided alcohol because of her nervous condition. When maybe it was nervous people who should drink. There were Soviet women, she'd read, having babies in water these days. A softer transition, and surely adults needed their own soft transitions —

'Is that what you've heard, Mrs. Mackey?'

167

'That's what Hubert says, that you're a close, personal friend of the president's. But what do I know? I mean,' she giggled, 'what does Hubert know?' Warmth was spreading through her and putting her in a giddy, almost superior mood. 'Maybe I know one thing,' she said, feeling mischievous.

But Mr. Gonzalez didn't ask her what it was. And later, she couldn't quite remember what it was that she knew.

★ ★ ★

While people mingled and drank and gossiped, Mr. Mackey, stone sober, waited in the foyer for the ambassador. Mortified at the rundown condition of Gonzalez's lodge, Mr. Mackey planned to greet His Excellency, pull him aside, and explain the situation. 'Humor him,' the National Lead rep had said, 'but don't tell him a goddamn thing.' It was more than humoring Gonzalez to let him host Nicaro Nickel's welcoming party. Mr. Mackey had wanted to have it at Cayo Saetía, for the simple and right-headed reason that Saetía was where United Fruit had their company parties, and United Fruit had been running a business in eastern Cuba for fiftysome years and knew a great deal about how to do things. But Gonzalez had sent out invitations before Mr. Mackey could stop him.

When His Excellency arrived, Gonzalez seemed to appear out of nowhere. He was right there at the door next to Mr. Mackey, and to Mr. Mackey's dismay, Gonzalez took the ambassador by the arm and walked him into the party as if the two of them were old friends. Mr. Mackey trailed behind them, feeling invisible. Gonzalez and His Excellency were laughing. Mr. Mackey took a deep breath and decided to insert himself. He approached. They both fell quiet, and Gonzalez excused himself to greet other guests.

Mr. Mackey introduced himself and cut straight to the chase.

'The word is this Gonzalez character is Batista's hatchet man,' he said quietly, leaning in close to the ambassador, his hearing still a little muffled from the quinine incident.

'Mr. Mackey, don't forget that he was approved by the U.S. government,' the ambassador said coolly. 'They wouldn't let just any gorilla buy twenty percent of the company's shares. Batista is promising no strikes, no labor laws, no taxes, no problema. The way I look at things,' the ambassador said, 'he's *your* hatchet man, Mr. Mackey.'

★ ★ ★

Mrs. Lederer watched as a group of Cubans filtered into the party, low-level managers that Gonzalez, as the men all said, had wrenched into the hiring scheme. The Cuban wives were gaudy to a degree that seemed like deliberate satire, she observed with restored confidence in her own custom-tailored silk organza dress, after her moment of doubt in the presence of chic Mrs. Mackey. In their heavy and probably costume jewelry, red lipstick, paint-on beauty marks, foundation, and rouge thickly troweled over their dark complexions, the Cuban wives looked to Mrs. Lederer almost like drag queens in a Hasty Pudding production. She detected a mishmash of fragrances — Fibah, Arpège, Chanel — a blended overkill that seemed the moral equivalent of Long Island iced tea, a cocktail drunk not for the taste, but as an insurance policy against sobriety. Many of them were in fox-fur stoles. Or probably rabbit, dyed to look like fox. This on a night when the temperature might drop to a chilly eighty-six degrees.

Mrs. Lederer wondered out loud if Mr. Gonzalez was planning to serve them Cuban food. She said she thought she smelled garlic, that same odor that drifted from the servants' quarters on Sunday afternoons, when their cook, Flozilla, was off and prepared her own meal on a hot plate. She said garlic made her nauseous and she'd half a mind to ask Flozilla to stop using it.

'You let your servants cook native in the house?' Mrs. Billings asked.

'Well, I mean, they can cook what they want to feed themselves,' Mrs. Lederer said, 'as long as they serve proper meals to us.'

Mrs. Billings said there was no place for garlic and boiled yucca in her house. She'd trained her staff to cook reasonable American dishes, and now all she had to do was train them to eat reasonable-sized portions. She said her servants ate enormous piles of food.

The others listening concurred, and Mrs. Lederer asked how it could be that none of the servants were a bit fat, while she and Mr.

170

Lederer were constantly on reduction diets.

Mrs. Mackey offered timidly that she'd read in the *Tips for Anglos* brochure that you could consume more calories in the tropics. But whether you had to be *from* the tropics for this to be the case, she wasn't sure. She was just rejoining the group after her tour with Mr. Gonzalez. Despite his pariah status among the others, she'd been strangely reluctant to abandon him. In fact, he'd abandoned her, excusing himself on account of the ambassador's arrival.

The brochure had included a list of difficult questions Americans should be prepared to answer when traveling in uncivilized countries. *If you are a democracy, why do whites and blacks eat at separate lunch counters?* The brochure didn't propose an answer, as if the answer was obvious, and the issue was only that a person should expect the question. Mr. Mackey said it was a trick question, and that all you had to say was that democracy had to do with separate branches of government, checks and balances and voting.

One woman said she'd heard that girls went through puberty at a younger age in the tropics and that those with preteens better keep an eye on them. Another said she'd read that women's cycles were affected by the equator, but she couldn't remember quite how, something to do with the moon and tides. Blythe Carrington, in earshot and now thoroughly adjusted by three, or maybe it was four bowls of that delicious rum drink, was thinking how funny it would be when these birds discovered they were in the latitude of the three-week menstrual period. Swaddled interminably in jumbo-sized Kotex, they would all bleed and bleed. You couldn't stanch the flow of things in a humid swamp. Sweat was probably this moment soaking the lining of every wife's party dress. Just as sap was surely oozing from the dark and leafy manchineel trees that hung over the pathway to Gonzalez's ghoulish and primitive rattrap. Manchineel sap was poisonous. It left fluid-filled blisters on any human skin it touched. And there were the mosquito bites, which wept crusting tears of amber pus for a month and scarred permanently. There was so much for these women to discover about the tropics, Blythe Carrington thought with angry anticipation, a bitter optimism in the future promise of other people's discomfort, discomfort she already knew, and had the advantage of having accepted long ago.

★ ★ ★

Tip Carrington was flirting with the perfumed bevy of Cuban wives, speaking Spanish, telling each of them how lovely she looked, asking where his wife could shop to look as chic and elegant as they did. The Cuban women draped their furs down around their lower backs. Perspiration beaded on their upper lips, caking their makeup and giving their décolleté a particular, reflectant glow. They looked to Tip Carrington as delicious as bowls of ice cream beginning to melt. Something you better lap up quickly, before it puddles.

Just then, Blythe Carrington walked past. She

glared at her husband with her bloodshot, Windex-blue eyes and headed for the bar.

'Do you ladies shop in Havana,' Tip Carrington asked, 'or do you have to go all the way to Paris for this caliber of elegance?'

The women giggled. They shopped at La Época, a middlebrow department store in Holguín, two hours from Nicaro by car.

Tip Carrington continued on his rounds with the cocktail shaker, stopping to refill Mr. Lederer's and Mr. Mackey's drinks. 'So, Carrington, where'd you pick up the Spanish?' Mr. Mackey asked. 'You sound practically like a goddamn native.'

'A native, sure. Of upstate New York. I picked it up on engineering jobs. This is what South America will do to a man,' he said with a laugh. 'Ruin him.'

★   ★   ★

Dinner was served, but served too late, after a certain high-water mark of alcohol consumption had been reached. It became an afterthought, a ritual lost in the general drift of drunkenness. The next day, Mrs. Lederer recalled vaguely that they'd been served starchy cubes of something or other, everything oil-drenched and stinking of garlic, and that she and Mr. Lederer had shared a table on the riverfront covered porch with the ambassador and Mr. and Mrs. Billings. Mrs. Lederer had asserted herself among them after being snubbed by the woman from French Guiana — the name was Fourier, she remembered too late. Mrs. Fourier hadn't really

173

snubbed her. She'd been perfectly polite, which made it worse. In the hazy recall of that drunken evening, Mrs. Lederer had a distinct image of herself, the ambassador, and Mrs. Billings dumping their 'dinner' straight into the river when no one was looking. And she and Mr. Lederer, home from the party, eating midnight sandwiches at the kitchen table.

Whatever was remembered or forgotten of that meal, in the excess of Mr. Carrington's martinis, they all remembered the ugly scene between him and his wife.

'Dinner theater' is how Marjorie Lederer later referred to the incident.

The two of them had argued at the table, in front of everyone.

Mrs. Carrington had stood up.

Her husband tried to get her to sit back down. She wrenched away from him. 'You humiliate me! Don't you see that?'

If Tip Carrington did see, he didn't say. He didn't say anything.

'I'm sick of it,' she slurred. '*Sick sick sick* of it!'

The servants had been in the process of bringing out coffee and dessert. Carrington tried to act casual. He dug in his pockets for a cigarette. 'Who's got a light? Lito, got a match?' he asked, mock-cheerful, an unlit cigarette dangling from his lips.

Mr. Gonzalez, seated at the end of the table, leaned over to hand him a pack of matches.

As Carrington stood to receive them, his wife slapped his face and sent the unlit cigarette flying.

174

He bent down, calmly picked up the cigarette, and asked Lito Gonzalez again for a light.

Everyone was quiet as he was handed the matches, took one out, struck it against the side of the matchbox, and lit his cigarette.

'Okay, let's liven things up. This is a party, right?' he said, exhaling smoke and waving the match to extinguish it. 'Does anyone have a joke? Mr. Lederer, got a joke?'

No one spoke.

'No? No one's got a joke? Okay I've got one,' Carrington said. '*I* have a joke. Here goes: Why is a Cuban wedding cake made of shit?'

They all looked at him.

'Because it keeps the flies off the bride.'

Again there was quiet.

'Ha . . . ha . . . ha. My husband, the comedian,' Blythe Carrington said. 'It's tasteless, right? And everyone's *heard* that joke. But you people aren't in on why my husband thinks it's funny.' She looked around the table. 'It's only not funny to you 'cause you don't get his sense of humor.'

She stood up and walked heavily across the porch. Before she passed through the doors and into the lodge, she said something else. It was difficult to hear because she said it quietly and the river that ran under the porch rushed loudly, swollen from the recent rains. But Mrs. Mackey thought she heard correctly.

'It's only funny if you know my husband's Cuban,' Blythe Carrington said. And with perfect ease, she opened the ill-fitting screen door that had been sticking all evening and slipped through, careful not to slam it behind her.

9

The ice was broken between them, but La Mazière still enjoyed sitting in the back of the Pam-Pam Room, observing her like she was a mysterious specimen, which in a way she had remained.

He'd been in Havana three months now, since his arrival just after the March coup, studying her in his own calm fashion, from up close and from afar, biding his time, his instinct telling him she wasn't just amusement and flesh, but might, just might, assist him in attracting ex-president Prio as a client. Although how, he wasn't sure.

His own contact to Prio — the same gentleman who had originally apprised La Mazière of the coup via telex from Havana to Paris — had promised 'heavy business' for La Mazière, supplying weapons to the instigators of a new insurrection. But now this same contact was claiming the situation was hopeless.

'It looks like there is no insurrection,' he said in hushed tones when they met one afternoon in the dark lobby bar of the Hotel Nacional, empty except for the little Indian man who was always there, despondently sipping his Harveys Bristol Cream, a deposed maharaja too absorbed in his own troubles to bother eavesdropping on anyone else's. 'The former president is really down in the dumps,' the contact said. 'He's just not motivated to fund an overthrow.' Even the newspapers had acknowledged Prio's wilted morale. The morning after the coup, the headlines read PRIO QUITS, despite the fact that Prio was technically ousted.

La Mazière had business to attend to in Ciudad Trujillo and was planning to depart the next day. Between Rafael Trujillo, leader and generalissimo of the Dominican Republic, and François Duvalier, a Haitian insurgent with presidential ambitions, La Mazière had a regular beat in the Caribbean. From Havana to Ciudad Trujillo to Port-au-Prince was about the shortest sequence of flights in the world. And maybe, when he returned, something in the Cuban situation would have shifted.

★ ★ ★

He purchased his tickets at the Air Cubana office near his hotel and then went to the Tokio, taking up his regular station in the back of the Pam-Pam Room. As he was ordering a drink, a man who looked familiar entered the club, though La Mazière could not place him. He was tall, pale, and freckled, with a companion who couldn't have been more than a teenager, with soft doe's eyes and hair on his upper lip so pubescent it looked like cupcake crumbs. The taller one, La Mazière realized, was Fidel Castro, a trigger-happy politico who had made himself a public nuisance since Batista moved into the presidential palace. He and his younger companion — an obvious queer, La Mazière presumed — waited by the bar, awkwardly, as though they'd never been inside a place like the Tokio. It turned out they were waiting for Rachel K, who led them to a booth in the back of the room.

La Mazière had seen Castro's photograph in the news magazine *Bohemia*, which printed it alongside a letter Castro had drafted, as his own lawyer, to Cuba's Urgency Court, in protest of the coup. It was such an inspired piece of political rhetoric that La Mazière had cut it from *Bohemia* with a pair of scissors. 'I, Fidel Castro Ruz, resort to humble logic,' the letter began. 'I pulse this terrible reality. And the logic tells me that if there exist courts, Batista should be charged. If he should not be charged, and continue as Master of State, Major General, President, Civil and Military Chief, Owner of Lives, Farms, Women, Cattle, and Whores, He Who Flicks Upon the Island His Droit de Cuissage, then there do not exist courts. Nor logic. I repeat: I pulse this terrible reality.'

'I pulse this terrible reality' was peculiar language, almost sensual locution, and yet there was coherence. Castro had made 'pulsing' a transitive act, to sense and to monitor, to take a pulse. On the same page as Castro's letter, below it *Bohemia* had printed the court's reply: 'In response to the petition filed contesting the revolutionary coup resulting in General Batista's presidency, the Urgency Court rules that Revolution is the source of law.' At which point Castro apparently gave up filing legal affidavits and began organizing public protests. During the largest of these, on the steps of the university, he fired several shots into the air and one at Batista's secret service, who were across the street taking their demitasse. No one was hurt, but Castro became an instant enemy of the new regime.

He and his teenage companion stayed in the booth with Rachel K for what seemed to La Mazière like quite a while. When the curtain finally opened, he watched the three of them file out. Each shook Rachel K's hand as though one had just sold the other a used car or a piece of real estate.

★ ★ ★

'Formal handshakes among a gangster, faggot, and a variety dancer,' La Mazière said to her later that evening. 'It's certainly peculiar.'

She was silent.

'Or perhaps it isn't peculiar. But you might be careful. What would Batista think?'

'He's not much of a thinker.'

She explained that the Castros — the younger one was Fidel's brother Raúl — had come to the club asking her to connect them to Prio.

And would she?

'I said he's in Miami and wants to be left alone.'

★ ★ ★

It vexed La Mazière that Fidel Castro should want anything to do with the former president. Castro was responsible for sending in the mole who photographed Prio's Green Room cocaine exploits. After Prio was exposed and humiliated, Castro tried to bring impeachment charges against him.

179

On the plane to Ciudad Trujillo the next morning, it occurred to La Mazière that Castro wanted to get to Prio for the same reason he did. Prio had money — this everyone knew, his only brave act before leaving having been to empty the coffers of the Cuban National Treasury. Castro had motivation and followers. He was likely plotting to try to overthrow Batista, just what La Mazière had hoped Prio would be doing, when he'd arrived from Paris in the first place.

He would reapproach Prio upon his return to Havana, either through his contact, or better yet, through the girl, and let him know that his own lack of motivation was no longer a problem. Someone else was motivated. All Prio had to do was release the funds, and La Mazière would arrange the supply of weapons that this leftist gangster Castro and his followers, assuming they existed, would need to begin their campaign.

It was an artful logic, putting together people who shared a common enemy. Or maybe it was a crude logic, but one to which La Mazière was attached. Artful or crude, these logics created demand on all sides, for large shipments of Tula Tukarovs and tea bags, of Camemberts and carbines.

'What the hell are Camemberts?' President Trujillo asked him when they met later that day at the Dominican palace.

A French cheese, Sir Benefactor, La Mazière resisted saying. 'The tommy gun — you know, with a round magazine. Like a Camembert wheel.'

180

Trujillo, it turned out, had been hoping to buy piranhas, to stock the Massacre River, which divided his country from Haiti. No Rhine, joining two cultures under the mystical reign of one great emperor, the Massacre River was the only reason the entire hunk of land had not gone up in flames.

Trujillo was wearing a heavy crust of eye makeup, bordello-fringe epaulets drooping off his shoulders. On a previous occasion he'd received La Mazière dressed in a shako and white satin breeches. Breeches that must have been slightly too tight, because Trujillo kept tugging at the rise and shifting in his chair as he quizzed La Mazière for details on Napoleonic headgear. As if being French, La Mazière should know the difference between First and Second Empire officers' bonnets. When in fact it was Trujillo who knew the difference among varieties of office bonnet in all their elaborate details, the questions having been merely a pretext to his own discourse on the subject.

La Mazière suggested that instead of preoccupying himself with piranhas, he might consider a more direct action, such as cooperating with the insurgent doctor François Duvalier, who was attempting to overthrow Haiti's president.

'A Negro?' Trujillo asked, incredulous.

'Naturally. He's Haitian.'

Trujillo shook his head. 'Through the misfortune of history we are forced to live next to them. But maybe — ' He closed his eyes and thought for a moment. A sun shaft poured into the room, sending starbursts from the gold buttons on the generalissimo's coat. 'Maybe I see your point, Mr. La Mazière. Either we play a role in the direction of their governance, or we abandon them to their instincts.'

It was a successful trip all around, Trujillo buying weapons for Duvalier and his revolutionary movement, the Haitian president alerted to the danger — by La Mazière, who had more or less created this danger — and everyone scrambling to protect himself.

★ ★ ★

While La Mazière was away, the Castro brothers had come back to the Tokio to see Rachel K, asking again to be put in touch with Prio. She'd agreed, she explained to La Mazière, and sent a telex to Miami. Prio's response was just what she expected:

WHAT IS POINT? STOP.

'I think he's depressed. He told me his house is a coffin. All he does is play canasta with the ancient retirees in his neighborhood.'

'Perhaps you could send him another telex,' La Mazière said. 'Tell him there's someone who can provide real hope, a professional who can supply the weaponry he might be looking to buy if he ever wants to come home. Tell him that with proper support and guidance and the fervent efforts of this untutored gangster Fidel Castro, *of whom we're all suspicious* — important to include that detail, to reassure him — he just might be able to eject Batista.'

La Mazière expected her to take it in stride

182

that he was involved in a violent and illegal business. He was right. She worded the telex just as he instructed and asked him nothing about his own role, supplying weaponry.

A week later she received Prio's response:

HANDSOME CHANGED HEART. STOP. PUT ME IN TOUCH. STOP.

10

Miss Alfaro, the Nicaro schoolteacher, had a piano that Everly could have walked a quarter mile to play anytime she wanted. But she and Mrs. Stites both pretended it was out of necessity that Everly come by boat to Preston on Saturdays.

After she played they ate lunch together, Mrs. Stites having arranged for the cook to prepare whatever Everly requested. She didn't want to ask for anything special, but Mrs. Stites insisted. 'Whatever you want, dear,' Mrs. Stites said. 'Right, Annie? Annie is a wizard in the kitchen, and anything you want that we have, I promise, she can make it. And if we don't have it, you let me know the week before, and I'll be sure she orders it from the almacén.' Everly suspected the cook resented her and this game of preparing the lunches Everly thought up. Once, she asked for grilled cheese, and when it arrived open-face, Mrs. Stites detected Everly's disappointment and sent the sandwiches back, after pressing Everly for how she wanted them cooked. 'Fried in a pan?' Everly replied sheepishly.

The cook was an enormous Jamaican woman who moaned as she ate her own meal, sitting in the kitchen after she finished serving Everly and Mrs. Stites. Either the cook was in pain, or what she was eating was so delicious that she had to express herself. One day the cook served a chocolate cake for dessert. Everly hated chocolate, and the cake almost made her retch, but she faked that she liked it and ate as much as she could, afraid that otherwise it would be sent back. Mrs. Stites got the impression that chocolate cake was Everly's favorite and had the cook serve it every Saturday. Everly and Mrs. Stites would sit eating the powdery dreadful cake in silence, nothing but the sound of a grandfather clock's tick. Mr. Stites was off on his company rounds. The two boys had Saturday engagements, boxing and tennis and golf lessons, or fishing excursions. Everly was Mrs. Stites's Saturday engagement, but they didn't have much to say to each other. Everly would leave worried that she hadn't quite fulfilled whatever it was that daughterless Mrs. Stites wanted from her, though Mrs. Stites was perfectly nice, always gentle, soliciting Everly's opinion on various matters as though she were an adult. 'What do you think of this pattern, dear?' she'd ask, holding up a swatch of checked fabric that she was thinking of using to have new curtains made. 'Should I go with that, or something more plain? I have this purple fabric as well.' 'Maybe the purple,' Everly would venture, secretly thrilled but pretending it was normal that someone needed her opinion before making an important decision. 'Then it's settled,' Mrs. Stites would say, 'the purple it is.'

If K.C. showed up after lunch, Mrs. Stites suggested that he and Everly play together, but she sensed that K.C. didn't want to play with her. He was a boy, caught up in a boy's world.

185

One afternoon, he'd planned to go fishing with Hatch Allain and some of the other Preston boys. Mrs. Stites insisted that K.C. bring Everly along with them. Everly sat at the rear of the boat in a clammy orange life jacket, which neither Hatch nor any of the boys had to wear. K.C. dove over the side, laughing and splashing, swimming behind the boat. 'Careful, now,' Hatch said when Everly leaned over in the damp and bulky life jacket to touch her fingers to the water. Hatch said there were sharks, and that the water was dangerous, too dangerous for a girl. They steered into a reef and the boys caught octopi, which looked like dripping wet ladies' wigs.

One afternoon, Mrs. Stites suggested that K.C. take Everly out on a popshot — a little open railroad car that you pumped with a hand lever. K.C., two of the Allain boys, and Everly piled on. One of them somehow put tar in Everly's hair. She was walking up the path from the Nicaro dock, almost home, and realized that she'd been absent-mindedly pulling at these mysterious sticky clots on the ends of her hair. Her mother and Flozilla washed the tar out with gasoline, and the parts they couldn't clean, they cut out with scissors. Everly said that K.C. might have done it. 'Why would that angel of a boy put tar in your hair?' her mother asked. No one was an angel. Except maybe Duffy, who walked around so softly spying on people that she practically floated on wings. All night Everly smelled the gasoline in her hair. Even while she was sleeping she smelled gasoline. 'At least your hair's not long,' her mother said. There had been a girl in Everly's class in Oak Ridge with hair that fell to her waist. People said it was 'fine,' meaning it was silky and delicate. The girl leaned over one of those automatic washing machines like Everly's mother wanted to buy — round, like a drum. It was in the spin cycle, and the top had been removed. The spinner in the machine grabbed the girl's hair and ripped it right off, along with her scalp.

K.C. delivered a note of apology in his own writing. Mrs. Stites had probably made him do it, but the fact that he'd consented seemed an apology enough. Everly understood why he might not want his mother doting over a child who wasn't even related to them. When the Lederers hired Willy as their new houseboy, Everly started making excuses so she could stay home and follow Willy around on Saturdays, instead of pretending to be a model child for Mrs. Stites.

★ ★ ★

Every afternoon, Marjorie Lederer had Willy clean the dust from the outside of the house with a garden hose, clean the dust from the windows with crushed newspapers and vinegar, and wash the Studebaker. But the dust always settled again on everything by the next morning. It churned twenty-four hours a day from the nickel plant chimneys, sounding like a giant waterfall. Dust hung in the air, and on overcast days it smudged the bottoms of the clouds a dirty red. At night it hovered low and mixed with the fog that crept in off the bay. Cars would come up the road where the Lederers lived, blurry in the thick fog, headlights making two lit cones.

The town was a pinkish red, and the jungle beyond it was green. Everly's father was color-blind, and said he saw red as green and the reverse. He claimed he couldn't tell the difference between the two colors. Everly found this hard to believe, although she didn't think he was lying. He'd get dressed and come in the kitchen and she and her sisters would make a game of telling him he had to change because his clothes were unmatched. What color, Everly would ask him, is the dust from the plant? 'Red!' Duffy would shout. 'I don't know what color it is,' her father would answer. Everly tried to picture colorlessness and only came up with gray.

⋆ ⋆ ⋆

'You got to get the television box, Mr. Lederer,' Willy had said.

'The RCA. Or get the Du Mont, it's the biggest. No one here going to have a Du Mont. You going to be the first, Mr. Lederer. The only one.'

Willy was right about the television. No one else had a Du Mont. The Lederers were the second people in Nicaro to have any television at all, never mind the largest model available. The first *Americans*, Everly's mother said, because Lito Gonzalez had one before the Lederers, brought it back from Havana in the trunk of his enormous Cadillac.

Willy had read about television in *Popular Mechanics*. He looked at all the Lederers' magazines, even the boring ones such as *Forbes* and *Time*, flipped through the pages as if he would know it if he came upon something interesting. He seemed to be absorbed in what he was reading, confident that he could recognize what was worth paying attention to. Everly picked up her parents' magazines and turned the pages, looking for what she guessed Willy might look for, wishing she had that same confidence. She suspected that the best way to pay attention to Willy was to be as interested in everything as he was, do whatever she saw him do. She watched him turn the pages and looked at his pink palms. Willy's hand was black. The pink was on display, tender-looking, like a hand that had been pricked with pins, or plunged in scalding or icy water.

Willy said television would be the new way to learn about things and keep up on the world. He said Cuba needed news, and maybe American news would be better than the news from Havana, which was all biased. What did biased mean? That it isn't news, he said. It's what President Batista wants people to hear. He explained that Cuba didn't really have a free press, that the newspapers were all censored by the government, and any news that made the president look bad wasn't printed. It was important to keep up on politics. If you didn't, you chose, by not choosing, to accept the way things were. Everly wondered about her own parents, who never mentioned politics. Were they choosing for things to stay the way they were? Maybe they weren't hungry for information the way Willy was. Willy said that Cuban radio was as bad as the Cuban newspapers, but at least it was good for tuning in to dance music. Batista censored the CMQ news, and all they had for talk programs was a faith healer. Willy said lots of people practiced superstition instead of putting order in their lives. Willy didn't waste money on lottery tickets and holy water. He had plans, not pipe dreams. 'I save my money, and who knows? Maybe someday I get my own house. If you spend it on lottery tickets and holy water, you guarantee you end up with nothing.' On his day off, Willy polished Mr. Gonzalez's Whitewall tires and picked up odd jobs from the other Americans. Word had gotten around that he could fix things, appliances and even cars, and that he was a patient tutor of Spanish and French. 'How come you know so many things?' Stevie asked. Everly knew why. Because he listened, and because he was smart. She could tell that when he worked around the house he was absorbing everything. He had a trick of not looking at whomever it was he was listening to most intently. If someone was having trouble, Willy was right there to help. Like when George Lederer, working at home one afternoon, was trying to adjust the tabletop fan on his desk and the fan wouldn't stay in the right position, just kept flopping over and blowing papers around. He grew frustrated and started banging the fan on the desk. Willy asked if he could have a look.

He got a screwdriver and carefully tightened the spring on the fan.

★   ★   ★

Everly's mother arranged a kids' party to debut the Du Mont television — Nicaro kids, the Stites boys, and a few others from Preston. The Allain children were not invited, and Panda cried because she wasn't allowed to come. Duffy's mean streak had compelled her to announce to Panda that the Lederers owned the largest television in the Western Hemisphere and would be watching cartoons and eating cupcakes the next Saturday. 'Do you even know,' Stevie asked Duffy, 'what a hemisphere is?' 'A place,' Duffy said. 'It's a *place*!' Stevie was of the growing opinion that Duffy was turning into a monster. Stevie had developed a habit of flirting with Tico Leál, a Cuban employee at the nickel plant. Duffy spied on her older sister, going so far as to lie flat on the floor outside Stevie's bedroom, her ear to the draft under the door. 'Shhh . . . ' Duffy said to Everly, who caught her one afternoon and asked what she was doing. 'Stevie is talking to someone,' Duffy whispered. 'A man — he's in the yard talking to her through the window.' One afternoon Stevie opened her bedroom door, and practically stepped on Duffy. Stevie told her to knock it off, and said that if Duffy ever mentioned a word to their mother, she would live to regret it. 'Are you threatening me?' Duffy asked. 'Definitely,' Stevie said. Duffy seemed satisfied by the answer; a threat was a threat, and

191

she kept her mouth shut, at least for a while. Tico Leál continued to visit Stevie at the window, and elsewhere, too. Everly saw them in the bleachers of the Nicaro baseball diamond, kissing. Stevie started sneaking out her window at night. From her own bedroom, Everly would hear Stevie's window sliding open. Everly didn't think Duffy was a monster. Duffy was 'amoral,' which meant neither moral nor immoral. Morals were learned, and Duffy hadn't learned hers yet. And maybe there was something to be said for a child who was a monster. She would make a good killer, because she didn't care and it wasn't her job to care. If you told Duffy to slam someone over the head with a heavy book, or maybe a brick, she would immediately do it. Not just gladly, but with delight.

Willy and Flozilla put out snacks for the television party, little roulades they made with one of Marjorie Lederer's precious canned hams. When Willy and Flozilla retreated to the kitchen, K.C. said to Everly, 'Your houseboy. I swear I know him. He was Mr. Bloussé's boy.' K.C. said that if it was the same person, he'd come to the Stiteses' house when K.C. was a tiny boy.

After everyone had left that afternoon, Everly told Willy what K.C. had said.

'I don't know any American child,' Willy said.

'But he says you were Mr. Drussay's boy.'

'I don't know a Drussay.'

'A man from Haiti, he said, who brought workers over.'

'You mean Mr. Bloussé? I'm not his boy.' Willy shook his head. 'Not for a long time.'

Willy's people were from Haiti, but he'd been raised by this Bloussé — a white man from France. The man brought groups of Haitians over to cut sugarcane for the United Fruit Company, and he'd taken Willy with him all over the Caribbean. He'd taught Willy to speak English and proper French, not like a Haitian but like a French person spoke it, and to do arithmetic so that Willy could help with his business, organizing boatfuls of Haitian laborers to go here and there working for foreign companies. Willy said he didn't remember K.C., but he remembered going to the Stiteses, and there might have been children there. 'The big house,' he'd said to Everly, 'on the end of the avenue.'

'You know Willy!' Everly said to Mrs. Stites the next Saturday. They were sitting together, about to play a Bach two-part invention that Everly hadn't practiced sufficiently. It was exciting having Willy around her house, and she had to partly concentrate on him — where he was and what he was doing — which made it hard to focus on anything else.

'Who's that, dear?'

'*Willy*,' Everly said. 'He visited you when he was a boy. With Mr. Bloussé.'

'I do know a Mr. Bloussé. He came with his family. Three girls. He didn't bring anyone named Willy. Shall we begin?'

Mrs. Stites didn't remember him, Everly later realized, because he wouldn't have mattered when he came to her house. He wasn't a guest. He was the help.

Willy referred to him as mister, Mr. Bloussé. Had Willy worked for him? Or was he more like a father to him, since he raised him? Somewhere in between, Willy said. It was hard to explain. Mr. Bloussé told him what to do and he had to do it, so he supposed it was more like he worked for him. But Mr. Bloussé taught him languages and sent him to a tutor for reading and writing, which made him more like a son. And eventually he'd left, just like a boy leaves a father to go out on his own. 'Did he pay you?' Everly asked. 'He raised me,' Willy said. 'That was the payment.' He said Mr. Bloussé shipped people over to Cuba from Haiti to cut sugarcane. 'Like cattle,' Willy said. 'They made almost nothing, I mean *nothing*, for backbreaking work, while Mr. Bloussé is living like a king in Le Cap. He's white, but he choose to live in a black world, where he rules everybody. Even his own wife. He married a black woman and she's his servant and wife both. Slave and wife both, just like his cane cutters. They are worse off than servants because they owe him for the ship passage and they never make enough cutting cane to pay him back. The daughters were his servants, too, just like the wife. Everybody running around bringing Mr. Bloussé this and that. The wife, she knows he can put her out in a second, and she's back to selling discount underwear on the streets of Le Cap, where he found her to begin with. We're all running around like he owns us. Like we're his property. I got tired of it and decided I was through.'

194

Everly didn't understand how a man could have a wife who was also his servant. Daughters who had to work or they would be put out of the house. But it didn't seem like she'd understand any better by asking Willy to explain. It was something she'd have to figure out by thinking about it. It was a different world. It almost didn't seem real.

So he'd just left? 'That's right,' he said. They docked in Cuba and suddenly he knew he was done being Mr. Bloussé's boy. He tended people's flowers around Santiago and learned Spanish. He remembered Preston and how beautiful it was, because Mr. Bloussé had taken him there. Very fancy, he said, with pretty gardens. He figured you could have a fine life in Preston, and that he would go there and look for work as a gardener. He hitchhiked from Santiago, and the man who gave him a lift said there were jobs in Nicaro, because the nickel mine was reopening. 'Now I work for your father,' he said. 'He pays me and when I'm finished for the day I'm finished for the day.' Being raised by Mr. Bloussé had meant he was never finished for the day, and that he was always owing. You have to make a clean break sometimes. No good-bye, just the act of good-bye.

Was Mr. Bloussé sad when Willy went away? Willy shrugged. He hadn't seen Mr. Bloussé since the day he made his decision, at age fourteen, and he was twenty-one now. They never saw each other again? Willy said there was a Willy who traveled with Mr. Bloussé, and there was this Willy talking to Everly and clipping the Lederers' hedges, the Willy who lived on his own, and in the evening worked for no one but Willy. They weren't the same person, and he couldn't see Mr. Bloussé and not be the old Willy. They would have nothing to say to each other unless he wanted to go back to being Mr. Bloussé's boy.

★ ★ ★

'I was sent to be your driver,' Willy had said to her father, a week after their arrival in Nicaro. He'd stood at the back door with his cap in his hand, a navy blue newsboy's cap.

Her father said he didn't need a driver.

'Then I'm your houseboy,' Willy said. He'd heard that none of them spoke any Spanish. 'You need a houseboy, sir, if you don't speak the Spanish language. I can speak it for you.' The smile on his face was so broad, so contagious, that George Lederer couldn't turn him away.

Her mother said that although Willy was lazy and preferred delegating chores to doing any actual work, you couldn't help but like him, his gentle manner and that dazzling smile, and that they'd be lost without him. Everly heard the lady from French Guiana say he was 'compelling.' What did it mean? 'That she's attracted to a Negro,' Stevie whispered. 'He's not a Negro,' Duffy said. 'What is he, then?' Stevie asked. 'He's Willy.' None of them was attached the way Everly was. 'You follow me around like a little dog,' Willy said, and patted her on the head. She didn't mind.

Marjorie Lederer still didn't speak any

196

Spanish, although she practiced her French every afternoon. She'd been practicing her French every afternoon for as long as Everly could remember, but she never seemed to advance to another level. She'd say things to Willy in French, give instructions like she was helping him out, since English, her mother said, was Willy's third language. But Willy didn't understand her mother's French and would repeat words in what must have been the proper pronunciation, asking if that was what she'd meant. 'Yes,' Marjorie Lederer would say, and repeat Willy's pronunciation. 'That's right. You say it perfectly now.' He had a way of making everyone feel good. Her mother's French wasn't proper, but she was trying. Willy was complimenting the effort.

The Du Mont television worked, but it didn't get good reception. When Everly's mother wanted to watch something important, Willy was sent up on the roof to hold the antenna this way or that, so the picture would stay clear. The week after they got the TV, Queen Elizabeth's coronation was televised. 'Live,' her mother kept saying, which Everly found confusing. Wasn't everything live? Or did it mean seeing in present time something that was evidence the present had taken place, like the photos and souvenirs that Stevie collected to put in her scrapbook? Maybe it meant you could experience something and see it as a memory at one and the same time. Stevie had a photo album with clippings about the queen, the Duke and Duchess of Windsor pasted onto its matte black pages.

Underneath, in white grease pencil, details like *Gala Christmas party, Bois de Boulogne, Dress: Givenchy, Dec. 1951*. Everly sometimes took the book out, but more for the amusement of snooping than any real curiosity about the duke and duchess, who seemed wooden and unreal, characters mentioned in ads, like the one in the *Havana Post* for El Louvre, the big ice cream parlor on La Rampa. 'Try our rum raisin, the Duke of Windsor's favorite!' The coronation went on and on, Queen Elizabeth sitting under hot lights and sweating visibly, in a huge crown and a long dress that looked scratchy and uncomfortable. It was raining in Nicaro, hard, and her mother had Willy up on the roof adjusting the antenna, his foot wedged against a drainpipe so he wouldn't fall.

Stevie and their mother sat glued to the set. Everly went out on the porch and shouted questions to Willy through the rain, until her mother said he could come down, that the coronation was over.

⋆ ⋆ ⋆

Willy said his family was still in Haiti, but it would be impossible to find them. He said he wasn't sure of their last name, couldn't remember it. He'd been with Mr. Bloussé since he was six years old, and on his identification his name was Willy Bloussé. He didn't have papers for traveling and doubted he could go to Haiti. Didn't he have a passport? He showed her what he had: one pocket-worn yellow index card, his name typed on it, stating that he'd been vaccinated for communicable diseases, the Nicaro doctor's signature underneath. 'You have to vaccinate,' Willy said, 'if you want to work in a white person's home. Everybody have to vaccinate.'

His father had come over to cut the cane in Cuba when Willy was little. When his father returned, there was a problem. Willy hadn't known what the problem was, but it had something to do with Mr. Bloussé. Mr. Bloussé came to the house and spoke to Willy's father, and when Mr. Bloussé left their house that day, Willy was sent with him. Wasn't Willy sad to leave his family? There were ten children, he said, and they ate nothing but boiled yucca. The boys had to cut sugarcane and there was no money to go to school. Without Mr. Bloussé, he never would have learned to read. And anyway it was his own fault, he said, getting sent with Mr. Bloussé, because he'd dreamed of escaping so he wouldn't have to cut the cane. When he was little he'd wished he was Chinese, anything but what he was. 'The Chinese are clever,' he said. 'You don't see them cut cane. They grow vegetables, work in the sugar mill, sell ice cream. They find a way to make a life without cutting the cane.'

'Guanabana! Carombolla! Mamoncillo! Limone! Mango! Piña! Plátanos!' The Chinese came to the Lederers' door every afternoon, selling fruits, vegetables, fish, tools, soaps, and laundry supplies. Willy showed Everly how to choose a ripe pineapple, how to cut it with her knife, and make a perfect spiral of the outer skin, which was patterned like fancy leather upholstery. Could you save it and use it for anything? No, she discovered. It immediately rotted. You could tell that a pineapple was ripe, Willy explained, if it was veined with red like a bloodshot eye. After school, she'd go home and buy one of the blood-shot pineapples from the Chinese vendor, Lumling. They were small, a one-person pineapple, and she'd eat the whole thing and feel like she was eating something that had to do with Willy.

Sometimes, when Everly and Willy were the only ones home, he turned on the radio and danced in the Lederers' kitchen with a broom. 'La Pachanga' was his favorite.

When it came on, Willy turned up the radio and danced, swaying and twirling like the broom was a real person. Everly would giggle and beg him to dance again. Please, one more. He'd spin the broom around and dip it low, then hold it close, he and the broom moving side to side like a man and a woman. He looked to Everly like a movie star, with his narrow waist and broad shoulders, muscular but so slim and graceful. He demonstrated all the dances. Cha-cha. Pachanga. Rumba. Mambo.

How did he learn so many dances? 'At the Club Maceo,' he said, swaying with the broom, 'in Levisa.' Was it like Las Palmas? He said it was sort of like Las Palmas, but it was for colored people. The blacks didn't drink like the white people did, but they were more lively. They liked to dance more, he said.

Everly pictured Willy dancing at the Club Maceo. Not with a broom. With a woman. She tried to push this image out of her mind but it kept returning. Sitting at the kitchen table eating the deviled eggs that Flozilla prepared, she'd be suddenly unhungry, stricken with sadness, picturing Willy at the Club Maceo, dancing the pachanga with black people who didn't drink too much or act silly like the Americans at Las Palmas. She pictured the people in the Club Maceo dancing elegant dances, romantic and dignified. Willy had a whole life away from the Lederers that she didn't know about and couldn't see.

★　★　★

'You got to get the wet bar,' Willy said to her father one day.

When he worked behind the new wet bar, Willy wore a white bartender's jacket with a black bow tie. He mixed stingers and sidecars, pink slippers and old fashioneds. He knew all the cocktails.

After she was sent to bed, Everly could hear her father's voice booming to Willy to fix Charmaine Mackey another Tom Collins, or telling stories about his childhood, offering details that didn't seem to follow from what anyone else had said. 'They put a red ball on the front of the trolley when the pond was frozen thick enough for skating. That's how we knew! They had a red ball — ' And Marjorie Lederer interrupting to change the topic of conversation, asking the lady from French Guiana whether she preferred Cézanne or Pisarro. 'Gauguin,' the woman said. 'Such beautiful bodies — '

The men all liked to bring Charmaine Mackey another Tom Collins. She was pretty, with the face of a young child. She had large eyes, a nub of a nose, and plump lips. People said she was the prettiest woman in Nicaro, and Everly figured there was an extra thrill in a pretty woman getting drunk, and another extra thrill if you were the man responsible, the one who brought her another Tom Collins.

Once, at Las Palmas, Charmaine Mackey walked past Everly on her way to the powder room and lost her footing. She started to fall and clutched Everly on her way down, pressing hard on Everly's shoulder. Everly was only ten and small, but she managed to hold Charmaine Mackey up. She looked at Everly in a peculiar way, as though Everly didn't exist, was just a block of something, furniture that could take all the weight she gave it.

She righted herself and asked Everly if Mr. Gonzalez had arrived. Everly said she didn't think so. She'd never seen Mr. Gonzalez in the club. He didn't seem friendly with the other Americans. Charmaine Mackey looked disappointed. She turned and teetered down the hall. Everly felt bad about disappointing Mrs. Mackey. People must have been waiting for Mr. Gonzalez. Maybe there was some special reason he was coming that night. Everly decided it would be her job to spot him when he arrived. She would go and tell Mrs. Mackey, wipe away the disappointment, and make Mrs. Mackey pleased. But he never showed up, and then it was time for the Lederers to go home. That might have been the only time Charmaine Mackey had ever spoken to Everly. She barely spoke to anyone.

* * *

The Carringtons lived next door, but Everly had to walk down the front path to the road and around to the proper entrance, rather than just cutting through from the Lederers' front yard to theirs, because the cactus fence bordering the Carringtons' yard was prickly and you couldn't climb over it without getting lanced by cactus spines. Val said the cactus fence was called 'catch the nigger.' 'Atajanegro,' she'd said, and translated for Everly. Everly tried to forget its name. One day Willy pointed to it as he trimmed the Lederers' hibiscus. 'Isn't that wonderful? A fence made out of plants. It's a special cactus, only grows in Cuba.' It made the ends of her fingers ache with sadness. The same fence Willy thought was wonderful, other people were calling 'catch the nigger.'

Val and Pamela themselves weren't quite white, though this was supposed to be a secret. 'Latin,' Val said. 'One-quarter Latin.' According to their mother, Val added, they were white, just like Mrs. Carrington. We're white, like our mother.

Everly walked around the fence and knocked on the Carringtons' front door. The Carringtons had invited the whole family to a cockfight. Willy had advised them not to go, but her father thought it would be rude to decline.

The Carringtons' houseboy answered and called

to Val. She came out of her room dressed in only a slip and told Everly to come in, that she wasn't ready yet.

'You don't care if he sees you in your underwear?' Everly whispered, sitting down on Val's bed.

'Why should I? It's just Roosevelt.'

The bedroom door was open. Roosevelt was polishing the hall tiles with a rag, his eyes on the floor. Everly figured he had no choice, with Val standing there in her slip, sixteen and with a body like a grown woman.

'Where's Pamela?'

'Not coming,' Val said.

'Why isn't she coming?'

'She's going to Preston. I can't say why.'

There was always something secret and dramatic happening with Pamela, who had begun announcing that she was not one-quarter Latin but in fact half-Cuban. Val rolled her eyes and said it was a phase Pamela was going through, an embarrassing phase. She spoke angrily to Pamela in French. Pamela spoke angrily back, in Spanish. 'My sister is losing her mind,' Val said. 'And she's adopting that hideous singing Spanish, like a barefoot guajira.' One Saturday, coming back from Mrs. Stites's house, Everly had seen Pamela down by the seawall with K.C. Stites's boxing coach, Luís Galindez.

'I bet I know why she's going to Preston. To see Luís Galindez.'

'What do you know?' Val said. 'You're ten years old. And you're not even interested in boys yet.'

'I'm interested in boys.'

'Tell me who, then.'

'It's a secret.' She knew what not to share. Not with Val Carrington or anyone else.

★ ★ ★

One of the two cocks immediately began losing. It was on its side, blood spreading underneath, its chicken body huffing up and down like a fireplace bellows. A man jumped into the ring and pried open the cock's beak and blew air from his own mouth into the bird's lungs. The bird stood up, matted and dazed, and took a wobbly step. The man fluffed up its feathers and steered it toward the other cock, who tore it apart and killed it for good.

They were served chicken after the cockfight. It wasn't clear to Everly if they were eating the birds that had been fighting, or chicken that came from some other place. Mr. and Mrs. Carrington began to argue as they ate. Everly's mother said the Carringtons habitually broke the rule of a 'unified front.' People fight, Marjorie Lederer said, it's reality, but you do it in private. When they were finished eating, Mr. Carrington stepped outside for a cigarette. Everly's mother went to the ladies' room. Her father got up to pay the bill. ('How did we get stuck with that bill?' her mother later asked.) It was just Everly, Stevie, and Val at the table when Mrs. Carrington started talking, more to herself than to them.

'He thinks I'm full of shit when I say I can quit anytime,' Mrs. Carrington said, 'but he doesn't know the first thing about drinking. About people who drink.'

'Mom — ' Val said, embarrassed. 'Come on, Mom.'

Mrs. Carrington continued as though she hadn't heard. 'Every day I quit drinking. When I decide to have my *last drink*. I get to the last drink and I quit. Every goddamn day. And he thinks I don't know about last drinks. About quitting. I know all about that.'

Mrs. Carrington picked up the drumstick on her plate as if she hadn't noticed it was there until just then. 'But,' she said, gesticulating with the drumstick, 'this place *fits* with drinking, so what's the point of quitting?' Everly wasn't sure if she meant the chicken and cockfight place fit with drinking, or Nicaro, or maybe Cuba. Her mother would have voted the chicken and cockfight place, which she later commented to Mrs. Fourier, the lady from French Guiana, was terribly vulgar. Mrs. Fourier said she'd been to a cockfight herself, in Santiago. She found it 'extremely compelling.' But more compelling, Mrs. Fourier said, was the voodoo ceremony she and Mr. Fourier had attended in Regla, across the bay from Havana, where they'd witnessed chickens being sacrificed. Intoxicating, she said, as long as one ignored the hissing steam and the flames from the Shell refinery that loomed over Regla. 'The dances of the possessed, the drumming — it was all so *human*,' she said. 'You could smell the humanity. Like a musk.'

★ ★ ★

'I told Mr. Lederer not to go, that he won't like it,' Willy said, shaking his head, after Everly reported the grisly details of the cockfight. 'I said 'Don't go.''

Willy had the chairs in the Lederers' living room upside down and was painting the bottoms of their feet with clear nail polish, her mother's idea. Something about not scratching the floor, which made no sense to Everly because her mother had already ordered new furniture, so the upside-down chairs would be replaced. Mrs. Billings had come over for tea and commented, as she selected a seat in their living room, that it was clear where George parked himself. She pointed to a broad, bottom-shaped indentation in the Lederers' eiderdown couch. After that, Everly's mother ordered rattan, which is what everyone else had. It's so much cooler, Marjorie Lederer said. 'And people's bottoms don't leave prints in it!' Duffy added.

Everly told K. C. Stites that she'd gone to a cockfight in Mayarí, and K.C. said that in the mountains above Nicaro they had cockfights with men instead of roosters. Stevie teased Everly and said that K.C. had a crush on her. Everly wondered if telling her creepy stories was K.C.'s version of the men bringing Charmaine Mackey another Tom Collins. Trying to do something to her, the way the drinks did something to Charmaine Mackey.

'They put the men in the ring,' he said. 'It's just like cockfights, with spectating and betting.'

She tried to wipe away the scene of two men fighting to the death but kept seeing it. Her mind did this sometimes, acted mutinous like a bunch of drunken sailors, making her see gruesome things that took away her appetite and made her feel dirty on the inside.

She dreamed she was watching actors on a stage. Two men, who argued over a woman. They were dressed alike, in dark suits like her father and the other managers wore. They were shouting, and Everly understood that they were no longer acting, but arguing for real. The men took off their jackets, ready to fight in their white shirts and neckties. They struggled in a sort of awful dance. One man picked the other man up and shook him violently. The other man began to split apart. Milk jetted out of him at the seams where he split. The other man kept shaking him, milk flying in all directions.

11

Rachel K hadn't realized she'd take pleasure in such a thing. 'Zazou,' Fidel called her, and said the resistance couldn't operate without her. Especially now that he and Raúl were both locked up, serving time for their attack on the Moncada army barracks in Santiago.

It was up to her, Zazou. She had a magic way with Prio, Fidel wrote to her from prison, flattering her. Not just to his changed heart, but also to his wallet. Prio was pledging millions to overthrow Batista. The other girls at the club squealed when they saw pictures of Fidel in *Bohemia*, midspeech, his finger in the air, next to reprints of his famous prison declaration. He was brave and good-looking and Rachel K was lucky, they said, lucky indeed. What an honor to be guapo Fidel's confidante. But of the two brothers, she secretly preferred Raúl, partly because of his homosexual put-on. Fidel was far more likely, she guessed, to go that way. Too bristlingly macho to be truly interested in women. While Raúl batted his eyelashes and swished around like a Chinatown cross-dresser, then told her he was packing a weapon and tried to put her hand on his crotch to prove it.

The other girls wanted to help, too. There was plenty for them to do, as Fidel explained in a series of notes that Rachel K received through an elaborate system of intermediaries. At a bar near

Havana Harbor, a glass of rum was served with a note underneath it, a cardboard coaster with facedown messages in pencil. Certain clients, Rachel K explained to La Paloma and the other dancers, could be cultivated. Business leaders, for instance, who didn't like Batista. Things changed quickly at the Tokio, as the dancing and the lights and the music stayed the same. Money was collected, as well as petards, time bombs, and jars of phosphorus, Colt revolvers and ammunition, gallons and gallons of jellied gasoline.

★   ★   ★

'I've been getting this vague feeling,' La Mazière said to her, 'that something bad is supposed to happen to you.'

He'd shown up at the Tokio unannounced, having been away for several months. He told her he was in town on business, but the truth was he could have gone straight from Miami, where he'd just met with Prio, to the Dominican Republic, where Cuban insurgents were stockpiling weapons and running a rebel training camp. La Mazière had no pressing business in Havana. He was there to see her.

The feeling had come to him in fleeting moments. He knew she was in the underground — in a sense, he'd nudged her in in the first place — but she wasn't candid with him to what extent she was involved. Perhaps it was a taste of his own medicine. He'd been plenty coy with her over the two years since they'd met. He'd come and gone without warning, never explaining what he was up to, sometimes not because information was sensitive, but for other reasons, for style and for aesthetics, because honesty was so clunky and irrelevant, like a cumbersome piece of furniture. Why not throw a sheet over it and move on to the business at hand?

'This is your fantasy?' she asked. 'Something 'bad' is supposed to happen to me?'

'I have my fantasies. That's not one of them. They aren't so dull as a simple morality tale, 'cabaret dancer meets tragic end.' I loathe morality tales.'

'What's the dancer's tragic end? Tell me what happens. I'd like to know what I'm in for.'

'Oh, I don't know,' he said wearily, as though it wasn't worth getting into. 'Any number of scenarios, really. Let's say the dancer is caught playing both sides and gets snuffed out by Batista's henchmen. Henchmen who have their way with her beforehand — or after, depending on their own fantasies, of course.'

'And nothing bad is supposed to happen to you? Trotting around and conducting your dubious 'arrangements'?'

'The dubious arranger gets away, is how it goes. He escapes to a remote location. Lies on a chaise longue, under a palm tree, on the banks of a slow-moving river. The credits roll — '

'And the girl is long dead.'

'Generally, yes.'

'That's actually fine with me. You know why?'

'I have a sense.'

'I'm not afraid of that end.'

'Right. That's the sense I have.'

He liked her reckless attitude, even if it was an act. It seemed a form of intelligence to claim not to care what happened to oneself. Survival instincts are a kind of stupidity, an animal stupidity.

★ ★ ★

She'd left, to get ready for her show. He watched as the sad bartender played canasta with a dancer. The bartender won, but his face remained dolorous, as if winning were a burden, one more sad duty to perform. It occurred to La Mazière that he hoped she would find a way to avert the demise he'd just narrated, if only to forestall the dull cliché of one more showgirl disposed of.

PART THREE

12

NICARO NICKEL COMPANY
NICARO, ORIENTE, CUBA
CIRCULAR NO. B-21

Hubert H. Mackey   Oct. 23, 1955
General Manager
GSA Mining Interests, Tropical Division

To all management:

Attached is a photograph of D. L.
Mazierre. This man is a political agitator of
the worst type: an extremist suspected of
supplying arms to political uprisings in
North Africa and the Caribbean nations of
Haiti and the Dominican Republic. He is
believed to pose a genuine threat to the
stability of American interests here in
Cuba. His description is as follows:

30 to 34 years old
Native of France
Unmarried
5' 11"
150 lbs.
Race: white
Eyes: gray
Hair: brown
Complexion: pale, as if suffering some ailment

Smooth-shaven
Small mouth
Sometimes wears glasses
Personal habits: drinks occasionally
Is given to frequenting low resort

Mr. Mazierre has been known to travel
repeatedly between Havana, Santiago, Port-
au-Prince, and Ciudad Trujillo. There is
evidence he has been on the northeast
coast of Oriente. Be on the lookout for
him and any other roguelike individuals
attempting to agitate among our employees. If you see anything suspicious, report
it directly to management.

Yours truly,

Hubert H. Mackey

He didn't look dangerous, Everly thought, with
his boyish and mischievous face. Dressed in a
coat and tie, with shiny prep-school hair
perfectly combed but curling slightly upward
— not subduable with hair cream, like he might
not be subduable by the men who were
supposed to be on the lookout.

There were two photos, a side and a front
angle. He looked handsome and agreeable from
both angles, and what, anyhow, was 'low resort'?

She stared at the photos, taped on the wall
outside the company's executive offices. She and
the other students milled in the hallway as Miss
Alfaro spoke to Mr. Carrington, who was

guiding their class field trip around the nickel operation.

'Looking fresh as a daisy, Miss Alfaro,' Mr. Carrington said.

Miss Alfaro blushed. She was unmarried, and Everly's mother said she didn't get invited to parties because unmarried women were a problem.

'What kind of problem?' Everly had asked, but her mother hadn't answered.

'Always so exquisitely put together, Miss Alfaro,' Mr. Carrington said. 'I'm curious where you shop, so I can tell my wife. You travel to Havana?'

'You tease me, Mr. Carrington.'

'No, really. You renew my faith, Miss Alfaro. In the educational system. I had no idea schoolteachers could be so . . . chic and attractive.'

He was flirting with her in front of the whole class, and Everly suspected Miss Alfaro was enjoying it, even if it embarrassed her. She was certainly pretty, or at least she had all the signs of prettiness, what Everly's father called 'vavoom.' Bleached blond hair with a beauty parlor flip on the ends. Red lipstick, narrow skirts, and high heels — as high as the ones Stevie had put on that morning. Their mother had said to turn right around and change into something more appropriate for a field trip to the mine. No one said out loud that the high-heeled shoes — and the seersucker dress and the rouge Stevie had on — were for Tico Leál, who worked at the mine. There were kids in Everly's class who said that Miss Alfaro's curtains matched her carpet, meaning she dyed the hair between her legs the same platinum blond as her head hair. Everly didn't believe it. It seemed impossible that any of the kids would have seen it in order to know. And if an adult saw it he wouldn't say 'curtains' and 'carpet' and he wouldn't tell a kid about it.

★ ★ ★

They rode in an open ore car, Everly bouncing along under the hot sun, thinking about the man with the shiny hair and small mouth, chanting to herself.

Given to frequenting low resort. Low resort. Low resort. Given to frequenting low resort. Low resort. Low resort. Given to —

The mine was so high above Nicaro that they could see the whole town. Mr. Carrington pointed out the nickel plant on the bay, and the sugar mill smokestacks across the channel in Preston. Cayo Saetía in between, where they went for company picnics, and beyond the fence around Nicaro, the shantytown of Levisa. It was huge compared to Nicaro, with soft-looking huts made of palm leaves, jammed in together and leaning in all different directions. Smoke rose up here and there from between the huts. Willy lived in Levisa. He came to Nicaro on foot and every day Everly watched for his familiar gait, slow and rhythmic, as he turned onto their road. Willy said everybody in Levisa cooked their meals outside, over wood fires. Or with alcohol, if it was raining. But the alcohol stoves, he said, were dangerous.

218

They could blow up and burn your face or burn your hut down if you weren't careful. All the servants lived in Levisa, except for the ones who lived in servants' quarters, like Flozilla, whose room was off the Lederers' kitchen with its own tiny bathroom — a toilet and a tiny sink. The people from Levisa came down to the river by the main highway to bathe and wash their clothes, the women rubbing wet, soapy clothes on rocks, boys and men fishing from the banks without poles, just line wound on spools. It looked so close to Nicaro, right across the main road at the edge of town. She had never been there.

Beyond the nickel plant, she could see the roped-off area of Levisa Bay where they swam. There was a mesh wall around the swimming area, which had been Mr. Carrington's idea. One day Portuguese man-o'-wars had floated in, hundreds of them slopping over the rope on a high wave, everyone screaming and splashing their way out of the water. Everly had seen a photograph of a fish caught in the tendrils of a man-o'-war. The caption said the tendrils grew to be sixteen feet. The fish was paralyzed and would be eaten, but it looked so relaxed. Sometimes you didn't want to be able to move. You just wanted to be held. The same book had illustrations of parrots that were native to eastern Cuba. But they'd been extinct for four hundred years, the book explained, because a Spanish conquistador and the men of his court had eaten them as a delicacy. It seemed that 'delicacy,' the way the book described it, meant not rarely, like

219

on a special holiday, when you'd eat a Dubuque ham or a pot roast, but as often as possible until there were no more parrots. They were conquistadors. They'd come a long way and were ready to gorge themselves. Everly couldn't imagine that anything so showy and beautiful would be tasty. The metallic blue and emerald green of a parrot's feathery coat made her think of something bitter and not meant to be eaten, like talcum powder or pencil erasers. The delicacy hadn't been so much about taste. The point was to eat a bird that talked. She imagined the Spanish teaching the parrots to repeat cruel and offensive phrases. The parrots squawking, 'Get out of here! You're ugly and stupid! I hate you!' The Spanish would then get so angry they'd kill the parrots. 'Take that, you rotten bird. Who do you think you are, talking to me that way?' And then they would eat them in revenge. It was terrible to think about, but it was interesting, too. Because it meant that eating was no longer about filling up. Making hunger go away. It was more like a court proceeding, with punishment and justice.

They could see a huge ship coming into the Nicaro dock. Mr. Carrington explained that it was there to pick up the nickel ore and take it to Louisiana for processing. Men were rolling carts down the seatrain track — a track that led to nothing, until a ship was docked, and the carts rolled from the track onto the ship.

No children were allowed on the dock when shipments were coming in. It was dangerous, her mother said. A grapple iron could swing around and kill you, just like that. Once, Everly and K.C. had sneaked onto the dock to watch an enormous ship anchoring. Workers from the ship began unloading heavy-looking bags of some-thing, the bags sending up clouds of dust as they whomped into piles on the wooden dock. There was funny, blocky writing on the ship's side, an unreadable alphabet that looked like barbed wire. The workers were shouting in a language that was all consonants crushed together. They had big, muscley arms and hoisted the heavy bags hand to hand, one to the other in a chain. Some of them were wearing head scarves tied under their chins, which seemed peculiar until Everly realized they were women. With large, heavy breasts, hanging low like they weren't wearing brassieres. Her mother said if women didn't wear brassieres their breasts would drop. Everly guessed this had happened to the foreign women on the Nicaro docks. Everly was eleven and flat-chested, but her mother made her wear a training bra so her breasts would learn, from early on, not to drop. Her mother said she might just develop overnight, the way Stevie had. She said Everly was 'making progress' and she might just yet turn out to be a looker, against all odds. Everly wasn't sure if her mother was compli-menting her or hurting her feelings. Stevie wore a woman's-sized dress now, and had a woman's-sized bust and hips. The Lederers, who still didn't know about Tico Leál, said they better watch her, because it was that age for trouble. Stevie saw Tico in secret. Once she came home and told Everly that Tico had

221

pressed himself against her and she'd felt his thing. What thing? 'If you don't already know,' Stevie said, 'you're too young to find out.' Once she thought about it, of course she knew. But when Stevie said it, Everly didn't realize. You can know something but not the codes of when it's being referred to. When their parents finally did learn about Tico Leál, two years later, they talked about 'nipping the situation in the bud.' But by then it was too late for that.

Everly and K.C. had watched the foreign women tossing the bags hand to hand. They were all women, even the captain. K.C. said they were Russian. Where were the men? He said they all died in the war.

That night, the Russian women had come into town. They were at Las Palmas. The Lederers' house was close enough to the club that Everly could hear faint shouting and laughter and stomping. Her father returned with a cube of smoked pig's fat wrapped in newspaper that the captain had given him.

'Did all the Russian men die in the war?' Everly asked.

'A lot of them,' her father said.

Mr. Carrington made them put on hard hats for the tour of the mining area. He took extra-special care to fasten the chinstrap of Miss Alfaro's hard hat. Miss Alfaro said she felt like a tomboy in the hard hat, and Mr. Carrington assured her that nothing could make Miss Alfaro look like a tomboy. Everly's hard hat was too big. It smelled like the sweat of a grown man and kept slipping down over her eyes. Four hundred men, Mr. Carrington told them, worked the mines. Seven days a week. A different shift of men worked at night. They saw men shoveling ore into railcars, rags tied around their heads to protect them from the sun. Not under their chins, like the Russian sailor women — more like Ali Baba, rags tied around and around, the ends tucked in. They bent over and struck at the hard earth with axes that had a sharp tooth on the end. Chink, chink, chink. 'This is called strip mining,' Mr. Carrington said. It seemed a gargantuan task, to scoop out the earth by hand. The workers glared at Miss Alfaro in her tight skirt and hard hat. Stevie had prepared for the field trip as if it would be a date with Tico Leál, but there was no sign of him. The operation was huge, bigger than any of them had imagined.

A labor boss sat in the shade of a tree, watching the workers. A single tree, the rest of the land rust-colored and sun-baked and treeless. Maybe they left the one tree there just for the labor boss. He wore green-tinted eyeglasses, and a gun in a holster hung from his belt. He sat perfectly still, holding a glass of cane juice. He looked awake and asleep at the same time, like a lizard.

★ ★ ★

She lay in bed that night moving her mind around the features of the agitator D. L. Mazierre. The adults said 'troublemakers' about people who were causing problems for the company. But Willy made it sound like the troublemakers were the good guys. They just wanted to be paid fair wages and to live in decent conditions. He said unions were legal in Cuba, a tradition, part of the way things were run. But if you worked for an American company, you were not allowed to organize a union. He said that people were organizing anyway. It was a secret that he was confiding in her. Everly was so thrilled to be trusted by Willy that she never would have told anyone, no matter what.

D. L. Mazierre was involved. Maybe he was coming to organize the workers so they could have fair wages. In the photograph, there had been numbers on his shoulder. They looked like a military stripe, but they must have been for identification, like the numbers men held up in post office wanted posters. In Oak Ridge, it had been her hobby to look at the wanted posters and scan the people in line to see if there was a match. Whenever she had a fever, she dreamed the same dream, that she was in a prison that doubled as a mausoleum, with human bones lodged in its sandy floor. Real prison was probably even worse than her fever mausoleum-prison, and she couldn't blame the men in the post office photographs for escaping. 'Wanted' on the posters did not mean desired.

Given to frequenting low resort. Low resort. Low resort. Given to frequenting low resort —

Outside, wind stirred the banana leaves beyond her bedroom window. The leaves brushed against one another and cast a papery sound. The wind gusted, and the banana plants made shadows on her bedroom wall like mad puppets. Willy said that after a soaking rain, if you stood under the leaves and listened carefully, you could hear the bananas growing. What sort of sound did they make? A damp pop and creaking, he said. He explained how they grew, that you planted an 'eye,' and then the eye bore fruit for several seasons. He knew all about gardening and tropical species of flowers, even their Latin names. He ordered seeds from catalogs and planted them in tidy rows that alternated in color. A pale, salmon-colored trumpet vine next to deeper orange heliconias and flamingo flowers, which were like Valentine hearts cut from shiny red patent leather. Along one flower bed edge, white butterfly jasmine as an accent. He pruned the flamboyán tree that grew outside the Lederers' dining room windows so that it bloomed longer than anyone else's on the manager's row. Vermilion sprays of color flocked the windows and formed a carpet of brilliant leaves on the ground below. When the sun shone into the tree, the windows were ablaze in orange flames. The women who came to tea at the Lederers' were envious. 'Where on earth did you *get* him?' they asked. 'He speaks French and he's handsome — that smile, it's practically like a drug — and he's got the greenest thumb.' 'Not to mention,' the lady from French Guiana said, 'those beautiful hands.' Willy planted a night-blooming cereus in the Lederers' yard, right underneath Everly's bedroom window. It wouldn't bloom for several years, he said. But eventually it would produce an enormous ivory flower with a strange, sweet smell. One evening, it would open at dusk, bloom until dawn, and then close, never to open again. Years from now its first bloom would open and fill her room with fragrance, he said, but Everly would be gone by then. 'I'll be here!' she protested. 'No you won't. You'll be in college, a university, getting your degree.' 'Maybe I'll stay in Cuba,' she said. 'Maybe I won't want to go.' 'That's silly,' Willy said. 'You have to go.'

★ ★ ★

The wind gusted like a personality, quieted, then gusted again. Duffy was snoring gently in her bed across the room.

Everly thought she might like D. L. Mazierre to come and agitate them, even if she didn't know what was involved. She felt sure he was one of the good guys that Willy talked about, on his way to help.

Maybe low resort meant rough areas, the kinds of places her mother would tell her she wasn't allowed to go. Like Gamble Valley, where the Negroes lived in Oak Ridge. Timothy Hodgkiss had said his father went to Gamble Valley to buy splo. 'What's splo?' Everly had asked. 'You know, moonshine.' But she was only eight, and didn't know what that was, either. 'My father says the county is dry,' Timothy Hodgkiss had said, as if to explain. She didn't press on, although she knew that what she imagined was wrong. Moonshine, something too bright, like a metal car-door handle hit by the sun. They didn't need moonshine in Cuba because everyone drank rum. 'Ron,' the Cubans said, the Spanish word making the drink seem somehow thinner and more watery, with an 'n' rather than an 'm.' Anyone could buy rum, even a kid. Just walk up to a bar and order it. And there was marijuana growing everywhere, which K.C. had pointed out, to roll into cigarettes that the cane cutters smoked. She'd seen them smoking marijuana cigarettes, she could tell by the smell, the cane cutters whetting their machetes with a rock and molasses, sitting on the side of a road that Everly was not supposed to go down because there were shacks along it where adult things went on.

When they'd first arrived in Nicaro, her mother said that Everly and Duffy's bathroom, with its pink and black tiles, looked like a bordello. 'What's a bordello?' Everly had asked. 'A bathroom with pink and black tiles,' her father said. The first time she was invited to Val and Pamela's, she pointed out to Mrs. Carrington that they, too, had a bordello.

'Excuse me, child?' Mrs. Carrington said.

Everly's face went hot. 'The tile pattern in your bathroom, isn't it bordello?'

After Mrs. Carrington excused herself 'to powder her nose in the bordello,' Val explained that it wasn't tiles. It was a place where men paid money for certain services. 'What kinds of services?' 'Sex,' Val said. Now she was older and knew what sex was. It was possible her sister had tried it with Tico Leál. But back then, she'd pictured a thing that came in a box, like

227

something you purchased from Sears, folded and wrapped in tissue.

She supposed that if Gamble Valley were low resort, a bordello could be low resort. But buying sex didn't seem like something D. L. Mazierre would do. He'd be busy agitating.

13

Charmaine Mackey was near the ice factory when she saw Lito Gonzalez coming up the road in his white Cadillac. She felt a strange rise in something — her heart rate, maybe — when she realized his car was slowing, and that he would stop to speak with her.

His window went down. Did she need a lift?

She explained that she was out walking on purpose, for exercise, which suddenly seemed like a ridiculous activity. The Cubans didn't walk anywhere unless they had to.

Another car pulled up behind Mr. Gonzalez's, the driver honking impatiently. It was Mrs. Carrington. Probably stocking up on ice.

Charmaine felt caught. Doing what, she wasn't sure, but in a perverse instinct to prove that she had nothing to hide, and hadn't done anything wrong in speaking to the greasy Cuban millionaire, she put her hand on the passenger side door handle and opened it. Said she'd take a ride after all, and got in next to Mr. Gonzalez.

They proceeded up the road, Mrs. Carrington, behind them, turning left onto the manager's row. The interior of Mr. Gonzalez's car was enormous, white leather upholstery that reminded Charmaine of the sleek, plush lining of coffins. But what a waste, to line a coffin in white leather. This was an interior you could actually enjoy. Mrs. Billings was wrong about Mr. Gonzalez's taste in cars. It was a wonderful car, and she wished she could tell him so, but she couldn't think of how to say it without relaying the insult, in order to pay him the compliment.

'I was heading up to the mine, Mrs. Mackey, but I can take you anyplace you need to go.'

'Do you think I could come with you?' she impulsively asked. 'I've never been up to the mine.' It was absurd of her to ask. But there was something about Mr. Gonzalez that put her at ease, perhaps too much ease. He was so reserved that he brought out something assertive in her. The Americans in Nicaro were friendly in an overbearing way, with their smiles and warmth and handshakes — sometimes even hugs, which almost hurt Charmaine Mackey's nervous system. She was standoffish because she had to be, because it was too intense to be embraced by acquaintances. Mr. Gonzalez was not friendly or unfriendly. He let her take the lead, and she did.

'There isn't much to see at the mine, Mrs. Mackey, and it's no place for a lady. It's dusty and hot and unpleasant. And not so safe these days. There are rebels nearby. Perhaps your husband has told you about the situation?'

'He says it isn't anything to worry about. My son, Phillip, went up there last year on a class field trip with Miss Alfaro, and found it fascinating, just — '

'Is that what he said?'

'Yes, he had a wonderful time. He likes Miss Alfaro quite a lot. All the children do.'

'I meant your husband, Mrs. Mackey. He said the situation was nothing to worry about?'

'He said they're just a few bandits.'

Hubert had said nothing to her about bandits. She was repeating what she'd overhead him say to someone on the telephone.

Mr. Gonzalez said he hoped her husband was right, but with all due respect, it wasn't likely.

She was silent, thinking it best to feign that she knew what he meant in claiming Hubert was wrong. If they weren't bandits, what were they? She felt sure Mr. Gonzalez knew, and that he would lower his opinion of her if he understood how little she herself knew.

When he dropped her off in front of the bakery, a made-up errand she invented to give the impression that she had some structure, things to do, she felt somewhat abandoned, as she had at the welcoming party, and then disturbed by her regret at having to leave the upholstered cocoon of his car.

She stood outside the bakery and watched his long, white car move slowly up the road. When his car had disappeared around a bend, she turned to enter the bakery and discovered that it was closed and locked.

It must have been after 2:00 P.M., she realized. Rain was falling in a fine veil, almost a mist, but coming down steadily. The air had turned chilly, and the water on the bay was a dull bluish-gray, and choppy. Birds were dropping low in the bushes beyond the road, the way birds do when the rain is about to fall harder. How do they know? They just know. Charmaine had no umbrella. Her feet, in a pair of flimsy Capezios, were soaked now, and cold. She watched the dull, choppy water, thinking school would be over soon, and Phillip wouldn't take the boat out in this weather. He'd come straight home, go into his room and shut the door and study his nautical maps and fishing magazines. She'd pretend to be busy to avoid the servants, who all terrified her, boisterous and confident people who could have bossed her around and told her to mop the floor or fix them a snack and she would have. At five-thirty, Hubert would come home and grumpily cap off all possibility of conversation by responding in a terse and dismissive tone that his day went fine, that there was nothing worth mentioning.

She heard a car rounding the bend. Someone else, too late to buy a loaf of bread. But it was the white Cadillac. Mr. Gonzalez, coming slowly back down the road toward the bakery.

He stopped in front, his window down.

'You're back,' she said.

'I remembered, when I got home and looked at the clock, that the bakery would be closed.'

'Yes, it's closed. Oh, well. I hadn't realized what time it was. Aren't you going to the mine, Mr. Gonzalez?'

'I was. But now it's raining, and the road is turning to mud. I don't like taking this car through the mud. I'll go tomorrow in a company jeep.'

He looked at her carefully, like he was gauging something.

'Why don't you get in,' he said.

It was not a question. Her hands, in the pockets of her sweater, were shaking. But it

232

wasn't the bewildered shake that set in when others barraged her too-sensitive nervous system. Her hands were shaking with excitement.

★ ★ ★

Mr. Gonzalez's house was dark and orderly and quiet. They turned on no lights and left the curtains closed. His butler and housekeeper, he explained, both had the afternoon off.

It was an afternoon of time outside of time, although it couldn't have lasted more than forty-five minutes. When she arrived home, the kitchen clock showed 3:00 P.M. Phillip was nowhere to be found. She'd walked from Mr. Gonzalez's, understanding that of course he couldn't drive her home, but feeling slightly rebuffed that they separated with so little chivalry on his part. He'd simply said good-bye, turned, and gone inside, as she set off in the rain on foot. Still, she was elated.

As the days became weeks, the elation started to fade. She grew anxious that the chance of another visit to his home was growing more remote. When she saw him around Nicaro, he behaved as he had before that afternoon, polite and formal. Once, they were alone together outside the plant's executive offices. She had just dropped Hubert off, and was on her way to send telexes to boarding schools, to inquire about enrolling Phillip. They chatted briefly, but Mr. Gonzalez was distant. It was an opportunity, a moment when they were finally alone together. He didn't seize it. He asked if he'd be seeing her

233

and her husband at the club, for the Saturday dance. Her and her husband. Was he speaking to her in code? Letting her know that if it weren't for Hubert, they could have more afternoons like the one when he'd rescued her from the closed bakery? At the club that Saturday, she scanned the entrance all evening, waiting for Mr. Gonzalez to appear. He never did.

Twice she went to the bakery just after 2:00 P.M., knowing it would be closed. She stood in front, thinking if only rain were falling in a fine veil, as it had that day, his white car would appear. He would come down the road and invite her to get in it, and take her to his home, where they would turn on no lights and leave the curtains shut.

She understood that Mr. Gonzalez was not what many women would dream about. People said chemical, about attraction, and she supposed it was that. It had been immediate when she'd spoken to him during the party at his hunting lodge. Since their first conversation, she'd been waiting to speak with him again. He never came to the others' parties, never to their club. She knew her attraction to him was real because there was no need to tell herself that other women would approve, which is what she'd told herself before she married Hubert — that many other women would have married him. No one would approve of Lito Gonzalez, and she didn't care. He was up to no good, they declared, a greasy Cuban so-called millionaire, a word they uttered with invisible quotes around it, as if no one could reasonably believe he was

234

any kind of millionaire. He was overweight. His hair smelled pungently of men's cologne. But he caused a feeling to well in her, an electric anticipation.

She didn't really believe that standing in the deserted parking lot of the closed bakery would summon his car down the road. She stood in front of the bakery because it brought her closer to that afternoon at his dark and quiet house, which was disappearing into the past, as if it had never occurred.

She thought she knew every moment, the notepad on his bedside table, the cold cotton sheets. After months had gone by, she remembered addressing him as Mr. Gonzalez, even as she'd reclipped her stockings, chattering nervously and sensing, suddenly, that he was waiting for her to leave. She'd called him Mr. Gonzalez, and he had not bothered to correct her.

★　★　★

One afternoon she'd been shopping at the almacén in Preston and was planning to get a ride back to Nicaro on the United Fruit launch, the *Mollie and Me*, when she saw the familiar white Cadillac parked at an angled spot in front of the United Fruit Company offices. She was ecstatic, and decided she'd take a seat on one of the benches in the square and wait.

Finally he came outside, shading his eyes from the noontime sun. She couldn't tell if he'd spotted her, but then he was walking toward her. He sat down and asked if she needed a ride back to Nicaro, as if it were an old routine of theirs. All those lonely afternoons hoping she'd run into him. A few times, running into him only to encounter disappointment. Just, 'Good afternoon, Mrs. Mackey,' and nothing more. After all that, this was so easy!

She got in his car as if they were a couple, two people who'd already been together, though not for long, because electricity was pulsing through her the way it only does when love is new. She decided she would not call him Mr. Gonzalez. But she couldn't bring herself to say Lito, either. She called him by no name. He called her by none, either. Later she couldn't decide if it was impersonal or intimate that they both used 'you' as their mode of address.

He did not invite her to his house, but parked on an access road halfway to the mine. That wonderful leather interior, with a very roomy backseat. He was not exactly gentle that afternoon. In fact, he was rough. He grabbed her and pinched her arm and then the inside of her leg, so hard that he left a bruise. But his roughness seemed exactly right. The way he'd grabbed her, it meant he was paying attention. *To her*. She celebrated the beet-colored bruise on the inside of her thigh, and mourned its disappearance.

A few weeks later, she waited in his car while he conducted business at the Mayarí courthouse, then followed him into a ravine behind the pool hall. They made love on the ground, under the midday sun. She lay on a bed of pine needles, whose scratchiness had the same intoxicating effect as his rough pinches when they'd done it in his car.

After each incidence, he made her wait and wait and wait to see him again. But by now she'd grown somewhat used to the waiting, and considered it a part of their courtship. She sensed that the waiting, his ignoring her for weeks and even months, abided some logic that was remote to her but not to him. The courtship required profound patience on her part. It tortured her, but torture was part of infatuation.

Hubert continued to talk about Gonzalez as if he were an unconvicted killer. How unlikely that she, Charmaine, had an intimate thread to the person her husband and the other Americans despised. Hubert swore that Gonzalez would be their undoing. Hubert said — not to her, but to Mr. Lederer and Mr. Billings, though right in front of her because she didn't count, was too stupid and batty to understand — that Gonzalez was working with the rebels, and also making deals with Batista, trying to build a pressure cooker and bring combat right into Nicaro, to drive the Americans out. Her lover, whom they were talking about. And if they only knew. Maybe he was doing all of that, but he told her nothing. He was rough and hasty and never spoke her name, which made him that much more attractive and mysterious.

She imagined years from now, when Phillip was grown up, that maybe she could ask him about Mr. Gonzalez. Phillip had been caught using his boat to ferry rebel arms and supplies across Saetía. Hubert spoke to Phillip and decided to send him away. He said little about it to Charmaine. She suspected that her son, a clever and gifted boy, a sensitive boy, probably understood a great deal about what was going on with the rebels and mysterious Mr. Gonzalez and whether or not he was involved. Someday, when he was all grown up, Phillip might explain it to her.

14

Christmas in Havana

The morning we were leaving, Del kept us waiting. His bags were packed and in the hall with mine and Mother and Daddy's, but there was no sign of him.

Crushing season was set to begin just after the New Year, and people were going to Havana or Miami or New York to get a proper holiday before the sugar mill started running around the clock. This was December of 1957, just before the big cane fire. Before anything, really, had started to go wrong. We were going to Miami for the annual shopping spree, then to Havana as guests of Deke and Dolly Havelin.

Del knew what time we were supposed to be at the airstrip to meet the company plane. He'd gone off somewhere earlier that morning. I stuck around the house. Curtis Allain came by, and we killed time pitching rotten fruit at the mamoncillo tree, trying to get bats to fly out of it — they sleep in mamoncillo trees. The Allains weren't going anywhere. I think Rudy and Hatch were supposed to be around all the time, keeping an eye on the mill. I can't imagine the Allains going on a vacation anyhow. Pearly sure didn't like to go anywhere, not even to Mayarí. 'Can't blast her out of there with dynamite,' Rudy joked. Mother had gone up to Nicaro that morning.

The roads were good, and Hilton Hardy took her in one of the Buicks. She wanted to bring a Christmas ring to the Lederers, and she'd bought a gift for Everly — I think a bottle of perfume. Mother had invited Everly to come with us to Havana, but she couldn't for some reason that I don't recall, and Mother was sad about that. As I said, she had a real soft spot for Everly Lederer. She had our piano tuned religiously, even after Everly stopped coming over to play it. Mother felt that she had a unique personality — very 'individualistic' is what Mother said. She loved us boys to death, but I think it was a special treat to have a girl around.

When Del didn't show up on time, we all figured he was off sulking. Daddy had enrolled him in military school in Georgia starting in the spring, and Del didn't want to go. He was too old for the Preston school. I was almost too old for it, and would be enrolling at Ruston Academy in Havana the next fall. Del had been doing Calvert home schooling system by mail. After Phillip Mackey was caught helping the rebels, Daddy said it was proof enough to him that the humidity was making these older boys soft in the head. Del would go to the States and have a drill sergeant teach him some common sense.

We'd waited maybe thirty minutes when Daddy started getting anxious. 'Screw him,' he said. 'He's sixteen and he can take care of himself. Let him eat cat food.'

The entire staff of servants had the week off, except the company guards and Ho, the

Chinaman who tended our flowers.

Of course, Mother didn't want to leave without him. But you didn't cross Daddy. Hilton Hardy put the suitcases in the Buick, and we left. Daddy gossiped to Mother about Mr. Carrington's embezzlement troubles. Mother usually had a taste for these things, but she was too preoccupied about Del to enjoy the scandal. 'Bought himself a brand-new Cadillac. What a jerk. Can't even be discreet.'

On the plane, Daddy talked about Deke and Dolly Havelin and how they'd probably do a roast beef and Yorkshire pudding. He seemed in a fine mood, and I guess it was peculiar, given that his oldest son had run off, but I didn't always understand Daddy.

★　★　★

Aside from Del getting shipped off to military school, everything seemed normal to me that Christmas. Daddy must have known the situation was worse than a few ruffians in the hills, as Batista was claiming, but he hadn't told us. He never told Mother anything because Mother couldn't keep a secret. It wasn't her fault, Daddy said, it's biology, just how women are.

United Fruit put out their 'Jungle Bells' issue of *Unifruitco*, with pictures from the masquerade at the Pan-American Club, everybody goofing in ridiculous costumes. A lot of people just switched roles — husbands dressed up as wives, women in pants with mustaches drawn

241

over their upper lip. I went as the Lone Ranger, and Daddy let me carry a real pistol. Daddy wore a tall, pointy white hood with eyeholes cut into it and insisted he was dressed like a Spanish Holy Week penitent. He could be perverse like that. The year before, he'd gone as a guajiro. After that, everybody started doing it. It's an easy costume, just smear dirt on your cheeks, cut jagged hems on your pants, hitch them up with a rope, and walk around going 'Sí, señor.' I'm not saying it's polite. But this was a different time.

Mother's flamboyán tree was blooming a brilliant red and made things feel Christmasy even if the air was a wet ninety-one degrees. I'd never had a white Christmas anyhow. Christmas for us was Hatch taking all the boys fishing at Saetía. Splashing around in crystal-green, waist-deep water, warm as a tub. Eating pounded octopus we brought back, a typical Cuban feast except for Mother playing carols on the piano after dessert, and Annie's traditional no-show. On the evening of the twenty-fourth, Mother let Annie go down to Mayarí to visit her family. Christmas morning, like clockwork, she'd call person-to-person from the Mayarí post office saying she'd missed the bus up to Preston and would have to wait for the afternoon coach. Mother would sigh. 'Just take the rest of the day off, Annie.' It was a game. Annie pretending she missed the bus. Mother pretending she was exasperated.

One Christmas I answered the phone, and the operator said, 'Josephine Courtland is on the line.' I said we don't know anyone by that name.

242

We'd always called her Annie. I didn't know that Mother had made up a new name when I was little because I couldn't say the real one.

★ ★ ★

Daddy's pleasure over Mr. Carrington's troubles was part of a long tradition of his, hating the people in Nicaro. He said the place was a mess waiting to happen. He partly blamed Lito Gonzalez, who was a Cuban investor in the nickel mine. Having Gonzalez around meant the nickel company had to comply with Cuban labor laws, which to Daddy was sheer idiocy. Daddy said it was a conflict of interest to have a Cuban in management, and that the Americans in Nicaro were green and naive fools. When he heard that Hubert Mackey took too much quinine and went deaf in one ear, Daddy thought that was just hilarious. He said the Nicaro people were no different from the cows we got from Argentina, which didn't know the difference between alfalfa and Johnson grass, which is poisonous, so they ate the Johnson grass and got sick and died.

★ ★ ★

East Egg — is that what it's called? Deke Havelin was a wealthy and successful rayon magnate, and El Country Club, where the Havelins lived, was our version of East Egg. It was over the Almendares River, which divided the city, and mostly rich Americans lived out

243

there. El Country Club was gated and private, with a lake, a golf course, and palaces that were built in the twenties, during the Dance of the Millions, when everybody made a killing in sugar. Imitations of Versailles, with long, mirrored hallways. Promenades lit with frosted globes as big as the globe in Daddy's den, which lit up on the inside and gave off a ghostly blue when you shut off the other lights. Deke was a friend of Daddy's, and Christmas at their place in Havana was a real to-do, certainly more exciting than staying in Preston and decorating a breadfruit tree.

Daddy took me to see Sugar Ray Robinson fight at the Havana Sports Palace. The famous Cuban boxer Kid Chocolate, who had been world champion in the thirties, was master of ceremonies, which was a thrill. When Daddy had work to do, Mother and I swam in the salt-water swimming pool at the Yacht Club. They had a tiled bar on one end, and you could sip a virgin banana daiquiri without leaving the water. If it was high tide, waves lapped over the pool's seaside wall and sent you bobbing like a skiff. It was odd to be there without Del, but I have to admit it was also a relief. By then, Del and I weren't close. He was moody, and always off with Phillip Mackey, fishing with a group of young Cuban employees from the nickel mine. At dinner he would argue with Daddy, say contrary and ugly things out of nowhere. I think he got a lot of it from Phillip.

'Did you know Batista force-feeds people castor oil?' Del asked once of no one in particular. 'Isn't

244

that nice, Mother? Maybe we can ask him about it next time he comes for dinner.'

'Listen to you,' Daddy said. 'Maybe you need a little castor oil yourself. Maybe I'll talk to Batista about it.'

That quieted Del for the rest of dinner. But as we were eating dessert, he started up again. 'Father, how much do we pay that gorilla?'

Daddy ignored the question and asked me about my schoolwork, as if Del wasn't worth answering.

As Del was getting up from the table he said, 'Don't you think it's funny that we teach them agriculture, and none of them own any land?'

That's when Daddy blew up.

'You got a problem with how things are run around here, then get off your ass and do something about it!' He slammed his fist on the table and made all the silverware jump. 'Instead of sitting there with a linen napkin in your lap like a goddamn pantywaist, eating grub I pay for, the flan you asked your nanny to make you like you're five years old. Go do something. You have no idea what you're talking about. Nothing but a spoiled goddamn brat.'

⋆　⋆　⋆

Mother, Daddy, and I went to see Xavier Cugat at the Cabaret Tokio that Christmas. Their main theater was outside, but air-conditioned. I don't know how they did that. We sat under royal palms, colored searchlights crisscrossing red and green, parrots flying over us, cutting through the beams of colored light. A flock of them lived in the palm trees at the Tokio. We'd seen Xavier Cugat perform many times. He'd recorded the 'Chiquita Banana' jingle for the company's radio and television spots, and he was friendly with Daddy.

Xavier Cugat kept a little Chihuahua in his coat pocket. The band started, and finally he walked out, everybody clapping, and the dog jumped from his pocket and trotted around the stage. When I was little, I got up from our table and went and sat on the edge of the stage and played with Xavier Cugat's little dog while he was performing. No one minded or said a word about it. That Christmas, Mother and Daddy ribbed me about getting up onstage, but I'd outgrown that.

Daddy took us to the Floridita for dinner after Xavier Cugat's show. The dining room was full and we didn't have a reservation, so they seated us at the bar. You might know that the Floridita was Hemingway's hangout. Sure enough, just after we ordered, his raw, pink face filled the mirror above the liquor bottles. Daddy said Hemingway was crude and obscene. He talked about him like they were mortal enemies, but Hemingway walked right by us and I don't think he knew Daddy from Adam.

I ordered lobster. The lobster they brought me was pregnant, and when I cut into it an orange liquid oozed out — the eggs. I didn't think I could eat it, but Daddy said I should think of a pregnant lobster as a delicacy. That anything unseemly could be made tolerable if you told yourself it was a special thing, an exclusive thing. Like caviar, he said. I told him I hated caviar, and Daddy said it wasn't about taste, it was about having things that other people couldn't have, and there was a certain burden in that.

Hemingway parked himself at the bar and began chatting with his neighbor on the next stool, a slick-looking fellow in an expensive suit and tinted glasses. Somebody put coins in the jukebox, and Augustin Lara started singing 'Mujer.' That song was on our jukebox at the Pan-American Club. It was a popular song, and apparently Hemingway knew the words. He asked the bartender for change, and then punched in selections himself, still singing along with 'Mujer.'

He sat back down, and 'La Pachanga' came on. That was another popular song. Hemingway was doing the whistle parts along with the song. He turned to this slick-looking guy, who was sitting at the bar minding his own business.

'You do the pachanga?' Hemingway asked.

The guy nodded like he didn't really understand, then looked away.

'The pachanga,' Hemingway said, louder. 'Like the song. Or maybe cha-cha? If you know cha-cha, you can learn pachanga.'

'I'm afraid I do neither.' He had some kind of European accent.

'A rumba, then?' Hemingway was humming and snapping his fingers.

The fellow shook his head. 'I sit at the bar. That's what I do.'

'Don't get huffy. I asked if you do a pachanga.

Who says men can't dance?'

I felt bad for the guy. It seemed like he wanted to be left alone. But those are always the ones who get the onslaught. Then again, if you really want to be left alone, you have a drink in your room, by yourself.

'Look, ah, I'm not a friend of the family, shall we say.'

'I've got news for you: I go to Paris — I sleep at the Ritz — and everybody over there — you are French, aren't you? — every one of them is a friend of the family. Even the women. So how about some cha-cha? Because the rumba — have you heard? They're talking about outlawing it.'

'Is that so.'

'But they shouldn't.'

'Oh, no?'

'It's a crime to outlaw the rumba!'

Hemingway wasn't exactly shouting, but his talking voice was louder than the music and the room murmur. I think everyone in the bar was listening, the way I was.

'Even if it's so sexy it forces people,' Hemingway said, 'to do naughty things. That's the curse of the rumba, and I've seen it. Men hiking up women's skirts and humping them right on the dance floor. It's probably happening in some back alley right now. I mean this second, while I'm sitting here talking to you. Me, I've got a back problem. Still make love good, but not standing up. Do you know why they shouldn't outlaw the rumba?'

'I couldn't say.'

'Because people need diversions. Sex is a

248

healthy diversion. A very effective diversion.'

'I suppose I can agree with you there,' the Frenchman said.

Hemingway insisted they toast. 'To humping.'

They held up their drinks.

It's a typical scenario, drunk people carving out worlds as they get drunker, making pacts about what's important and what isn't in a couple of lost and forgettable hours. But when you're thirteen, you don't realize it doesn't count, that both those men could enter the bar the very next day and act as if they've never seen each other before. Perhaps repeat the conservation word for word, as if for the first time.

They were still talking when the waiter brought the dessert cart around and did the flambé routine for us. It was Mother's favorite part of going to the Floridita. She said they made the best flambé in town.

'I'll confess,' Hemingway said, 'that I cannot dance rumba to save my life. Like I said, this damn bad back. Listen to me — *I* said this, *I* do that — too many goddamn 'I's. You know what I should do? Every time I want to say 'I,' I'll substitute something else, 'Your Operative,' or maybe 'This Task Force.' In any case, 'Your Operative' is not a skilled dancer. What he knows is fiction. It's a very unhealthy diversion. Unless you can give it a high moral tone, which 'This Task Force' has failed to do. We need more poets. I once broke a poet's jaw. I feel bad about it, but he asked me to. More or less. Do you write poetry?'

'I don't think so,' the Frenchman said. 'In fact, no.'

249

'Because you smell like a high-level civil servant, see, and they used to send us poets. Poet-diplomats, like Perse. Or Valéry — '

'Claudel,' the Frenchman interjected.

'Exactly! Let me buy you another, my friend. Double whatever he's having. And a double for me as well. And a Ballantine's, because I'm very very thirsty. What was I saying? Oh, yes, men who type poems on embassy stationery. Send alexandrines to the State Department. Or just a single phrase. A wonderful question. It's a gift to ask the right question.'

'This is a fact,' the Frenchman said, and then they were toasting their doubles to the art of questions.

'Hell is breaking loose in French West Africa,' Hemingway said.

'Indeed it is,' the Frenchman agreed. 'Indeed it is. It will be quite interesting to see what evolves. A can swollen with botulism. Sometimes there is a healthy botulism, you know. A 'good' botulism — '

'Like I was saying,' Hemingway said, cutting him off, 'hell is breaking loose in French West Africa, and Saint-John Perse sends an embassy report back to France, one sentence. A single sentence. And it's a question: 'Is the Pink Lake of Dakar pink, or is it mauve?' That's his report!'

'I can tell you that it's mauve,' the Frenchman said.

I don't think Hemingway was listening.

'They used to send us diplomats,' he said, draining his drink and starting on the Ballantine's, 'who didn't dare talk about the price of sugar, the price of nickel, insurgent stunts on wireless radio. They sent us men like Perse, who asked, instead, what has the world given us 'but this swaying of grass.' They used to send us poets. Now they send us guys like you. Who don't even dance the pachanga.'

★   ★   ★

A driver took us down Calle San Rafael after dinner. They had fake snow and an elaborate manger set up, with life-sized department store mannequins that El Encanto donated from its window displays. The fanfare was all for us Anglos. The Cubans don't make such a big deal about Christmas — they have the Three Kings, that's in early January — but the president's wife gave out gifts on Christmas morning to children from the slums. It goes without saying that there were huge divisions between rich and poor in Cuba. You could look at a map of Havana and wonder about these massive areas, with ominous names like Cueva del Humo — cave of smoke — but the way the city was laid out, we never passed through a single slum. Mrs. Batista handed the gifts out herself, on the front lawn of the presidential palace. Hundreds of kids came to receive them. When the president and Mrs. Batista arrived at the Havelins' party, Mother complimented the first lady on her Christmas gift tradition. Mother said it was this type of gesture — modest and specific — that just might save the world.

The Havelins' party was formal formal

— greased hair, coat and tie, white bucks. Daddy wore a tuxedo and joked that you could take the hillbilly out of Mississippi but not the reverse. Mother had on a white bouffant gown. I remember it. She leaned in to kiss me, and the puffy fabric of her skirt made a soft, crunching noise. Dolly's father, Mr. Becquer, had commented that I'd be a lady-killer someday. Mother leaned in and kissed my forehead and said I was her peach and still a one-woman boy. The ambassador was there — not available when your plantation is burning down, but right as rain at a bash with champagne and movie stars. In his white suit, thinning hair plastered back, a tall fellow with coat-hanger shoulders. Face so suntanned that even by expat standards he looked ridiculous. He was a snobbish type with a Yale class ring, and when I think of him and Daddy in the Havelins' living room, sitting in club chairs with cocktails in their hands, tuxedo or no, Daddy does seem like a hillbilly by comparison. Daddy may have been the Cuba manager of United Fruit, but he was in backward Oriente, not Boston or New York. The people who mattered in Ambassador Smith's world were the financiers and CEOs, not the guy who hires the agronomist, deals with the day-to-day of cane crushing, of labor politics and revolt.

A guy was playing Gershwin melodies on the Havelins' grand piano. He stopped playing, and Dolly Havelin clinked a spoon against the side of her glass. People quieted down, and servants circulated the room with trays of poured champagne, making sure everyone had a glass. The servants were done up like French maids, in short skirts and little starched pillbox hats.

Dolly Havelin clinked her glass again to get our attention. Deke Havelin stood up and spoke.

'Everyone have a little bubbly?' Deke asked.

'We've got a special guest here tonight I'd like to toast. I'll give you a hint: Who's the most important man in Cuba?' Deke looked around. 'Not you, Smith.'

Everyone laughed, including the ambassador.

'I refer, of course, to President Batista.'

Batista and his wife were sitting at a special table, decorated with crepe. They both smiled a lot, which I realized later was about photography. People who are used to having their picture taken know to keep their faces placid and camera-ready at all times.

Deke paused to retrieve a little piece of paper from his tuxedo pocket. He unfolded it and read.

'One evening, one of the many lovely evenings I've had the enormous pleasure to spend with the president, he asked me, 'Deke, what do you *really* think of Cuba, an American like yourself, who's spent so many years here? Do you love it as your own country?' Well, I didn't have to think twice about that one. 'Claro que sí,' I said to the president.'

I don't know if it was ceremonial — you know, acting — but Deke wiped tears from his eyes.

'I'll make this short. It's quite an honor to call this marvelous country home. And now, to call myself Cubano. It's just wonderful. I feel like I'm dreaming. And so I want to make a toast.' Deke

253

held up his glass. 'To President Batista, and to Cuba, which the Havelin family always has, and always will, love *as our own*.'

Everyone raised a glass in the direction of the president's table.

'And by the way,' Deke said, 'Dolly and I broke out the good stuff, so drink up now and you won't feel a thing later on, when we start uncorking the rotgut.'

People laughed, and there was a lot of applause. The pianist started in on a tune, and Deke twirled Dolly around the dance floor as everyone watched. He dipped her dramatically, and everybody laughed and applauded again.

Batista had offered Deke Havelin Cuban citizenship, and Deke had accepted. I knew it had something to do with wealth and keeping it protected, but I had no idea Deke was in serious legal trouble in the States. I was thirteen, and suddenly in that wild state that puberty flings boys into, and preoccupied with other things — girls, for instance. There were some pretty ones at the Havelins' that day, and I felt like I was noticing girls for the first time in my life. I guess there were kids my age who were into all that before I was, but I was a late bloomer. Maybe it had to do with Mother, something complicated about my loyalty to her. I married very late, after Mother had already died, and perhaps there's a reason for that. Desi Arnaz and Lucille Ball were at the Christmas party — they were friends of the Havelins, friendly with Daddy. Mother and Daddy had gone to their wedding reception in Santiago. I was hot on the heels of a niece they brought to the party, Elisia Arnaz, a pretty girl with white-blond hair like mine, who talked with a lisp that made her sound like she was from Spain except I don't think she could help it. For years I'd watched how Phillip Mackey operated, and I remember adopting his style a bit to flirt with Elisia Arnaz. Phillip had this way of looking girls right in the eye, even if he wasn't that interested.

I was wrapped up in looking Elisia Arnaz in the eye as if I wasn't afraid of her, and it didn't occur to me that Deke Havelin was giving up his American citizenship. I figured it was like Batista was giving him the key to the city, a purely ceremonial thing.

Dolly's family, the Becquers, had come from Philadelphia, but they'd been in Cuba for more than a century, since long before the Spanish-American War. They had their own mausoleum in Colón, the big cemetery in Havana — black marble with yellow Lalique windows, air-conditioning, and an elevator to the underground tombs. They'd bought themselves Spanish titles — Casa or Marqués de this or that, Gentleman of the Bedchamber of the Queen — which not only made them sound pompous and important but also transferred all litigation against them to Spain, causing so many delays that they could never be taken to court for anything, never had to pay any debts, and had built up a great deal of wealth back when Cuba was still a Spanish colony. Kind of like Deke Havelin getting out of his legal issues by changing passports. I don't think that's a coincidence: rich people are clever about holding on to money.

Becquer was originally Baker, but they'd been in Cuba so long they Hispanicized it. Deke Havelin didn't Hispanicize his name, but maybe he would have if things had gone differently.

★ ★ ★

Watching him twirl Dolly around the dance floor, I guess I figured it was a good thing Batista had done for Deke, if it meant the Havelins got to keep the mansion and the swimming pool with its bamboo cabañas, the gardens and tennis court, the fourteen-foot Virginia pine Christmas tree, which had come all the way from North Florida in a chilled shipping container, in the Havelins' living room with an avalanche of presents underneath it. Those were happy times. Why not take measures to make the happiness last?

During Deke's toast, Mother had sneaked out to the guesthouse. She'd been trying to get a call through to Del since we arrived in Havana, but with no luck. Naturally there was a telephone in the guesthouse — they even had a telephone mounted on the wall of each bathroom. That morning after the party I was in the bathtub and thought about calling Elisia Arnaz, but I didn't have her phone number. I probably wouldn't have done it, but I can't think of why they'd put a telephone in the bathroom, except to call up girls while you're in the bath.

Mother came back into the living room and told Daddy no one was answering.

'I called down to the Allain place and spoke to

Rudy,' she said. 'Rudy says they haven't seen hide or hair of him. They thought he was in Havana with us. And since the Mackeys are in New Mexico, I put in a call to Marjorie Lederer, who says that Phillip's boat is gone from the Nicaro dock. That it's been gone for several days.'

'Jesus, Evelyn,' Daddy said. 'This might be the time to cut him from the apron strings. He's an ingrate, and I will testify that I am enjoying his — what do you call it? The opposite of company? His absence.'

'But Malcolm — '

'And it's not like he's never borrowed that boat. He probably thinks he owns the fucking thing now that the Mackey boy is gone.'

Phillip Mackey graduated from a military academy with honors the next spring. Del set buses on fire, grew a beard, and took his orders from a seventeen-year-old commander, a suspected Communist, suspected homosexual.

★   ★   ★

When I think of Tee-Tee Allain, I think of my brother. Not that I think of her much. Sometimes, when I see women with that same blank look, I see Tee-Tee's face as Del handed her the chocolates on Valentine's Day. She always had that empty look. Maybe that's what did it for Del. It's a particular blankness, and I've mostly seen it on billboards for so-called gentlemen's clubs. The convincing ones have that same empty look. Like they know just how to void

257

themselves and not get in the way of some 'gentleman's' fantasy.

Tee-Tee floated around, oblivious, in the shadow of his obsession with her. That's the strange thing about love. Unless you return it, it's invisible. Even if you know someone is directing it at you, it's nothing but a dull reminder of your own indifference to it. One person impaling himself on his own obsession, the other wolfing down Valentine candies, playing dodgeball barefoot, her stringy hair in her face, staring at nothing, mouth partway open like she can't be bothered to close it.

Del gave up on her about a year before he disappeared. His last attempt was asking Tee-Tee to the cotillion. Phillip Mackey had already asked her, and I think her getting hung up on Phillip is finally what did it.

Daddy had arranged with our company lawyer, Mr. Diaz-Hart, that Del and I would take Mr. Diaz-Hart's two younger daughters to the dance. Mother wanted us to go with the Lederer girls, but it was a business thing for Daddy, and he'd already arranged it. Mr. Diaz-Hart's oldest daughter, Mirta, married Fidel Castro in 1948. The wedding was at the church right on the town square in Banes, United Fruit's other sugar mill town, thirty miles away. It seems absurd that Fidel would marry a society girl whose father's occupation was helping Americans avoid Cuban taxes and labor laws. They were rich, Americanized Cubans. They vacationed in the States, read *Look* and *Life*, and ate cornflakes for breakfast. The daughters dressed straight out of *Vogue* magazine. Mirta ended up sending divorce papers to the rebel camp. I guess she realized Castro wasn't going to be the husband who drives a new Buick and gives her a shopping allowance. I think he married her to put a notch in his belt. I mean, an enemy who's sleeping with your daughter has a certain advantage over you. But I also think he had something to prove, that even as he was destroying it, he wanted in to a social world from which the Cubans were excluded. Maybe he still wants in. When Castro was in Tampico planning his invasion, the story is he spotted this sparkling white yacht on the Tuxpán River and declared, 'Here she is — I'm going to Cuba in this boat.' That boat became famous: the *Granma*, which until 1959 the English-language dailies were calling '*Gramma*.' It was a pleasure boat exactly like our company yacht, the *Mollie and Me*. Eighty feet. Meant to carry twenty-five people, with lacquered teakwood trim and white leather tuck-and-roll upholstery. You invade a country in a PT boat, not a yacht with a built-in liquor cabinet! Castro later said the boat had come to him in a vision, and in a way it had: it was a vision of the *Mollie and Me*, which, of course, Castro had seen countless times anchored at the country club in Preston. They jammed eighty-five men on that little yacht. It almost sank, and then they shipwrecked, ran it aground northeast of Nicaro. If that's not stupid enough, as they fled into the mountains, Castro's men were chomping sugarcane, and they littered their own trail with chewed stalks. Batista followed the trail and sent

259

in planes. You can hide in a cane field if you're being pursued on foot. But from a plane it's impossible. You're Cary Grant getting mowed by a crop duster in *North by Northwest*.

At the cotillion, Del sat along the wall and stared at Tee-Tee the whole night and refused to dance with Alina, the Diaz-Hart girl. I danced with her, although she was a foot taller. She wore white cotton gloves, and her hands were bigger than mine. I took turns between her and the younger one. I didn't mind.

Del protested when Daddy first told us about the setup. He said the Diaz-Hart girls were 'shallow.' I didn't ask him how he knew Tee-Tee wasn't shallow, considering she never said a word. I was a kid. I didn't know about love, that you see someone and whether or not they say much, they make the world suddenly different, a mysterious and more alive place that you can access only through them. And the new, better world falls lifeless and flat when they go away.

Phillip Mackey danced with Tee-Tee during the slow dance. He went to put his tongue in her mouth, and she bit him on the face. He let out a loud yelp. Everyone looked over. She left a crescent of red tooth marks on his cheek. It looked like a dog had locked on to him.

I don't think Phillip had any special affection for Tee-Tee, and wouldn't have even if she'd let him put his tongue in her mouth, put his hand over the front of her dress, et cetera. And even the et cetera probably wouldn't have meant much: a lot of the older boys were getting their practice on the cheap. Daddy shut those places down, but they always reopened. There was a guy who procured small-town girls. They came on boats from Antilla. You'd see them with these dour expressions, fanning themselves in the heat. You know why they're called red-light districts? In Oriente, the brakemen would leave their railroad lanterns out front when they visited those places. If a train was coming in and they were needed, they could be called back to work. Sometimes at night you'd see two or three red lanterns glowing like buoys along the row of shacks where the girls from Antilla worked.

After the night she bit him on the dance floor, Tee-Tee started following Phillip Mackey around. When the Nicaro kids came over to Preston to swim in the pool, Tee-Tee would sit at the edge with her bruised white legs in the water, staring, glum and intense, watching Phillip go off the high dive. Phillip told everybody she gave him the creeps, that she looked at him like she wanted to hunt him down with an animal net.

Phillip's parents bought him a boat, and he and Del started going out fishing together. Suddenly my brother was obsessed with that instead of Tee-Tee. I once heard him chime in about the 'spooky broad' who wouldn't leave Phillip alone, no mention that he had spent years of his life obsessed with that same spooky broad.

Phillip kept his boat anchored in Levisa Bay, by the nickel processing plant. He and Del became friendly with the Cuban mine employees who fished off the dock, younger guys from the countryside around Mayarí. A couple of months before our Christmas stay at the Havelins', in

October of '57, there was a phone call to the Mackeys from Chatsworth — Chatty, the Saetía watchman who gave me my silvered conch. Chatty said Phillip was up to something. That's when the Mackeys sent him away.

★   ★   ★

These peculiar Cubans arrived late to the Havelins' party, ministers in Batista's government. Deke, Daddy, and the Cubans all went down to the billiards room. Mother went to bed. Desi Arnaz's niece Elisia — *Elithia*, she said, like she was missing her front teeth — and I snuck out for a late-night swim.

We were clowning and splashing; I cannonballed into the pool, innocent stuff. We got out, and Elisia pushed me into a cabaña. I remember that she was a pretty aggressive kisser. We were kissing, and she stepped out of her wet bathing suit, just rolled it down and stepped out of it, and put her arms around me. Her skin was cold where the bathing suit had been, but with a body warmth coming through from underneath the cold. I'd gone to second base with girls in Preston, but getting your hand in a blouse is not the same thing as a Cuban girl well into puberty standing in front you with a wet bathing suit looped around her ankle. The truth is, *Elithia* was ready for a lot more than I was. I wasn't one bit ready, as it turned out. It was cold. I was nervous. But she was sweet about it, and said we could try again. We didn't, but that second try happened about a thousand times in my mind,

262

and it wasn't at all awkward, as it would have been in real life.

The next morning rain was falling in a steady shower. Mother came and woke me. It took me a minute to remember about the night before in the cabaña. I wondered if Mother could tell. She always said that a mother can detect her son's presence, that she knows his smell like no one else does. If I'd taken a nap on the porch, she knew because she could smell where I'd laid my head on the pillows of the divan. I wondered if I smelled like Elisia Arnaz. Of course, I didn't want Mother to know anything about that, but then again it makes me sad to think of her as naive, as unable to detect the smell of a stranger on me. Mothers are possessive. Mine certainly would not have wanted to entertain the idea of me naked in a cabaña with some girl, high society or not. It would have been more palatable to her if it were a proper courtship with someone she knew and liked. I think she wanted me to date Everly Lederer, and I remember waking up and knowing I was betraying that.

A servant brought breakfast to the guesthouse on carts — poached eggs, bacon, guava juice, butter, and rolls. Mother said Daddy had gone to the Hotel Nacional early to get work done. Because he came to Havana on business so often, he kept a suite at the Nacional as an office. The Yacht Club was having its annual tea party — they hosted it every year, the day after Christmas, but Mother said she'd had enough socializing and would I like to go to the movies instead. One of the Havelins' drivers took us to

La Rampa for a matinee, Mother in a green rain slicker with a black velvet collar, me smelling secretly like Elisia Arnaz.

We saw *Jet Pilot*, and I remember thinking it was a pretty good film. Then we went to El Louvre for ice cream. There were these French places in Havana — the Tuileries, El Louvre — but they were just names. There was more French ancestry in Oriente, the descendants of the planters who started coffee operations in the Cristal, above us, after they were run out of Haiti by the blacks. The culture wasn't exactly what you'd call 'French' — there were Rousseaus and Carpentiers up in the mountains and in Santiago, but they weren't so different from wealthy Cubans, except they danced quadrilles and minuets, and their servants called you 'maître.'

El Louvre was famous for sherbet, but at Christmas you could get tropical snow — a frozen guanabana-flavored custard under a thick layer of flaked coconut. Nothing tasted so exquisite as tropical snow. They were also famous for delicados, cognac and ice cream whipped in a milkshake machine. It gives me a headache just thinking about a cognac milkshake.

El Louvre was elegant — marble tables, marble floors, waiters in formal jackets, a fountain in the middle of the room, nymphs with water bubbling out of their mouths. I spooned my tropical snow and Mother drank black coffee. She seemed preoccupied, and I knew she was thinking about Del. It was cruel of Daddy to make her leave him at home. Different from putting limits on her, as he sometimes did when she wanted to feed people at the back door.

When I went to use the men's room, I passed by an older man sitting with a much younger girl. I didn't look at them until I was practically squeezing by their table, and it wasn't until I got down the hall to the washroom that I realized the older man was my father. I didn't expect to see Daddy at an ice cream parlor and certainly not with a strange girl. The mind does things to correct for what doesn't make sense, and I just didn't think it was he. I came out and had to pass by them again. His back was to me, but it was my father's back. I thought there must be some mistake, but I didn't know what kind of mistake. She was eating ice cream and he wasn't, the way I was eating ice cream and Mother wasn't. But she wasn't a kid. She was probably in her early twenties, attractive in an unwholesome way, heavy makeup and high heels, that sort of bottle-blond, Lana Turner hair. Her clothes looked too tight. Walking back to the table, I listened to the voices and clattering dishes and had that dreamy, disconnected sensation that takes over in those moments in life when things turn suddenly queer.

I'm sure Mother saw them. They might have seen us, because when I sat back down, they were gone. Strange to think they'd rushed off like we were the police, or the Rural Guard, or what was worse, like we were total strangers.

★ ★ ★

Deke Havelin was the type of guy who joked loudly and in front of Dolly that he was 'married but single.' Or 'married but looking' — that was his other one. He came off like a swinger, rayon magnate, ladies' man. It was a performance. Dolly called all the shots, and he adored her.

Daddy told everyone about seeing Mother on the road in Indiana and saying to himself here comes this angel. Mother did everything right. She was attractive and elegantly put together, and she took excellent care of herself. Never lost her cool, rode her horse out into the countryside to take sick or retarded children to the company hospital. Mother was perfect, but people don't always want perfection.

Why Daddy was so reckless that afternoon still vexes me. Either he thought we were at the Yacht Club tea, which is where the Havelins were, or he just decided to take his chances. Or maybe he knew she could bear it.

People say you discover someone's secret and suddenly he or she feels like a stranger. The older man sitting with the girl didn't feel like a stranger. It was my father, equal parts old-fashioned gentleman and Mississippi hillbilly, white ducks and a demi-demi. Daddy, who was intimate with that girl like he was intimate with Mother, if he was intimate with Mother. I'll gladly remain ignorant about that. I don't know who she was or if he saw her regularly or what. But he was sitting like a patient father, that girl licking her ice cream methodically, seriously, the way kids do.

★ ★ ★

When we got home to Preston, Del's bag was still in the hall. Mother fainted. Hilton Hardy and Henry Das carried her upstairs while Daddy and I unloaded the car. Hilton and Henry normally refused to speak or even look at each other, something to do with Henry being part Hindu. There was all sorts of hairsplitting among those guys, Chinese, black, mulatto, what have you. Mother and Daddy thought it was cute that the chauffeur snubbed the butler. They talked about Henry and Hilton not mixing like it was sibling rivalry.

Daddy made phone calls. Crim, Mackey, Allain. He called Diaz-Hart. Even Lito Gonzalez. Lito Gonzalez spoke perfect English, but Daddy spoke Spanish to him on the phone. I'd seen him do that, speak Spanish to Gonzalez while Gonzalez responded in English. Daddy said Gonzalez was one of those types who cared only about money and hated Americans. 'Stab you in the back first chance he gets,' Daddy said. The phone rang, and it wasn't Crim or Diaz-Hart. It was Gonzalez.

After he hung up, Daddy said it looked like Del might have accidentally crossed into rebel territory and we would have to figure out a way to get him out safely.

★ ★ ★

A month later, our cane fields were torched. The blaze burned for almost a week, until rain finally fell and drenched the flames. Afterward, the workers slashed and crushed the burned cane,

267

fed it into the mill rollers in blackened, gummy masses. If they could get it all processed within a week, Mr. LaDue said, the stalks would still have some sugar content. The rain had turned the town into a giant wet ashtray, and then the mill was flowing burned sugar into the boilers. It was different from the smell of cane fields on fire. More acrid and metallic, like poisoned air hitting my tongue. It made me think about the warm, malty smell we were accustomed to, and how pure it was.

In an abandoned hut out in the cane cutters' batey, the Allain brothers had found stacks of notices calling for a strike, and flyers with arson instructions and diagrams: tie a kerosene-soaked rag to the tail of a rat and let him loose in the cane. A cat would work, too. That's why no one had come to help put out the fire. They were honoring the strike. Everyone came back to work, and because Daddy needed them, he didn't have a choice but to allow it. Daddy had me helping out, mostly just watching as workers unloaded cane cars, keeping an eye on his 'peóns,' as he put it. When I was little I didn't know what that meant. 'An animal that talks,' Daddy said. They saved what they could, but we lost almost three hundred million pounds of sugar. A quarter of the yield.

Batista's Rural Guard opened a garrison in Preston, and suddenly there were Cuban officers in khaki uniforms patrolling with guns, and they weren't shy about using them. That's how these things work. The crackdown *after* the ruin and hell-raising. Cubans had a five-o'clock curfew, no exceptions. To prevent people from hiding weapons, Cuban women weren't allowed to wear the sack dresses that were popular at the time, and the men had to tuck in their shirts. The Rural Guard raided an all-black club in Levisa, the Maceo, and took some of the men in for questioning. One of the officers came and knocked on our door late, after midnight. Henry Das answered, and the officer said they wanted to speak with me. Henry Das assumed they had the name wrong and meant Daddy, but the officer said no, we need to speak with the boy. Henry woke me. I got dressed and told Mother what was going on — Daddy was in Havana on business — and Hilton Hardy took me up to the Rural Guard station. They had all these black guys with their hands chained behind their backs. They brought one of them out. The captain, Sosa Blanco, asked, 'Do you know this nigger?' It was the Lederers' servant. That curious boy who'd come to Preston with Mr. Bloussé. Whenever I went to the Lederers he seemed to disappear, as if he were avoiding me. I got the feeling that he felt found out. Suddenly, he was standing there in chains, telling Captain Sosa Blanco, 'He knows me. This boy knows me. Tell them you know me.' I will never forget it. It was as if we'd been having a conversation all along, even if we'd never acknowledged that we knew each other from so many years earlier. There was no question of whether he was innocent or guilty. He'd seen no reason to address me out loud until that moment. It was judicious, to say the least. 'He's innocent,' I said, but there was only a question of who he was. Did a white person know him? If so, he goes free. If not, they shoot him along with the other boys and string him up in a tree along the main highway. I didn't see any dead bodies in trees. By then Daddy was adamant that Mother and I stay inside the gates.

I told the captain I knew him from when he was little, that his employer was an old friend of my father's. That boy was not stupid. He knew the name Stites would have more pull with the Cuban officers than Lederer or any other American in Nicaro. They let him go.

★ ★ ★

Despite the new laws and curfews in Preston after the fire, mill equipment kept getting damaged and stolen anyway. The rebels took tractors, and put sugar in the gas tanks of Daddy's Buick limousines. They raided his private freezers at the almacén. Daddy insisted on butchering his own meat, and he had the butchers down there wrap everything in white paper and label and stack them according to cut. The rebels left us not so much as a bag of gizzards. Maybe we have Del to thank for that. I didn't care about steak, but I hated to see my father in a rage. It got worse in the summer of that year, when someone tossed a Molotov cocktail into Daddy's Pullman car. There was nothing left but a charred shell. I went in there a few days after the fire. What a terrible thing, the velvet club chairs and couches just springs, like skeletons.

I always thought of the Pullman car as Panda's, never mind that they kept it locked after she installed herself in there and got grubby fingerprints on everything. She cut swatches out of the velvet curtains with scissors, and all the drapes had to be replaced because they didn't have any more of the old fabric. The Allains had to pay for the damage, but no one was angry at Panda. How can you be, at a serious little girl with a birthmark that made her look as if someone had slung a glass of red wine in her face? Mr. Flamm took it out of Rudy's paycheck a little at a time. The company was like that. Informal. They treated people as people, and families as families. If the workers had a beef with us, they were supposed to go to a Cuban guy first. His job was to try to settle things off the record, Cuban to Cuban. If a worker was causing trouble, stealing or drinking too much cane brandy on his break, this same Cuban had a word with him. A lot of the workers drank on their shift breaks instead of acting sensibly and eating a square meal. They made liquor from the syrup that was dumped after the last stage of centrifuging. 'La miel final' it's called — the final honey — and it has absolutely no taste.

Their problems with us, ours with them — the idea was to get things straightened out native to native. It was a very old-fashioned way of doing things.

The Rural Guard had a different philosophy. Jesús Sosa Blanco, the captain, had been let out of prison by Batista. Sosa Blanco had killed his wife, his mother-in-law, and his sister-in-law.

Batista released rapists and murderers — anyone who'd enlist went free. The Rural Guard was like a local, domestic version of the French Foreign Legion, who were good enough to do dirty work in the colonies, but not to be free citizens of France. At the end, when Batista sneaked off the island, in the middle of the night, resigned finally to the fact that he'd lost and the revolution was imminent, was there space for Captain Sosa Blanco, murderer and ex-con, on the DC-4? Of course not. He was tried in the Sports Palace, where Daddy took me to see Sugar Ray Robinson fight that Christmas. Thousands of people watched from the stands as a firing squad executed him. I watched it on CBS.

★   ★   ★

Revolutions start with fires. That's how it was in Haiti in the 1790s. In Cuba in 1844 they had La Escalera, when the slaves burned some of the larger Spanish cane plantations in Oriente. The slaves who led these revolts were called 'kings' and 'queens,' and they gave the signals to torch. When the rebellion was finally quashed, the Spanish executed not just its 'royal' leaders but also thousands of slaves, many of them probably innocent. Plantation owners tied the slaves to ladders — that's 'la escalera' — and whipped them to death. Of course, no one was whipped to death in Cuba in the 1950s, but what Daddy had to deal with wasn't all that different, except there weren't any kings and queens — only 'comrades' — and it wasn't Daddy who dealt out

272

punishments. This is a modern state, and they had secret police — the Servicio de Inteligencia Militar, or SIM — and the Rural Guard, led by Captain Sosa Blanco. But with a history of tumult and revolts, certain ideas, certain lessons, silt in — like the belief that it's necessary to crush these things before they get out of hand. And that the only effective way is with violence.

It was Sosa Blanco's idea that every native must have his hands waxed with paraffin. If the wax showed traces of nitrate, that person had fired a gun. They didn't bother arresting people. They shot them on the spot, or worse. On the roadside between Preston and Mayarí, Sosa Blanco burned five people alive, four men and a woman who all had nitrate on their hands. He hung them from trees and started a bonfire underneath like he was roasting five New Year's pigs. I wasn't supposed to know about that, but Hatch told Curtis, and Curtis told me. The thing is, anyone who works on a farm and handles fertilizer is going to have nitrate on his hands.

⋆　⋆　⋆

I started listening to the rebels' clandestine broadcast, Radio Rebelde, every night. We couldn't get any of the regular news. Our paper, the *Havana Post*, was mostly inked out in black. The only things they left for us to read were recipes for pineapple upside-down cake, want ads for light-skinned domestics, and silly columns about people like Deke and Dolly hosting charity balls. The censorship started to make the Americans uncomfortable, and I think it's the main reason why Batista got blackballed from the Yacht Club that spring. Daddy went to Havana for the vote. Who knows what else Daddy did in Havana? You'd think one or two would vote for the president, but it was all blackballs. Batista was a mulatto. Some people said he was an achinado, which is part Chinese. Of course, color played a part in his rejection from the club.

Clavelito was still doing his program, but I didn't hear his voice coming from the bohios when I rode my bike down there. Everyone was tuned into Rebelde to learn what was happening. Then the rebels put Violeta Casal on the air, so you got news and you got Violeta Casal.

Violeta Casal was a well-known actress who appeared in the print and television commercials for Pompeii laundry flakes. When I heard her silky voice reading the news reports over the radio, I had an image in my mind of the soap flakes model, a jiggly girl with dimples and dark, wavy hair. I thought about her a lot, and forgot all about Elisia Arnaz.

Violeta Casal announced that Fidel had ordered his own family's cane burned first because they, too, were exploitative landowners. I guess you can't call him a hypocrite. I don't think it was first, but they really did burn Ángel Castro's cane fields. Fidel's mother, Lina, was furious. The old man had died the year before. Daddy had gone to his service, at the church in Banes where Fidel married the Diaz-Hart girl.

Violeta Casal talked about miracles, but they were different from Clavelito's miracles, which involved winning the lottery, or cures for marital troubles, or hernias, or the chronic lateness that Clavelito said a lot of people suffered from. Violeta Casal declared that there were miraculous signs the rebels were triumphing. When the El Cobre copper mine above the city of Santiago was bombed, the only thing that wasn't damaged was the Black Virgin in El Cobre church. Its glass case was not even cracked, while everything around it was rubble. Violeta Casal said the Black Virgin was guiding the struggle and would save the Cubans from Batista's corruption the way she saved three miners in 1628. A ferocious storm had come in while the miners were out fishing, and their boat capsized in Nipe Bay. That's our bay. They were drowning when the Black Virgin came toward them on a block of wood. The miners grabbed on to the wood and floated to safety. The Cubans made her the patron saint of the island. They carried her to Santiago on the old horse trail that cuts through Ángel Castro's property. Blacks went to El Cobre to pray to the Black Virgin for healthy babies. Pardos, or lighter-skinned Cubans, prayed to the whitest saint they could find, hoping for light-skinned babies.

★   ★   ★

For a long time, we heard nothing from Del. Daddy said it was a family issue, and not to be discussed with the other Americans. This was especially hard for Mother, having to pretend that everything was fine when her son had

275

disappeared. Everyone knew about it anyway. Everly heard through the houseboy. You got the feeling that all the blacks had some inside key to what was happening. I started to wonder if Annie knew. But I doubt that she did. She was practically a part of our family.

★ ★ ★

A few weeks after the cane fire, a letter finally arrived from Del. This was in March of 1958. Del had been gone for three months, since Christmas. That was the moment when a person seemed like a stranger to me. Daddy with a whore is still Daddy. But Del's litany, I just couldn't attach his voice to it. He said the cane fire hadn't caused any more damage than the phosphorus that Batista's American-built bombers had dropped on the guajiros in the Sierra Cristal — humble people, he wrote, who were honest and working their own land, not land that rightfully belonged to someone else. He said he hoped Daddy was contemplating his association with tyrants and criminals, and that we should all be thinking about what justice meant.

The only part that seemed like the old Del was the postscript: 'As you both know, I hate to write letters. So I dictated this.'

15

A woman's voice, American, echoed up to her window, cutting through a steady drumming of rain.

'Why didn't you tell me?' the woman shrieked, plaintive and drunk. 'Why didn't you tell me?'

Rachel K had spread the postcards out on the bed. Every few months one turned up in her mailbox. *Greetings from the banks of the Tagus. Greetings from the banks of the Neva. Greetings from the banks of the Seine*, they announced. But it was always the same image: a lithograph of a woman reclining on an ottoman piled with cushions, a gauzy band of fabric draped across her hips so she wasn't completely nude.

On the back of each card: 'Greetings from the banks of nowhere, Christian.'

The stamps were smudged and faint, but a few she could make out: Algiers, Dakar, and Port-au-Prince, Haiti.

She put the cards away when she heard the familiar double honk of Batista's driver.

★ ★ ★

Batista was speaking on the phone. She took a seat on one of the sofas in the Green Room, its familiar gold and lime-green drapes and upholstery casting a different mood now that it was Batista's Green Room and not Prio's Green Room.

It hadn't been Prio's for six years now, but Batista still seemed ill-fit to its overbearing decoration, brocade everything, and giant chandeliers.

'I see . . . yes, thank you. This is wonderful news.'

Batista put the receiver back on its cradle.

'They've finally carted that moron off to jail!' He pounded his fist on the desk in satisfaction. 'Indicted him for conspiring against me. He thinks he can do what he wants because he's in Miami. But that asshole isn't going to get away with so much as jaywalking.'

The moron was Prio. He'd been charged with violating U.S. neutrality laws by financing Cuban insurgents. Batista had made a deal with the Americans, in exchange for Prio's indictment. The Americans requested that Batista lift martial law in Cuba, and he did. At least in Havana, at least for a few days. Oriente, he said, was out of the question. He hadn't trusted that the Americans would come through on their end of the deal, but as soon as Batista publicly announced the guarantee of rights, the lifted curfew, the Miami court issued a bench warrant. Police went to Prio's home and arrested him.

Rachel K had warned Prio that his own cook and butler in Miami seemed to be on Batista's payroll. 'You mean *Guillaume?*' Prio had asked in disbelief. He refused to believe that anyone who should be loyal wasn't. Just as Batista wasn't capable of understanding that none of the girls — Rachel K or La Paloma or any of the others — was loyal. They would never dare, Batista said, cavort with his enemies. But they did, and openly. He wasn't aware because it was beyond the scope of what he deemed possible, even as he made himself aware of every last detail.

He devoted the majority of his time to his paranoia, his fragile ego, to keeping meticulous accounts of who said what. He tapped telephones and offices, those of his wife, his ex-wife, his ministers, certain American businessmen, all the newspapers, and CMQ's Clavelito, whom he suspected of putting a curse on him. The 'Novel,' Batista called his daily log of wiretaps. He spent long hours every day listening to the Novel. Or reading it, if the wiretap was less sensitive and could be trusted to a secretary for transcription.

Though he'd sent for Rachel K, he became so involved in the Novel that night that he forgot she was there, sitting on a sofa near his desk. The euphoria of Prio's arrest consumed him. 'After that exciting news, I *must* listen to today's Novel developments,' he said, and eagerly slipped on a pair of headphones. Rachel K removed a small notebook and a pencil from her purse, to jot down brief notes. She was spying on Batista plainly and openly, as he spied on others with his elaborate contraptions.

Batista took notes and interjected comments, the reels of his recording equipment clicking with each forward revolution. He spoke loudly, the headphones muffling his ears to the volume of his own voice.

He preferred to listen to the Novel rather than to read it. And ideally to listen while it was 'hot from the oven,' which meant recent. The Novel was his obsession, and he loved talking about it. Reading it, he'd once told Rachel K, could sometimes lead to information that listening could not, because those phrases that had been uttered in a breathy or inconsequential manner, trailing off, or quickly added at the end of a conversation — they were right there, typed, and of equal importance.

The reels clicked forward, then stopped. Batista scribbled frantically with a pen.

'I knew it!' he said, and pressed rewind, then stop, then play.

He listened and nodded, making notations. 'You go right ahead. I'll see you here, for your 'special plan.'' He was talking to the voices coming through the headphones. 'I'll see you and raise you! Ambush *me?* You're already dead, bastard.'

Knows DR plan, Rachel K wrote quickly in her little notebook, while Batista was too engrossed to notice. The DR, or Directorio Revolucionario, was another insurgent group, who believed that storming the palace and assassinating the president was the most effective plan of action. Fidel and the M-26 were against it. Prio was for it. He gave money to the DR and to Fidel, increasing his chances by betting on two horses. Batista seemed thrilled at the discovery. The pen trembled in his hands. The Novel, Rachel K guessed, would be too boring for him to endure if it weren't for the masochistic promise of locating proof that he'd been betrayed. Like a jealous lover, he wanted confirmation of what he feared. The United

Fruit executive was always asking her about her other liaisons. The idea seemed to hurt him, and yet he pestered her for details. When Rachel K refused, he launched into his own lurid and elaborate descriptions, savoring yet disdaining his fantasies of her and other men, like a preacher savoring yet disdaining the sin of sodomy by saying 'sodomy' over and over again, as if the word itself might have some erotic effect. The executive's own repertoire consisted of two positions, missionary and laundress — which meant from behind. Rachel K disliked the laundress position, not because she wanted to look at him — she didn't — but because old men had pincers for hands, which reached around and clutched her in a brittle and insistent manner that she found unpleasant.

'You let two of these guys do you at once?' the executive asked her. 'They do you doggy-fashion? On all fours?'

She laughed at him and he laughed with her, certain that he was in on whatever was funny. Then he inevitably grew excited by the idea of these scenes, quit with the laughter, and ordered her to take off, as he called them, her drawers.

★ ★ ★

She'd fallen asleep on the couch in Batista's office by the time he finished with that day's Novel developments. He woke her but didn't gruffly escort her, as she assumed he would, to the secret chamber behind the bookshelves, furnished with a bed, Baltimore candy, and stacks of pornographic magazines.

He stood over her, distress creasing his face. She knew this crease, which grew more visible when he tried to suppress it.

'Who blackballed me,' he asked her, 'from the Yacht Club?'

He was upset about not being admitted to the right club.

'How would I know? As if I'm a member,' she said, unzipping him to end the conversation.

★ ★ ★

GOD AND BATISTA blazed in green neon letters from the roof of the palace.

That was new, La Mazière thought, looking up at the glowing message. And why not? Why not convert the palace to an evangelical casino, caboose your name to God's?

Rain was falling, and storm clouds had muted the afternoon sky. Reflections of the green neon and the red of automobile brake lights ran together and gleamed from the wet streets.

As he walked the Prado, he heard someone strumming an amorandola on one of the recessed benches, singing a song as he strummed.

'Bonanza bonanza, we'll all be rich! Bonanza bonanza, the sea is calm — '

La Mazière had been back in Havana two days, during which there were maybe thirteen blackouts, four movie theaters bombed, and a massive fire at the Shell refinery across the bay in Regla. Things had certainly progressed over the six months he'd been away.

The Prado's lamps flickered on. They were antiquated *papillons*, Parisian-style butterfly-shaped gaslights — a detail he hadn't noticed until now. 'Paris of the Tropics,' the hotel brochure announced under a map of the island. On the map, a drawing of a girl waist-deep in the warm waters of the gulf, an Amazon rising from the sea with a red gladiola behind her ear. On the Plaza de Armas, just like in Paris, one could purchase Obelisk and Olympia books, and obsolete French pornography — displayed right there in the bookstalls rather than sequestered in L'Enfer, on the top floor of the Bibliothèque Nationale. But the fragile pages, La Mazière had realized upon closer inspection, were speckled with mold, ruined from humidity. The door knockers at La Mazière's 'French-style' hotel had all turned green from salt air. And the enormous lobby mirror was blackening, its silvered tain oxidizing from constant moisture. Paris resituated to the tropics, with its humidity, deluges, and brine, was like a transplanted organ a body had begun to reject.

How he'd missed this blighted, ersatz 'Paris,' and he hadn't even realized it. But this is how it always was with La Mazière, even if he was in love with a city, as he'd been with Havana when he'd visited for the first time — the coup, the club, the girl. It was a marvelous city, but so was Caracas, and so was Dakar, Sidi Bel Abbès, and Ciudad Trujillo.

He had just made his routine triangle through the Caribbean, from the Dominican Republic to Haiti to Havana.

'Do you know why?' Duvalier, who was now president of Haiti, asked him on his stop in Port-au-Prince, a layer of rhetorical dust piling on the cryptic words like lint from a vacuum cleaner bag.

Duvalier reached up, his gaze ponderous and distant, and caressed the red and blue flag hanging from a pole in his office, its silk fabric billowing in the humid breeze coming through the iron bars of an open window.

'Do you know why the Haitian people love Papa Doc?'

La Mazière waited, understanding that the question was a pause for rhythm and not meant to be responded to.

'Because Papa Doc cured them,' Duvalier said.

They all referred to themselves this way, in the third person. As if their names were too grand to be contained by an 'I' or an image of an 'I.' Names that pointed to entities of which they, too, were merely humble subjects. 'Your Operative,' as Hemingway had said.

'The people crawled out of the hills and came into town walking like crabs, on the outsides of their feet. You see, the bottoms of their feet — ' Duvalier's voice broke, as if he were overcome with emotion. He cleared his throat and continued, his tone becoming angry. 'The bottoms of their feet were ravaged! So destroyed by yaws that they came out of the hills like crabs. Papa Doc healed their feet. Not with filthy magic. He did it with science.'

The people loved Papa Doc. And yet, as La

Mazière was there to inform him, an insurgent radio broadcast had been traced to somewhere within his own palace.

* * *

He turned from the Prado onto the oceanfront Malecón. Across the choppy bay, he could see the refinery fire in Regla burning greasily and unabated in the downpour. White-hot tongs of lightning spidered against the dark sky, followed by the sound of falling boulders. The rain surged harder. It gusted with such force it seemed to be eroding the medallions and scrolls on the buildings along the Malecón, as if their ornate facades were made not of sandstone but of a substance more like sugar, crumbly and solvent. La Mazière had no umbrella. Already soaked, he took his time, walking slowly, the rain dominating and releasing him.

A lone man turned from a side street onto the Malecón and walked behind him by a few paces. He and the man continued this way for several blocks, and La Mazière wondered if he were being followed. But then the man's heels ceased their clicking on the wet pavement. He must have ducked into a building. Perhaps La Mazière was just being paranoid. His meeting the night before with a bizarre character named El Extraño, a supposed contact for Prio's Directorio Revolucionario, had him spooked, though feeling spooked went with the territory of La Mazière's chosen life. Prio's insurgents were training in Miami, and Fidel Castro's in the

Dominican Republic — two groups that might at any moment turn against each other and against La Mazière, and both were being tracked by a third danger, Batista. There was Duvalier and the fomenting insurgency against him, with La Mazière in the middle, playing both sides. And President Trujillo in his self-named ciudad, with no idea that Cuban arms were being shipped from Miraflores Airport, on Trujillo's own commercial airline. The list went on. It was sometimes dizzying, arming various warring factions, feeling hunted by the mere sound of heels behind him on the pavement. But it was a life to which he was attached, a way to poke his finger into the more interesting but otherwise invisible folds of the cities he roamed.

La Mazière had met with El Extraño at a chicken-dinner-and-cockfight joint near the Havana airport, a place that proved even more vulgar than the concept had sounded. He sold El Extraño the reels of a French film on the planning of assassinations, warning that the film might be useful, but then again was a bit like reading a book to learn how to ski. The allusion had been lost on this Extraño, who seemed strangely unable to communicate by metaphor.

'I mean you don't just set off for the Alps,' La Mazière said, attempting to explain.

'I'm not going to the Alps,' El Extraño replied, eying La Mazière suspiciously. 'Who told you that?'

'I was speaking, you know, figuratively. I meant, you don't read a book about skiing and assume you're an expert skier. These things take practice. They require experience, planning, and caution.'

'This is Cuba, for fuck's sake. You see any snow? Nobody skis here.'

El Extraño's face shone, coated in sweat. All through dinner he'd jerked his head around every time someone shouted in victory from the cockfighting arena. Why so nervous? La Mazière wondered. Is this guy setting me up?

'What about the other stuff?' El Extraño asked. 'When and where?'

'You tell me what other stuff.' La Mazière kept his tone cool and even.

'You know.'

'If I know,' La Mazière said, suddenly tempted by his own weakness for petty word games, 'and you know that I know, then you know, too. So remind me: What do I know?'

'Goddamnit. What is this?' El Extraño said angrily. 'What the hell is going on here?'

'Perhaps you can tell me, because — '

'This meeting is over.' El Extraño stood up. 'You come back and talk to us when you mean business.'

Watching him weave among the tables toward the exit, La Mazière thought he better play it safe and meet with the rebels' arms procurement officer himself, even if it meant going all the way to Oriente Province.

For the sake of discretion he'd checked in to the Hotel Lincoln this visit, rather than the Nacional. As an added precaution he had the taxi driver take him from the chicken place to the Floridita, a few blocks from the Lincoln. The

Floridita would be full of Americans — it was Christmastime, high tourist season — and if any of El Extraño's people were tailing him, they would stand out.

Without at first realizing it, La Mazière chose a seat next to Hemingway. Within minutes, Hemingway turned and asked him to dance. It wasn't the first time. Hemingway never gave up asking, men and women both, as if the people at the Floridita were indistinguishable to him and he couldn't be bothered to take note of a minor detail such as gender. No one would ever dance with him. It was Hemingway's routine to ask, and a willing dance partner might have wrecked the cosmic balance of his serial life.

La Mazière was busy mulling the probability that El Extraño worked for Batista, and wondering who had set him up for such a trap. But Hemingway persisted in engaging him in conversation, launching into a muddled discourse on poetry and diplomats, La Mazière thinking that Hemingway should stick to the topics of humping and the use of 'I.' He seemed to miss the point about Saint-John Perse, who wasn't a mere foil to logic, sending oblique questions as diplomatic correspondence. Perse was from Guadeloupe, and his poems were filled with succulent memories of an idyllic childhood in the tropics, coco plums and the cool hands of yellow nurses, the smell of clay and violets, sour milk, and fresh butter. But what Hemingway quoted was no sultry rumination, but Perse's treatise on violence and loss, based on Xenophon's *Anabasis*, the story of ten thousand

Greek mercenaries hired by Persian barbarians — not for their civilized refinement, but for their gifted brutality at waging war. Mid-expedition, the mercenaries' Persian employer is killed. They are suddenly stripped of purpose, wandering deep in the core of an unknown land, outside of place, of law, torn away from their own selves. Trapped, with no leader and no adequate provisions, they are forced to go north, into the rugged and snow-covered mountains of Asia Minor. They survive on the principle of discipline alone, and must invent their own nomad laws, their own destiny, which, once invented, is the path they were meant to have taken. A route that cannot be found without the mercenaries first being lost. 'The sea! The sea!' the rearguard soldiers cry out as they near the end of their journey. They've risen to a rocky promontory, their shrieks so frantic and pitched that Xenophon, down below, assumes they are being massacred. But no, they have spotted a sliver of the ocean's chalk-blue bed rising up beyond jagged peaks, the water that will take them home.

Xenophon and his soldiers could not have been closer to La Mazière's heart. Their abandonment and discipline were his; their wandering, too.

Lost in the Russian steppes, where his Waffen regiment was pulverized and scattered and he became an animal, eating raw horseflesh and sleeping in the snow, he'd seen no sliver of home, only a landscape blanketed in whiteness and death. He'd won a 'frozen meat' medal, but he'd as soon eat actual frozen meat than fight Bolsheviks again. He understood painfully well that you couldn't re-create a moment of ignorance that preceded misery, a luminous winking bubble. Ten thousand soldiers setting off to make fortunes, or one man in his Citroën driving toward the Bavarian town of Wildflecken for elite Waffen officers' training, his papers stamped with a wet, inky swastika, a profound and electric violation of Frenchness. Confessing publicly, after the war, had meant coming to terms with the stark fact that his luminous winking bubble had floated in a tide of darkness. And yet he still yearned for a luminous bubble, for an impossible time of privilege and turmoil. All he could do was keep going until he found a bubble somewhere on the map.

Don't talk to me of Anabasis, he'd thought, sitting at the Floridita bar, if you're only going to quote the swaying of grass. He doubted Hemingway had any comprehension of the homeland that Perse and Xenophon both referred to, a crossroads of will and wandering where new enemies, new wars, new and unknown lands — Port-au-Prince, the streets of Havana, and maybe, now, the mountains of Oriente — were, in fact, the watery promise of home.

★ ★ ★

The rain let up, and wind was vacuuming out the last low, ragged clouds as La Mazière continued along the Malecón, looking back periodically to be sure no one was following him.

The moon appeared, glowing like a quartered orange section that had been ever so lightly sucked, its flat edge thinned and translucent.

He turned and headed up La Rampa, in the direction of the Tokio. He assumed she was still there, still in her zazou getup, her legs painted in prison chain-link, as smearable as when he'd last left his handprints on her soft and unathletic thighs, six months earlier.

The same bartender was working, his face in its same melancholy key, which reminded La Mazière of Chopin. Not Chopin's face, with the potato nose, but the preludes, lugubrious music for which he had a weakness.

He sat at the bar and ordered a pins 'n' needles, the blue, morphine-laced drink that had become his Tokio habit. The sweet, toothpasty flavor of the drink and the familiar smell of the Pam-Pam Room, ashtrays and liquor and tuberose oil, plunged him into the full atmospherics of sense memory, the nights he'd spent observing the girl and her zazou act, and eventually investigating for himself, only to discover that her odd combination of remoteness and availability went several layers deep. At times he'd suspected she was *only* layers, like an onion, and if he peeled them away, to get to some kernel, some essence or truth, he'd end up with just a pile of glossy, eye-stinging skins, an odor on his hands that was difficult to wash away. People said lemons, but the lemons never worked: a hand would smell of onions until it was finished smelling of onions.

She played indifferent, as he did, or as he was. But then again, she opened herself in a way that

291

was almost alarming. He'd felt it every time he'd been with her, this girl who would be, he was sure, no fun to spank. There'd be no threshold of resistance. That's how people like her win, he thought. By caring just that much less than whatever you ante as indifference.

He asked if the 'dancer from Paris' was working, which amused him, even if the irony was lost on the morose bartender.

'Tonight we have La Paloma,' the bartender said. 'She's very good, very nice. If you want to see La Francésa, come back tomorrow.'

I'm not disappointed, he thought, leaving the club. It's simply an annoyance, walking all the way here in the rain, trying to keep the gift, which was boxed and in a plastic bag, from getting wet. It was a child's size, but he suspected it would fit her, a batiste cotton dress that had reminded him, when he saw it in a shop window near Duvalier's palace in Port-au-Prince, of the tiny girls who ran under dogwood branches in the Bois de Boulogne, wearing frocks that were stiff and white like bonded paper.

Two men left the Tokio just after he did. As he walked, he thought he detected their presence behind him. He stopped on a corner a few blocks from Rachel K's apartment. He looked both ways, and at the street signs, pretending to be lost. When he glanced back, the two men were sitting on a bench, languidly smoking cigarettes as if they'd been there for hours.

He turned left, toward the Barrio Chino. From the corner of his eye, he watched the men hurriedly stub out their cigarettes.

The streets of the Barrio Chino were crowded now that it was no longer raining. He wove among the prostitutes and bags of rotting vegetable scraps from the chop suey houses, heat rising off the ripe pavement in gossamer waves of steam. The Barrio Chino was no pretend glamour, no pretend France. It was a marketplace of dour, pockmarked girls, and boys refashioned as girls.

'Hey, you,' one of the boy-girls said, and came close, walking alongside him. 'You're coming with me.' She hooked an arm smoothly through La Mazière's, encircling him in a musky cloud of perfume. They strolled together.

'You see, I'm just a dumb tourist looking to entertain myself,' La Mazière was telegraphing to the two Cubans who were so obviously trailing him. 'Just a dumb tourist looking to 'restore morale,' shall we say, in the Barrio Chino.'

'Where you taking me, honey?' the hooker asked him, her Adam's apple moving up and down, barely disguised under a satin neck ribbon.

'Just let me escort you.'

Despite her sashay, she exuded a virility that the perfume and heels couldn't conceal. Try to rip her off, he thought, and I bet she transforms into something more aggressive and male than I am.

'Go where I go,' he said, 'and I'll make it worth your while.'

'And I'll make it worth yours.' She looked him up and down approvingly. 'My while and your while will go perfect.'

Walking with her, it occurred to him that the male virility was not a mistake, a thing she'd accidentally left showing. It seemed, instead, an integral aspect of what made her hard to refuse. The Adam's apple, her wiry arms and willowy height, the louche appeal of caked mascara rimming huge, dewy eyes, with a shadow of dark stubble on her upper lip.

It wasn't his thing, but he understood that it was certainly someone's. Promising tits and ass and tuberose perfume, and at the same time covertly promising something else, but openly-covertly promising this something else. If she were perfectly covert and convincing as a female, what would be the point?

On his flight to Havana, La Mazière had met an Englishman who'd insisted that the male Kabuki who performed in drag were more feminine than any woman. 'I've just come from Japan,' the Englishman said. 'And if you could see these artists — the Onnagata, they're called — why, they make women, especially Western women, hardly seem like women at all.'

La Mazière doubted going to Japan would convince him that femininity was the art of walking in stilettos, that it had much to do with poise or surfaces, makeup and neck ribbons. Whatever female essence was, he had caught it only fleetingly, a thing women reflected when they were least aware. He couldn't have named this quality but suspected it had something to do with invisibility, a remainder whose very definition was predicated on his inability to see it. Like dust, a particle too fine for the sieve of

294

his comprehension. It occurred to him that the hooker posed an amusing solution to this problem, by covering feminine mystery in familiar layers: artifice, and also maleness. Underneath the layers lurked the promise of 'woman,' but the layers were a safety net, a guarantee of putting off getting to 'woman' — whatever she was. For those who didn't care to know, there were these sublime creatures in the Barrio Chino.

He and the girl jaywalked toward a theater offering LIVE EXTREME SEX, or advertising it. It isn't extreme if it happens for an audience, was La Mazière's feeling. Frosted bulbs ran in relay around the theater's sign like a circling electric tongue. In Paris this was called 'life show,' which seemed more poetic and terrible. As if what it promised was a glimpse of the secret reality that subtended all life, and to which all life could be reduced: two paid performers copulating on a square of linty, hot-pink carpeting.

'You're lovely,' he said, handing her a generous stack of bills. 'But I must run.'

Instead of entering the main theater, he darted up the wrong stairway, to be sure he'd shaken off the men following him.

He found himself in a hallway outside a large room, where three Chinese musicians were playing marvelously atonal music, or what he'd thought was atonal music, until he figured out they were tuning their instruments. They were diminutive men with kitty-cat faces, and there wasn't the slightest trace of sex in the room. The scene moved him, with its smell of rosin dust, the men producing whiny and plaintive strains in

295

this curious rehearsal space. A sign on the theater doors facing the street had announced *Gentlemen Only Please*.

Here they are, La Mazière thought, watching the three musicians play, sandwiched in a building between people viewing sex and people having it. *These* are the gentlemen.

★　★　★

Rachel K never knew where Fidel's underground would send her, or who she'd meet on these errands, and the mystery lent each task a certain surreal excitement. Fidel's Havana contacts sent her to Miramar, land of the American executives, to keep an Argentinian race-car driver company. They'd kidnapped him on the eve of the Cuban Grand Prix and were holding him hostage, no real purpose but attention, worldwide publicity for the rebel cause. Someone had brought in a television and offered to let him watch the race, but the Argentinian said he could not, that it would depress him to witness what he'd been strongly favored to win.

Sometimes she'd meet contacts who turned out to be aides from the palace, men she'd seen with Batista. She guessed that the president could have tracked their betrayal, found clues in the Novel, if he hadn't been so obsessed with those parts that were personal, the insults, social exclusions, and petty hierarchies. Batista was upset that the place-card seating for a dinner at Ambassador Smith's had situated his wife next to Madame Masigli, which he suspected was meant to emphasize how much more glamorous and refined Madame Masigli was, compared to the first lady. He worried that his barber disliked him, that his aides were cheating him at canasta, not that they were plotting his overthrow.

On one errand, Rachel K met with a professor from the now closed university. A gentle, older man who asked why they called her Zazou.

It was French, she said. Something from World War II. At which point he went to the shelf and pulled down a book, flipped through it, and read a passage, nodding. 'Yes, of course!' he said, delighted. 'They were dissidents — what a wonderful quotation you've chosen.' He was a lonely history professor. He invited her to sit, and began talking about wars and revolts and various European underground movements. He recited facts about the Zazou, reading from the book, their ethnic background, the yellow star, their work with the French Resistance, when they were deported, the Gypsy music to which their name referred, how they were linked to another group, a German equivalent called the White Rose. He went to the shelf and retrieved another book, offering to show her photographs, which is when she said she had to get going. He told her to visit anytime she wanted. 'We'll discuss history,' he said. 'Various codes and uniforms of protest and refusal.'

She appreciated the sound of 'White Rose,' two words dusted with something clandestine. But knowing the details of history would ruin things. It was the vague brightness of the word 'zazou' that she liked, a word and a few details:

paint-on stockings and grenadine with beer. White Rose, in her own mind, would be something other, surely, than what the professor had tried to explain: a flower made of wax, voluptuous and fragile. A German girl with short black hair and Japanese face powder. A mouth like a bloody stamp.

★ ★ ★

'Hello, mademoiselle.'

She feigned indifference, standing in the doorway to her little apartment. Not inviting him inside, or asking where he'd been the past few months. They both understood it was a form of affection.

La Mazière took her hand, put his lips to it, and kept them there in a protracted kiss.

Her legs were painted in crisscross diamonds. She wore a tight black dress and heels. 'You weren't on your way out, were you?' he asked.

It was her habit to be made up even when she was home alone, like having music on, a kind of ambience, the mirrors in her room responding that she was still herself, with or without a witness.

'No. I was waiting for an ambassador. I heard one was coming through, on his goodwill tour.' It surprised her how easy it was to slip back into these roles.

'My goodwill tour; yes, of course.'

★ ★ ★

The batiste cotton dress he'd brought her was a size too small, its capped sleeves squeezing her upper arms like blood pressure cuffs.

'I'm going to burst out of this.' She was laughing, twisting to emphasize how tight it was. 'I'm performing a ballet recital or something?'

'Just be still,' he said, and began tossing things off the bed — shoes, newspapers, piles of clothes, a long, auburn wig.

'You're still a messy little girl. That hasn't changed.'

'Had I known an ambassador would be dropping by, I would have tidied things up a bit.'

He stepped over the wig, which lay on the floor like the debris of some sort of domestic violence, picked her up — she hardly weighed anything at all — and tossed her on the bed.

'But anyway, tidying,' she continued, as he took off his jacket, his shoes, and set his tinted glasses on her nightstand, 'is for desperate people.'

'In fact, I prefer you messy,' he said, and tugged her downward by the legs so that her head was off the pillow and flush to the bed. 'It makes you seem vulnerable.'

The dress was thin cotton, a fine weave, cool and silky to the touch. Meant to be worn with a slip. Her body was faintly visible beneath it, the sheer white fabric with an underblush of flesh.

He pinned her down and proceeded with his pantomime, pretending he was taking something from her, a thing she was too fresh and young to understand, this girl in her white batiste dress. Underneath the dress, a body that was solicitous but vulnerable, laid out for his inverse ritual of passing through what was lewd to get to what was innocent, through inverse to get to verse. It was a cheap fantasy, and he hated his propensity to cheap fantasies, but he allowed them all the same.

★ ★ ★

Of course he was attractive. And he had the uncanny gift of making her feel as if time and everyone in its viscous grip were frozen, and only she and he were sentient and unfrozen. But on each visit he had paid her, at the club, or her apartment, she had been surprised to see him, having assumed he'd left the island for good.

He'd come and gone unpredictably for the past six years, since just after Batista took over. If he bothered to say good-bye, it was a canned charade, kissing her and proclaiming that he took his Little K wherever he went, that the version of her he carried along with him was just as real — 'more real,' he'd say. A refined essence to honor and elect as company, after the coarse materiality of their body-to-body conversation. A fine conversation, he'd amend. In fact he enjoyed conversing with her body immensely. But the two of them as entwined flesh was only one aspect of things, he'd declare, and the ethereal mingling that took place in her absence was another.

He seemed to have an arsenal of these performances. Not unlike her own performances, for which there were as many scripts and stages as

there were reasons and affects. The role of walking to buy milk, of dancing for the men at the
club, of giving the underground information — where
Batista would be, at what hour — and preempt-
ing meaning with a Frenchman by understanding
that there was none.

★ ★ ★

'How can I truly adore you, you and your body
both,' he said, 'if I don't allow them to marinate
properly in my imagination?'

They were saying their good-byes.

'I hate to go,' he said, 'and I hate that the
distance is so integral.'

'Oh, I hate it, too,' she could have replied in a
syrupy voice, playing along. But their game was
beginning to tire her.

'What you do mean, 'integral'?' she asked.
'Maybe you could just speak plainly. For once.'

'To love. Integral to love. There, I said it.' It
surprised him how easy it was. But easy, he
knew, because he was leaving. It was a tautology,
of course, that whatever he took or mistook for
love necessitated absence from the loved one.
But this circular reasoning had become like a
perfect wheel, motoring him here and there
among various realms of tomcatting and novelty.

She scoffed. 'Let's not devalue the term.'

'But I don't — '

'Darling, this isn't love,' she said in a
mock-consoling voice. 'And I don't buy your
pretend belief that it is. Unless you've managed
accidentally to seduce yourself. The hypnotist

who put himself under.' She snapped her fingers, to wake him from the spell.

Prio had insisted he loved her, but it was all part of his gloomy narcissism. One more injustice he was forced to endure. And there was the deluded United Fruit executive. 'I'm so sorry, dear, I just couldn't get away,' he'd say, as if he and she were anxious lovers finally able to continue with their tryst. She'd seen him a few days before, on his Christmas vacation with the family. He took photos from his wallet and handed them to her, his pincer hands slightly trembling. Two tow-headed sons and a handsome wife, the wholesome type of woman whose cosmetics kit probably consisted of a bar of Dove soap. 'Saw her on a road in Indiana and told myself here comes an angel,' he'd said. And in apologetic tones, 'Sooner or later, you needed to see these. No getting around reality. And I don't mean to make you feel bad, but this, what you and I have, it's got limits.' She liked to think he was perverse, showing her photos of his 'angel' to let her know that she herself was not one. Because the other explanation was that he was profoundly dumb.

'You're cynical,' La Mazière said to her, as if he'd suddenly realized it.

'And you're not?' She laughed.

'To the contrary. I believe that the briefest of interludes can be love.'

'You call it love because you don't pay me.'

But even paid transactions, La Mazière resisted saying, could be affairs of the heart. Where was the heart actually located, and who

302

could say what touched it? His own was impetuous and abstract, and many professional mistresses had touched it.

'Call it love if you want,' she said. 'I'll call it see-you-next-time. Perhaps you can bring me Dalida's autograph. Your little Miss Egypt.'

'Little' was not how he thought of Dalida, his sometimes girlfriend back in Paris. She was a major pain, a grand hysteric whose sudden pop stardom was now one more source of anguish in her absurdly tragic life. But occasionally she amused him.

'You know that I won't be seeing her, that I'll be right here, in your country. 'Your country' — how silly of me. I forget that my Miss K is French. Never mind her K name and that lovely Manouche face. Or maybe she's German Jewish, with those sensual lips.'

He pressed on her lower lip, which felt buoyant and soft and warm under the pad of his thumb.

'What a coincidence,' he said. 'You're French, and Dalida — did you know? — despite the Miss Egypt title, is Italian. Two European girls, both performers, both what they call 'exotics.' And yet you couldn't be more different. But surely you aren't jealous — '

'Oh, please. I was serious. I love that song 'Bambino.' They play it forty times a day. Or they did, before Batista shut down the radio station.'

'I'm going to pretend that you are jealous. Because the idea pleases me very much. My tough and unfeeling little K, lighting a candle in my absence. Perhaps shedding a tear.'

303

He traced his finger down the side of her face, the path of this imaginary tear.

'But I fool myself. To think my chilly Miss K will cry over me. A girl who has to sleep without blankets *to feel any warmth at all.*'

He looked at her steadily through the tinted glasses.

'And do you know what? I adore this chilliness. It's irresistible, just irresistible — '

He leaned in.

She let him kiss her.

Then she pushed him out the door and shut it.

16

Radio CMQ-AM 670
May 1, 1958 10:00 P.M.

(Café Pilon spot)

(Theme music, 'La Agua de Clavelito')

Good evening, brothers and sisters.

As some of you who tune in to my show are aware, our government has decided to crack down on hope. On healing. To limit, or perhaps eradicate, miracles. To fine and regulate those whose earnest claim is to facilitate in the name of dreams.

Should the people be barred from dreaming?

It's your choice, people of Cuba:

Am I, Clavelito, a man or a nerve wave?

A fraud without special powers? Or a magic vibration that can travel through the water and into your thoughts no matter who you are and where you are?

Which do you want me to be?

Call me a man, and the possibilities collapse.

17

D.L. Mazierre, with his small mouth and gray eyes, did not come to agitate in Nicaro. Three years had passed since Mr. Mackey posted the letter outside the nickel company offices. Everly never thought about him and his handsome looks anymore, though his photograph was still taped in the hallway. Mr. Mackey had added a second photo of him, wearing tinted glasses like the people in Stevie's movie magazines. But there were many other photographs outside the nickel plant offices — the Castro brothers: the older, freckled one; and the younger one with the Chinese face, pretty like a girl, with longish, feathery black hair.

Now Everly breezed down the hall to her father's office, passing photos of workers who had quit suspiciously with no notice, suspected agitators and rebel leaders, understanding that they weren't magic angels coming to transform her and everyone else. Into what, at age eleven, she hadn't been sure, but she'd expected D.L. Mazierre to try to contact her somehow. She'd imagined him waiting behind a tree as she walked home from school, stepping out quickly to tell her something. Or standing outside her open bedroom window and relaying his mysterious message — whatever it was — after everyone else was asleep. It was a child's fantasy that she no longer harbored.

Willy said the mine employees wanted fair wages, fair treatment, and that's what the rebels were promising. She herself had seen how the miners worked, seven days a week under the boiling sun, a labor boss with a gun in the shade of the only tree. The mine was a dirty secret that made the young and handsome men in the photos seem like heroes.

Mr. Mackey had said the rebels were bandits, an annoyance to nickel operations. But then his own son, Phillip, was caught helping the bandits, and the Mackeys panicked and sent him away. Mr. Stites's oldest son, Delmore, had run off to the mountains to join the cause. People talked about his disappearance vaguely — said he was 'in rebel territory' and not that he was a rebel — but everyone knew.

The agitators were getting bolder now. They torched thousands of acres of United Fruit sugarcane, a fire that coated Nicaro with cane ash and blackened the sky for days. They tried to sabotage the rail lines that ran from the mine, trundling nickel ore down to town for processing. Mr. Mackey said the rebels would be subdued and that the company must play its part. Anyone remotely suspicious was arrested and handed over to the Rural Guard. Everything had changed.

Like the new Cuban guard at their Friday night double feature, *Fuzzy Pink Nightgown* and *The Big Boodle*. The new guard wore a holstered gun and a machete — a guampara, Willy called it. He stood stiffly by the theater entrance and didn't sit down once, not even during intermission. The Nicaro theater was outdoors, a low wall and a screen with folding chairs. Rain began to fall steadily during the second film. George and Marjorie Lederer got up to leave and said Everly and Stevie could stay if they were nutty enough to sit through a movie in the rain. Everly decided she was nutty enough. She munched rain-dampened popcorn and spied periodically on the smoochers in the back row, Pamela and Luís Galindez, and Stevie and Tico Leál. Luís Galindez held Pamela's hand and fawned over her the same way Tico fawned over Stevie. Stevie and Pamela both went to Cuban dances and wore their socks rolled down and their hair teased up in the front the way the Cuban girls did. Stevie drew a fake beauty mark on her chin with an eyebrow pencil. She learned the pachanga and danced it with Tico, though neither of them were as good at it as Willy. Willy's pachanga was the real one, everyone else's just a watered-down imitation. The Lederers worried that Stevie was becoming too Cubanized — that was one thing. Dating a Cuban was beyond what they'd imagined. When Marjorie Lederer found out, she was furious. How could this have gone on, right under her nose, for *three whole years?* Everly's mother wanted to have Tico fired from the nickel plant. Fired *immediately*, she said. George Lederer refused. He said Tico Leál was one of Gonzalez's hires, and it would stir up too much trouble the way things were now. They were all nervous about Lito Gonzalez. Mr. Mackey thought he was working with the rebels, cutting secret deals.

308

'So you're firing me, instead!' Stevie shrieked. They were sending her back to the States. In two days she'd be getting on a bus for Havana, then flying to Miami, where the Vanderveers would pick her up and drive her to an all-girls boarding school in Tennessee. 'Te quiero,' Duffy kept repeating, imitating Stevie. 'Te quiero, Tico. Mucho mucho,' and then she made kissing noises. But it wasn't funny anymore. 'Duffy, shut up!' Stevie shouted. 'She's just a child,' their mother said. 'Leave her alone.' Duffy cried and burrowed against their mother. But when she turned her head to the side, still sniffling, Marjorie Lederer rubbing her back, she looked not just comforted but also satisfied.

Luís Galindez and Pamela vacated the back row, to continue their smooching someplace else. Would the Carringtons send Pamela away for dating a Cuban? Everly didn't know where there was to send her back to. They were American, but they'd never lived in America. And Mrs. Carrington didn't seem to care what Pamela did. It was mostly Val who was upset. The romance with Luís was all she talked about now, as if Pamela had betrayed her. Maybe it was like that with twins — they had to share everything, including choice in boyfriends.

Everyone left the theater but Everly, Stevie, Tico Leál, and the new armed guard at the entrance, who stood stiffly and didn't watch the film. It boggled her that someone could patiently stand in the rain and let the time pass with nothing to wrap his mind around. But maybe patience, she thought, didn't mean being

309

unbothered by waiting and boredom, but the opposite: that patient people were exceptionally bothered. Perhaps the guard was able to let his mind bump and drift like a blank white cloud because he'd given up believing that distracting himself was of any use. She suspected that patient people understood the horror of boredom best of all, and thought it was hopeless to pretend there was some way to make it bearable. Which meant patience was actually hopelessness. And impatience, a kind of hope — making the effort to fill time with something, by turning your head to watch the movie, for instance. The guard did not turn to see the film. He confronted his waiting head-on, patient and hopeless, rivulets of water running down the sides of his face.

★   ★   ★

'You're almost fourteen, and it's time you quit hiding behind this tomboy act and let everyone know you're a young lady.'

Stevie was gone, and now it was Everly's job to be the eldest daughter, the young lady. 'I gave her a Seconal and put her on the overnight coach to Havana,' her mother repeated in every phone conversation about Stevie. 'It's for the best.'

Everly was going to a pool party for K.C. Stites's fourteenth birthday, and the other kids would be in shorts and pullovers and tennis shoes. Her mother wanted her to wear a dress. Everly didn't have the heart to explain that it only emphasized their own lower social status to go fancy and formal to a pool party. People with something to prove went fancy, and those with nothing to prove let their kids wear whatever they wanted. Pullovers and shorts. But because it would please her mother, she put on the stiff white kitten-heeled patent leather shoes, which dug into her feet and made them bleed, and carried the matching purse, although she couldn't think of anything to put in it.

How can these things let everyone know I'm a young lady, she wondered, if they seem so unlike me? But maybe they were her, she thought, and she just didn't know it. If she'd never seen a mirror, she wouldn't recognize herself in one and would have to learn what she looked like. Without a mirror she'd be as blind to herself as the eyes on Mrs. LaDue's peacocks, which weren't really eyes, just blue-black blots. Mrs. LaDue treated the peacocks better than she treated Poncho. 'Poncho needs discipline,' Mrs. LaDue said. 'He's an unruly child.' Everly doubted that a grown monkey had the character of a child. Poncho had taken to spitting at Mr. LaDue, and now they wanted to get rid of him. No takers yet, despite the four-season wardrobe with accessories — belts, ties, hats, socks, and shoes, even monogrammed handkerchiefs — that Mrs. LaDue was offering complimentary to whomever might be willing to adopt Poncho. Everly put on the dress and kitten heels and hoped they would have the same effect as learning what she looked like in a mirror. Her mother said she looked just darling, that she was

311

starting to fill out and come into her own. Later, after they'd moved back to Tennessee, Everly was elected May Queen and her mother said she wasn't a bit surprised. But her mother *was* surprised, which was why she insisted on denying it. She'd always said that redheads were not conventional beauties, but an 'acquired taste.' So I'm like aspic, Everly thought.

She'd had a dream about a woman who walked through a room wearing nothing, just a towel held up to her front. *What a lovely way to assert yourself* was her dream sentiment, watching the woman stride through the room, her backside bare. When she woke up, it still seemed lovely, even if it was a nonsense dream. Maybe the dreams she had about going to school in her underwear — everyone had them — were not about anxiety, but about wanting to be naked, and in front of everyone.

The day of K.C.'s party, there was a get-together for the adults as well, at the Pan-American Club. A matinee, the people in Preston called daytime parties. Everly's father was tired from working all week and didn't want to go, but her mother said he should do more hobnobbing. And that he should wear a bracer.

'Dear, I'm not wearing a girdle,' her father said. 'It's ridiculous. Men wearing girdles.'

'It's not a girdle,' her mother said. 'It's a *bracer*.'

Her mother had ordered it from the Sears in Havana. George Lederer's reduction diet wasn't working, so they'd fired Flozilla, whose cooking was too fattening. Before she came to Nicaro,

312

Flozilla had been a cook for Batista's brother over in Banes. Batista was overweight. You could see his belly when he appeared on television. Marjorie Lederer was convinced that the president's belly was connected to Flozilla's cooking and that Flozilla made people fat.

Everly didn't miss Flozilla, who had been nice sometimes and mean other times. Like when she told Duffy, who believed her, that the ñáñigos would get them when they were sleeping, and boil them down.

'Why?' Duffy asked, beginning to panic.

'To get a powder,' Flozilla said. 'Boil you down and extract it. A special powder they need from white children's bodies.'

Everly pictured translucent grains, like uncooked rice, in the paper fold of an envelope.

When Duffy caught a fever, Flozilla said white children got sick because they weren't hardy. 'If you grow up in the bush,' Flozilla said, 'eat guava, go barefoot, bathe in the river, you strong. Strong enough to fight off a fever. But you not strong,' she told Duffy, who shivered under a pile of blankets. 'You weak. And you sick with a fever.'

They still hadn't found the right cook. One of the women who came to interview had good credentials, her mother said, but she was an albino. Everly's mother said a Negroid albino was the saddest thing in the whole world. Too sad to have in the house, although she'd been pleasant enough. Nothing sadder, her mother said, than a Negroid albino.

Their laundress had been cooking, filling in

until they could hire someone new. But she knew laundry and not cooking and burned everything. Everly had started going to the club after school, filling up on cheese and crackers the bartender gave her. Gouda cheese and saltine crackers, on a plate she'd carry over to the little library in the corner, where she sat in one of the club chairs and looked for the hundredth time at the books on the shelves, all donated by the U.S. government. They were mostly biographies. *The Life and Leadership of Rafael Trujillo, President of the Dominican Republic*. A painting someone had done of Trujillo decorated the inside cover. Under the image was the mysterious caption 'Photograph of His Benefactor by R.R. Martinez.' *The Life and Fortune of James D. Dole, Pineapple King*. Everly had read it twice. James D. Dole had married Mrs. Belle Dickey of Honolulu and made enormous profits once he figured out how to can pineapple. 'After they began canning the fruit,' the author said, 'the life of James D. and Mrs. Belle Dole was one long, sweet song.'

One sweet song. Like canning syrup. How dull, a life that was only one song.

★　★　★

The servants had built an elaborate sunshade of palm fronds on the patio of the Preston pool. They'd hung Chinese paper lanterns from the sunshade, pink and yellow and baby blue, which bobbed in the wind. One long table was decorated with bunting and streamers, with a

314

place card at each table setting. 'You're right here, dear,' Mrs. Stites said to Everly, patting the seat next to hers, 'between me and K.C.' Mrs. Stites leaned close, close enough that Everly could smell her flowery scent. She said she was glad Everly was there to celebrate with them and that it hadn't been an easy time. With Del gone and everything so — she sighed — *unsure*. Her eyes welled with tears. 'Anyway,' she said, retrieving a handkerchief, smiling weakly and blotting the tears, 'I'm so glad you're here, Everly. And you look lovely. Doesn't she look lovely, K.C.?'

K.C. was just sitting down. He looked at Everly, at the white handbag in her lap, and said yes, she sure did look lovely. He said it carefully, like he was speaking to Everly and not to his mother. Everly's face went hot.

When the party was over, K.C. insisted on escorting her to the dock. The other Nicaro kids were walking in front of them. They were near the seawall when he stopped her. He said he had something to give her, that it was private and he didn't want to give it to her in front of the others. They could hear people drifting out of the Pan-American Club, which was right next to where the Nicaro yacht was anchored. Mrs. Billings's high-pitched voice. 'No, really, I mean it. *That's* what he said! I swear to you — you can't *make* these things up.' K.C. reached into his pocket, retrieved something, and placed it in Everly's hand. It was smooth and metal, a mechanical part to something. It took her a minute to figure out what it was: a gold faucet handle.

'From the water closet,' he said, 'in Daddy's Pullman car. I stole it when I was little, on one of our trips to Havana. It might seem like a crazy gift, but I've hung on to it all these years. Now they've destroyed Daddy's Pullman car, and it's all that's left.'

He was looking at her, and she wished he wouldn't. That he would just give her a minute to absorb what was happening.

'You know that Mother has always liked you, Everly. She thinks you're something special. Anyway, this little object means a lot to me, and I wanted you to have it.'

Everly thanked him and put the handle in the purse her mother had wanted her to carry, which now held one thing. K.C. was a golden boy, had all the confidence in the world. Girls were always declaring crushes on him. He was good at sports. Did well in school. His father ran the entire town and yet he wasn't spoiled, always good-natured and loved to show people around and tell them about the sugar operation and how it was run. 'We' and 'ours' and 'the company,' he'd say, proud of everything. He should have wanted to date a blond tennis star from Ruston Academy in Havana, one of those girls with tan arms and charm bracelets, a jaunty ponytail with a scarf looped around it. The kind of ladylike girl Everly's mother nagged her to be, and that she wasn't.

Something about that day, giving in to the kitten heels, the dress, and the attention from K.C., changed her. She didn't mind the attention. It didn't embarrass her the way it

316

would have even the year before, when she'd squealed with horror at Stevie's suggestion that she go to the movies with Tico Leál's younger brother. In fact, attention from boys was okay. Nice, even. A redhead was an acquired taste. Not conventionally attractive. She'd been told this her whole life. Maybe it was to her advantage, because it meant she wouldn't attract boys who wanted conventional.

If K.C. liked her, there must have been something to like. What about Willy? she wondered. If K.C. saw something, what about Willy? 'Thank you K.C,' she imagined herself saying, 'but I can't accept this. Because I'm spoken for.'

* * *

The Americans said the guards in Nicaro, the new guard at the movie theater, the guard patrolling the managers' row, made them nervous.

'Thugs,' Mrs. Billings said.

'You know Batista let some of them out of prison. Murderers and rapists keeping the peace.'

'Charming. Just charming.'

'I mean, is this really *necessary?*'

Because they'd all complained, there'd been no guard on the boat to Preston that day, and no guard on the boat home.

As they approached Nicaro, Everly could see people standing along the dock, as if waiting for them.

'What's going on?' Mr. Mackey asked.

Behind the people were cars and jeeps parked at angles. Vehicles were not normally allowed on

317

the dock, unless they were authorized to unload supplies.

'That looks like our Studebaker!' Everly's mother said. Dusk was descending and it was difficult to see the color, but it did look like their car, dark green, with the bullet nose, parked next to some sort of tractor with a curious metal structure built onto it, and guns pointing out.

As the boat got closer, they saw that the people were Cuban rebels. They wore army fatigues and berets, and M-26 armbands. They smiled broadly and waved at the Americans like a curious greeting committee. They did not look scary or menacing, although some of them had guns. They looked like people who were just back from a very long camping trip, dirty and tired but happy. Everly scanned them as the boat pulled up to the dock, hoping to identify some of them from the pictures at the nickel company offices. She looked for D.L. Mazierre. He didn't seem to be among them, though one did resemble a photo from the offices. He had a soft smile and dark, pretty eyes, his beret cocked sideways. It was Raúl Castro. He smiled and helped Everly out of the boat. He called her 'linda,' and retrieved two M-26 armbands from a jeep and gave one to her and one to Duffy.

A rebel who spoke English explained that the American men would go with them into the mountains but that no one would be harmed. It was simply 'procedural,' and there was no reason for alarm. They thanked the Americans for being so cooperative and apologized for having to take the men, promising again, as they directed them

318

at gunpoint into the vehicles, that no harm would come to them. Everly's father was led into the backseat of his own car, which a rebel started by opening the hood and touching two wires together. Her mother watched, tears streaming down her cheeks. 'I really think they mean it,' Everly said, trying to console her. 'Mean what?' 'That they won't hurt them.'

After they'd left, Mrs. Billings screamed that it was an outrage. Ambassador Smith would be equally outraged, and she was going to telephone him immediately. Two days later, someone from the ambassador's office finally contacted her and said the ambassador didn't see what the wives in Nicaro wanted him to do. What could he do? Mrs. Carrington called the consul general in Santiago, whom she'd known from the U.S. embassy in La Paz, Bolivia. He arranged a mission up to the camp, to negotiate with the rebels. Eventually Fidel Castro called for the Americans' release.

* * *

Her father said he'd enjoyed himself immensely during his three weeks in the mountains. They were good people, fighting for a reasonable cause, and had treated him well. Too well, he said, patting his belly. He and the other Americans had eaten delicious food that the local guajiros brought into the camp every day. Three meals a day, without fail. Roast pig. Fried plantains. Arroz con pollo. Picadillo. Coconut cakes. All washed down with prú, a homemade herb drink, her

319

father explained. Or sometimes beer, which the rebels went to great lengths to acquire for them, and then cleverly kept cold in a stream.

The guajiros up there were clearly rooting for the Castro boys, her father said, and you couldn't help but sympathize. He'd slept on a mattress and eaten like a king and dipped his feet in the cool stream where they kept the beer supply. It was excessive and terrible, he said, what Batista's people had gone and done in Levisa. The Rural Guard burned it to a smoldering, flattened wasteland as retribution. Thousands of people were homeless. Others, who hadn't been able to escape, were killed in the fire. Retribution for what? her father asked, pointing out that even Mr. Mackey had a ball, though Mackey would never admit it. Too busy insisting that Raúl was practicing Marxism out of books. Mr. Mackey drafted letters to the State Department, warning them that the rebels in the hills were Communists. No one, Mr. Mackey complained, seemed interested. The other Americans, including Everly's father, mooned around talking about Raúl's future wedding to his aide-de-camp, Vilma Espín, which they'd all been invited to attend, to be held in Santiago sometime after the triumph. 'You're hoping for a revolution, so you can go to a wedding?' Marjorie Lederer asked him. The question seemed to stump George Lederer, who shrugged and said nothing.

* * *

Willy was living in a navy barracks now, on a special ship sent to house the servants and mine employees after Levisa burned. He told Everly that no one got on the ship without proper ID. Guards roamed the bunks all night long with flashlights, waking people up and shining lights in their faces, demanding to see their papers. He said the guards barely let you close your eyes in there, and when he finally did manage to drift off, rats nibbled on his toes.

George Lederer had gotten Willy a job in the nickel plant. He said Willy was a quick study and that he could learn metallurgy. Willy had pointed out that the locks on the company boats got ruined because they were brass on the outside and iron on the inside. Her father told the story over and over, marveling that Willy knew something about metal. Her father wanted to train Willy as a technician, said he was trustworthy and no troublemaker. But he got resistance, as he put it, 'from on high.' Willy was given a job, but Mr. Mackey arranged for him to work in the furnace room, where he'd get zero technical training, her father said sadly. 'They'll promote you eventually,' he told Willy, 'I promise.' On the weekends, Willy still came to work for the Lederers. 'Why are you up so early? It's Saturday,' Willy asked Everly. She wanted to be near him every hour he was there.

Willy said the furnace room was hot, very hot. But he was thankful to go to the plant. It was safer to be near the Americans. 'Safer than what?' she asked. 'Than being out and about,' he said, 'where you might find trouble.' 'You mean like with rebels?' 'I don't know anything about that,' he said, not looking at her. She suspected he was lying. Why would he lie? Because she was an American, and worse, the daughter of a nickel plant manager who didn't protest his assignment to the furnace room. She wished Willy hadn't lied. She wanted him to confide in her. It was selfish but she couldn't help it, just as she couldn't help disliking the idea of him dancing at the Club Maceo, Willy off, and working for no one but Willy.

Mr. Bloussé and Willy were not father and son. She didn't know what they were. Willy was what Mr. Bloussé had ended up with, a six-year-old boy. If Mr. Bloussé didn't think of him as a son or treat him like a son, he must not have wanted one. And yet he'd wanted Willy, gone and taken him after his visit with Willy's father. Everly imagined that Mr. Bloussé had become attached. Willy was a magnet, and Mr. Bloussé got to have him all to himself. She, too, wanted him to herself. Willy with no time off, no time away from the Lederer house, and no secrets. No Club Maceo. I'm a sick and monstrous person, she thought. She wanted him to be free and constrained at the same time. She wouldn't have wished this contradiction of wants on anyone, not even herself.

Five years now Willy had worked for the Lederers. Planted them the most exquisite garden in Nicaro, Everly's own night-blooming cereus, which would open one night, deep into the abstract future. When she was younger, he'd taught her the names of all the flowers and trees, taught her to fish with a hand line, how to make cashew wine and juice from guanabana, taught her words in Spanish and French. As she got older, he'd explained the basics of Cuban politics, the basics of labor politics. But her world and his were no closer. They were farther apart. She was dressed up in her mother's Jane Powell fantasy, and returning from a golden boy's birthday affair. Willy slept in a navy barracks where an armed guard patrolled the rows and rats bit his feet. Like all colored people in Nicaro, he was scared and cautious, and he lied to her like any colored person would lie to any white.

For five years he'd danced with a broom in the Lederers' kitchen. And once at Las Palmas. Put a coin in the jukebox and played 'La Pachanga' when no one was around to tell him Negros weren't allowed in the club. It was a show for Everly. Willy with his warm, broad smile, his graceful form, dancing with a broom. An unspoken secret that the broom was Everly, it was Everly he twirled around and dipped low.

'Thank you, K.C.,' she had said, as she'd put the gold flush handle from Mr. Stites's private Pullman car into her purse. *Thank you, but I'm spoken for.*

It was about as naive as thinking it's a lovely gesture to walk through town naked.

18

He lay under the tarp, exhausted, vaguely hungry, vaguely horny.

Women floated past, and he reviewed them one by one. Because he had access to none at the moment, he could choose any he desired. It was a fantasy, and the only obstacle to fantasy was his own mind, sometimes noncompliant.

She was almost like the German girls he'd met on his Rhineland travels, La Mazière thought when he got to Rachel K. Cold and unapologetic, these girls who used up all the hot water, didn't cry, ate their share of a meal. Rachel K never said thank you, a sensible etiquette he'd also witnessed in SS officers at the elite Waffen officers' camp of Wildflecken, where he'd trained after his enlistment. It charmed him to no end, the idea that what you needed was simply given to you, a deserved reapportioning that gratitude would only demean.

But underneath his pleasure at her frosty manner, La Mazière found himself wishing Rachel K had expressed a bit more regret at his departure. A sweep through his past, and half the women were clinging and crying. Even the baker's daughter who kept a hideous lolloping rabbit in a cage next to the bed, a girl with an exterior like the thick hard crust of bauernbrot, or a stale kaiser roll, had begged him not to leave when it was time for him to report to

Wildflecken. Rachel K had shoved him out the door, shut and latched it. He'd stood in the hallway feeling slightly stunned, until he decided he didn't care and needed to return to his hotel and pack in order to leave Havana by dawn, before Extraño's goons, or someone else's, caught up to him. But in that instant, he'd stood and listened, trying to discern her movements from inside. Footsteps, things set here and there, water running, a match struck against emery, the poof of a gas flame, a pot set over it as if she were making coffee. The sounds told him that her life continued with the door shut against him, and would continue after he was gone.

Rain hammered the tarp above him, which sagged under the weight of water rapidly pooling in its middle, threatening to douse his already damp bedroll. He reached his hand up and pushed, bowing the plastic tarp. Water ran off it. A moment later, he felt the cold water soaking into the ground beneath him. He closed his eyes and wished himself elsewhere.

Nothing like a wet bedroll to make a man long for a dry and comfortable place to sleep. He thought of his suite at the Hotel Lincoln, but this image led him to her again, shoving him out the door, and to what came next — the spooky figure sitting in the hotel lobby as he had checked out at 4:00 A.M., a gentleman in dark sunglasses, his face pitted with acne scars — why did they always have acne scars? — no doubt waiting for La Mazière. He asked the concierge to call him a taxi, then said he had to run back upstairs where he'd forgotten something, and

325

instead went down to the basement. He exited through a fire door behind the hotel's laundry room and skulked alleys to the rental car facility five blocks away.

Forget the Hotel Lincoln, he thought as he again pushed water off his tarp. 'It is an indignity to be chased around from hotel to hotel,' the little maharaja had said to him one evening at the Nacional lobby bar, after La Mazière suggested that the maharaja could get himself to Monte Carlo, where he wanted to relocate, without proper authorization, rather than wait for the visa the government of Monaco was reluctant to issue him. 'Some people make a life,' La Mazière had responded, 'of being chased from place to place.' Still, the maharaja was right. It was an indignity.

He thought of his Paris apartment, in the Seventh Arrondissement. Its closets filled with naphthalene-redolent suits, fresh from the cleaners and protected in sheaths of filmy plastic, waiting patiently on cedar hangers. Which lucky one would he choose? This is a fantasy — he can select whichever he wants. Dark blue, made in Hong Kong, a fine summer wool. Just out of the bath, clean-shaven, hair with a daub of pomade, he removes the suit from its plastic and puts it on. Takes it for a walk down the Boulevard Saint-Germain.

He parks himself at the Café de Flore, an outside table. Orders herring. A Pernod. Observes the girls. One, with her hair swept up in a patterned scarf, a lovely neck, Mediterranean skin, modestly curvy, good waist-to-hips ratio, and elegant

326

hands. She's pretending to read a book. He offers her a cigarette. Leans over with a lit match, breathing her perfume, then ignores her for a measured spell. He watches Sartre, sitting at a nearby table with his notebook, his eyes leering off in two different directions, the equivalent of looking at nothing. Sartre is with a couple of attractive women. He always is, despite his ugliness — or maybe because of it, some unique method of compensating for ugliness by being the first to declare it. La Mazière reads through the stack of newspapers he's purchased at the kiosk on his way down the Saint-Germain, *Le Figaro, Le Monde, Rivarol*. Looks up, and what does he know? The girl with the elegant hands has moved to his table.

He and she catch a matinee. It's his habit to go to matinees whenever he's in Paris. After the matinee they attend another 'matinee,' at his place.

As she dozes or pretends to, he gets up from the bed. Naked, he opens his windows to the fresh air, the sounds of rush-hour Paris. The sun is setting. There are a few high clouds now, fanning out and tinged in pink like quilt batting soaked in punch. Such mild weather. Hohenzollern weather, the officers at Wildflecken would have called it. The gauzy white curtains blow in, then get sucked out the windows and flap around. Announcing in their gauzy wind flap — what? That the gentleman standing nude at the window of 5B has just fulfilled a handful of duties that his noble heritage allows, and even requires. Walking a well-tailored suit down the Saint-Germain, drinking, smoking, lurking, and bedding working-class girls from the Café de Flore, who are always soft and amenable.

But if his noble heritage ordains that he seek softness, he is also, and often, a man who sees a dirty hole in the ground and has to put his hand in it.

★ ★ ★

'Your tarp, señor,' a rebel said when La Mazière arrived in the mountain camp, handing him the moldy shower curtain.

It still had the plastic loops meant for a pole mounted on a bathroom wall. He threaded a length of twine through the loops and propped the thing as best he could between two bushes. He slept on a hopscotch of sugar sacks under his open-sided 'tent,' which barely protected him from incredible volumes of rain.

Though he had never planned on staying, he'd done the right thing by going to Oriente. His suspicions about El Extraño, sweat-shiny as a greased pig, had been correct. El Extraño had taken the film reels La Mazière had given him, instructions for killing Batista, directly to the president. Prio's men stormed the palace and found it stuffed with waiting SIM — the secret police — who ambushed, killing every last attacker, thirty men in all. Now they were attempting to snuff out Prio's Directo-rio Revolucionario, and everyone remotely involved. Had La Mazière not left Havana when he did, the SIM would have picked him up. He'd saved his own life by departing, and for a destination

328

that was untraceable. He'd rented a car under the name Chris Person and set out on the Carretera Central with an unfolded Esso map flapping around on the passenger seat.

In Palma Soriano, a small town deep in Oriente Province, where the temperature was a good fifteen degrees hotter than in Havana, the sky somehow lower, the sun closer, the air so heavy with moisture it was more fish tank than greenhouse, he returned the car and waited at a dingy stucco motel for his pickup contact. He paid for a room, showered, and went to sit in the shade of the motel patio, which aproned a swimming pool ringed in algae. To his surprise, there was a group of people clustered on the far side of the pool. From the front, the motel reeked of lethargy and desertion. He hadn't heard any voices from his room and figured there were likely few if any other guests. The group was absolutely silent, hovering in a semicircle around a camera on a tripod. It was aimed at two men dressed like Cuban rebels in army fatigues and M-26 armbands, except they looked possibly American, pale and clean-shaven. A microphone dangled above their heads. Nearby, a young blonde sat on an aluminum patio chair, having makeup applied.

'Cut!' someone yelled.

He wouldn't have expected to encounter Americans, or film crews, this deep in rebel country, at the foothills of the Sierra Maestra, which rose dramatically just beyond town, checkpoints and road-blocks at every turnoff. The man who'd yelled 'Cut!' waved to La Mazière.

'Come on over,' he called, 'if you insist on watching. My only rule is absolute quiet while we're filming.'

The man introduced himself, pronouncing his own name grandly, as if it would explain everything. It didn't, and La Mazière immediately forgot it.

'I'm an actor,' he said, when he saw the lack of recognition on La Mazière's face. 'A film of mine, *The Big Boodle*, is currently playing at theaters all over the island. Though I don't recommend you see it.'

'Oh, no?'

'It isn't a good film. And the theaters have all been bombed. Though perhaps a violent interruption of that sort might have improved the plot.'

Her makeup complete, the blonde walked toward them. She was spry and leggy and didn't seem much more than eleven or twelve years old. Her lips were painted trollop red. Her hair was teased up into a whipped confection, a giant meringue reaching for the stars, with pin curls like inverted question marks swooping down over her ears. And she wore the shortest shorts La Mazière had ever seen. As she bent over to tie her shoe in a manner that seemed oddly solicitous for a child, the shorts crept up to reveal quite a bit of slender, well-formed buttock.

'This is Woodsie,' the actor said.

She cracked her gum and nervously touched her hair in the manner women did when they'd just had something new and unfamiliar done to it at the salon.

'What sort of thing are you shooting?' La

Mazière asked, watching the girl.

'A motion picture,' the actor said, 'about the revolution. About these brave young people fighting for their freedom, and the women who are assisting them.'

The actor seemed unable to speak without using an absurd Dictaphone voice, as if everything he said were being recorded for posterity.

'The film is called *Assault of the Rebel Girls*. I wrote it myself. Originally, I planned to use actual rebel girls, but they weren't quite, shall we say, Hollywood material. So I cast Woodsie.'

'I'm the lead,' the girl said, fingering one of her pin curls. 'Daddy says I'll be a star. They're going to know me in Hollywood. All over the place.'

'Your father?'

'Oh, please!' She jabbed La Mazière lightly in the rib cage. 'My *real* father wouldn't make me a star. My real father wouldn't buy me a pair of shoelaces!'

'We planned on using documentary footage,' the actor said, 'but our cameraman had problems. A fire melted some of his equipment, and so we've set up our own rebel theater here in Palma Soriano. Restaging things, see, after the fact.'

'After the fact? But the war is not over,' La Mazière said. 'It's far from over.'

'Yes, that's true, and this is part of what has made our project so interesting. More of an art film, really. I'm thinking we'll take it to Cannes. It's fiction, a faked version of a real war, and yet.

And yet. It is taking place *amid* the real war, against it, as its own fictional backdrop. A war it depicts, against this very war. Yesterday a grenade bounced into our film set, and we all had to duck for cover. I have a rash. Manchineel bushes. Terrible itching, which has spread to certain places . . . very unpleasant, I assure you. Woodsie has a flesh wound.'

The girl swung her long, tan leg up and held it in the air for La Mazière to inspect. A gauze bandage was taped around her calf, blood soaking through its crisscross weave.

'We've thrust ourselves in war's midst,' the actor said, 'And only if you've been through it as we have, can you understand the terror of the hunted — '

A film hand interrupted, informing the actor that there was a problem with their microphone. They would have to reconvene later in the day.

'Woodsie, dear, you go to the room and take a nap,' the actor said. 'I'll have someone fetch you when it's time for your scene.'

She turned to La Mazière. 'Nice meeting you,' she said, and cracked her gum for punctuation.

The actor sighed and shook his head as he and La Mazière watched her skip off.

'Young people need all the sleep they can get,' he said. 'Ten, twelve hours a night. The heart at that age — it's still growing.'

He paused, as if lost in thought, and then added, in a voice more intimate and wistful than Dictaphone, 'My Woodsie's heart has quite a bit of growing to do. I don't know what sort of thing you go in for, my friend, but children can be terribly cruel. I've spent many a night mending my bruised and oversized heart with whatever I can find. My Woodsie gives radiant joy, but then she takes it away.'

The actor offered to buy him a drink. A daiquiri, he said, pronouncing it *dye*-quiry.

'Meester Person! Meester Person!' the desk clerk called across the patio. 'You have visitors.'

His contacts, two rebels who waited in front in an idling jeep, had arrived just in time to spare him from a Dictaphone sermon at the motel bar. He gathered his things and checked out.

★ ★ ★

Rain began to fall that afternoon, en route to the rebel camp. It only invigorated him, wet glancing on his face, green whirring past, the old familiar thrill of bumping along in a military vehicle bristling with weapons that his hosts, Hector and Valerio, two cheerful comandantes — captain and first lieutenant, respectively — had picked up from an abandoned army cache. Valerio expertly guided the jeep up steep, muddy roads, steering carefully around ruts as deep as the graves at Père-Lachaise, then gunned it to eighty kilometers per hour over washboard. La Mazière, impressed, asked who was supplying their vehicles. 'Batista,' Valerio said, steering with his knee as he reached to wipe the windshield with a rag.

The invigorating sprinkle turned to a heavy shower as they arrived in camp. The rain continued for several days, making the roads impassable. In addition, they were now blocked by the Rural

Guard. Anyone who'd found his way into the mountains would not be finding his way out until further notice. La Mazière was trapped, the entire camp forced to wait out the rain. Hector and Valerio visited his tarp for long and competitive chess games, and rambling conversations about military strategy and the various women they'd each known. La Mazière would hear the two men's exuberant woops echoing through the trees, their call, the mimic of a mockingbird's, announcing they were on their way with one of the chess sets Valerio carved out of coconut fruit. Because they turned brown and limp within hours, Valerio was always working on a new set. He and Hector would crawl under La Mazière's tarp, laughing, dripping wet, Hector booming, 'El Francés! Today I will finally take your king.'

One afternoon Hector said something about the girls in Havana working for the underground, that there were some hot ones willing to give a rebel his good-bye 'gift' before he set off for the mountains. 'And what a gift,' Hector said, grinning. 'Those girls are professionals.' He could have meant any girl, there were scores in the underground, or he could have made it up, and yet La Mazière had an uncharacteristic moment of jealousy, wondering if Hector meant Rachel K. Hector was tall and good-looking, with soft pre-Raphaelite curls and large brown eyes. La Mazière resisted pressing for details. The second time it came up, he asked Hector if he had a particular girlfriend in the underground. No, Hector said. La Mazière was not comforted, and developed a strange attachment to Hector, simultaneously admiring and distrusting this handsome fellow who might be screwing his zazou.

★ ★ ★

Despite being trapped in a soggy mountain camp for several days — twelve or thirteen, so many that he'd stopped counting — there were moments when La Mazière genuinely enjoyed himself, destroying his new friends at chess, and also canasta, which they taught him, and regaling them with stories of the Russian steppes, of smoking bitter tobacco that burned like hay, and seeing Mongolians on horseback come over a high mountain pass, men with rusted, czarist-era pistols and woven wool saddles. But unlike Hector and Valerio, neither of whom seemed bothered by their miserable living conditions, La Mazière was growing tired of being constantly wet and cold and hungry. For the past week, food rations had consisted solely of stale cassava bread. Mosquitoes attacked brazenly at all hours, leaving unpleasant lumps on his face and hands. And he suspected his feet might be rotting, though he hadn't removed his shoes in several days to look. They were issued hammocks and no longer had to sleep on the ground, but this was a minor improvement, the uncomfortable canvas sling making La Mazière feel like someone else's privates, crammed into a pair of damp swimming briefs. He tried to remind himself that the need for happiness was a mutilation of character, and that comfort and pleasures so quickly

335

turned insipid. *Why don't you join me for a dye-quiry?* At least he wasn't in a drab and depressing motel, 'safe,' and making hash of something real and unsafe. *Only if you've been through it as we have, can you understand the terror of the hunted* — The thought of those people, turning history into a poolside burlesque, made him glad to be where he was, in the heart of the action.

After twenty days of continuous downpours, the rain finally let up. At the same time, Fidel Castro began a vigorous public relations campaign on Radio Rebelde, which was broadcast from La Plata, far south of them, but it came in clear enough. La Mazière's unit gathered around the wireless each evening as Castro publicly invited journalists from *Look, Life, Newsweek,* and *The New York Times* up to the mountains, reading their names over the radio momentously, as if they were lottery winners, and then challenging them to witness for themselves who the rebels were and what they were fighting for. The public relations campaign was apparently working, American journalists lounging in Fidel's camp, smoking cigars, flirting with the sexy soap flakes model who ran the radio station, and watching Castro kiss the feet of campesinos. La Mazière could have easily grafted himself to some sort of neutral convoy and made it safely to an airport.

Yet he stayed. He had never planned on such a thing, fighting with bearded Cuban revolutionaries, half of them teenagers. But a definitive moment occurred in which he saw the potential for something grand.

One afternoon, two lieutenants returned from scout duty with a captured member of Batista's Rural Guard. An actual POW, gagged and bound with baling twine. Hector was napping, so the lieutenants came for instructions to La Mazière, regarded as something of an authority, an exotic who might harbor knowledge.

'What do we do with him?' one of the lieutenants asked.

'You know what we're supposed to do,' the other said, his voice trembling. 'All Rural Guard members are enemies of justice. They're . . . they're supposed to be assassinated — '

'No no no,' La Mazière cut in, tsking and shaking his head gravely. 'They are not to be assassinated.'

The lieutenants both looked at him.

'The proper term,' La Mazière said, 'is executed.'

'These are not the same thing?' one of them asked.

La Mazière launched into a discourse on the critical distinction between the two. As he spoke, other rebels wandered over, until he had almost the entire unit of thirty men gathered around him, listening. One was spitting pistachio shells — they'd finally received more than stale cassava as food supplies — but lectures were no time for snacking. La Mazière shot him a look, and the offender quickly put away his bag of pistachios and stood at attention. Execution, La Mazière continued, his voice rising to be sure everyone heard, was an act of intent, purpose, and exactitude. Assassination was a far lower act, an act of opportunity, or worse, 'necessity' — a word he said as if it were a soiled, smelly rag he held between two fingers. Execution was a *ritualized* killing, he emphasized. It was never, ever, an act of necessity. It was always an act of choice, a calculated delivery of justice. And only by the elevated loft of choice, he explained, could the act of killing take on symbolic meaning. Killing, he said, had meaning, voluptuous and mystical meaning that should never be squandered. An execution was a rhetorical weapon, a statement that could not be disproved, just as a man could not be restored from death.

The rebels were quiet. Awed, he assumed. He decided the act itself should be part of his impromptu lecture, a complete lesson.

He called the camp chaplain, who gave the Rural Guardsman his last rites. Watching the chaplain trace an oily cross on the prisoner's forehead and place the Eucharist on his tongue, meager provision for the afterlife, La Mazière thought of the chaplain at Wildflecken, who rode a white horse and wore a silk soutane, his crucifix and iron cross jangling together on their separate gold chains.

When the captive's last rites were completed and he was properly blindfolded, La Mazière took out his knife and cleaned it on his pant leg until it shone.

'Wait!' one of the younger rebels called out. 'Shouldn't he have a trial? I mean, I'm not saying he isn't *guilty*. But shouldn't we be like a court, and judge him guilty? Sentence him before we do this?'

La Mazière sighed, summoning the patience he needed to teach this clueless boy the basic concepts of law and judgment. 'I will explain this once,' he said, 'so please, all of you, listen. This is a popular uprising. A popular movement. The people do not 'judge' in the same manner as courts of law. They do not hand down sentences. They throw lightning bolts. The people do not condemn Rural Guardsmen, or traitors, or kings. They drop them back into the void.'

And then he quickly swiped his shining knife across the prisoner's neck. Even with his eyes covered by the blindfold, the man's face expressed jolting surprise. Under his chin, a quaking smile of red opened up.

Two soldiers vomited in front of all the others, no time to turn away and disguise their weakness — physiologic, beyond their control — and because of this, all the more shameful. La Mazière pretended not to notice, as he might have pretended not to notice a woman's inept methods and obvious sexual inexperience. People must be allowed to learn.

That night, as they dipped fried plantain chips into a pot of beans, a meal a campesino's wife brought into camp, the men were quiet. Hector normally provided their dinner entertainment, regaling them with dirty jokes. *I asked her if she smokes after sex. She turns to me and goes, 'I don't know, I never looked.'* Instead, Hector ate sullenly and said nothing. After dinner he pulled La Mazière aside.

'You sure know how to take the pachanga out of it, man.'

La Mazière said he wasn't sure what Hector meant.

Pachanga was an attitude, Hector said. A revolutionary movement with pachanga was a lively movement, with a certain spirit — the spirit of fun. Killing Batistianos as a lesson for the men wasn't what Hector would call fun.

La Mazière replied that fun is in the eye of the beholder. And if they wanted to goof off, play stickball, forget about the goal of taking over the Cuban government, they should let him know, because he'd been under the impression that they were serious.

'We *are* serious. But there was no need to kill that guy. What about the concept of prisoner of war?'

Concept indeed, considering that Hector had neither captured nor been one. 'By all means tell me,' La Mazière said, making no effort to disguise his contempt for Hector's ignorance, 'about prisoners of war. The concept, at least — '

'Look, man, the father is extremely upset. He thought he was being asked to demonstrate last rites, as in, show the soldiers a hypothetical scenario.'

La Mazière responded that last rites were last rites. Would the chaplain be happy to see prayer regarded as a hypothetical scenario — *if* I were sincere, I'd get on my knees and appeal to God, but I am not, and so this is a *demonstration?*

Hector didn't argue. La Mazière wasn't sure if he'd convinced him, but he didn't care. He probably had more sympathy for that unfortunate Rural Guardsman than all of the others in camp put together. He couldn't explain this to Hector or anyone else who hadn't graduated from indulgent and idiotic 'concepts' to life itself, in its full spectrum of necessary horrors.

* * *

Hector and Valerio no longer came to his tent for games of chess, and certain soldiers, in particular the boy who'd suggested they hold a trial for the Rural Guardsman, kept their distance as well. He'd been with the unit two months now, and an obvious schism was growing, between those ready for intensity and those ready for stickball.

A week after the execution, after word got back to him about the incident, Raúl Castro sent their unit a letter of commendation. Raúl declared, as Valerio read aloud, that the future dream of a new society required not compromises, the distorted 'fairness' of the old system, but new and severe measures. They were lucky to have on their side this Frenchman with impeccable military training. If he were willing, Raúl would name La Mazière their unit's official tactical adviser. When Valerio finished reading, some of the soldiers looked down stoically. One of the boys who had vomited during the execution clapped robustly.

* * *

His new advisory role uncorked a flow of memories, a mode of being in which La Mazière began to marinate, and happily. Remembering

341

tricks he'd learned as a Waffen, which he shared with the soldiers.

Tape your glasses to your face before you jump, La Mazière instructed, the basics of parachuting, to a squadron being sent on sorties to sabotage army garrisons and sugar mills.

They will open a manhole cover, he explained. The light above you blinks red. When it stays red, drop into the black. Don't think about it. Just look at the red light and drop.

Don't try to prevent yourself from falling when you land. Bend your knees and roll. If there is a pond near your landing site, wrap your chute around a rock and sink it.

If you run out of water, suck on bullets.

Always cook off grenades before lobbing them, so they can't be lobbed back. No more than two seconds, he warned. And never, ever, throw them up stairwells.

From the primitive conditions he'd encountered when he'd first arrived in January, the activities of La Mazière's unit began to approximate something like modern warfare. In the late spring they finished building their own airstrip in the mountains, and by May they were receiving regular shipments of M-1 and carbine rifles, artillery, mortars, and ammunition — thousands of pounds of weapons whose sale La Mazière himself negotiated, before he had any plan to roll up his sleeves and train the men who'd be using them. With these shipments came proper machining tools, which resourceful Valerio and a team of helpers utilized to convert an enormous tractor into a tank. They welded on thick plates of steel

342

and mounted every caliber of rifle they had, and, to La Mazière's horror, a catapult, which would launch a single bowling ball they'd recovered from an abandoned American social club. The plates of steel were of mismatched sizes and shapes, the guns loose in their turret holds. Their contraption flopped along the steep, muddy road toward camp like a metal shack on wheels. A group of men tumbled from it, excitedly making mockingbird calls.

'I am amused,' La Mazière said to them, 'and even somewhat impressed. However, it is a clumsy thing. *Terribly* clumsy.'

The men's faces, all triumphant smiles as they'd dismounted, fell in disappointment.

'I thought that you more than anyone,' Valerio said, 'would applaud the project.'

'It's a living expression of the living creativeness of the proletariat!' another soldier protested.

Others chimed in.

'Who cares if it's clumsy?'

'Yeah, we'll blow their asses up!'

La Mazière was beginning to lose patience with the general disregard in camp for the importance of aesthetic as well as military control. He had suggested to Valerio that making swamp shoes out of reeds wasn't, perhaps, a top priority, and this ridiculous 'tank' is what Valerio made instead. More than once, he'd been forced to explain to Valerio that chess games were for rainy days, not every day. Here he was, summoning his old wartime fitness, his finesse, a French killing machine, and he was surrounded by men who argued with their hands but were reluctant to use those same hands to pull a simple grenade pin, preferring to strap on Valerio's homemade swamp shoes and tromp around the cow lilies, shouting with glee through boqui toquis, as they called their two-way radios. He was not averse to the cult of nature, to grounding a political cause in the facticity of the earth. But the rebels' rural habits were laziness and leisure in place of discipline. None was interested in midnight hiking, as the Germans at Wildflecken had been so fond of doing. None was game for a brisk, predawn swim in a cold mountain stream. They had little taste for discipline in itself and the transcendence it promised. They could not even clean and properly oil their weapons, and so much worse, they had no understanding of the lyrical qualities of violence, and avoided it as best they could. Twice now, Hector had asked La Mazière to 'show them again' when they'd encountered prisoners who had to be dealt with, Hector claiming that the soldiers still had not quite perfected the technique, and that he didn't want them to squander the meaning of the killing that had to be done, asking could La Mazière please go over once more how 'the blade of popular justice' worked, and demonstrate once again how the act was properly carried out. The idea of someone making him, La Mazière, conduct others' dirty work like a regular low-life hit man was, of course, unthinkable. They were merely too weak to do it themselves, and needed someone strong to do it for them.

He retreated to his tarp and drew diagrams,

thinking, scratching out his failures. He came back to them with a tank design that was far more elegant than their rattletrap. No catapult. No wobbly turret holds. Just one spare and tasteful flamethrower with two thousand pounds of pressure.

'What shall we christen it?' he asked them.

'The *Queen*!' Valerio shouted, and so it was.

Watching them practice their maneuvers in the *Queen*, La Mazière contemplated how odd it was that in chess, the consecrated object, the king, on which the entire game hinged, was in fact all but useless, sheer vulnerability, an inert symbol, while the queen was the truly desired object, with powers that were leaps and bounds beyond what any other chess piece possessed. When did this curious reversal of terms take place? And why? And what did it mean? Valerio's hand-carved coconut queens were obscene caricatures with lusty proportions. But this did not diminish their importance to the game, their innate dignity as instruments of victory. A queen whose maker had beleaguered her with huge breasts and protruding labia could still move in any direction, still glide over the board with thrilling velocity and ease en route to triumph.

★   ★   ★

Raúl, leader of the Frank País Second Front covering all of northeastern Oriente, was their commander. But they'd seen little of him, until the tractor-tank was perfected and a plot hatched to roll it down into the American region and take

345

gasoline, which they badly needed, and hostages, which they didn't need, but might prove a brilliant publicity stunt. They would abduct nickel company men and sugar company men and bring them up to the rebel camp. Show them a good time, offer tours of the damage caused by Batista's bombers, and win the Americans' sympathy.

This plan, though officially Raúl's, had actually been hatched *by* an American — Raúl's sidekick, the prodigal son of a United Fruit manager. The boy, accompanied by a small detachment, came to La Mazière's encampment to go over the details. He was a brooding sort who bit his lip, with longish hair that hung into his eyes — perhaps meant to look like Raúl's mop of hair, except that his was the white-blond of a Scandinavian. When La Mazière first heard about the scheme, he thought it likely to end in disaster, the rebels ambushed by the Rural Guard, or accidentally getting one of their charges killed. But hearing the American boy's ideas, he grew less skeptical. It wasn't a bad plan. Actually rather clever, the way this kid — Comandante Stites was his name — proposed dividing one column into two, just at the foothills of the Sierra Cristal, half the men crossing the Levisa River and going around and into Preston to take sugar company employees, the other half descending from the nickel mine, where worker sympathy meant they had all the lookouts and cover they would need, and into Nicaro, to nab unarmed managers like tender chickens and escort them back to camp.

La Mazière worked with Comandante Stites

on rearguard maneuvers, offering what knowledge he had on offense and retreat. Both men would be at the rear of a rear line — La Mazière because he was too valuable to be risked, and Stites because it was his own clan on which a front guard would descend. The boy had wanted to lead the operation. Understandable. It was, after all, his creation. But best, La Mazière advised, to give orders invisibly. Luckily, he was able to convince Stites without saying out loud what he saw as a likely outcome, if this boy wound up face-to-face with his own people, his own father, who was the head of the sugarcane operation in Preston. The strategy of keeping him in the rear of the rear line was classic Mao, or maybe Mao by way of Sun Tzu. During peasant uprisings, Mao never sent PLA units to roll tanks over the people of their own prefecture. Instead, he sent them to other prefectures, where the faces and names of the people crushed beneath their tanks were unfamiliar. Separating the American comandante from his American captives was prudent, a way of maintaining the rebel image as an unknowable multitude — not a boy with hair in his eyes, who might be vulnerable to the last-minute bribe of a warm bed and a hot meal, a Jamaican nursemaid drawing his bath. La Mazière could all but see it: 'Come on home, son.'

For the most part, Comandante Stites was severe and serious. A good marksman and tidy draftsman of military graphs, who was not fond of loafing or resting. He rose before dawn, as did La Mazière. Stripped, as La Mazière stripped, both men diving into the mountain stream near camp, Stites athletically surging upstream, switching from crawl to backstroke in a stoic but companionable one-upmanship, La Mazière responding with a muscular butterfly technique. Stites would then follow suit and transition to butterfly, the two of them throwing their arms and shoulders forward, propelling themselves through the cold water with everything they had, relishing this predawn agreement between men.

The way the American boy brooded and flipped his hair out of his eyes, occasionally reminded La Mazière of the rich and insolent American teenagers who showed up in Paris with their Swiss boarding school chaperones, lining up outside the Louvre, or occupying too many tables and ruining the ambience at the Café de Flore. But Comandante Stites meant business. The stakes for him were unique, and no doubt fueling his brooding focus. He clearly bore a grudge, perhaps not having outgrown the child's play of breaking, or simply soiling, the law of the father. Comandante Stites seemed especially keen on having his father's inner circle taken up to the mountains. Keen on having his father's steak freezers raided, and cutting off his hometown's telephone lines and water supply. As if the magnificent cane fire the boy had masterminded was not enough. His reputation had been built on that event, which had occurred just after La Mazière first arrived in the mountains. The other rebels revered the act as a grand sacrifice of the boy's own paternal empire. La Mazière found it slightly more dubious. Oedipal battles must be waged carefully, not compulsively.

Though who was he to say which really was bigger, the cosmos of infantile emotion, or the actual cosmos? Either way, the blaze made a devastating impact, more than the Americans likely realized. Fire, La Mazière knew, is alchemical. It changes everything. And long after it's extinguished, a fire may continue to burn and corrode.

★ ★ ★

The Preston and Nicaro abductions were successful. And quite fun, as it turned out. Rebel military posts became theatrical stages, everyone performing for the benefit of the captives and the American journalists who quickly followed. On the day a *Life* magazine correspondent arrived, La Mazière convened with several men behind a cluster of scrub pines and arranged for the men to crisscross the camp, changing shirts, removing a hat, donning a hat, grouped in different combinations — five men, seven men, and so forth — to create the impression that each time they appeared they were a new battalion passing through. The captives were split into small groups, which were easier to manage and guard. On Raúl's orders, La Mazière went from unit to unit to supervise security. Some of these units, to his pleasant surprise, were commanded by women. Real women, who smiled and flirted. One was particularly good-looking, and when he saw her swinging hair, her open feminine gaze, smile dimples like two delicate divots in the surface of a pudding, he thought he might be able to engage in softer pleasures in the midst of the more stringent pleasures of war.

He'd been surrounded by men and consumed with military tactics for the past five months, since he'd arrived that rainy afternoon in January, and he'd all but forgotten that intimacy and war occasionally coincided, if in a less than genteel manner. Of course, the Nazi joy division was a myth. One that served, like so many wartime myths, to allow for licentious fantasy under cover of redemptive guilt. There had been no roaming units of Aryan blondes, packed into wagons and delivered like milk. But there had been, of course, a soldier's 'droit du cuissage,' as La Mazière liked to think of it, one of the spoils of war. Over the grueling weeks he'd been trapped behind Russian lines, living like an animal and sleeping in the snow, there was an occasional farmer's wife who gave herself freely while her husband was marched out back and pistol-whipped in a pig stall. He remembered one in particular, hoisting herself onto the kitchen counter and lifting her muddy skirts. It was a gamy union — this was the war, and bathing a dim memory — but an enjoyable union all the same. Gamy, after all, was sometimes a pleasure of its own. He had even chosen gamy on occasion. But the 'base pastoral' of the kitchen-counter screw with the farmer's wife could exist only as a lesser value, an inferior pleasure, because it had not been selected in lieu of other pleasures, other varieties of feminine grooming or lack thereof. The highest pleasures, he knew, were those for which he gave up another. Not pleasures of opportunity, but of sacrifice.

The dimpled commander wore tight-fitting fatigues, her rifle strap bifurcating a decent-looking set, two mounds larger than his two hands could have cupped. Though any set, at that point, would have looked decent to him. When she grazed his arm with her own, he assumed it was a green light. He gestured to the woods, attempting to negotiate a discreet romp with this well-endowed commander. She became angry, almost hysterically so, yelling at him that she was of higher rank, and accusing him of demeaning her and betraying the democratic principles of the revolution, then marched off to 'write up' the incident. As if an indispensable leader like himself was not immune to a petty write-up. He was utterly immune. Nonetheless, his heart sank. How disappointing, how tiresome, to be scolded by a woman. Who in any case was dressed like a man, and had suddenly transformed from a warm and receptive female to a power-mad shrew. The incident cast a dreary mood over him.

He reminded himself that he could easily leave, trade in his hammock for a comfortable bed in the Seventh. Fly from Santiago to Port-au-Prince and then direct to Paris, and in three or four days' time have all the female comforts he wanted. See Dalida, his Miss Egypt, her torpedo bra and long legs, the depression that gripped her in a manner he found fascinating, an interest that wasn't quite empathy, but not cruelty, either. Something else, a brackish mixture of the two. Dalida suffered acute and sustained anxiety attacks that lasted several weeks and felt, she told him,

'Like I've dropped something priceless and fragile, and it's about to hit the floor and smash into
a million pieces. There's nothing I can do — I've
already dropped it and it's going to smash into a
million pieces. That feeling. It's just left my hands.
It's just left my hands.'

On second thought, he could avoid Dalida.
Not tell her he was back, and embark on simpler
engagements. Lurk at the cafés and pick up
working-class girls, bring them to his apartment,
and eject them just as quickly, explaining that he
looked forward to savoring the memory of their
company as much as or more than he'd savored
the company itself, offering his shopworn theory
about passion necessitating absence.

He thought of his indifferent and less
predictable zazou. Of course, Hector hadn't
screwed her. La Mazière was simply falling prey
to the pathetic notion that everyone must find
her desirable because he did. But going to
Havana to see her was out of the question. The
SIM would put a bullet in his head. And anyway,
he'd committed himself to this fugitive world,
even if its women, with their prick-teasing
attempts to humiliate him, were enough to make
him long for an Englishman's Kabuki drag
queen. Even if these soldiers had not quite
mastered the mystical potentials of violence, the
gifts of merciless discipline, and still could not
grasp the basic and vital concept of militiae
species amor est — warfare as a kind of love, as
Ovid had said. Ovid might have said the reverse,
that love was a kind of warfare, but no matter.
Both were true.

The rebels controlled most of Oriente at this point. The central province of Las Villas was almost theirs. After its capital, Santa Clara, fell, they would make their push into Havana. Thousands and thousands of acres of sugarcane were burning. Buses and trains were burning. Every tobacco-curing shed in eastern Cuba was burning. He loved revolt. It was his favorite part of revolution. He had to stay, at least for the grand debouchment from the hills.

★ ★ ★

Fidel Castro visited their camp one afternoon and delivered an impromptu speech about diet and nutrition. In times like this, Castro said, when camps were short on food — La Mazière's had had none the past two days — it was important to remember that termites were edible. But terribly bitter, La Mazière discovered, when the unit commander ordered the cook to prepare a batch to please Castro. The bitterness of a hundred Fernet-Brancas converging in one spot on the back of his tongue. He covertly spit them out and suggested they borrow a cow from the local campesinos, to be paid back after their triumph. Three rebels set off on this task, but all they managed to rustle up was an emaciated colt. They tied the rangy colt to a post, and it was La Mazière who had to put the thing out of its rangy misery. He shot it and hung it upside down, explaining that this was preferred, so the juices from the head would not drain into their meat. He held a butchering clinic. Skin it warm, but wait for the body to properly cool before cutting. Make one vigorous slice into the armpit, and yank the shoulder. Like this, see, *away* from the carcass. To remove the round, we locate — here — the ball-and-socket joint that connects the leg to the pelvis. Sever the joint with staccato knife strokes. The neck, by the way, is wonderful for jerky, if you like that sort of thing.

As the horse meat was broiled, Castro and La Mazière sat in the shade and chatted, watching the men cook and bring order to the camp. It was understood that neither Castro nor La Mazière were men who did chores. Both had graceful, uncalloused hands, with trimmed, clean fingernails. La Mazière kept a paper clip in his pocket for this purpose. To have dirt under his fingernails was to lose his sense of self, as he had discovered in that miserable Russian prison, where his paper clip was confiscated.

The meal that evening, like all their meals, was egalitarian in character, everyone sitting together, officers of the highest rank taking their share last. But in this performance of equality, La Mazière knew, his and Castro's separate and far higher status was all the more preserved.

★   ★   ★

Late that night, La Mazière heard a rustling of his plastic tarp. He opened one eye but didn't stir. Castro lay down beside him, quietly, carefully. The camp was silent, soldiers all sleeping, the only sound the rhythmic stridulations of insects.

For a long time, Castro was still and said nothing. La Mazière lay there, in the humid bosom of night, moonless and black, sensing the commander's concentration, his restive and alert mind discerning the shape of La Mazière's own alert mind.

'Mazière,' Castro finally said.

'Yes.'

And then Castro was upon him. In one simple roll, the heavy weight of his body over La Mazière's. A thin, scratchy blanket between them. He smelled the faint scent of garlic on Castro's breath. His beard was softer than La Mazière would have expected, though he wasn't generally in the business of expecting beards. He felt a vague throbbing, not his own. It was Castro's. A pulsing that was unmistakable, persistent, but then again calm. As if they both understood that there was no need to attend to it, this critical mass of blood, a throbbing, and that they would let it throb against La Mazière, who lay on his back under Castro, and under the plastic tarp, no sound except the drone of insects.

Some secrets cannot be said but only sung, like those of La Mazière's ancestors, the great troubadours of medieval France, who sang the secret heresies and chronicles of the Church of Love, which no one dared speak out loud. Some secrets cannot be said but only danced, like those of the rumba, the licentious dance that Batista kept threatening to outlaw. Other secrets, La Mazière knew, must be felt, and faintly. As possibility, and nothing more.

At some point Castro's secret throbbing may

have become two throbbings. But it can be difficult to discern what is one's own and what is another's. As in first aid training at Wildflecken, when La Mazière had learned never to take a pulse with his thumb, which has its own pulse.

In that position, they, or at least he, began to feel the promise of muffled, guerrilla sleep, a deep animal space where no person could follow, not even a man lying upon him.

The light above you blinks red, La Mazière had told the soldiers.

The light blinks red. Keep your eye on the blinking light. When it stays red, drop into the black.

He began drifting.

Don't think about it. Look at the red light.

When it stays red, drop into the black.

Look at the red, and drop in the black.

Drop in the black.

He did.

★ ★ ★

When he woke the next morning, Castro and his retinue were gone.

19

They let him go after only five days on account of his migraine headaches, and yet Tip Carrington did not feel free. They were kidnapped, true. But all he and the others had to do, all day long, day after day, was laze in hammocks. Chew horse jerky, which wasn't half bad. In fact, it was rather delicious. Play chess and smoke cigars. Raúl had announced to them and to the world, via Radio Rebelde, that he'd brought them to the hills so they could contemplate the effects of Batista's bombs — purchased, Raúl stressed, from the U.S. government and dropped from American planes that refueled at Guantánamo, an American military base.

Raúl gave the kidnappees liquor, which the rebels themselves didn't touch. And he threw them a Fourth of July pig roast, a regular bash. During the pig roast, a drunk and sunburned George Lederer practiced fast draw with the Cubans, shattering coconuts. After that the Cubans called him 'Desperado' and let him wear a holster with a loaded gun.

They were divided into little groups. Carrington was placed with Hubert Mackey and a Mr. LaDue — an agronomist from Preston whom Carrington had known only vaguely before their capture. An armed guard watched them at all times, or at least most of the time: a lovely mulatta with a perfect inverted-heart ass.

Carrington worked on the guard for several days. Because he was a native speaker, and Mackey and this LaDue were nonspeakers, nothing but sí and no, they badgered him to try to negotiate a release. Carrington figured that Mackey and LaDue didn't really want him to negotiate their release. Displaying some effort was a formality, to confirm that the situation was out of their hands.

He showered the guard with every manner of flirtation he had in his arsenal, mirroring her funny Oriente singing-style Spanish, trying this and that, aloof or pandering.

'What's she saying?' Mackey would ask. 'Tell her we're willing to speak to the Government Services Administration. The State Department. Tell her we'll get a letter to Eisenhower, for Christ's sake.'

'You seem Andalusian to me,' Carrington relayed to the guard, Mackey listening intently to what he assumed was a translation of his message. 'Your features, they're so delicate.'

'Tell her we'll do what we can to stop the refueling,' Mackey said. 'Promise whatever they want, and we'll deal with it later.'

'Aren't you overheated in those heavy fatigues?' Carrington translated. 'Why don't we lose these two jerks and take a swim? There's a stream up here, I've seen it on nickel company maps.'

The guard giggled and shook her head.

'What, you don't swim? I will teach you! I was a lifeguard in college.'

She was finally warming to him just the tiniest bit — enough to give him hope to carry on with his campaign — when one of Raúl's lieutenants told Carrington they were letting him go.

'You're a free man,' the lieutenant said.

'Why me?'

'Because of the headaches. Raúl feels it isn't right to hold an ill man captive.'

Carrington had detected the headache coming on the day they'd been taken. A building and convergence of telltale signs: the tunneling vision, a sensation that ice crystals were forming just inside the top of his skull, then melting painfully away. By the time he and the others were riding into rebel territory, their hands bound with twine, Carrington was succumbing to a full-blown migraine. A species of gloriously awful headache he'd suffered, in times of stress, for most of his life.

No matter. He'd enjoyed the cigars and horse jerky and the heart-shaped ass, even if he'd had to lie still for several days, a damp cloth over his forehead, his vision interrupted by spooling white patterns. The rebels had made him a special comfy headache bed with extra padding and pillows. And the episode itself wasn't nearly as bad as others he'd endured. Like when he and Blythe and the girls were chased out of Bolivia, the British crackpot who ran the mine threatening to dynamite it clear into the sky so that, he'd declared, '*no one* would have it.' As a driver sped them to the airport in Sulaco, Carrington had become convinced he was a monkey yoked from the neck up in a hole cut into the center of a dinner table, Asian men eating from his head with special utensils. A monkey in a table, and yet a woman nagged at him from somewhere nearby: 'Welcome to your lousy life. I said it was coming down and you didn't believe me! Too busy carrying on with some whore — '

He was feeling much better, Carrington told the rebel lieutenant who'd come to announce his freedom. Much better indeed.

'So you can make the trip down the Cristal no problem,' the lieutenant said.

'I suppose so, yes.'

Regret was rising in him, but he couldn't say wait, I want to remain a hostage, please —

'We'll send you in a jeep for part of the way. With a guide. You'll have to walk the rest.'

'Rosa?' Carrington asked, perking up.

'No, no. Rosa stays in camp, guarding the others.'

★   ★   ★

Two days into captivity, Rosa left them unwatched in order to tend to some emergency.

Mackey and LaDue decided to start a signal fire, hoping someone would see it. Maybe one of Batista's pilots, in one of the American planes that thundered overhead now and then.

LaDue turned out to be just as incorrigibly square as Mackey. Both of them were industrious Boy Scout types. They'd gotten their fire lit right away, then excitedly run off to collect more brush to keep it going.

360

'Only green kindling!' Mackey had shouted. 'Better for smoke!'

As if being commanded by an alien voice, his own, but so much more gruff and assertive, Carrington had lifted the damp cloth from his eyes, risen from his bedroll, walked over, and dumped dirt on their signal fire. Then he quickly laid down again and replaced the eye cloth.

He was lying still, a sick man, a migraine sufferer, when LaDue returned with a handful of kindling.

'Dern it!' LaDue said. 'Dag-dern it! Hubert, our fire is out!'

Carrington heard the brush of a body against leaves on the path. Rosa, returning.

★   ★   ★

He had been left to walk part of the way down the Cristal, just as the lieutenant had warned him. Scratched by brambles and covered with mosquito bites, he was on a mining road that led straight into Nicaro. The town was below him. Safe, American, twinkling. He could see the yellow glow of nighttime windows, the tiny white lights on the processing plant, the blinking red signals on the smokestacks. The signals were red at night and white in the daytime, blinking to warn planes of their existence. He could feel the mist from the bay on his unshaven face, hear the sound of the smokestacks spewing their thick columns of dust.

Then he was under the oak trees that lined the managers' row, and the whoosh of dust pushed

361

from the chimneys was louder, the mist wetter. He'd never noticed how odd the oak trees were, there in the middle of a jungle. Someone's idea of home-away-from-home. Not his. He would have advised something local, algarroba or tamarind. But he hadn't been in on the construction of Nicaro. That was 1942, and they were living in — he couldn't recall, exactly. Lima, perhaps.

He could see his own driveway, the Cadillac parked in it, a kind of nudity right there in front of the house, reminding everyone of his troubles, the public accusation that the car was not rightfully his. It wasn't, but lots of things in Preston and Nicaro didn't rightfully belong to the people who owned them. The problem was the paper trail he'd left.

All the lights were on in the house. He cut around the side of the Lederers' place, wanting to see his whole house, take it in somehow, before going inside. Three weeks he'd been away. His return was inevitable, so why not resist it for a moment? When a romance was called off, usually by him, there was no reason not to sleep with the girl one last time. One or two or three last times, because the affair was officially over. And when he'd finally succeeded in seducing someone, there was no reason not to put her off. Because she was now guaranteed to submit. Inevitability always produced this in him, a juvenile instinct to stall and resist.

He walked across the Lederers' backyard and into his own, pushing through the hibiscus bushes that divided the two properties. The sound of crunching foliage and snapping branches was loud enough that if someone were on the back veranda, or listening carefully from inside, he would have been heard.

He walked across the damp grass and stood behind the stout trunk of a bottle palm, looking into the windows of his own house.

The curtains were open, and he could see into the dining room. Dinner had been cleared away. Lights hanging from a fixture over the table blazed into the empty room.

★ ★ ★

They had all been drunk that afternoon. Not just he and Blythe.

Getting into the *Mollie and Me* for the trip back to Nicaro, he wasn't even sure why they'd gone to Preston. Just a lot of stingers and shouting and something about the Stites boy's birthday, which was elsewhere, but Malcolm Stites ran things, and so the festivity of his brat's birthday party soaked in like a stain and everybody was at the Pan-American Club for an occasionless afternoon of living it up.

Malcolm Stites's other son, the older one, was in the mountains somewhere, fighting with the rebels. A fact that had seemed perverse, almost astounding, until Carrington got up there and learned that there were all sorts of American boys volunteering. Six teenagers from Guantánamo had robbed weapons from an armory on the base and made a run for it. And there were foreigners helping to train various units. Soldiers from a nearby camp had come through one day. There was a Frenchman with them who seemed to be in charge, slightly shifty and moreover an annoyance, as Carrington got the distinct feeling that Rosa was flirting with the guy. *I'm* your hostage, he'd thought, and asked her in a weak voice for a glass of water, emphasizing his special needs as a migraine sufferer.

Carrington had behaved himself for the most part that afternoon at the Pan-American Club. There were no appealing women to ogle, much less seduce, just sexless Preston matrons rouged like corpses and stinking of baby powder. The exclusive Pan-American Club, no Cubans allowed, nothing but dowdy white women, the older ones in hats crusted with what looked like candy and cockatoo feathers bobbing as they nodded their heads, minding everyone else's business, gossiping about this or that. About him. *Did you hear? Playing it off with that phony name. His mother-in-law's, apparently. Well, I'd certainly call that liberal. I mean really stretching it, taking your mother-in-law's name!*

Blythe had been drunk, but for once not overly drunk. On the ride home, the two of them had sat together on one of the yacht's banquettes. Like a regular couple, a married couple, people who choose to be in proximity.

'You're sunburned,' he'd said, touching her shoulder, making a colorless thumbprint that reflushed a painful bluish-pink.

'And you're as dark as Roosevelt,' she replied, flicking her cigarette butt off the side of the boat.

Carrington looked at his arm.

364

'Roosevelt — may I remind my pale and lovely wife? — is a Negro. And hey, look on the bright side. If you'd married a Negro, they would have figured it out a hell of a lot sooner.'

They all knew, but still he felt that he was waiting for the other shoe to drop. Not sure what it would mean that they knew. It might mean nothing.

What would mean something was the embezzlement charge. A silly thing, really, just a car. Just one Cadillac he'd bought with company funds. I'll return it, okay? Be punished, possibly serve a little time in some white-collar facility. But there was more, a lot more, and he had to keep pushing the more out of his mind so he could stand on this one charge and feel honest with himself. That's what truth was. Establishing a truth in your mind, and declaring this truth to everyone else. If the truth he declared mirrored what he saw and felt inside, then it was true, period. And the more the others accused him of lying, the easier it would be to insist on his honesty. Because then it was no longer about denying one niggling detail, it was about defending character, and any man will defend his own character no matter what he's done.

It was just a car and he'd been planning on returning it, he was rehearsing silently on that boat ride home from the Pan-American Club. Cold began pinging under the top of his skull. Ice crystals forming, and then melting painfully away. Just one car that he'd been planning on returning.

From his station behind the bottle palm, he heard a door slam inside the house.

'¡No me puedes decir lo que hacer!'

It sounded like Pamela. Her voice and Val's weren't easy to distinguish, but only Pamela would speak to their mother in Spanish.

'Fine!' Blythe Carrington yelled back. 'I won't tell you what to do. What's the use? You seem to think you know. But you don't. You don't know anything.'

So everyone still existed. His life still existed. It had simply gone on without him.

'I know some things, Mother. I know we were chased from the last place and the one before it. It's happening here. Luís says the rebels are going to win. And I know that you and Daddy live a lie.'

'I've got news for you, Pamela: it isn't a lie anymore. Not after you told *The New York Times* reporter that your father — I mean 'Señor Guzman' — is Cuban.'

His daughter had outed him in *The New York Times*? Carrington wasn't opposed to children. Not to the general idea of them or even his own. They certainly had a talent for broadcasting whatever the parent suppressed, and maybe that was as it should be. You paid up front with children, to see what came next. If they stabbed you in the back, set the nest on fire, chances were you deserved it.

'You blame *me* for telling the truth! Should I lie, Mother? Is that what you're saying? We should all lie, that's best? Just because you're a racist. You and Daddy both — '

'Daddy and I have tried to get by and keep him employed so you and your sister — both of you are spoiled rotten, by the way — can continue burning through the money he makes. You think they would have hired a Cuban engineer in Nicaro? You've been taking something if you say yes. Because they would never have given him a job. You're an ungrateful brat going through a phase, and I won't tolerate it. It's enough to make me want to defend the bastard.'

'I'm not talking to you anymore, Mother. Why don't you go *fix yourself a drink?*'

He could hear it all so clearly. It was like his wife and daughter were actors on a stage, performing for his benefit. And how peculiar it was that he, their secret audience, could so easily step from behind the bottle palm, walk up to the back porch, to the servants's entrance, and suddenly and irreversibly enter this scene.

The ease of it froze him. He couldn't move and didn't dare. It would only take a second, the simplest of gestures, to enter the house and end his sabbatical. Be found instead of missing.

'You go ahead and ruin your goddamn life. Marry him, for all I care. But don't come crying to me about your cunt-addicted Latin husband.'

'Not every Cuban man is Daddy,' Pamela yelled back. 'That's your own special problem.'

Suddenly Blythe was standing in the dining room under the blazing lights, still as a mannequin. Carrington had been listening and not looking. It seemed almost as if she'd been there for a while and he hadn't noticed. She was looking in the direction of the kitchen. What was she looking at?

The house was quiet now. She turned, walked slowly up to the large plate window that faced the backyard, and gazed out.

She was looking right at him!

He froze. But then he realized that the lights were all on, and she probably couldn't see him. She probably couldn't see much at all, other than the glare of the lights on the glass.

She would only see him if she turned out the dining room lights. Funny how that was the case. That she'd have to put herself in darkness in order to see.

He stepped from behind the bottle palm and stood facing the house, no tree or shrub between him and the window where his wife stood. He was wearing a white shirt, the same white shirt he'd been wearing since the day he was kidnapped, and despite its filth it was picking up the moonlight and glowing like radium. If she turned out the lights, she'd see him plain as day.

If she wanted to see him, it was all she had to do — turn off the lights.

Keep the lights on, she would not.

She gazed out the window.

What felt like a great deal of time passed. A half hour, an hour, he wasn't sure, him staring at her and her staring back, still as a mannequin, her face close to the glass.

And then it occurred to him: *she was looking at her own reflection*.

She stared at the glass and Carrington stared back. Blythe, I'm right here. I'm back. They let me go on account of the migraines.

He put his hand up, palm out. He wasn't sure of the meaning of this sign. Peace, or hello, or no hard feelings.

She'll turn out the lights if she wants to see me.

It would have been that simple. Just turn them out.

It was all she had to do.

PART FOUR

20

'Our life here isn't particularly violent,' Mrs. LaDue said, after Mrs. Billings made the comment that it was.

The LaDues, the Billings, and most of the other Americans were at the Pan-American Club. This was December of 1958, near the end of this in-between era, after the Spanish ate the parrots to extinction, and before the Russians brought Marxism along with their smoked pig's fat. Built brutalist architecture and ran the nickel plant.

'I'm not saying there isn't violence,' Mrs. LaDue continued. 'But *violence* and *violent* — those are different. It's the difference between incident and *intent*.'

★ ★ ★

Some features of this era: Georgian estates in sugarcane fields, saltwater swimming pools reflecting tessellated rectangles of sunlight, and an open-air movie theater with love seats in the back row.

★ ★ ★

Although there was the plantation boss, Mrs. LaDue remembered — Hatch Allain. A decent man, really, even if it's true there was a killing connected to him. It seems he did it, she remembered; that was the connection. But that was in Louisiana and a long time ago. And Mr. Flamm the paymaster was killed, true enough. But that was the blacks, and their love of chopping people up with those horrific machetes they carry around. They really do look like savages, and it's the strangest thing to hear them speaking French —

★ ★ ★

Also in this era, after the Spanish, who cooked their parrots so slowly they remained alive as they were pulled from the oven, and before the Russians, who took the scrubbers off the chimneys and let the red dust rain down: Batista with a secret cavity behind a palace wall. The Fuck Room, he called it, though not in mixed company. An aristocrat's mausoleum with an elevator to the 'basement.' And the addition of cheval-de-frise — jagged pieces of bottle glass in brown, green, and clear — mortared into the tops of the low walls around the Spanish colonial buildings, to prevent vagrants from sitting.

★ ★ ★

Mrs. Billings said loudly, for everyone in the club to hear, that she was sick of all the violence.

'To *here*,' she slurred, and put her hand up to her neck.

She'd wanted to leave for some time now, but her husband resisted. They all did. No job in the

374

States would pay them like the nickel company paid them, they said. Or make them mining executives despite the fact that none of them had Ph.D.'s. Or give them enormous ranch-style homes, enroll their children in private school, on the company tab. No salary in the States would buy a staff of seven servants. Where's the company yacht, her husband asked her, when we're living in a midwestern shithole?

★   ★   ★

Also in this era, before the Russians and their brutalist apartments, and after the parrots, who looked up from the dinner plates as their wings were sawed off with serrated knives: a supply of what are called black pineapple grenades — philological proof of destruction's devotion to the tropics.

★   ★   ★

The Americans who hadn't gone to the Pan-American Club that evening were at home. Some watching television, others listening to the faith healer as he made his bootleg radio broadcast. His was the only program on this time of night. Unless you wanted to listen to the rebels, which few Americans did. The rebels, too, broadcast illegally, from their camp up in the mountains. Bearded ruffians who instructed people to burn sugarcane. Who announced, in advance, their own victory.

Mrs. Billings was drunk, as everyone was, most of the time. She was not a person to be taken seriously, the type of woman who bleaches her hair and then dyes it dark again, to get that coarse, ratted, bedroom effect.

'I said I'm *sick* of all the violence,' she repeated. Then she started an argument with her husband. Some women are very skilled at that. As soon as he began to fight back, she dropped her drink on the floor as a diversion.

* * *

A constant in all three eras: syphilis, tobacco, and trees with fruit whose flesh was the pink of healthy mucus membranes, a fruit that smelled like women's shampoo.

* * *

'Put a glass on the radio and my voice will serenade it,' the faith healer told listeners. Those who were lucky enough to go to the studio had their water serenaded with the beam of his green plastic flashlight. 'Buy lottery tickets with numbers ending in six. In four. In zero. Drink the agua serenada before you go to sleep.' It was a procedure for winning the lottery. The week before, the finance minister had won the lottery and used the money to buy a house in West Palm Beach. It seemed he expected to be relocating sometime soon.

'Why aren't *we* relocating?' Mrs. Billings asked her husband.

'Because we haven't won the lottery,' he answered drily.

It was almost Christmastime, and there were humans hanging in the trees beyond the security fence. Mrs. Billings had put up a cheerful breadfruit sapling in the living room — the refrigerated shipment of Virginia pine had not been able to get through because the bandits had blocked the roads eastward. She decorated the breadfruit tree with strings of tiny lights and hollow metallic balls and sang 'Jungle Bells' and other carols with the children.

★　★　★

Local fragrances, in addition to the flesh-pink shampoo fruit: the feminine traces that lingered in the powder room of the Pan-American Club (Arpège, Fibah, and Colony), and the fetid jungle breath beyond the club's meticulous gardens (rot, rot, and rot).

★　★　★

The faith healer had been condemned by Batista. Superstition was bad for the country's image. What they needed was to modernize, to at least appear modern, and thereby regain the confidence of the ultramodern United States, whose support for his presidency was eroding.

Batista accused the faith healer of feeding listeners false hope, like baby food, like liquor, a set of baroque and empty promises. He didn't realize that the faith healer was working in his favor, that faith kept everyone happy, or at least preoccupied. Too busy hoping to be cured of debt, malnutrition, and broken hearts to cause any trouble.

★ ★ ★

After the business of dropping her drink, Mrs. Billings felt somewhat calmer. She said to her husband in a defeated voice, 'I wish everybody would just be quiet. It's too much. All this talk of phosphorus and ammonia. I can't keep it straight — what we have, what they have. I'm not a goddamned chemist.'

Her husband was scooping up the remains of her drink, which was now just the base of a glass surrounded by broken shards.

'The rebels have the phosphorus,' he said, 'and we've got the ammonia.'

'But what the hell does it matter?'

'Because phosphorus is a weapon. The rebels are threatening to drop it from airplanes, to start fires. But it's just a threat, to get our attention. You know all about threats. Don't you, dear.'

He set the broken glass on the bar, gesturing to the bartender to make her a new one. 'And ammonia is a target. Those tanks near the bay? They'd explode — I mean hypothetically. It's a scare tactic. Nothing is going to happen. Except that some of us will have hangovers tomorrow.'

'All problems have a solution,' the faith healer announced. 'We all have a right to succeed in business, in study, in sports, in gambling, in love.'

There were new laws. Palm readers, hypnotists, and self-appointed gurus were convicted. Also, vendors who sold magic powders, aphrodisiacs, and remedies by mail. Batista banned broadcasts on divination and the interpretation of dreams, on anything that stimulated beliefs opposed to civilization. Only the lottery numbers were okay.

★ ★ ★

Mrs. Billings had gone to the powder room. She looked at herself in the large mirror above the washbasins.

Sometimes you just have to give in, she knew. She didn't want to live in a midwestern shithole. What is more beautiful than Oriente? the Americans all said. What air is more tender? What flowers more brilliant and exotic? What company parties more fun and carefree? What life is better than theirs? 'If you can just hang on, this is all going to blow over,' the men said to their wives, as if they'd rehearsed these lines. What did she know about what would and would not blow over?

There was plenty of liquor at the Pan-American Club. There was caviar and cream cheese on crackers, with a squeeze of fresh *limone* — delicious, although she never figured out why the Cubans called them that, since they were not lemons but limes. There were deviled eggs and vol-au-vents. Fetching, tiny electric lights in pink, green, and white, strung along the gleaming mahogany bar. Just for them, their club, their holiday. And she was in a new gown, chiffon, her favorite fabric, that wonderful rustling material that made her want to go home and pretend her husband still —

★ ★ ★

A thunderous rip of pops erupted from somewhere inside. The chandeliers swung in the rooms where the ceilings hadn't vaulted, and then sagged, threatening to collapse. Mrs. Billings, Mrs. Mackey, and the Carrington twin, the one who hadn't run off with the boxing coach, were all in the powder room when the explosion occurred. Better accustomed to their own club back in Nicaro, all three women reeled straight into the enormous mirrors that were mounted on the walls of the powder room lounge. Panicked and confused, they mistook the silvered glass for open space *(Euclid still applied, if not to history, at least to the layout of the Pan-American Club)*.

The mirrors crashed to the floor. The women ambled aimlessly, sliced up, blood batiking their faces. 'It's broken,' the Carrington twin said, holding her hands over her nose, which flumed garnet down her chin.

* ★ ★ ★

Mrs. Billings wandered into the foyer, glass crunching under her heels. There was music in her head, jangly and instrumental, with a high-pitched and chimey aftertrace. Music you'd pump out of a hand-crank organ, she thought, but pictured no monkey. The monkeys here didn't work — they hung from their cages, blinking at you with their moist, human eyes. The music was getting louder, more high-pitched around the edges. She felt a hand on her arm: her husband's. But she couldn't see him. Blood flooded her vision. And she couldn't hear him, on account of that crazy music.

She said, 'Can someone please turn that down? Can someone please turn that down?'

She said it as loud as she could, but the music drowned her out.

21

Radio Clavelito Independiente 710 AM
December 3, 1958, 10:00 P.M.

Good evening, brothers and sisters.

I have not abandoned you. In fact, the tragic actions of the state have only made me stronger.

They can shut down CMQ, but not Clavelito. The radio band is large. I will keep moving. Discontinued, though only temporarily, are my extrasensory telephones, no longer purchasable by mail order. We hope to make them available again soon. We are aware of the waiting list, and more importantly the need for this vital equipment. But on this issue the state has legislated, and established prohibitive fines.

Should I be fined for offering, at long last, a use of technology that isn't a lazy convenience? Would you rather have a wafflemaker? That's what the state would prefer. That you spend your money on wafflemakers.

Clavelito has not abandoned you. This important work, supplying faith where there is little, shall continue. Partly thanks to the support of you, my listeners, who understand what the state does not, that the true condition of radio has only one equivalence: not 'imaginary' participation, but the rain outside your window.

Brothers and sisters, collect this rain.

22

The dance at the Pan-American Club was not a good-bye fete, although some people later thought of it that way.

It was just a Saturday night party — Daddy's idea. I think Daddy wanted to prove that everything was business as usual, despite the rebels and some of the disturbances we'd experienced. Few people were giving up and leaving. We were staying, of course. The LaDues, I know, were staying — Mr. LaDue was like that, an old workhorse, loyal to Daddy no matter what. The Allains were staying, although they didn't have the same options as the rest of us.

There was only one twin at the club that night. The other had run off with Luis Galindez. Those sisters always came together to Preston, dressed alike, a thick collusion between them. Seeing just the one gave me this feeling that things might be beginning to unravel. It was Nicaro I thought was unraveling — not Preston. Nicaro was closer to the rebel encampments, and everything there was more complicated because of Gonzalez. We were an American town, and foreign-owned property in a time like that becomes a safe haven. Nicaro should have been a safe haven as well, but they had a Cuban investor, so it wasn't purely American-owned. There were rumors that Gonzalez was using the nickel mine as collateral, playing Castro off against Batista and cutting deals with both sides. People felt that Gonzalez was up to something, but they didn't know what.

I'm not sure why I didn't think Preston was unraveling. Del had been gone for almost a year, and running off to fight with Cuban rebels is a lot more serious than Pamela Carrington falling in love with a boxing coach. The rebels had blocked the main road down to Mayarí. We still had our social life — you could yacht over to Nicaro or Saetía anytime you wanted. Take a company plane to Miami. But if you wanted to go anywhere south or west or east of us, meaning to the rest of the island, you were out of luck. Castro had a lot of power by that point. He could stop our operations anytime he wanted. He was demanding that we pay fifteen cents on every bag of sugar, and yet we couldn't process the cane to pay him. We had no gasoline to run the mill, no oil to run the railroad. Much of the track was destroyed, making it impossible to get the cane to the mill. And half the blacks we needed to cut it were gone. The rebels were shutting off our water supply intermittently, to demonstrate that they could. They were threatening to burn down every last acre of sugarcane on the island. They could have done it. They had planes and their own airstrips in the mountains, and they'd been starting fires all over the island by dropping payloads of phosphorus-filled Ping-Pong balls from airplanes. Daddy kept telling everyone to be patient. He said gasoline was on its way, oil was on its way, and he was negotiating a deal that would work in our favor. The rail tracks were being repaired. We'd have a cutting season, he said. It would simply start a bit late, a late but fantastically profitable cutting season. If we gave up, he reminded people, we'd have no cutting season.

Maybe he was right. From the television news, life in Havana seemed fairly normal, the first lady preparing for her annual holiday gift giveaway on the palace lawn, the mayor of New York City and his family vacationing with the du Ponts in Varadero, and ads for a Christmas spectacular at the Cabaret Tokio. We weren't going to visit the Havelins, with the situation in Preston so precarious, but the Havelins wouldn't be in Havana anyhow. A month earlier, in November, Batista had appointed Deke Havelin Cuban ambassador to Brazil. There were photos of the Havelins in the *Havana Post*, dressed to the nines, flying off to São Paulo. Deke was quoted, saying how proud he was to represent Cuba and so forth — his party toast all over again, wiping a tear from his eye. I'm not sure how much Spanish Deke even spoke, much less a word of Portuguese.

That day of the party there were Cuban stevedores unloading a ship on the Preston dock wearing nothing but underwear and their shoes. You never saw any Cuban wearing shorts, much less their underwear in public, but that's how tight security had gotten. A shipment had come from England delivering weapons for Batista's Rural Guard, and they didn't want any funny business. 'Goodness,' Mother said, and turned away, embarrassed, as she and I walked past the dock. We were on our way to pick up some medicine for Panda at the almacén. That's how Mother was, always tending to people's needs. Panda was sick. Mother said she heard that Dr. Romero suspected tuberculosis. Mother put the medicine on our account, and I took it down to the Allain place. They had Panda in the living room, lying on a couch under a pile of blankets, pale and coughing, with dark pouches under her eyes. Mars took the medicine and thanked me. She said Dr. Romero had just been to check on Panda. He'd said that Panda needed to be under the care of someone who specialized in respiratory illnesses, and they should get her to a hospital in Miami as soon as possible. I doubt that Dr. Romero understood the situation. Mars asked me about hospitals in Santiago. It would have been difficult to get to Santiago, I told her, because of the roadblocks.

Rudy went to speak with Daddy at his office later that day. Daddy came home and told us there wasn't much he could do. 'Makes you realize,' he said, 'how well the company takes care of its own. We sure as hell don't judge people on whatever happened in the deep past. Hold it against a man because there's a little smudge on his dossier, a bit of shoe polish.' He was going to do what he could to get both Allain families transferred to an operation in Central America, maybe Tegucigalpa. Mother said why not have Mars take Panda to Miami? She didn't commit any crimes. Daddy said they were all wanted now, for harboring a fugitive. I understand Daddy's point about the shoe polish smudge, people being forgiven and allowed to

386

start over. But in Hatch's case it wasn't such a minor smudge. A lot of people in Preston were under the impression he'd killed a black man, just some worker on a Louisiana cane plantation. The fellow not only wasn't black, he was a fed — an ATF agent. Hatch apparently had an argument with this guy, a bootlegging investigator. Ironically, they were at a bar, drinking. There was some kind of dispute that escalated into a brawl, and Hatch ended up beating the guy to death.

* * *

Daddy always felt that the employees couldn't really relax at parties so long as the boss was looking over their shoulder. It was his custom to go to the club, spin Mother around the dance floor a turn or two, and then leave so everyone could enjoy themselves. I decided to make it a short evening as well. I'd gone to the party hoping to speak with Everly Lederer, but the Lederers hadn't come. For months now I'd had this feeling that something had been there between me and Everly all along, and that all we had to do was call it out. I guess it was foolish and romantic, this idea that she'd been a favorite of Mother's, and that we'd known each other since the Lederers had first arrived, when I was nine and she was eight, and that there was something special in trusting what seemed fated. I hadn't seen her much all fall, ever since my fourteenth birthday, in June, when I'd given her the keepsake. I figured she was thinking about things and would eventually come around. When she didn't show up at the club that night, it crossed my mind that maybe she was dating someone in Nicaro. 'Who would want to date Everly Lederer?' Curtis had said when I wondered out loud one day if she had a boyfriend. 'She's a gawky tomboy, walks around with that spaced-out look like she's focusing on something invisible about two feet in front of her face.' The spaced-out look had grown on me. If Tee-Tee Allain's face was a shield against the world, shutting off any speculation as to who she was or what she cared about, Everly's funny look was not intentional, as if she was unaware she had any look at all. Lost in thought, a naked look. Maybe everyone has that look, but they know to cover it. Hearing Curtis's comment, I'd become convinced it was the right thing. Who would want to date her? Only me, it seemed.

While Daddy took Mother out for a quick spin on the floor, I sat at the bar next to Mr. LaDue, who was entertaining some of us with stories about being up in the mountains with the rebels. Someone asked him what he thought had happened to Carrington. Mr. LaDue said poor Carrington had been sacked out with a migraine the whole time they were up there. Maybe he was wandering around in the woods, Mr. LaDue said, ill and confused.

★　★　★

Mother, Daddy, and I were walking toward home, about to turn onto La Avenida. It was a

388

very hot night, as humid as it gets in Oriente. A dense, rhythmic buzz of insects surrounded us. We had flowers in eastern Cuba that bloomed at night, and there was a heavy fragrance in the air as we walked, made more intense by the heat. Mother breathed in and said the butterfly jasmine was opening, and how gorgeous, that smell —

Boom! we heard. Another boom. And then another. And then people screaming.

★　★　★

Bombs detonated in our social club. It was a rude awakening, even if no one was hurt too badly. They'd been planted in a couple of rooms that weren't being used, but also under the dance floor. Miraculously, the bombs detonated while everyone was taking a break, sitting down to cool off because of the humidity, or at the bar getting a refresher. A few people were cut up. Val Carrington broke her nose, rammed right into the wall of the women's bathroom. But there were no serious injuries.

What else would blow up? Everyone was in a panic. Daddy called the consul general in Santiago. He'd secured the release of our kidnapped employees, proving himself to be a lot more reliable than Ambassador Smith. The consul general said he'd been told they were having problems over in Nicaro as well. I don't think he gave too many details. All we knew was that Nicaro was under attack — we assumed rebel attack. We didn't know until later that the U.S. Navy was sending a

389

rescue ship up the coast from Guantánamo. Because of the bombings, and the situation in Nicaro, which the consul general said could escalate, there would be a mandatory evacuation of all Americans around Nipe Bay.

Daddy said chances were the U.S. government was panicking for no reason, and we'd evacuate and then come back to Preston and life would settle down. We didn't have time to pack much, grabbed a few things and stuffed them in suit-cases. It was 10:00 P.M., and we got on the rescue ship at four the following morning. Daddy made phone calls and sent his secretary, Mr. Suarez, and a few other guys around to tell people to be ready to leave. Daddy tried to get through to Nicaro, but their switchboard was down. The people who'd been in the club were taken to the Preston hospital, stitched up, and treated. The Nicaro folks among them would have to be evacuated as they were. Val Carrington had two black eyes, an ice pack held to her nose. Mrs. Billings's head was wrapped in surgical gauze. She was wearing a fancy getup, a long gown with a matching capelet, with blood crusted into her hair and over her ear. She seemed dazed, like she'd really had her bell rung, and Mother took special care to try to calm her down after we got on the ship.

Hatch came up to our house while we were packing. He told Daddy that he and Rudy and the families would stay and look after things. Daddy reminded him that the evacuation was mandatory and said that navy officers would be clearing the town.

'But they're taking everyone to Guantánamo, sir,' Hatch said. 'I'm not going to Guantánamo.'

Daddy had just been on the phone again with the consul general and had a better idea of what was happening. He told Hatch that Nicaro was being strafed by Cuban military bombers and that the rebels had moved into town and were firing back. There was a battle going on right in Nicaro, and the American families there were in serious danger. Later we found out there were no rebels in Nicaro. Only Batista's bombers, strafing the Americans. The mistake was no accident. It was a situation that Lito Gonzalez had carefully arranged. He called in the attack, claiming the rebels had occupied the town and that all the Americans were safely inside the mine. He didn't care about their lives. He knew the Americans would be evacuated, and he planned to take over the nickel operation.

'This is chaos,' Daddy said, 'and you can't stay, Hatch.'

I think it was mostly because of Panda that the Allains decided to risk it and get on the ship with the rest of us.

23

Charmaine Mackey had rehearsed the conversation so many times in her mind that having it for real would not seem so radical, or risky, or outrageous.

She would go to his home, knock on the door, announce herself to the butler, and ask to speak to Mr. Gonzalez.

Hubert had left for the shindig at the Preston club without her. As they had gotten dressed for the party, she'd mentioned not feeling well, and Hubert said angrily that she was never feeling well, and why didn't she just stay home. She hadn't argued with him. He'd sighed heavily, knotted his tie, and put on his coat and wristwatch, his movements angry and deliberate, as if he were punishing her, when in fact she wanted to stay home. He patted her on the shoulder as he left, to indicate a breath of forgiveness in the stern policy of leaving her behind.

How outraged Hubert would be if he knew what she thought about. He'd come to believe that he and Mr. Gonzalez were fighting some sort of war. He said Gonzalez was scheming to drive them all out and take control of the plant. 'He wants my job,' Hubert said, 'and he's not getting it.' Charmaine couldn't help but feel that none of it was about the nickel company, or Gonzalez hating Americans, as Hubert insisted.

She sometimes believed that it was about her they were really fighting over.

She took off her party attire and put on something plainer, more appropriate for a neighborly visit, a cotton dress that she thought looked vaguely Cuban because of its cheerfully romantic print — huge, floppy red hibiscus flowers — and the white, nubby sweater she'd been wearing that first day, when he'd rescued her from the bakery. That was years ago now, but he might remember the sweater. She was daubing on a tiny amount of perfume when she heard the deafening screech of a low-flying plane passing over the house, and then the staccato yap of Mrs. Billings's poodle.

On her way to Mr. Gonzalez's, more planes flew over, so low they rang her ears and stirred up the dust on the road. She looked up but couldn't see any lights. They usually had those lights on the wings. Maybe clouds were blocking them. But the sky was a black velvet carpet littered with stars. There was no cloud cover. These mysterious low planes were flying with their lights off.

At his door, she did as she'd rehearsed, announced herself to the butler and asked for him.

He looked surprised to see her, not happily surprised. 'Why aren't you at the club in Preston?' he asked.

She felt a moment of doubt. He wants me to be at the club — why aren't I at the club? 'I didn't feel like going. My husband is there, and I thought perhaps you and I could talk — '

'Mrs. Mackey, did you hear the planes?'

'Yes, I heard them.'

'It's the Cuban military. They're strafing. This is extremely dangerous. It's not safe to stay in town.'

She could barely focus on what he was saying. Partly because she didn't understand this word 'strafe,' what it meant. Something to do with weapons. She could only concentrate on what she had come to say to him. It had dominated her thoughts for a long, long time. Her hands shook every time she thought about him, every time she thought she might run into him in town. She was overflowing with the need to confront him. It had taken weeks of rehearsing and storing up courage. She couldn't back out now.

'Mr. Gonzalez, I don't love Hubert. I don't love him. And I would be willing to leave him if you think that you and I — '

'Mrs. Mackey,' Mr. Gonzalez said with a smile, but she immediately saw that it was not a friendly smile, 'you're a foolish person. I don't hold it against you. If I believed, as you say, that you and I could be together, don't you think you would know? Don't you think I would have told you?'

'But . . . maybe I thought you *had* let me know. We have been intimate, after all — '

'In a car — years ago. Behind a squalid pool hall. Is that how a man treats a woman he hopes to marry? You come from a strange culture, Mrs. Mackey. If I wanted you to leave your husband for me, that's not how things would have gone.'

Her heart felt like a heavy person was standing on it. Her throat was closing in. She told herself to be brave. 'But I thought maybe because of Hubert . . . that you didn't want to — '

'You think I actually care about your husband? What Mackey thinks? It only takes one incident, and a husband is humiliated. One incident, of another man with his wife, and he is a, how do you say it in English? A *cuckold*. You should go and pack now. They're going to evacuate — I heard just before you rang, on my shortwave.'

A plane thundered over, low and deafening.

'Why are they 'strafing' us, Mr. Gonzalez?'

'Because the rebels have taken over the town. They have endangered American lives, and the military has no choice but to respond. Their planes are being shot at by rebels.'

She hadn't seen any rebels. Or heard any shots. She'd heard only the planes. 'But Mr. Gonzalez, there are no rebels in town — '

'You should go, Mrs. Mackey. They're evacuating all Americans, and you and Hubert will have to leave.'

'Oh,' she said, almost laughing, and then shook her head emphatically. 'Oh, Mr. Gonzalez, Hubert isn't going anywhere. He's convinced that you want to replace him. He says it won't happen over his dead body. He will not go. I can promise you that.'

'It isn't safe to stay.'

'He'll risk it. He's said over and over that if every last American goes, he'll stay to run the plant. You don't know Hubert, Mr. Gonzalez.'

'It won't be a risk. It will be a certainty that

something happens to him, Mrs. Mackey. A certainty. It won't matter how it happens, because there are so many possibilities. Shot, accidentally, in rebel cross fire. Or shot, accidentally, by the Rural Guard. In any case, shot. That's what he chooses if he stays.'

She could feel that she was about to cry, and once she started she wouldn't be able to stop. Gonzalez hated them and wanted them gone. It didn't make her appreciate Hubert any better, it just carried her to a new depth of loneliness and misery. Nothing was ever how she thought it could be. She turned around, her hands dug in the pockets of her sweater, and walked down his porch steps and out of his yard. She heard an airplane, invisible above her, scraping against the black sky.

24

Pepé Le Pew was joining the French Foreign Legion. It was Duffy's turn to pick the television program, and she always chose cartoons. She lay on the couch, sick with a cold. It didn't seem so serious, but Marjorie Lederer thought they better stay home and keep an eye on her, especially after people said the Allain girl was walking around with tuberculosis.

'Just because we're staying home doesn't mean you have to,' Marjorie Lederer told Everly. 'Mrs. Stites called. She and K.C. are really looking forward to seeing you. Val is going. Why not go on over with Val and have a bit of fun?' Everly didn't want to go, wasn't in the mood to put on a dress and have Mrs. Stites tell her she looked lovely and coerce K.C. into agreeing. Lately, despite all the worry and the way her parents talked at home about the situation in the mountains, the tension up at the mine, the adults all seemed overly gay, almost hysterical, insisting on throwing parties and having a good time regardless of whether they actually were.

Everly was on the floor, reading and watching television at the same time, a skill she'd been working on. Willy said it was possible to do two things at once as long as you decided which was the rhythm and which the melody. Your mind would sort out how to organize and absorb two different activities as long as you labeled one of them major and the other minor. He listened to music and read *Popular Mechanics* and said he could sing and write a letter at the same time, do addition and subtraction while making corn bread. He said if Everly practiced, she might get to where her mind could absorb two melodies or two rhythms — things of equal value — and lose nothing of either. But that this was an advanced level.

'I want to forget,' Pepé Le Pew said, disconsolate about something. Everly and Duffy had missed that part. Pepé Le Pew was in a Foreign Legion enlistment office. He signed on the dotted line. Then he was stinking up the bunks, and men with anchor tattoos and little French hats with pom-poms were running for their lives with clothespins on their noses. They left him to defend the fort all by himself. Poor Pepé Le Pew. He couldn't smell himself, but who really could? And no matter how the story changed, the object of Pepé Le Pew's affection was never real. Not once did they give him an actual skunk to be in love with. She was always an illusion, a cat that had somehow gotten a white stripe of paint down her back. But if he ever did catch the skunk-disguised cat, he would see that she wasn't what he'd thought, and that all along he'd been running after an illusion. Maybe by dodging him, the cat and the people who made the cartoon were saving Pepé Le Pew from an awful discovery, possibly worse than heartbreak —

An airplane roared over the house, rattling the window shutters and the liquor bottles on the cart in the living room. There was a loud plunk on the veranda. It sounded like something metal.

'What on earth?' Marjorie Lederer said, coming out of the kitchen.

A three-foot bomb had dropped right on their veranda, then rolled down the steps and into the yard, without detonating.

It looked like a smaller version of the laughing-gas tank at the dentist's office, drab and metal and tapered on one end. They weren't to go anywhere near the front door.

George Lederer called the security office at the plant. The rebels had apparently come into town to steal gasoline, and Batista was strafing them. Right in Nicaro, he was bombing and strafing them. They could hear the planes flying over and out to the bay, turning around and flying over again. 'If only we had a basement,' Marjorie Lederer kept saying. 'There's no basement — where do we go?'

'This is American property,' George Lederer yelled into the phone, 'and we're being attacked by the Cuban military? How can they bomb us? We've got goddamn ammonia. They hit those tanks by the bay and this place will go sky high.'

*　*　*

Mr. Billings, the head of company security, instructed everyone to seek shelter in the mine. Mrs. Carrington, who hadn't gone to the party in Preston, either, fetched the Lederers in her husband's Cadillac, which the company was allowing her to drive while they sorted things out. A compassionate gesture, Everly's mother had said, in the wake of Tip Carrington's disappearance at the hands of the rebels.

When they got to the mine it was already crammed with people — Cuban nickel company employees and their families, the guajiros who squatted in burned-out Levisa, Jamaican servants, even the Chinese vendors. She didn't see Willy, and heard someone say that the servants who slept in the navy barracks had been told to stay put.

★ ★ ★

So much of it was a blur, the false alarms that the mine was under attack and they would all have to relocate, followed by announcements that they were to remain where they were. In the early morning, a ship's horn sounded over and over, a U.S. Navy vessel taking them to safety.

'Only Americans,' a plant security officer announced. '*Solo* Americanos.'

They needed to get from the mine to the dock, but the Cubans panicked and tried to prevent them from leaving. Pushed and shoved them and blocked the road. 'What about us!?' they shouted. Everly knew so many of them — the women who worked in the bakery, and the men from the ice factory near the bay, Lumling, who came by with his cart every afternoon selling little pineapples. One of the gardeners from the club slashed the tires of Mr. Carrington's Cadillac as they tried to get in it.

'If you leave they'll bomb us!' a woman cried,

grabbing Everly by the shoulders. 'There's nothing here for them to protect if you go. You can't go.'

★ ★ ★

They were taken out in dinghies to a giant ship. To board it, they had to climb a tall ladder. The United Fruit people, and those from Nicaro who'd been at the party in Preston that evening, were staring from along the ship's railing like zombies, bloody and stitched up and wrapped in surgical gauze like boxers after a fight.

Everly's mother struggled on the ladder. She slipped and almost fell. Mrs. Carrington, the next person down, caught her. Later, Everly's mother said that Blythe Carrington was as strong as a man.

The navy ship moved out toward sea slowly, waiting for mines to be removed from the mouth of the harbor. It was morning now, but the fog on the bay was so thick it sopped up the rays of the rising sun and cast a gloomy, opaque white light. As the ship moved out of the harbor, the mountains above Nicaro began to fade, purplish-gray apparitions dissolving in a sea of milk.

There was no red haze of nickel oxide, Everly realized, as she watched Nicaro recede. The chimneys were cold, the plant shut down. The town was clean of its usual coating of dust. The clouds weren't stained and dirty. There was no fine silt on the surface of the water. It's so nice, she thought sadly, without us.

401

On the open ocean, she could see an aircraft carrier in the distance. It shadowed them all the way to Guantánamo. Duffy cried and said she forgot something. Everly's father asked her what could be so important. 'My corals,' she said through tears. Duffy collected things and put them in old cigar boxes that the bartenders from the club gave to her. Pieces of coral, shells, dead insects. Even a decomposing bird, which the Lederers insisted she remove from her bedroom. She buried it in the yard but then dug it up a week later, telling Everly she wanted to see what had happened. There was almost nothing left of it, eaten by the teeming, tropical earth.

Something about the opaque fog, the disorienting experience of being on that drab and enormous ship, the bandaged survivors from the bombing in Preston, made everyone dazed and quiet. Even the Allains, the loudest people on earth, were silent and grim. They huddled around Panda, who was laid out on a navy cot, sick and coughing. Her feet stuck out from the end of the blanket they'd wrapped her in. She was wearing Giddle's old tap shoes, the black patent leather scuffed and dull, the metal plates bolted to the soles ground down unevenly. It must have been a privilege of illness to wear the coveted tap shoes.

Only Mr. Mackey was speaking. He was outraged, he told Mr. LaDue, who kept touching a cut on his forehead. Mr. Mackey shouted angrily that it was Lito Gonzalez they had to thank for this, that he'd orchestrated the whole thing, called in the Cuban army to drive them out. Mr. LaDue nodded, but it seemed as if he'd already given up, and that Mr. Mackey was just filling the air with irrelevant facts. Mrs. LaDue stood quietly by, holding Poncho in her arms. Poncho was dressed in one of the white double-breasted jackets that the bartenders wore at the Pan-American Club. Someone must have put it on him during the rescue. Maybe he was cold.

Poncho climbed down out of Mrs. LaDue's arms. He came across the deck toward Everly and Duffy and peeked down between the ship's rails at the water. 'Hi, Poncho,' Everly said tentatively, hoping he wouldn't stay long, that he would lose interest and pay attention to someone else. He gazed up at her, hanging on to the railing with both hands, like a bored child. Then he began to swing back and forth from the railing. 'No, Poncho,' Everly said. She tried to pull him away from the rail, but he was too fast. He was on the outside of the rail now. Everly grabbed his furry, warm arm and tried to pull him back onto the deck. When he lunged to bite her, she let go. She'd forgotten that Poncho didn't have teeth. He slipped from the rail.

Luckily, he landed in a lifeboat that was strapped to the side of the ship a few feet below the deck. He stood up in the lifeboat. They were traveling at full speed, and the ocean, far down below him, moved swiftly past, greenish-black in the early morning light. Standing in the little boat wearing just the bartender's jacket, he

403

looked like a small, hairy man nude from the waist down. People ran to the rail to see what had happened. Mrs. LaDue pleaded with him in a cracked and desperate voice. Mr. LaDue rushed off to get the purser for help. 'Sweety, please come back up here. Can you climb up the rope? Mommy loves you. Please, Poncho, *please.*'

He was so close, just a few feet below them, but he refused to climb back up. He looked out at the horizon, as if in a moment of great contemplation, or faking a moment of great contemplation, knowing he had a rapt audience, keeping them in suspense as he stood there, balanced in the lifeboat. He did not look at Mrs. LaDue, though she pleaded with him. Not until the very last moment, when he looked up at her and smiled a broad, gummy smile. Then, in one swift movement, he knocked his head against the side of the ship, forcefully. It made a loud smack! Everyone gasped. Mrs. LaDue screamed. Poncho took a wobbly step toward the side of the lifeboat. Like a sleepwalker, or a drunk, he was leaning over the side. He leaned farther and farther until he went over, headfirst.

The whole episode was so seamless and precise — the smack, those shaky steps toward the edge, then going over and plunging into the water. Almost choreographed, Everly thought, but a terrible choreography.

He was facedown, floating on the water. The ship was moving fast, and Poncho was almost behind them. They all watched, Mrs. LaDue in hysterics, as the white bartender's jacket ballooned with air. Then the white jacket began

404

to fade into the depths of the greenish-black water.

Mrs. LaDue was screaming for them to stop the ship and turn it around. Everly remembered that it would take several miles for a large ship to stop when it was going full speed, something she'd read, though she couldn't remember where.

Afterward she kept imagining the feel of Poncho's gummy mouth on her hand, if only she'd kept it there. If she'd held on to his arm as he'd bitten her she could have pulled him safely back onto the ship. She closed her eyes and saw the scene and felt his mouth clamping onto her hand, that lunge when she'd known he would bite her, leaving the hand there and letting it happen. Over and over she imagined it. Just leave it there and let him bite. Knowing he couldn't puncture the skin, couldn't hurt her, didn't have teeth. Still, every single time she wanted to pull her hand away.

★   ★   ★

They had a modern medical facility in Guantánamo, and Panda was admitted and put under the care of an American doctor. Mrs. LaDue also was seen by an American doctor, who gave her a sedative. They were placed in plain, almost barren guesthouses across from a dusty baseball diamond, and ate American hamburgers and American-style soft-serve ice cream that evening at a military mess hall. The Guantánamo street signs were in English. The commissary sign, too,

405

where they had *Playboy* magazine on a display rack. One of the Nicaro boys stole a copy. There were American sailors everywhere. By the second day, Val Carrington was already dating one.

An immigration services official arrived in the afternoon that second day, sent by the U.S. government to assist them. He collected their passports, would handle all their paperwork, and help them repatriate. The process would not be quick, and everyone was asked to be patient.

Two days later they were summoned in alphabetical groups. *A* through *L* was the first group. They waited in line outside a Quonset hut. Genevieve and Giddle Allain were doing handstands and cartwheels. They both wore shorts under their dresses so they could practice without flashing their underwear. Val whispered to Everly that the Allain sisters were wearing her old shorts. 'Mother must have given them a bag of stuff I didn't want anymore.' Val thought it demeaned them, but it didn't. The shorts were madras and they looked good on Genevieve and Giddle, both girls upside down, skirts over their heads, Giddle walking on her hands.

People looked at their watches. It was after 8:00 A.M., and no one had come to open the hut. Finally an immigration services official arrived with three military policemen. They walked up to Hatch Allain and pulled him aside.

No one could hear what they were saying, but everyone — *A* through *L* — could see what was happening. The policemen handcuffed Hatch. Then they walked him past all the other

Americans, right past his own family. Hatch smiled and spoke to them. Maybe it was the only dignified thing to do, with everyone staring. He said to no one in particular that the little monkey might have had the right idea. And then the immigration official and the military police led him into the Quonset hut and the door was shut behind them.

What was the right idea? Everly thought about it and thought about it, and finally it dawned on her that maybe Poncho had been trying to escape. To *get* someplace, into some other life, away from being Mrs. LaDue's pet monkey. Like the Chinese railroad workers Everly had read about, who hung themselves from nooses to try to get back to China, as if suicide were a form of travel, like air travel or sea travel. She didn't know where Poncho had been trying to go. Hatch would be going to prison.

* * *

There was a lot of killing time at the guesthouses, people hoping to send telegrams and make calls. But the telegraph machine was intermittent and the phones were dead.

Everly was sitting on the guesthouse porch when Mrs. Carrington returned with a letter. Everly asked if it was news of Mr. Carrington, and added that she hoped he was okay.

Mrs. Carrington gave the oblique reply that Everly shouldn't worry about Mr. Carrington, that he'd be fine, just fine. Then she went into the room she was sharing with Val, and returned with two photo albums that she set on the porch table in front of Everly.

Everly figured it was memorabilia, like Stevie and her Duchess of Windsor scrapbook, Stevie and her Cuba scrapbook, with maps and restaurant menus and articles from *Unifruitco*, photos of all three Lederer girls at the Preston pool. Stevie had taken the Cuba scrapbook with her when she'd left for boarding school.

'Go ahead, open it,' Mrs. Carrington said.

They were black-and-white photographs of ports and other industrial sites, mounted on matte black paper, each photo labeled and dated in white pencil. Montevideo, 1942–43. Caracas, 1945–47. Sulaco, 1950. Page after page, hundreds of photos.

'All the projects my husband worked on,' Mrs. Carrington said.

Suddenly Everly envied this instinct to document life as it happened, and wished she'd documented hers. All the ports Mr. Carrington had helped to build, and he had proof. They had been forced to leave, and Everly had documented nothing of the past seven years. She could barely remember Oak Ridge, where she'd lived until she was eight. She only knew Nicaro, and she had nothing of it to show, the clothes on her back, the white purse that for no logical reason she had grabbed at the last minute before they were hustled into the mine. Inside it was the gold faucet handle K. C. Stites had given her from Mr. Stites's Pullman car. Because Duffy was still upset about her box of coral, Everly gave her the faucet handle. A decade later, she wanted

it back, but by that time it was lost. Duffy might
have just thrown it away, not understanding what
it was or that it was worth keeping. And isn't that
why you gave it to her, she thought, to transfer it
to someone for whom it would have no value?
But now I've changed my mind. They were all
grown up by then. Why did Everly suddenly
want it? As some sort of proof, though it seemed
strange to want proof of affections she'd never
been keen on requiting. K.C. had placed the
faucet handle in her hand. In that moment she'd
felt every moment of every afternoon she'd spent
with Mrs. Stites, and the doubts that had traced
each of the moments, the unpleasant feeling of
being appreciated but not known, not known at
all by these people who were too different from
her. She'd thanked K.C. and put the faucet
handle in her purse, but she had not wanted it. If
Willy had given it to her it would have been
different, but he never would have. Willy had
danced with a broom like he was dancing with
her, twirling the broom around, swaying with it
from side to side and dipping it like it was a girl,
but not just any girl, his hand supporting the
small of her back, and the girl trusting him and
leaning low. It was either more subtle than a gold
faucet handle or more forward, maybe outra-
geously forward. Either way, it was all she was
going to get. She hadn't even been able to say
good-bye to Willy. The servants in the navy
barracks were locked in, for 'security,' as the
evacuation took place. Everyone was being
pushed into a group, lumped with the rebels or
the government or the Americans. She had to be

with the Stiteses and the LaDues and the rest of them, as if they were her people, and separated from Willy and the Cubans, who were not her people.

K.C. had kissed her on the cheek when he and his family left Guantánamo for Haiti. An awkward, dry kiss they both knew meant good-bye, and not the beginning of anything. Maybe she wanted his affection, but not to return it. Yet she sensed that by not returning it, it would dwindle. Everything did.

'He's probably one of those Bay of Pigs fanatics,' Stevie said when Everly wondered out loud what had become of K.C., two years after they'd left Cuba. 'Totally conservative. You can't even *talk* to those people. They won't reason. They're hysterical with greed.' Tico Leál had become one. Stevie ran into him at a party in New York City in early 1961. Stevie was a beatnik by then. She wore black turtlenecks and white lipstick and talked about exploitation and revolution, quoted Jean-Paul Sartre and Franz Fanon. She said Tico Leál pulled her into a bedroom and opened what looked like a violin case to show her his machine gun. 'Some of us have a plan,' he'd said.

★   ★   ★

Everly made her way through Mrs. Carrington's album, port after port, aerial shots from so high up they looked like maps rather than photographs. When she was finished, Mrs. Carrington placed the second album in front of her,

410

presented it as though there were a formal order, looking intently at Everly. She's gauging my reaction to something, Everly thought, opening the second album. But what?

★　★　★

A week after the evacuation they were in Miami, staying at a motel across from a Pickin' Chicken, where they ate dinner at an outdoor table, under a sky the deep pink of women's crème blush.

Everly would be going to her grandmother's in St. Louis. Marjorie and George and Duffy would stay with the other grandmother, across town. Neither had room for all of them, and thank goodness Stevie was at boarding school, her mother said, tuition paid by the company through the end of the year. Marjorie Lederer kept announcing that they were ruined in a manner so insistent that Everly began to wonder if there was a certain pleasure in insisting such a thing.

They finished their Pickin' Chicken and returned to the motel to watch the coin-operated television set mounted in the corner of their room. Fifty cents per hour, which Marjorie Lederer said was highway robbery, but they wanted to see the CBS special report on Cuba and their own evacuation. *'The town of Palma Soriano has officially fallen under rebel control, according to Cuban news sources.'* There was television footage of roadblocks and tanks, people cheering in the streets. Then an old Hollywood actor, the star of a film Everly had seen in Nicaro, waving from a silver sports coupe with gull-wing doors. Cubans flowed around and past the exotic car as if he and it didn't matter. The actor told reporters he'd helped rebels take the town, and for his efforts they were awarding him a special combat medal.

Marjorie Lederer sat at the motel room desk, itemizing their belongings from memory, every last appliance and piece of furniture, for which she expected, she said, full compensation.

'From whom?' George Lederer asked her.

'Your employers. The U.S. government. Lito Gonzalez. National Lead.'

'Dear, my employers stand to lose a hundred million dollars on their investment. And Lito Gonzalez ran us out of town, if you believe Hubert Mackey.'

'*No one was hurt in the evacuation of American citizens from the Nipe Bay area on the northeastern coast of Oriente Province,*' a CBS reporter said. '*Though one woman, apparently overcome with sadness at being forced from her home, needed medical assistance.*'

'That's not why,' Duffy said. 'It's because Poncho cracked his coconut! He cracked his coconut!'

★　★　★

Everly did as Mrs. Carrington instructed and opened the second of the two photo albums.

The first image was of a woman posing against a rock, wearing a halter shirt and short shorts, Cuban, with hair that looked like it had been ironed flat to tame its curls.

'She's pretty,' Everly ventured, unsure what she was supposed to say.

'They're all pretty, dear.'

Everly turned the page. Another woman, in a sheer blouse and tight skirt, also Cuban, posed against what looked like the very same rock. The next page, another, same rock. The next page, yet another, every single one of them smiling like she was smiling for a lover. 'We both know I'm sexy to *you*.'

'He said he wanted the pictures for when he was old and depressed,' Mrs. Carrington said. 'To remind himself of the good times he's had.'

Her husband's secret catalog of mistresses. Mrs. Carrington seemed strangely proud of the photographs, as if they belonged not to Tip Carrington but to her.

'My husband loved life,' Mrs. Carrington said, as though he were no longer living.

My husband loved life. And she had proof.

25

They were riding into United Fruit territory, a convoy of jeeps and cars and buses, some forty rebels comprising a handful of units that had converged in the foothills of the Sierra Cristal, outside the city of Holguín. La Mazière was a hero, and there was a designated spot for him in one of the open jeeps.

Campesinos along the road gave the V for victory sign, shouting 'Mau Mau! Mau Mau!,' a term that had recently become popular, an allusion to Kenyans fighting to drive out colonial British rule — rebels who, like the Cubans, were shaggy and unkempt. They waved back from the jeeps as they rolled down the rutted road, La Mazière a Mau Mau, too, thanks to a shortage of razors in the mountains.

Some of the younger men fired their guns into the air. You waste those bullets now, La Mazière thought, but you'll want them later, for the cascade of reprisals.

They descended the foothills of the Sierra Cristal and reached Birán in the early afternoon, stopping for a brief visit at the Castro hacienda. Señora Castro appeared on the porch in a black lace mantilla and cat-eye glasses and clutched Fidel like a lover she had believed she'd lost forever. La Mazière sat in the shade of a grove of giant algarroba trees with Hector and Valerio, laughing as a younger rebel from their troop

414

entertained them by chasing a nervous rooster across the lawn. Several maids and a butler came out of the house, the butler outfitted like the maître d' at Maxim's, in a crisp white jacket and bow tie, white gloves, a starched tea towel folded perfectly over his arm. The maids and the butler in his formal attire served cane juice from frosted-glass pitchers, wonderfully cool and sweet. La Mazière and the others sipped their cane juice, waiting for Fidel and his mother to finish their brief and Oedipal embrace.

The procession continued toward Preston, for a local-boys-make-good celebration. They detoured through the cane cutters' slum on the outskirts of the town, a miserable-looking place with an open sewer running along a dense collection of primitive palm-leaf huts, hundreds and hundreds of them, possibly thousands. People flooded out of the huts and surrounded them. Women cried and hugged husbands who'd been away fighting in the mountains. Barefoot children and toddlers in raggy diapers climbed over the tanks, boys and girls putting on the armbands that rebels flung from the jeeps. Someone even fitted one around a newborn baby's head, M-26 in red and black banding its young and tender skull.

They parked the vehicles in the center of town, in the midst of what seemed to La Mazière a rather impressive colonial enclave. On their way to Preston, they had circled through Nicaro, the other now-empty American community in the region. It looked like a caricature of middle-class values, a town through which a toy train snakes, absurdly tidy, though its white houses were stained a faint pink. At first La Mazière suspected it might have been due to the tint of his eyeglasses, but then he realized that the entire town was coated in a fine reddish grit. Beyond the town, a workers' slum. But the Nicaro slum, unlike Preston's, had been burned to the ground, a remnant of the Rural Guard's campaign of terror, which had worked against them and made every Cuban in the region a rebel sympathizer.

Preston was far more obvious and immodest than Nicaro in its wealth. The homes were enormous, with wraparound porches shuttered in varnished louvers, plantation estates that he guessed were modeled on those in the American South. The gardens of each enormous home were showcases of tropical foliage, the teeming verdure of Oriente crimped and strangled into picturesque mise-en-scène. Beyond one of the avenues a flawless green carpet rolled into the distance: a golf course, and adjacent to the golf course, polo fields.

Fidel gave a speech on the main plaza, more angered and moving and animated than any of the speeches the commander had delivered over Radio Rebelde, to which La Mazière's unit had listened or half listened while eating their nightly mess-tin ration of rice, bananas, or horse meat.

The three men who remained from the town's Rural Guard station stood uncomfortably to the right of Castro's retinue while the commander spoke. As surprised as anyone that Batista had fled, they were now abandoned to their fate. Castro had offered them amnesty if they gave up their guns, and what choice did they have? They stood, abject, stripped of their weapons, feigning enthusiasm for the transfer of power, trapped in an awkward fact of civil war: that the enemies often have no choice but to remain, either to be integrated, punished, or disposed of. La Mazière himself had avoided such a fate by enlisting in the Waffen, departing Paris as Germans and collaborators lined up to board transport vehicles fleeing east, to Sigmaringen. As he was driving out of town he'd seen the author Céline waiting in one of those lines, hurriedly stuffing his cat into a cardboard carrier.

They were gathered in the heart of imperialismo, Castro announced to the assembled rebels. Castro pointed to a set of offices, three-story buildings painted a mustard yellow. 'La United,' he said, aiming an accusatory finger at the buildings, as if the name alone were an indictment.

This town, Castro said, was the location of his own childhood dreams, this very place where they were gathered. Off-limits and American, it was the site where his imagination had been ignited, and roamed. Freely, he said, but in the freedom of dreams. The town of Preston was make-believe in its distance from his life just a few kilometers away, in Birán, make-believe in its luminosity, its impossibility. But real in its control, its ownership of everything and everyone.

'Off-limits and American,' he repeated. 'But of course, as many of you know, we Cubans were invited to cut the cane.'

There was laughter.

'Invited to lose an arm feeding the crushers at the mill. Invited, most graciously, to be fleeced

417

by the company store, whose prices were unspeakable exploitation, invited into a modern and more efficient version of slave labor. But you and I were not allowed beyond those gates over there,' he pointed, 'where the managers lived. 'La Avenida,' with, take note, the definite article. *The* avenue, but, of course, only for some. You could not walk down it. You were not allowed to swim in the company pool, go to the company club, use the company's beaches. You could not fish in their bay, Saetía, or go to school with their children, or date their daughters, or God forbid, should you get sick, be treated at their hospital. You could not own your home, which you yourself had built, own your own plot of land, which you worked with your own shovel, your pick, your hoe.'

He said that he'd spent his boyhood gazing from beyond the scrolled iron gates that enclosed La Avenida, gazing, he said, at a mirage overlaid with black arabesques, the wrought-iron bars of a fence through which he'd looked. A small boy, wanting only to glimpse a magical place.

That was all he'd wanted as a young boy, and it was all he'd been given.

'There is another man,' Castro said, 'whose destiny was shaped by La United: Fulgencio Batista.'

People booed and hissed.

'Let me make myself clear. Batista and I,' Castro said, 'are opposites. We both gazed through the fence, he in Banes, myself here. I grew up to hate imperialists. He grew up to love them, and learned to ingratiate himself on their terms. Became president and accepted their bribes, no less humiliated than a cane cutter! We are opposites. My father was a landowner. Batista's father was a guajiro who squatted on company property. Batista was born in a dirt shack, with nothing, like the men who worked my father's land. Born in a dirt shack. His destiny was to humiliate himself for the American landowner. Perhaps a man cannot change his destiny. Perhaps he has no choice. My own destiny was to evict the American landowner — '

There was cheering and applause and shouting.

'Viva Castro!'

'Viva La Revolución!'

The Rural Guardsmen standing at the front smiled uncomfortably. One managed a limp clap of his hands amid the ocean of applause.

Castro asked if a Señor Suarez was in the crowd, and if so, would he please step forward. A delicate-looking man in spectacles moved toward the front, people making room for him to pass.

Señor Suarez, Castro explained, had been left in charge by the Americans. For the first time in history a Cuban would be running the mill. For the first time in history, La United would pay their taxes. It was almost crushing season, and they would have a glorious harvest.

'This revolution,' Castro said, 'is for the cane cutters. It's time for them to take their cut. And for Cuba to take hers.'

He said the revolution was beginning, but that it wouldn't be an easy process, that it was a road full of danger.

'So many times now,' he said, 'our revolution has been betrayed. In 1898, when the Americans invited themselves to rape our Cuba like a waterfront whore. Disposable, syphilitic, and worthy only of contempt. In 1952, when Batista betrayed the people. Again and again, those who claimed purity of heart turned out to be thieves and riffraff. For the first time in four centuries, this republic will be free. For the first time ever, it will be true to its revolution. Fatherland or death: it is our choice.'

Despite the romantic tone, La Mazière appreciated Castro's obvious love for revolution as La Mazière himself loved it, purely, and for its own sake. True revolution was attitude and passion, not ideas and ideology, something Castro seemed to understand well. It was an epic of methods, not aims. Aims would come later, but what form they'd take was anyone's guess. In his radio speeches, Castro had spoken repeatedly about a New Man, who didn't fit into the old commonplace sloth of bourgeois democracy. He talked about a classless and authentic society, true to its cultural heritage, true to its heroes, in which virility, not privilege, was revered. He told his audiences they were the true elite, the unshaven, the unwashed, whose spirit is forged in action. The elite, he said, is not the man who uses the correct dinner fork. The elite is the man who knows how to eat with his hands.

Castro's words gave off faint echoes, La Mazière thought, of Drieu and Brasillach, minus certain more drastic elements. Not that Castro's vision was the same as Drieu's or Brasillach's.

But his idealism, like theirs, was radically unstable, as was all idealism.

There was an impromptu party after Castro's speech, in a rounded building with enormous windows that jutted over the bay like an ocean liner. Behind an elegant mahogany bar were signs in English describing variously flavored daiquiris — pineapple, coco, and lemon-lime.

In the center of the club's tiled dance floor there was a charred cavity, and another hole in the hallway where the bathrooms were located, shattered mirror fragments underfoot. The place had been bombed but not wrecked. The jukebox still worked, and music blared from it, a deluxe-model Wurlitzer stocked exclusively with Cuban songs — a detail of the place that La Mazière found oddly touching. He read it as some shred of desire, on the part of these now absent Americans, to assimilate, to claim that the Cuban music was as much theirs as it was anyone's, because they loved it as much as anyone else loved it. Even if a love that derived from proprietary was a kind of profound ignorance, it touched him all the same. The Americans had clearly loved the foliage, the daiquiris, the Cuban music. He could feel it in their empty town, the ghostly imprint of their naive and imperialist love.

Soldiers and locals, mill workers and cane cutters and their children all danced, careful not to step in the charred hole in the center of the tiled dance floor. They did the mambo, the pachanga, the cha-cha-cha, or rather 'cha-cha,' as La Mazière had learned this Cuban dance was properly called, the third 'cha' one more American excess.

People went behind the bar and made themselves drinks, American whiskeys and English gins. La Mazière, too, helped himself to the American whiskey. Having gone without such luxuries for several months now, his constitution was almost virgin to its eighty-proof. The warmth spread quickly through him, his cells catching fire in a manner that was entirely pleasant.

The rebels would be going to Santiago to pay their respects to the Black Virgin, then onward, in a slow and meritorious caravan to Havana. Batista had fled two days before, on New Year's Eve, and overnight the revolution had come to fruition. The rebels were the state as they danced in an abandoned American social club, drinking English gin and doing the mambo, careful not to step in the dance floor crater.

La Mazière began to feel himself receding from the scene, as if he were not a full participant in these festivities, a mind that was not part of their collective fabric, their revelry, but attached to something outside it.

He stepped onto the club's veranda and gazed at the endless blue water. Nipe, the largest bay in Cuba, so integral to the weapons shipments he'd arranged. There were smaller fishing boats and pleasure craft tied along the dock, and larger vessels, a barge and a United Fruit Company freighter anchored offshore. What was beyond the blue? The Bahamas, he guessed, to the north. And south and east, around the crenellated corner of the island, Hispaniola. Duvalier and his humility. Trujillo and his makeup.

The rebels were the state, and overnight. A transition that was not unlike a man waking up to discover he'd somehow married his mistress. A gesture that would surely kill the allure of romance, of luminous desire, in the very fact of its guarantee. Like killing the allure of a new government, a new power structure, in the very fact of its installment. He gazed at the watery horizon, indulging in a childlike wonder at the simple fact that there were unseen worlds beyond the blue. '*The sea! The sea!*' the soldiers cried out. He felt an old familiar hunger beginning to announce itself, the desire to dissolve back into civilian life and witness the rest of this thing, the completion of revolution's arc, from a cozily anonymous vantage.

He knew this part of the equation, the end of an arc, the waking up, the exorcism. Purges, kangaroo courts, justice. Lots of justice, for which the rebels would wish they'd saved those sky-aimed victory bullets.

★   ★   ★

He slipped out and headed toward a destroyed railcar sitting on a pair of tracks beyond the sugar mill. He walked along the tracks, which cut through an ocean of silver-green sugarcane, and eventually reached the main highway. He was in remote territory, but someone would have to come down the road sooner or later. Perhaps an American family who hadn't left in the mass exodus, optimists pressing their luck. He could claim he'd been a hostage in the mountains, kidnapped along with one of the groups that Raúl had held for several weeks. He'd explain that he was a Frenchman, wanting only to return to Paris.

He had little luck. The rebels had sealed the eastern half of the island, and almost no one had fuel. The few who did were not stopping. He walked until well after dark, and spent the night in a cane field.

Late the next morning, he was drudging along the side of the highway, the sun burning a hole in his back, when a car stopped — a roomy, brand-new Buick sedan, a wealthy Cuban family inside. They gave him passage all the way to Havana and asked no questions, which he found remarkable in its gentility, its politeness.

The journey was twenty hours, with lengthy delays at checkpoints manned by rebels glowering officiously, despite their rusted weapons and mismatched uniforms. One particularly insolent young soldier had been eating an enormous piece of bread, crumbs tumbling down the front of his shirt as he demanded the driver's identification and an explanation of their 'movements.'

'Who's he?' the soldier asked, pointing at La Mazière. 'A médico,' the driver said. 'He was helping in the East.' La Mazière stayed quiet, impressed at the gentleman's spontaneous tact, regretful that a devolution into bureaucracy was already taking effect. After a battery of questions, the soldier waved them through.

Gazing at the series of mirages that pooled up

ahead on the highway, one after another, La Mazière understood that while he missed Paris, he wasn't so anxious to return. Paris held no mirages, just familiar comforts, Dalida, whose wet, gleaming eyes offered an alluring violence, and yet her melodramas, silly and uncomplicated, bored him terribly after more than a few hours in her presence. Even her beauty was static and predictable. Rachel K's, on the other hand, was somehow transitive. It acted upon him.

My Woodsie gives radiant joy.

He thought of the blue-lit body, the firm-jelly breasts. Watching her, pleased and amused, from his table in the back of the Pam-Pam Room.

He'd never conceived of a dalliance with a fellow troublemaker, an insurgent, if that's what she was. The gulf of secrets he kept seemed disarmingly mirrored in her, a girl who might keep her own gulf of secrets. She was rarely forthcoming about anything. She'd claimed, more than once, that she wasn't Cuban. 'And yet you speak only Spanish,' he'd said. 'You say 'Lucky *Strye*' when you want a cigarette. And the way you operate, friend of this and that politician, thug, and revolutionary . . . you're certainly a savvy foreigner.'

'Like I've told you,' she'd said, 'my grandfather was from Europe. I take after him.'

To which La Mazière had replied that she seemed not only Cuban but quintessentially so. He was lying. He didn't know what she seemed. If anything, she looked middle European, ghosting some ethnic riddle, a living clue that someone, at some point — a grandfather,

425

perhaps — had been roaming someplace he didn't belong. You might as well be the brochure cover girl, La Mazière said to her, for — forgive him — that tacky rapture-promising tourist slogan 'Caribbean fleshpot.'

'Maybe it's only your rapture,' she'd said.

★　★　★

'I can't thank you enough. I think this is where I get out.'

They were caught in a traffic jam, amid the victory cavalcade of cars, trucks, motorcycles, and jeeps. In front of them, a confiscated Sherman tank was being towed on a flatbed truck.

La Mazière waved good-bye and set out walking along Máximo Gomez, a wide boulevard with chipped, pastel-painted porticos. Above the colonnades were enormous Spanish-colonial homes painted in rich creams, custard yellows, pale pinks, and pistachio greens, like rows of éclairs and meringues in a patisserie display case. He walked in the shade of the porticos, passing newspaper stands and lottery ticket hawkers, vendors selling peanuts, cane juice, and candy.

Block after block, he floated in the heady rush that came with reentering a place that was familiar but had been temporarily forgotten. He walked quickly, in a state of euphoric anxiety, as if the city's existence without him must somehow and suddenly be recaptured.

He stopped at a barbershop for a shave. He'd had the momentous shave after the deprivations of war before. The shave of shaves, more momentous than that first sip of whiskey. The faint gardenia aroma of the lather, a tacit agreement among barbers and men that fragrance was acceptable, even desired, as long as it remained faint. He lay in a green vinyl chair, his feet propped, his arms on the armrests, his eyes closed for this meditation, the passage to a groomed state of being.

As he reached the Prado, patting his smooth cheeks and damp, trimmed hair, he heard an amorandola, the same musician strumming it who seemed always to be there, on a recessed bench under the laurel trees, singing the same song that La Mazière had heard him sing before.

'Bonanza, bonanza, we'll all be rich! Bonanza, bonanza, the sea is calm — '

★ ★ ★

The sea was not calm, La Mazière was pleased to observe, as he got closer to the presidential palace and the heart of the old part of town. When he turned onto Zulueta, he encountered an energetic mob of boys and men with sledgehammers, systematically decapitating the parking meters that lined the street. Coins vomited onto the sidewalk and were promptly scooped into plastic bags. A man held the head of a parking meter up in victory, and in one smooth movement, like a javelin thrower, lobbed it through the plate-glass window of a clothing boutique. Others knocked out the remaining jagged shards of glass, and people climbed in and began undressing the mannequins, trying on clothing and taking what they wanted, leaving the mannequins nude, their joints turned in inhuman directions, heads lolling. La Mazière remembered being amused to learn that it had once been illegal in the United States for display window mannequins to go unclothed. A ridiculous and prudish law, and yet he admired it, in its passion for symbolism. That people had faith in a plastic model to carry some threat of real nudity? Marvelous, he thought, it was just marvelous.

He drifted toward Vedado, wondering which way the buoyant looting would go, erupt into mob rule, or be immediately quashed.

Near the Hotel Nacional a house was being ransacked, furniture tossed from second- and third-floor windows, expensive-looking things, and none of it was being salvaged — perfectly good furniture, a television, refrigerator, a tabletop radio. A woman in curlers and house slippers dumped kerosene from a large can onto the home's defenestrated contents. Someone threw a match, and thin blue flames rolled like liquid over the pile, which quickly grew into a face-warming blaze. The home had belonged to Colonel Ventura, La Mazière overheard, Havana's police captain.

The looting subsided later in the afternoon, when Castro sent orders that anyone caught stealing would be shot. Castro called a general and immediate strike, which effectively kept people off the streets. The casinos were closed. The shops were closed. The hotels were open. La Mazière 'checked in' to the Nacional — he attempted to pay, but the clerk would not accept his money,

428

explaining that he was leaving to honor the strike, and the cash registers were locked. Take a tip, then, said La Mazière, but the boy would take nothing, said to enjoy the hotel, and that everyone should have something gratis this special week. No one, though, would be in to clean the room.

'You can be sure of that,' a voice said. La Mazière turned around. It was his old hotel barmate, the forlorn little maharaja.

'I was given no choice but to break into the linen closet down the hall,' the maharaja said, 'and change my own bedsheets.' He'd heard the new government would be sealing hotel safe deposit boxes any day. It was the final straw, he told La Mazière. He was getting a flight to the Dominican Republic and hoping for the best. La Mazière wished him luck, wondering why people who seemed so broken by their own uprootedness would choose to live in hotels.

As the clerk handed him his room key, La Mazière asked if any of the cabarets were open.

Most, the boy said, were closed.

What about the Tokio?

The Tokio was closed. The owner of the club fled the island yesterday. They're all getting on planes. They've had a lot of bad luck at the Tokio, the boy said. The piano player's hands were blown off earlier in the month, a bomb under the lid of his baby grand, a terrible tragedy. And one of the Pam-Pam Room dancers, murdered by the secret police.

Did the boy know which of the dancers?

He'd heard she was Batista's mistress, but he

didn't know her name. He didn't cavort with those kinds of girls, he said, because his mother believed they were harlots and that they all had the pox, and if he ever so much as stepped foot in one of those places —

My Woodsie gives radiant joy. But then she takes it away.

26

Mother felt that we were abandoning Del. She said nothing tore her up more than the thought of her son coming home, hoping to clean up, be fed a sandwich and reunited with his loving mother, and to find the house empty and locked, the whole town vacated. It broke her heart. But going to Haiti meant at least we weren't so far away. Haiti was only a hundred miles east of Guantánamo. From the balcony of the Hotel Mont-Joli in Le Cap, where we were staying, Daddy pointed toward the blue horizon and declared to Mother that if she squinted carefully she could see Preston. 'Yes, I see it!' Mother exclaimed, 'that cluster of green — those are the palm groves of Saetía, right?' Daddy nodded and said he believed she was correct — Saetía, surely.

You couldn't see Preston or Saetía from the balcony of the Mont-Joli. What Mother saw was Turtle Island, just west of us, and it wasn't actually so green.

★ ★ ★

Daddy said the move to Le Cap was temporary, but he had Hilton Hardy and Henry Das pack up and ship us most of our belongings from Preston.

Daddy was optimistic. He'd helped broker the

deal with the weapons from England. The Cuban government just needed some support, he said. The State Department had abandoned Batista, but with England's help he might regain control and stamp out the rebels.

If Batista's government crumbled, Daddy was prepared for that. He had guys deep in negotiation with Castro. In the middle of a war, there's always time to stop and talk about taxes and tariffs and who's going to collect what. Not that different from what he accused Lito Gonzalez of doing, but Daddy didn't endanger American lives the way Gonzalez did, radioing that the town was being attacked by rebels so that Batista would send bombers over. Gonzalez hoped to take over, but that didn't last long. I heard he escaped to the Dominican Republic in the Nicaro yacht when Castro and his government started killing Batistianos.

No matter who came out on top, we would wait in Le Cap until things settled down. Life would eventually return to normal. The company had worked with every government, installed or elected, it didn't matter, since 1898. We'd work with Castro.

★   ★   ★

If there was nothing to see from the balcony of the Mont-Joli, from the top of the massive fortress south of Le Cap, one could actually glimpse the eastern tip of Cuba on a clear day. I took a trip out there by myself one afternoon and roamed the citadel and the ruins of

432

Sans-Souci, King Henri Christophe's palace. It was four stories of crumbling pink bricks, grass growing up among its foundation stones and what remained of the enormous stairs. The brick mortar was pink, too, supposedly made of limestone, molasses, and cow's blood. Sans-Souci had been ravaged by time and a couple of earthquakes, but even pristine it was difficult to imagine that a pink palace built of sugar and blood would be inspiring to a population of freed slaves. They had a new king, black instead of white, on a new gold throne, importing his robes and crown from France, his Lipizzaner stallions from Vienna — the idea of it is absurd and nightmarish. But maybe it's unfair to blame a black king for mimicking French notions of empire. King Christophe built Sans-Souci while Napoleon was conquering most of Europe, and why should anyone expect democracy in Haiti before it happened in France?

★　★　★

I asked Daddy if we would visit Mr. Bloussé. Didn't he live in Le Cap? Daddy looked at me and said, 'Who?'

My entire childhood, this figure loomed large, I mean mythical, in the jodhpurs, the cuff links, the slicked hair. Adventurous and elegant Mr. Bloussé, who spoke a French that anyone could understand, the pronunciation was so refined, who arranged for so many workers to come over and cut the cane, brought bottles of cognac to Daddy, entertained us with grand tales, always

433

followed by that mysterious boy who ended up working for the Lederers. And the Great Scandal of Bloussé's colored family.

How could Daddy forget? He brushed me off, and the subject was dropped. Over the weeks we were in Haiti, I wandered the port at Le Cap, watching men unloading the ships that came and went. They were the darkest people I'd ever seen. Their sweat-coated faces shone like black patent leather. And they had these strange haircuts, everything shaved but a tuft on top of their heads, like we were in tribal Africa. I walked the narrow streets, past wrecked mansions that had been built by the French in the eighteenth century, before the blacks deposed them, ripped the white from the flag and left only the blue and the red. I couldn't get Mr. Bloussé out of my mind. I kept picturing scenes from the stories he told in our parlor. The native voodoo practices, human sacrifice, and ceremonies presided over by an adolescent who was dressed half man, half woman, in a top hat and tails and lace skirts. I suppose it was a hermaphrodite, but I wouldn't have understood that as a child. People planting a lemon tree at the gate to protect their house from yellow fever. And one fellow who asked Mr. Bloussé to bring him an almanac from Paris. Mr. Bloussé did. He gave this guy an almanac and the fellow hid it from his village and declared he was controlling the sky. 'There will be a lunar eclipse on October thirteenth. The sun will set at seven fifty-nine on Thursday. A blue moon will appear in July.' And they all think he's a god on earth, dictating the heavens.

The life of this exotic gentleman, Mr. Bloussé, seemed dashing and sophisticated, and also savage. It fascinated me. Mr. Bloussé was Haiti. They were the same thing, and I felt him everywhere.

27

La Mazière told himself there was a chance it wasn't Rachel K. Batista probably had dozens of mistresses.

He had more than dabbled in this revolution, but he was so much less vulnerable than she. It was a war he engaged in lightly, almost anonymously, and then slipped away, sure that no one would miss him. Now was the time for nationals, not Frenchmen. He understood that for her it was not a game. She was betraying Batista, and moreover, she was disposable. When boys had been murdered by the Rural Guard in Santiago, their mothers flooded the town plaza, demanding justice. In Havana, when a student disappeared, his parents rushed to radio CMQ, where they waited to go on the air and call his name, pleading for his safe release. No one would have called her name or pleaded for her release.

If something had happened to her, he'd go back to Paris as soon as he could get a flight. The Pan Am office in the lobby of the Nacional was still open, but the airport, a clerk told him, was closed for security until after Carlos Prio arrived later in the evening. Only one terminal was functioning. The other had been torched.

He left the hotel, walking in the direction of La Rampa and Rachel K's apartment.

Certainly his reasons for wanting to see her, for hoping she was unharmed, were selfish and narcissistic. But love was both.

Six years earlier, just after he'd met her, on a trip to Africa he'd watched women wading into the Pink Lake of Dakar with salt pans balanced on their heads. A blissful scene, and yet he'd been unable to truly enjoy the silver opacity of the salty lake, the women nude from the waist up, dipping their pans in the water, because he'd felt a nagging emptiness. 'Greetings,' he'd written her, 'from the banks of nowhere,' not having realized that nowhere was anywhere she wasn't. He wasn't sure if it was the special fate of wounded dreamers or simply what it meant to be alive that he hadn't understood this until it was perhaps too late. His mind was riddled with remote compartments, like the caves at Lascaux that could be entered only by lowering oneself, dangerously, with ropes, the walls inscribed with nonsensical images of men with erections and bird masks, bison with their guts spilling out. He wanted to see his own birdmen and bison, whatever form they took, and had always told himself love was banal comfort that didn't lead to any cave, any recess of understanding. It was a mutilation of character that prevented men from reaching greatness, and should be kept minor. Little passions, as insignificant as little deaths, as the French called climax.

The streets were ghostly. The strike had worked surprisingly well. Soldiers had ridden through the city announcing Castro's message through bullhorns, and aside from a group of boys attacking a pay telephone with baseball bats, La Mazière saw few people.

He walked quickly, suddenly convinced that Rachel K might be the key to something, never mind that the idea of a person as a key was ludicrous sentimentality.

She'd proven herself to be arbitrary and mysterious, even unkind. There were times when he'd appeared, unannounced, and she'd acted as though she wasn't pleased to see him. Such a love object was no banal comfort. What if he and she could sustain their distance, but in proximity? Veil each other in lovely deceits, and put off the bewildering but highly likely possibility that love's true object was absence?

My Woodsie gives radiant joy.

The ice cream parlors on La Rampa were closed. The movie theaters as well, their marquees dark. He turned right onto Calle G, her street. She could be the one murdered, he knew, and he better be prepared.

He was so close now.

Little deaths.

There was only one death, and it was grand.

★   ★   ★

He saw the legs, painted in their prison chain link, dangling from the balcony of her apartment. That crisscross ink, smearable, but perfect and unsmeared.

The legs swung slowly back and forth, as if she

438

were lolling her feet off a boat dock.

He tried to subdue his elation. He had responsibilities, after all, a certain role to play.

He called up to her. 'Excuse me — miss?'

She leaned over between the rails of the balcony, blood rushing to her Manouche Gypsy or German Jewish face, the blond hair flopping forward.

She smiled, said nothing.

'I just thought I'd let you know that if you're waiting on the parade, it isn't until tomorrow.'

He was calm now, his cool and regular self.

'But I'm enjoying the other parade,' she said.

'Is that so.'

'The invisible parade. Empty streets, silence. Would you like to come up and watch?'

★ ★ ★

Her apartment was as messy as ever, a joyful mess. 'They left me in a room for a long time,' she told him. 'Suddenly a guard comes and yanks me up and escorts me out. That's it, I'm free. But it's strange, because I don't know why I got off so easily.'

'I know what you mean.' La Mazière thought of his own unforeseen amnesty, the yellow telex. He'd been thrilled, of course, even if his prison was not the worst. He'd been allowed to exit in street clothes, no escort, no handcuffs. When the prison gates slammed shut behind him, he'd stood under a sky so much more brilliant than he'd imagined that it was too bewildering to enjoy. He hadn't been prepared for the blue of

439

the sky, how stunning it was.

'¡GRACIAS A FIDEL! ¡VIVA LA REVOLU-CIÓN!' someone shouted from below her window, guiding cheers with a bullhorn. A chorus of voices joined in.

★   ★   ★

She'd been a brave and crucial part of the underground. Fidel had sent a message that there'd be a place for her in his revolution. She hoped so, she told La Mazière, because the casinos and cabarets were closed. No one knew when or if they'd reopen. Thousands of people were out of work.

The United Fruit executive cabled her from Haiti. He'd secured her an apartment in Cap-Haïtien and wanted her to go to the Nacional and retrieve valises full of Cuban pesos he'd left hidden in the closets of his suite. Sew the larger denominations into her clothing, he'd written — hide them wherever women hide things — and get on a plane. CAN'T WAIT. STOP. LIKE OLD TIMES. STOP.

But it wasn't like old times. A week after she got his letter, the executive's paper money was worth almost nothing. Castro had named Che Guevara finance minister, inciting panic among businessmen and a run at the banks. The peso plummeted. Prio, who had arrived in Havana on January 7, the same day as La Mazière, fled back to Miami on January 9, when Fidel announced he would expropriate Prio's country estate and convert it to an asylum for albinos, who desperately needed above all else *shade*, Fidel announced, from the incinerating tropical sun.

The morning after Prio left, Rachel K had been summoned to Fidel's headquarters at the Hilton. La Mazière was in her apartment drinking coffee and reading about the ex-ex-president's departure. Poor Prio, outraged and already condemning Castro, whom he'd helped bring to power. But there was a limit to La Mazière's sympathy. Toppling governments was not without risks. Prio losing his artificial waterfall was nothing compared to the guillotine.

She returned with an odd expression that La Mazière took for disappointment. Whatever place Fidel had planned for her in his revolution, La Mazière assumed it was a letdown, one that he had been waiting for. He figured she would come around to his own cynical feelings about the promises of revolution. Why couldn't he just enjoy the flux and tumult of sweeping change? Of history? He did enjoy it, in his own way. He had attended the public trials at the Sports Palace, entertained by the spectacle and ruthlessness of popular justice. That Castro was giving the Americans a run for their money — that was good, quite good. That they'd probably try to invade the Dominican Republic and knock off Trujillo — interesting, a bold tactical move. But logic was absent elsewhere. Castro, for instance, hosting a cookout for the new revolutionary air force at La Cabaña fortress, offering as barbecue a twenty-thousand-dollar breeding bull.

He clasped her face in his hands and said that

whatever it was they'd offered her — a job in a lightbulb factory is what he pictured, an ignoble and ridiculous bit part in their drably populist scheme — she shouldn't worry, that he and she could leave together.

'How would you like to go to Paris?' he asked. 'You've never been there.'

'I've never been anywhere,' she said.

Then he should take her to France, he announced.

He pictured her on the Boulevard Saint-Germain in her fishnets and heels, carrying her parasol on the Boulevard Saint-Michel, near the Sorbonne, a phantom conjuring of zazou in the birthplace of zazou.

I'll take her, he thought, to the Café de Flore, let her see the place for herself. Let her open the windows of my apartment onto twilit Paris. She'll stand there, watching the curtains flap around in the wind, moody and graceful apparitions, announcing in their movement — what?

That a certain Christian de La Mazière, occupant of 5B, has detained one final zazou. And if the rest of Paris wants to see her, wave hello or good-bye, all they have to do is look up.

She responded with only an inscrutable, luminous smile. Everything in her room seemed to glow with meaning — her eyes like a silent screen star's, the synthetic strands of a wig splayed on the floor.

The river of his thoughts flowed around her and the glowing objects in the room.

My Woodsie gives radiant joy.

'Paris,' she said.

'Yes.'

'Why would I want to go to Paris?'

'To see the world.'

But, she said, he talked about 'the world' as if it were all relative — no place and anyplace. Greetings, as he put it, from nowhere. This place, Cuba, was where she was from. It was all she knew, and she had no intention of leaving it. She'd spoken to Castro, and just as he'd promised, he'd reserved a special place for her in his revolution.

'Whatever it is, you can't possibly believe that — '

She was staying, she said. She added, in a gentle but imperious tone, that he might send her a card from his travels.

28

2004: Tampa

I have a bottle of cognac here, among the boxes that house Daddy's prized liquor collection from Preston. I ended up with the crates of crème de menthe and the little glass bears filled with kümmel. There's an entire case of Bacardi — the original Bacardi, made in Cuba, not like the fake stuff they put out now, which is made in Puerto Rico. The old Bacardi bottles are the size and shape of softballs, with nubby-textured glass and ruffle-edged bottle caps like on bottles of cola.

A whole case of the Bacardi, and I've never once dipped into any of it.

I don't think of it as something meant to be drunk, but a relic like all the other relics of our life in Cuba that I keep in this room, my den here in Tampa.

Del didn't express much interest in Mother and Daddy's stuff. The older son flies the coop. It's a classical model. The younger one stays in the nest, his mother's boy. After Mother and Daddy died, I put everything in here. Del said he would come up and have a look but he never has, even though he lives on Marco Island, a two-and-a-half-hour drive.

★   ★   ★

Mother kept immaculate records of our life. It's all here, in an old United Fruit accounting tablet that must weigh a hundred pounds. This morning I had to get the cleaning lady to help me move it.

My wife never came into this room, and I didn't much, either, the six years we were married. It's frankly overwhelming, though I hadn't meant to create any kind of mausoleum.

The big red lamp from the *Mollie and Me*. My silvered conch shell, which Chatty, the watchman at Saetía, gave me. It was Mother's idea to have it silvered, probably the very conch that Chatty blew the day I knocked Curtis's lights out. A framed image of the Black Virgin. I don't know who gave it to me, somebody who worked for Daddy. You can see the three miners and their capsized boat, the Black Virgin floating above the waves, to save them from drowning. A stack of old home movie reels, a hobby of Daddy's. I've looked at them a few times. Del and me playing catch with Daddy in the yard, riding our bicycles on La Avenida. You can see Annie, Hilton, and Henry in the background here and there. The prints are so scratched that in every scene it looks like it's raining. In some of them it *is* raining, and the only difference is that everything in the frame gleams with wet.

I pick up the conch shell, its inner spiral still a vibrant, fleshy pink, its white outer edge plated in silver. All these years and it never broke.

The phone is ringing. My answering machine will pick it up. I finally got one. Everybody was complaining that they'd call and my phone just rang and rang. I said, 'Let it ring. Call when I'm home.' But I must say, I like the machine. The phone rings once, the machine picks up, 'This is K. C. Stites, please leave a message,' and now I never have to answer. If someone insists on reaching me, they can come to La Teresita, where I take my lunch. Anyone who really needs to talk to me knows where I am. Five days a week, at eleven-thirty, seated at the counter with the green and black tiles, flirting with the waitresses. They call me 'Cuba' and I never have to order because it's the same thing every day.

*　*　*

Suppose you get only fifteen minutes. Would you travel three thousand miles to speak with someone you love for just fifteen minutes, if you know that it's the last time you'll ever see that person?

How far would you travel?

Suppose you could speak to someone you love who's no longer living. Would you cross a continent to speak to that person for just fifteen minutes?

You would.

When it's someone you love, the answer is that fifteen minutes is limitless if it means getting information about how to proceed without them. The chance of a clue is worth the journey. Because you don't know what that person will say to you. You can't guess what you might be turning down.

Just after my wife died, I came into this room and took an ancient phone book of Mother's from the shelf, black leather with gold lettering on the cover. The spine cracked when I opened it. On each page, twenty different kinds of ink and lots of crossing out. The people we'd known in Oriente moved around a lot after 1959.

The *Ls* — 'LaDue' — those folks were surely dead. 'Lederer.' They'd moved to Chattanooga, Tennessee. Everly and I wrote for a while, but like everything, that friendship had its time and place. I'd thought maybe she was the one, but what do you know when you're fourteen? We were not so alike. I think she knew it all along. I was too square for her, was the truth. I moved here, to Tampa, after college. I taught at a private school, ran the athletic program. I dated a lot of Cuban girls. I think they were a way to fight the homesickness. Weekends, I'd go over to the dances in Ybor City, the Cuban colony here. The music and the atmosphere reminded me of those native functions out in the batey that Curtis and I snuck into. I dated all kinds of girls, old, young, fat, thin. But I didn't commit until very late in life. I was fifty-four when I met my wife, on a public tennis court. She could murder the ball. Off the court, she was a kitten, ran a philanthropy, and was interested in museums, cultural things. Sharp as a tack and always cheerful, made everybody feel they were something special. Mother would have loved her.

I was in the *Ms* of Mother's ancient phone

book and found the name Charmaine Mackey, Phillip Mackey's mother. I had no idea if it was still the right telephone number, or if she was alive. As I said, my wife had just died. Twenty years younger, a knockout, and dead of cancer.

I don't know what drove me, but I picked up the receiver and dialed the number.

It had been disconnected.

Probably a number from 1963! I mean, ridiculous.

Ever since I was a child, old phone numbers have had this magnetic effect on me. Clavelito used to sell special telephones during his faith healing hour on radio CMQ. They were for calling the dead. He sold various things, planchettes and Ouija boards and something called a 'volometer,' which was for measuring a person's willpower. 'Psychic telephones,' Clavelito called them. I don't know how they were supposed to work. I wanted to see one, but it was a thing you mail-ordered, and as you can guess, they were expensive.

I picked up the phone and called information. It's nationwide now.

I suppose it's strange that I would want to call Phillip Mackey's mother, and not, say, any of the Allains. Maybe the Allains were too close to my childhood, and in another way too far.

When the operator answered I asked for Mackey, Charmaine Mackey. There was one listed in Carlsbad, New Mexico.

I felt like I was doing something you aren't supposed to do. Put it this way, I didn't go down to the Teresita afterward and start announcing to the guys at the lunch counter that I'd spent the morning stalking people I'd known as a child.

I've always been curious to know what went on with Phillip Mackey and Del before Phillip was sent away, how it was he and Del got mixed up with the rebels. I thought it might explain what went on with Del later, his decision to leave home and go up to the mountains to fight. Del does not talk about that period of his life. He said a few things to Mother when he arrived in Haiti a month after the revolution, but as far as I know, that was it. He never brought the subject up again. Now he's very conservative, very buttoned up. He's my own brother, but he leaves no opening to ask about the past. It's like he isn't the same person. If I ever bring up our childhood, he asks me if I've already seen the photos of his new boat. He doesn't encourage real conversation. His wife offers me a drink and they've got a new patio set they want to show off. The three of us sit down together and they smile at me with their dentistry smiles. My brother says he doesn't know about the rest of us but it's time for a dip in the pool and leaves me there with the wife. She probably has no idea about Del's complicated history. He's in control, and there's no window to ask questions, certainly not about things that his current life, in every aspect, contradicts.

I figured if I found Charmaine Mackey, I could ask about Phillip's whereabouts, then maybe call him or write him a letter. We never saw the Mackeys after we left Cuba. They didn't move to Florida like a lot of people.

I dialed the number for Charmaine Mackey of Carlsbad, New Mexico.

The phone rang once, and a woman answered. I could feel the particular muffled quiet of a very old person's home.

I say I'm hoping to reach a Mrs. Mackey, formerly of Nicaro, Cuba.

'Yes, dear,' she says. 'How can I help you?'

★ ★ ★

In a way I envy Del for not wanting any of this stuff. My brother moves through life and doesn't look back, drawn intensely into one thing, then another, each thing canceling out what came before it.

The wife he has now, it almost seems an indiscretion that anyone fathom Del pining for a person like Tee-Tee Allain. Del's wife wouldn't understand that girls like Tee-Tee exist, with her accidental charm, an accidental femininity, a despite-everything sexiness, dirty legs, wolf's eyes, stringy hair, and possibly crazy. Del's wife is the antidote, a trophy, very artificial. She's what he was supposed to want. I doubt he wants it, and I'd guess that is partly the point.

★ ★ ★

When Del turned up in Le Cap in early 1959, he'd seen Raúl Castro 'execute,' or so they were calling it — more than a hundred men in Santiago. Del was ordered to bulldoze the bodies into a mass grave, and I believe that's when my

450

brother's career as a 'barbudo' came to an end. He told Mother he'd seen body parts floating in the Levisa River that December just before he disappeared, peasants that the Rural Guard had chopped up and dumped in our river. Then he was ordered to dump people into a mass grave. Violence got him in and violence pushed him out.

A year after the revolution he was very anti-Castro, living in Miami and working with various parties to 'get the place back,' he said. Of course, that world turned out to be just as violent as Raúl's. Lito Gonzalez was involved in these movements to overthrow Castro, a Miami big shot. He went to start his Cadillac one morning in 1975 and blew himself to bits. There was a lot of infighting with those guys, a lot of disputes. I came across Lito Gonzalez's grave in Woodlawn Cemetery down in Miami. I was taking Rev. Crim's widow to put flowers on her husband's headstone. After we left Cuba Daddy remained close with Rev. Crim, who had conducted Methodist services in Preston and run the agricultural school. The dictator Machado is buried in that cemetery. So is the president before Batista, Carlos Prio. Prio blew his brains out. People said it was financial troubles. Deke and Dolly Havelin are buried there. They share a giant black marble mausoleum with the inscription, 'Cubanos de corazón.' Pretty sappy, but so was poor Deke, who'd given up his citizenship and couldn't return to the States, not until his relatives shipped him back to be buried in Florida. The family mausoleum at Colón Cemetery in Havana, where Deke had wanted to be laid to rest, was engulfed in ficus roots, its Lalique windows smashed and anything removable taken. Deke and Dolly had ended up living in the Dominican Republic. They were in São Paulo for less than a month, Deke relishing his grand appointment as a Cuban diplomat, before Batista fled the island and the curtain came down. The minute he flees, you're not ambassador anymore.

After the Bay of Pigs disaster, Del gave up agitating and got into weight lifting. He worked out with Steve Reeves on Muscle Beach. Now it's real estate. Del has done very well for himself. He lives on Marco Island, where the money is.

Feelings run high. Just sit at the Teresita for one lunch rush and you'll get the drift. People who feel that everything was stolen from them, and just because it's been almost fifty years now doesn't mean they have forgotten. They haven't. Nor have the companies. A company is like a person in that it has a memory, its own institutional memory. A company can wait and anticipate with more patience than a person. There are pending claims against the Cuban government that the Cubans ignore. Mining concerns like the old Nicaro Nickel Company keep meticulous account of what they lost. United Fruit became United Brands became Chiquita. CEOs came and went. The claim lives on, in a black binder somewhere at the Justice Department — $350 million at this point, with inflation. After every last person who worked for United Fruit is long dead and gone, still, the company will fight to get its assets back.

An assistant in Daddy's office, Mr. Suarez, ended up overseeing cane crushing and processing after we left for Le Cap. He was ambitious, and when they nationalized they made him administrador, which is what the Cubans call manager. Suarez was bright, and he got the whole operation up and working. When they were short on fuel, he had them running the mill on bagasse, which is cane trash. Suarez was competent, and yet Daddy said that up until 1963 he got a phone call every afternoon after Suarez did his rounds. He called Daddy every day, to run the numbers and report on what was happening. At a mill that was owned by the Cuban government! The company built the mill and the town and the culture around it. You extract the culture, and there's no purpose to the operation, no overseer, no witness. For whom is the sugar ground? Suarez couldn't accept that it was no longer ground for us.

Daddy died in 1964. I honestly think he died of a broken heart. You don't transfer someone to bananas or pineapples, just throw away immense knowledge and experience, when they've spent their entire adult life managing a sugar operation. He retired early and became very depressed. I went to military school in Gainesville, Georgia. It was September when I enrolled, and I cried myself to sleep every night because the leaves were falling off the trees. I'd never seen anything so terrible.

Some people say Hemingway killed himself because he was devastated that he wouldn't be able to go to Cuba anymore, after the U.S. travel ban. His first suicide attempt was the day Kennedy announced the Bay of Pigs on television. Maybe it's worthless to wonder why someone does such a thing, but I can believe that theory. It wrecked a lot of lives to seal the place off.

★   ★   ★

'Yes, dear,' Mrs. Mackey said. 'How can I help you?'

I explained who I was, slightly mortified for disturbing this ancient woman. She said she remembered me, but I don't think she did. I think she was being polite. Of course she remembered Mother and Daddy. We talked about the evacuation, where they'd gone from Guantánamo. She said her husband had wanted to stay in Nicaro, but Lito Gonzalez threatened to kill him if he didn't leave. I wondered if she had an active imagination, though a lot of people thought Gonzalez was trouble. She laughed about it, the way old people are able to laugh about serious things because they happened so long ago.

She told me she and her husband divorced just after they returned from Cuba. I said I was sorry to hear it and she said don't be, that it was for the best. He'd always made her nervous, she said, and he couldn't stand nervous women. She'd remarried, a gentleman from Puerto Rico, and they had a daughter together. I asked her about Phillip, curious to hear where he lived, what kind of work he did.

'Phillip has been dead for eight years now,' she said.

I couldn't believe it. I'd always had this vague idea that someday I would get in touch with Phillip Mackey and ask about him and Del and their involvement with the rebels, what Phillip thought of the revolution, Castro, everything. But it was too late. I called too late.

Now, that is an irony: Del lives in Collier County, two and half hours away. I would travel around the world to get fifteen minutes with my wife, with Mother. But I can't ask a living person to explain something to me.

It had never crossed my mind that Phillip Mackey would be dead, that Charmaine Mackey would be alive and tell me this. She said Phillip had been living in Paraguay — some of the people from Nicaro and Preston were serial expat types. I guess Phillip went that way, too. He got sick and tried to work through it, whatever that means. It doesn't really matter how he died. The Puerto Rican husband was gone as well, she said. The men always go first. I asked if anyone looked after her. She said no, that she had to take care of their daughter, who was handicapped. This is a woman who must be in her late eighties. Calling her felt like a real intrusion, asking her about her life from fifty years ago, and making her talk about the death of her son. But before we got off the phone she said she was glad I called and she hoped I'd call again. I never did. It's been three years now. I don't know if she's still alive.

I'm looking through Mother's United Fruit ledger. It's so fragile that each page I turn, the paper tears and starts to unglue from the binding. There are photographs, pressed flowers, letters, and telegrams. There's a picture of me in one of the school plays. I hated that play. I was a plum pudding. Mother made me do it.

Here's a program from the Cabaret Tokio, where Xavier Cugat used to perform. 'Air-conditioned,' 'national and international Stars' — they capitalized the *S* for some reason — et cetera. The telephone number is on the bottom of the program:

B-4544

Not something you can call. But what if you could?

People say Batista had a gold telephone, fourteen-carat, a gift from American Telephone & Telegraph — another company that has a giant lawsuit pending against Cuba. Maybe it's true about the gold phone, but people like to caricature guys like Batista, which makes them that much harder to see. Daddy kept his distance, regarded him as a thuggish sort, but he had a certain respect. Batista was not another peón, an animal that talked, a cartoon with a solid gold telephone. He was of mixed race and from very poor people — a class lower than the lowest class. He'd worked his way up to president. You have to allow people their contradictions, give them what they're due.

Del once said that Mother's sympathy for people, without any sympathy for what caused their circumstances, was not real sympathy but sentimentality.

Perhaps it's true. The fact is we went down there and we took. But I don't think it was Mother's responsibility to change that fact, or anything else. I don't think her sentimentality was any kind of crime.

Hilton Hardy became mayor of Preston. Castro renamed our town 'Guatemala,' but I can't imagine anyone who remembers it as Preston saying 'Guatemala.' That is incredible — our chauffeur, mayor of Preston! But that's communism. Ho Chi Minh started out as a fry cook at the Ritz.

I fish in the Caribbean all the time. I have a boat. I go to the Bahamas. I could easily sail clear into Preston Harbor, go and knock on the door of my very own house. But I never have. I understand that the town is terribly run-down, and I don't want to see that.

Everly Lederer and her sisters are the only ones who have gone back, as far as I know. She went to Preston and took photos and showed them to Rev. Crim's widow, who told me about it. I have Everly's phone number. Mrs. Crim gave it to me. But I haven't called her. Mrs. Crim said the photos were awful to look at. She said our house is a school and the Crims' house has about fifteen families jammed into it. Mrs. Crim said Everly told her that she and her two sisters were hoping to find their old houseboy. I wonder if it was that curious boy who'd worked for Mr. Bloussé. Apparently they found this fellow living in Levisa — Castro's 'revolution showcase.' The Rural Guard had burned Levisa flat, and Castro rebuilt it straight away and gave all the blacks real houses, with poured-concrete foundations and indoor plumbing. Mrs. Crim said Everly told her she wires the houseboy money every month, sends it to Mayarí, and the houseboy takes the bus down there to get it. She said Everly talked about this houseboy as if he were practically a blood relative. She goes back there every year to see him, and stays with him and his wife. At some point I'm going to call her. I'd like to hear about Preston, at least I think I would. Part of me isn't sure if it's the same place, now that we're not there, the company isn't there. I'll have to be good and ready when I call her. Mrs. Crim said she had the uncomfortable feeling that Everly was a sympathizer to communism. My thought was maybe she's just a sympathizer period, like Mother.

★　★　★

My phone is ringing again. Someone keeps calling and hanging up without leaving a message. It's a quarter to eleven. Soon I'll go down to the Teresita. It might be Red McGreevy calling, but I'll see him at lunch. The Teresita is what you call a joint, and all my buddies eat there. Red is old-fashioned like me, makes a call, and if he gets a recording puts the phone quietly back on the cradle instead of speaking into the machine. Too old to adjust to the new ways. He and I and some other guys are going hunting this weekend. They wanted to hunt just pheasant, but I insisted we hunt geese as well. If you hunt only pheasant you're done at nine in the morning and end up in the lodge drinking brandy the rest of the day.

★ ★ ★

Eventually the state went after Clavelito. They forced him not to sell any more mail-order merchandise, magic powders, and special equipment. Right before we left Preston, they took him off the air completely.

There were articles about it in the papers, housewives, his main fan base, up in arms. He was being charged with fraud, and part of the reason was those special phones for calling the dead. 'Selling faulty equipment' was one of the charges.

It seems silly to ban such a thing, much less prosecute someone for selling them.

Anyone who buys a psychic telephone doesn't really believe it's going to work. That all you need is $19.99. Buy the machine. Take it home. Plug it in. Dial a number and hear the living voice of someone dead and vanished. People buy things for other reasons. They weren't born yesterday. They don't need the law to tell them the equipment is faulty.

Let people learn for themselves:

You don't call the dead.

The dead call you.

459

Epilogue

There it was on the globe, a dashed line of darker blue on the lighter blue Atlantic. Words in faint italic script: *Tropic of Cancer*. She had crossed it more than once, but still she pictured daisy chains of seaweed stretching across the water toward a distant horizon.

And still there was the paradox of zones and borders on a surface that was fluid, that could float a bottle containing a message halfway around the world. During his exile at Guernsey, where the granite cliffs were shaped like kings, a monster, a nun's habit, letters reached the author addressed simply 'Victor Hugo, Océan.' Had the woman from Guernsey really invited the man from Dakar to dinner? It seemed unlikely for 1952. There was a detail a child might overlook: the man from Dakar would be black.

★ ★ ★

This time she crossed the Tropic of Cancer in an airplane. Her sister brought the scrapbook, but the flight from Miami was so short they barely had time to look through it. 'Prime rib, Harvard beets, whipped potatoes, a cold buffet with pineapple ring, and for dessert, rum raisin ice cream from El Louvre in Havana — the Duke of Windsor's favorite!' Their dinner menu from the SS *Florida*. 'We didn't stay at the Lincoln Hotel,'

460

the youngest said, the flames of the Regla oil refinery burning in the distance as their taxi sped along the Malecón. 'It was the Sevilla, the Graham Greene place with the Moorish tiles.' On the Air Cubana connection from Havana to Santiago, a stewardess passed out hard candies and paper cups of water. The seat belt signs were in Cyrillic.

★   ★   ★

It was 1999. They stayed at the Rancho Club Motel in Santiago, where their father had attended Raúl Castro and Vilma Espín's wedding reception a month after the revolution. 'I promised I would attend, and I am keeping my word,' he'd told Marjorie Lederer, though of course he was thrilled to attend. He returned from Cuba ecstatic, humming Danzón melodies. A marvelous, earthy affair, he said. He and Mr. Billings flew down together, George Lederer toting a Bundt cake pan despite his doubts that it was an appropriate wedding gift for revolutionaries. 'It's *cast aluminum*,' Marjorie Lederer said. 'It's a very good Bundt cake pan.' Everly was given the exact same model of cake pan when she married. She and Raúl shared kitchen equipment, a pan she never used and was sure he hadn't, either.

★   ★   ★

'Do you know a Willy Bloussé?' she asked everyone she spoke to their first day in Nicaro.

461

The Cubans on the old manager's row were mostly plant technicians. They made it quickly apparent they didn't associate with Haitians, people who'd been servants under the old regime, so she asked only Haitian men.

Their second day, as the sisters sat on the veranda of their old house passing around photographs with its new occupants, a man came walking up the road and stopped in front. She should have known from his slow, rhythmic saunter that it was Willy, wearing a navy blue newsboy cap like he'd always worn.

'When they told me 'someone named Everly Lederer is in town,'' he said, 'I didn't believe it. It was like a dream.'

★ ★ ★

The house of Willy and his wife, Malvina, was tidy, meticulously decorated with Malvina's fake flowers and Haitian dolls. But they had no telephone. Their electricity was out. Their toilet was in a dark corner, separated from the rest of the house by a plastic curtain. And they cooked on an alcohol burner out back behind the kitchen, under palm thatches. Race still mattered in Nicaro. Many other things were the same. The shampoo fragrance of ripe guavas, and enormous black butterflies like airborne swatches of scalloped velvet. The ammonia tanks next to the ice factory on the bay. Their club, Las Palmas, modernized and anyone could go there now, though they served only beer, and no one had money to buy it. The sisters went. Their beer was served in sherbet glasses. Why not? Everly thought, sipping her flat beer.

The flamboyán Willy had carefully tended was taller than their old house. Its vermilion petals spilled over the roof, partly caved in and covered with a frayed tarp. Willy laughed about the roof. He repaired his own with homemade tar and it didn't leak. Willy planted vegetables, machined parts to fix his refrigerator, welded his own hand-operated cane crusher and mounted it on a tree in his backyard. He offered them each a cup of cool, sweet guarapo. Willy was prepared for the future.

Pamela and Luís Galindez lived just up the street, in Levisa. Pamela was trapped in the past. 'When you leave, honk the Klaxon!' she said. 'Everyone will know I had visitors who came in a car.' She wanted Everly to send her clothes from Burdine's in Miami, but clothing from 1958. 'A cardigan with the shiny things — the sequins,' she said in rusty English, a language she hadn't used in forty years. 'And Capezios — or those moccasins with, what are they called, the *seeds* sewn onto them.' The last thing she said when they left: 'Everly, don't forget the slippers with the seeds! Size eight — '

★ ★ ★

Tip Carrington lived in Mr. Mackey's old house. He was retired, but for many years he'd been administrador of the nickel operation, a hero who figured out how to run the plant when they nationalized, famous all over Cuba, a 'personaje' honored by Fidel, given a house and a decent pension. A happy old man, slightly crazy, wandering shirtless in his nickel company hard hat. Baby pigs pattered around on the house's tiled floors, the same cream and blue tiles as the Lederers' old house, the same pink and black bordello bathroom. His wife, a mulatta from the countryside, was thirty years younger. She made rum in a still on the back porch, and the two of them drank it on the front porch. She drove her very own state-awarded automobile, which upset the neighbors greatly. 'She lets delivery people look up her skirt, to get extra loaves of bread,' they said. 'She doesn't wear underwear.'

★ ★ ★

Red dust was everywhere, so fine it was like a gas, under their fingernails, in the seams of their clothes, in the weave of paper money, a glaucous powder that coated their skin. There was more red dust than she remembered, but underneath the dust was the same jungle-green, a profusion of it. The sea as well looked green, under heavy-lidded clouds. Had it always been that color, or had its colors changed? The sea is a multitude, a roar of voices. And then again a silence, an absence of voices. The green water in Levisa Bay lapped softly, making almost no sound. In the crash of foamy waves that pounded the shores of Guernsey, the exiled author decoded messages from Dante, Marat, and Molière. *Don't forget the slippers with the seeds.*

Why is the water green? she wondered. Perhaps it had something to do with algae, or minerals, or light. The Red Sea wasn't red, but its surface, reflecting the mountains beyond it, sometimes appeared red. And whether it means red or something else — perhaps 'not mirrorlike' or 'very opaque' — the sea in the *Odyssey* is wine dark. It can be mirrorlike, silver as a mirror's surface, or black as its tain. Or blue. Like an eye, it both reflects and refracts the sky at which it gazes.

We do hope that you have enjoyed reading this large print book.

Did you know that all of our titles are available for purchase?

We publish a wide range of high quality large print books including:
Romances, Mysteries, Classics
General Fiction
Non Fiction and Westerns

Special interest titles available in large print are:
The Little Oxford Dictionary
Music Book
Song Book
Hymn Book
Service Book

Also available from us courtesy of Oxford University Press:
Young Readers' Dictionary
(large print edition)
Young Readers' Thesaurus
(large print edition)

For further information or a free brochure, please contact us at:
Ulverscroft Large Print Books Ltd.,
The Green, Bradgate Road, Anstey,
Leicester, LE7 7FU, England.
Tel: (00 44) **0116 236 4325**
Fax: (00 44) **0116 234 0205**

WHAT WAS PROMISED

Tobias Hill

Post-war London: Children run wild on East End bombsites, while their elders strive for better lives in a country beggared by victory. Clarence and Bernadette Malcolm have come five thousand miles in search of prosperity, but find that the Mother Country is not at all what it was promised to be; Solly and Dora Lazarus, too, are strangers in a strange land, struggling to belong even as they try to make sense of their past; and Michael and Mary Lockhart take with both hands all that the world owes them, whatever the cost. In the street markets and tenements of Bethnal Green the three families live and work together in uneasy harmony, until Michael shatters the balance between them, his hunger for betterment changing the courses of all their lives over decades and generations.

REMEMBER ME LIKE THIS

Bret Anthony Johnston

Four years have passed since Justin Campbell's disappearance, a tragedy that rocked the small town of Southport, Texas. Did he run away? Did he drown in the bay? As the Campbells search for answers, they struggle to hold what's left of their family together. Then one afternoon, the impossible happens. The police call to report that Justin has been found in a nearby town, and he appears to be fine. And though the reunion is a miracle, Justin's homecoming exposes the deep rifts that have diminished his family; the wounds they all carry that may never fully heal. When a reversal of fortune lays bare the family's greatest fears — and offers perhaps their only hope for recovery — each of them must fight to keep the ties that bind them from permanently tearing apart.

THE CHILDREN ACT

Ian McEwan

Fiona Maye is a leading High Court judge, presiding over cases in the family court. She is renowned for her fierce intelligence, exactitude and sensitivity. But her professional success belies private sorrow and domestic strife. There is the lingering regret of her childlessness, and her marriage of thirty-five years is in crisis. Now she is called on to try an urgent case: for religious reasons, a beautiful seventeen-year-old boy, Adam, is refusing the medical treatment that could save his life, and his devout parents share his wishes. Time is running out. Should the secular court overrule sincerely held faith? In the course of reaching a decision, Fiona visits Adam in hospital — an encounter which stirs long-buried feelings in her and powerful new emotions in the boy. Her judgment has momentous consequences for them both.

DAUGHTER

Jane Shemilt

Jenny loves her three teenage children and her husband, Ted, a celebrated neurosurgeon. She loves the way that, as a family, they always know each other's problems and don't keep secrets from each other. But when her youngest child, fifteen-year-old Naomi, doesn't come home after her school play and a nationwide search for her begins, secrets previously kept from Jenny are revealed. Naomi has vanished, leaving her family broken and her mother desperately searching for answers. But the traces Naomi has left behind reveal a very different girl to the one Jenny thought she'd raised. And the more she looks, the more she learns that everyone she trusted has been keeping secrets . . .